D0115281

Praise for *A Life Without You:*

'A tender, poignant story of love, loss and long-buried secrets. Katie Marsh's gorgeously heartbreaking, life-affirming tale grabs your heart and won't let go. A truly special book – I adored every twist and turn'   Miranda Dickinson

'A heart-clangingly powerful stunner of a novel. If you're looking for a book to make your heart sing, you've just found it. A triumph!'   Isabelle Broom

'A great read – heartwarming and funny in places and poignantly sad in others. A reminder to us all not to take our families or our memories for granted'
The Unmumsy Mum

'Touching, emotionally charged . . . A wonderful tale about love and motherhood, that leaves the reader basking in the warmth of hope'   Amanda Jennings

Praise for *My Everything:*

'This skilful debut novel offers an inspiring journey through love, loss and second chances'   *Sunday Express*

'Both devastatingly sad and blissfully romantic'   *Heat*

'Absolutely LOVED it! Such a beautiful book . . . Heartwarming and funny in places, and very honest'
Carrie Hope Fletcher

'A moving and thoughtful story about love and second chances'
Sunday Mirror

'This thought-provoking debut novel is both brilliantly funny and sad'   *Sun*

Katie Marsh lives in south-west London with her family. Before being published she worked in healthcare, and her books are inspired by the bravery of the people she has met in hospitals and clinics around the country.

Katie loves strong coffee, the feel of a blank page and stealing her husband's toast. *A Life Without You* is her second novel.

You can follow her on Twitter @marshisms, visit her website www.katie-marsh.com or find her on Facebook: /KatieMarshAuthor

Also by Katie Marsh:

My Everything

KATIE MARSH

A Life Without You

HODDER

First published in Great Britain in 2016 by Hodder & Stoughton
An Hachette UK company

3

Copyright © Katie Marsh 2016

The right of Katie Marsh to be identified as the
Author of the Work has been asserted by her in accordance
with the Copyright, Designs and Patents Act 1988.

All rights reserved. No part of this publication may
be reproduced, stored in a retrieval system, or transmitted,
in any form or by any means without the prior written
permission of the publisher, nor be otherwise circulated
in any form of binding or cover other than that in which
it is published and without a similar condition being
imposed on the subsequent purchaser.

All characters in this publication are fictitious and any
resemblance to real persons, living or dead is purely coincidental.

A CIP catalogue record for this title is available from the British Library

Paperback ISBN 978 1 473 61365 2
eBook ISBN 978 1 473 61364 5

Typeset in Plantin Light by
Palimpsest Book Production Ltd, Falkirk, Stirlingshire

Printed and bound in Great Britain by Clays Ltd, St Ives plc

Hodder & Stoughton policy is to use papers that
are natural, renewable and recyclable products and made
from wood grown in sustainable forests. The logging and
manufacturing processes are expected to conform to
the environmental regulations of the country of origin.

Hodder & Stoughton Ltd
Carmelite House
50 Victoria Embankment
London EC4Y 0DZ

www.hodder.co.uk

For mum and dad

One

That sandwich had definitely been a mistake.

Zoe pressed her hand to her clammy forehead and reached for her toothbrush. The pile of soft white towels by the marble sink mocked her with its fragrant perfection as she applied toothpaste and started to brush.

'Come on, Zoe.' Her dad knocked a brisk rhythm on the bathroom door. 'Chin up.' His voice was more a threat than an encouragement.

She spat and rinsed before straightening up and staring at herself in the mirror. Bad move. Even the over-zealous make-up artist hadn't managed to disguise the craters of exhaustion beneath her eyes.

'I'm coming, Dad.' She suppressed the latest in her seemingly endless supply of yawns. She and the small hours had become very good friends of late. She felt sweat prickling all over her body and tried to loosen the lace that clung to her neck. The material had other ideas, and after a small tussle, she gave up and ran cold water over her wrists instead. At least the nausea was ebbing away now. Just the pounding headache and the panic to go.

She dried her hands and straightened up, watching as the cream silk folds of her dress swirled elegantly towards the ground. She was dressed like a bride. Her sweeping chignon was certainly ready to be the centre of attention.

Part of her even felt like a bride. Expectant. Lucky.

It was the rest of her that was the problem. The persistent voice that kept asking whether she should even be here at all. Whether she and Jamie could ever really be happy after everything that had happened and everything that had been said.

Her stomach cramped again and she ran across to the toilet and bent over it. This wasn't quite the glamorous wedding build-up she'd been hoping for. She waited to see if there was anything left in her stomach. Apparently not. Small mercies. She stood up shakily and closed the seat.

More knocking. 'Zoe. I need to go down now.'

She could hear his impatience. There was no room in the wedding schedule for crises of any kind. Every second of the day was accounted for. No deviations allowed.

She inhaled and walked over to open the bathroom door. She tried a smile. He grinned back, apparently convinced.

'You're OK, then. I knew I could rely on you.' He looked her up and down, tall and imposing in his morning suit. His grey hair was waxed flat and his black shoes gleamed. 'I always can.'

She nodded. 'I'm fine. I just wanted to powder my nose.' Her stomach growled ominously, and she had to fight down another wave of queasiness. As he looked at her she could see the pride in his blue eyes. He always saw the best version of her. That was all she had ever shown him.

'Here you are, Zo.' Her sister held out a glass of champagne.

'Thanks, Lily.'

Maybe alcohol was the answer. Nothing else had worked so far. Not Rennies or deep breathing or listening to calming classical music. Zoe watched the bubbles pop and fizz right up to the rim as she closed her fingers round the stem. She took a cautious sip before putting the glass down on the dark oak coffee table. She exhaled slowly. She could do this.

Her dad smiled, and the pale scar on his chin curved upwards into a lopsided C. Northern Ireland, 1986. He could name the origin of every mark on his face and body from his many years of service. 'Jamie's a lucky man. I hope he knows that.' His voice held a note of warning. Jamie sometimes joked that he would actually have to save Zoe from a burning building or an assassination attempt to ever be deemed worthy of her in her dad's eyes.

'Right. Time to go.' He turned on his heel and marched towards the door. Then he stopped. Came back. Hugged Zoe so hard she could feel his heart beating against her ribs. The hug said he loved her. Said everything he never expressed in words.

He squeezed still closer. 'Here's to a wonderful day.'

Well, she hadn't been sick for at least five minutes, so things were heading in the right direction.

'Thanks, Dad.' She nestled under his chin, remembering the way she and Lily had peered out of the windows of a succession of army quarters, waiting to see their dad the hero arriving home. Noses pressed to glass. Voices raised as they competed to spot him first. Then the sweet crush of that homecoming hug.

He let her go, and she stood on tiptoe to kiss his cheek. 'I'm sure today will be perfect. I can't wait.'

She ignored her rapid pulse. The darkness whirling through her mind. People had been telling her for ages that you weren't meant to actually enjoy your wedding day. Maybe every bride felt like this. Overwhelmed. Unsure.

Her dad patted her shoulder. 'Time to get those ushers

in order. I'll see you downstairs in twenty minutes. Don't be late.' He walked to the door and opened it.

Zoe nearly stopped him. Nearly shared the worries gnawing away at her heart. But then she bit the words back. A lifetime of practice stood her in good stead. She was good at this. Good at keeping calm and carrying on.

Besides, she couldn't exactly do much right now. The flowers, the catering, the venue, the guests – the thought of stopping this marital juggernaut in its tracks made her want to rush to the bathroom again, lock the door and start digging an escape tunnel to Australia.

'We'll be right on time, Dad.'

As the door swung shut behind him, both girls raised their hands in a mock salute. They looked at each other and smiled, remembering a childhood of having to be precisely on time for everything, from trips to museums to games of football in the garden.

Zoe moved towards the huge sash window. Her chest was so tight she was struggling to breathe. She needed air. She tried to pull the window open. It didn't move. She tried again. The catch broke off and fell to the floor.

It really wasn't her day.

She turned away and started fanning her face with her hand. The grips holding her hair in place were starting to bite. She massaged her temples with her fingers. 'God, can you imagine what he'd do if we actually *were* late?'

'I'd rather not.' Lily shook her head vigorously, while fastening a silver pendant round her neck.

'Spoilsport.'

Zoe gulped as she thought of all the people waiting for her in the hotel conservatory downstairs. The guest list had grown and grown – from an original list of forty to the hundred and fifty people who would be milling around now. Her dad's friends. Their friends. Waiting for action. Waiting for her.

'Are you OK?' Lily put a slender arm around her shoulders, and her silver nails gleamed in the sunlight.

Zoe nodded. 'I'm fine. It's just that with Dad on full alert, it's not the most relaxing atmosphere in the world.' She tried to laugh but it came out as more of a shriek. Her whole body felt wired, tensed for a disaster that only she could see coming. She had jumped out of her skin earlier when Lily had slammed her suitcase shut unexpectedly, and the wedding photographer had long since given her up for a bad job and gone downstairs to take pictures of people who could actually smile.

Lily's voice was quiet. 'Are you sure that's all it is? Dad stressing you out?'

Zoe sat down on the edge of the vast double bed, the purple bedspread crackling beneath her. 'Yes. One of the ushers texted me earlier to say he's genuinely terrified. He thinks Dad's got an old army rifle stashed away in case any of them step out of line. I'm hardly going to be laughing giddily with all that tension going on, am I?'

This time Lily looked more convinced. 'True.' She slid a diamanté clip into her cropped blonde hair. 'I just wanted to check. Because, you know, you and Jamie are so great together. I'd hate it if anything has ruined that. And recently you've seemed a bit . . . jumpy.'

Understatement of the century.

'I know.' Zoe's heart gave a nervous flutter at the mention of her fiancé's name. They hadn't been great together over the past few weeks. Quite the opposite.

She kept talking, as much to calm herself as to convince Lily. 'I think we've just found the wedding build-up a bit difficult. Jamie asked me last week whether I'd like to elope

5

somewhere nice and peaceful like the Middle East instead.' She raised an eyebrow. 'I *think* he was joking.'

Actually she hadn't been entirely sure. And part of her had been extremely tempted to say yes. Instead she had panicked and changed the subject and things had spiralled until they were back at that night in May when he had found her in the darkness, staring at the flickering street light outside their living room. Feet tucked beneath her. Heart on the floor.

Things were still so raw. At times it seemed the wedding preparations were the only thing keeping them talking, distracting attention from the silence thickening between them. She frowned, stretching her neck from side to side, trying to ease the tension in her muscles. This kind of thinking was why she never let herself sit still.

Lily collapsed on to a majestic silver and purple armchair. The Carnegie Hotel really had gone all out on the design and furnishing of its honeymoon suite. The default setting was 'overwhelming'. The chandelier on the ceiling looked like it could be made out of actual diamonds, and the floor was so huge that Zoe could have brought her trainers and got in a good few laps to pass the time.

Lily looked at her thoughtfully. 'I can't blame Jamie for freaking out. His family seem so down to earth – this might all be a bit much for them.' She stood up and walked to the window, opening it with embarrassing ease.

The thrum of traffic came from far below as London got ready for another muggy July Saturday. The sun was shining. Everything and everyone was on track for a perfect day.

Except Zoe.

She looked at the clock. Time was moving on. Her stomach twisted with panic. She tried to push away the doubts and questions that were her constant companions now. 'You're right – his family are pretty down to earth. His mum bakes cakes and delivers Meals on Wheels. She won a couple of hundred quid in a raffle a few months ago, and spent it on a new garden shed.'

Lily stared at her lap. Zoe knew the images that would be playing in her head. Snapshots of someone who wouldn't be here today. A narrow face with mischievous brown eyes. A laughing mouth telling stories or ordering them to hurry up and get into the bath before they both turned ninety. A bright dress over leggings. Frayed flip-flops. Sunglasses tipped up above a thick fringe. Mum.

Lily sighed, and Zoe saw how rigid her pale shoulders were above the neckline of her green bridesmaid's dress. She stood up and went over to put her arm round Lily's shoulders. Her sister's eyes remained downcast. Zoe kissed her on the cheek. 'Thanks so much for being my bridesmaid today, Lil. I know it's hard, after what happened with Gary.' Lily's eyes filled with tears, and Zoe cursed herself. She should never have mentioned the G word. Gary was an overbearing accountant who considered not farting during dinner to be the height of romance. Lily had dated him for eighteen months.

Self-worth. Not her sister's strong point.

Zoe reached out and wiped the lipstick smudge off Lily's lower lip with a practised hand. 'I'm so happy you're here.'

Lily rallied. 'I just want to enjoy myself. Sod Gary.' She stood up decisively and reached for more champagne.

Zoe was impressed. 'Wow. You said his name without sobbing. That *is* progress.'

Her sister's face trembled again.

Zoe caught her hand. 'Too soon?'

7

'Too soon. It's only been a month.'

'Sorry.' Zoe reached out and hugged her sister. Their dresses creaked in protest and they separated rapidly.

Lily drained her glass. 'Don't worry about it. Besides, being your bridesmaid is my wedding present to you. God knows I can't afford anything else.'

Zoe laughed. 'You managed to get my dress done up – that's present enough for me.'

Lily nodded. 'True.' A rare mischief coloured her face, lifting her eyes, her smile, her skin. Zoe wished she looked like that more often. 'It's all my gym training.' Lily flexed a pale bicep the size of a comma.

She darted a sideways look at Zoe. 'So, do you still think it was the right thing? Not to invite Mum? No last-minute regrets?'

Zoe stiffened. She had been dreaming about Mum a lot recently. Not about what had happened between them. Not about the anger that was keeping them apart. No. Sweeter dreams. Deceptive dreams. Zoe standing on a stool at her mum's side, licking the spoon as they made chocolate cake together. Or her mum leaning over the bed at night, tickling Zoe's tummy with her long red hair. *Sleep tight, baby girl. Sleep tight.*

Guilt needled her yet again as she wondered how the rift had grown so wide, and how much of it was her fault. She summoned all her strength and forced the thought away. She had done the right thing. Mum had given her no choice.

'She wouldn't have come anyway, Lil. We haven't spoken for years, and we were never exactly the Gilmore Girls to start with.' She stared her sister straight in the eye. 'OK?'

'OK.' Lily nodded. 'It just makes me sad that you two

8

never see each other. Even after all this time. I know she said some pretty terrible things, but . . .'

'Yes. She did.' Zoe nodded, wishing she had simply told Lily the truth at the time. But now years of secrecy imprisoned her. 'Look, Lil, now isn't the time to talk about this.' She got to her feet. 'Shall we go down soon?'

'Sure.' Lily checked the time. 'Five minutes.'

There was a knock at the door.

'Shit. That'll be Dad again. What the hell's wrong now?' Zoe's skin was starting to itch. She just wanted to get down there and brazen it out. Push through the doubts. Ignore the jagged edges and snares of the past few weeks.

She opened the door.

'Jamie!' She instinctively slammed it shut again.

'Ouch.' She heard a muffled groan on the other side.

She opened it again. 'Shit. Are you OK?'

'I think so.' He prodded his face tentatively. 'If I'm very lucky, my nose might just about manage to pull through.'

She reached out and touched his cheek, smelling the cinnamon tang of his aftershave. 'Oh God, I'm sorry. I just . . .'

'Panicked?' He nodded. 'I know. I'm not meant to see you before we meet downstairs. But as you're someone who seems to actively despise superstition, I didn't think you'd mind. By the way, may I just say you look HOT.'

She met his eyes, and as ever, his presence lifted her, turning the world from drab to neon. A little part of her started to hope.

He leant forward and kissed her. 'Oh my God, I can't wait to get you back up here later. Look at that bed. It's so—'

She heard a discreet click as Lily disappeared into the bathroom.

9

His cheeks turned pink.

'Awkward. Didn't see her over there. Which isn't surprising, seeing as this room is bigger than our entire flat.' He walked around admiringly.

'Jamie, I . . .' She felt her face flush as words blocked on her tongue. Seeing him here, in the bright light of their wedding day, with his purple waistcoat and excited eyes, she felt the gap between them widen. He was ready for happy-ever-after. She didn't even know if she deserved it.

She looked down at her engagement ring. The diamond shone as he took her hand. 'Look, Zo, I'm really sorry to surprise you like this.' His green eyes met hers and she saw only conviction. 'Things have been so shit between us recently. And I didn't want to just . . . see you. Down there in front of everyone. Without saying sorry.'

'Sorry for what?'

'For everything.' Anxiety clouded his face. 'Sorry for being such a dick. For trying to make you talk about it all the time when you didn't want to. I just didn't know how to feel – I wanted an explanation, you know? A reason.'

She nodded. 'I know.'

He shifted from foot to foot. 'So I jabbered on like an idiot, talking about how stressed you were – making it sound like what happened was your fault. It's no wonder we kept fighting all the time.' He ran a hand through his spiky blond hair. 'I didn't know what I was saying. And I would never blame you. You know that, don't you?'

'It's OK.' Zoe examined the purple swirls on the thick carpet, running over them with the tip of her satin shoe.

'No, it's not.' He took her hands in his. 'I saw your face that night, remember? I've never seen you look like that before. So defeated.'

She had no words to answer him. Only memories from

long ago. Tears. Breaths. Hours spent curled on her side waiting for it to be over.

She swayed, and Jamie put a finger under her chin and gently raised it.

'Talk to me, Zoe.'

She stared at him and tried to put the words into an order in her head. Words that could make him see how confused she was. How unmoored. How there was so much she hadn't told him.

She was just opening her mouth when he ran the tip of his finger down her cheek.

The warmth of it stopped her in her tracks.

'I'm OK, Jamie.' She kissed him. 'Nothing to worry about.' She glanced at the clock on the wall. 'You have to get downstairs.'

'But I want to stay here and tell you how beautiful you are. And how proud I am to be with you. And—'

She pulled back. 'Shouldn't you be saving all this for your speech?'

'I've got more than enough to say. Don't you worry.' He smiled. 'Like the way you always remember to buy loo roll. That's my grand finale.'

He stole another kiss.

'Wow, that'll have them whooping in the aisles.' She stepped free and reached for her champagne, downing the entire glass in one quick gulp. She was used to being able to banish doubt. And today she would do so again.

'Jamie, you need to go.'

'First let me just do this. Because I'm mad about you.' He lifted her high in the air and whirled her around, and despite herself, she laughed.

'Watch out! I'm not sure my dress can take any more surprises.'

He put her down and peered at her approvingly. 'How the hell do I undo it, anyway?'

She felt her cheeks burn as she ran her fingers around the satin-covered hooks that tapered down her lower back. 'I have absolutely no idea.'

He reached for her again, and panic knifed her as the urge to confess returned. Then Lily came out of the bathroom. 'Time to go, sis.'

'OK.' Zoe nodded, inwardly relieved. In another second she would have told him. And there would be no coming back from that.

'I love you.' His eyes still searched her face.

He knew something was wrong. He was too used to seeing her coping. Never thrown. Never put off her stride. Whereas today she was unravelling, right there in the engagement ring that had cost him two months' wages.

'Enjoy the ceremony, Jamie.' Lily leant forward to kiss his cheek. 'See you on the other side.'

'If I make it that far.' Jamie grimaced. 'I think your dad may do away with me for daring to abandon my post just before the ceremony.'

'No he won't.' Zoe shook her head. 'It would ruin the table plans.'

Lily grinned. 'You made a joke! Great. You must be feeling better.'

'Better?' Jamie paused again. 'I knew there was something wrong.'

'Just go!' Zoe held the door open for him.

'I love you.' His voice was still audible as she shut it behind him.

Zoe took another deep breath. She was doing the right thing. She was. This was Jamie. The man with the slow smile who had captivated her four years ago when he ambled over to mend her work PC. The man who always had time to stand and stare. Who appreciated the little things. Frost on a leaf. Marbled clouds in the sky. The sunlight on her face in the morning.

Those were the things that mattered. Not the last few weeks.

Lily handed Zoe her bouquet.

'So what's he given you this time?' She gently flicked a speck of dust off Zoe's forearm. 'Yet more perfect jewellery? More hand-painted pictures of your favourite view or the place you met?' She sighed. 'He really does do his best to make all the rest of the men in the world appear to be complete and utter losers.'

'He just wanted to talk to me.' Zoe's jaw was so tense it felt like her teeth might crack. 'We've had a few . . .' She stopped. No point going into it now. Not with 'Here Comes the Bride' starting in five minutes.

Lily blinked. 'A few what?'

'Doesn't matter.' Zoe shook her head.

'Zoe?'

Lily's voice seemed very far away. Zoe poured more champagne, hoping it would seal the hole that was opening in her heart. She downed it in one.

Lily looked at her, concerned.

'Zoe?' she said again.

Zoe stared at her, poised to speak. At last. But then she swallowed the words down just as she always did, burying them deep, safe where no one could see.

'It doesn't matter.'

'Are you sure?'

'Yes.' Zoe nodded. 'Look, just humour me. I'm the bride. It's *my* day. OK?'

'OK.' Lily shrugged. 'Time to go.'

'Yes.' Zoe put her hand on the doorknob. This was her last chance. She could go downstairs, or she could listen to the voice in her head telling her that she wasn't going to get away with this. That she wasn't the woman Jamie deserved.

It took them both a second to realise that Lily's phone was ringing. Lily leant over and looked at the screen. She frowned. 'It's just Mags. I'll leave it. It can't be important.'

Zoe reached for the phone.

'Let's answer.'

'No, Zo. We have to—'

Too late. Zoe had swiped to accept the call.

Mags. Their mum's best friend. Zoe could still remember her dark hair blocking out the sun as she bent to dab on calamine when Zoe had fallen off her bike into the nettle patch.

Lily frowned at Zoe as she spoke. 'Mags? Hello? Now's not a great time, we're about to—'

Zoe leant closer to listen to the voice at the other end of the line.

Lily's voice was low. 'What?' A line appeared between her eyebrows and she put the phone on speaker.

Mags's voice crackled into the padded luxury of the room. A voice from another world. 'It's Gina.'

'What's happened?'

'She's . . .'

Fear flared in Zoe's heart. Fear that after all this time, all these years of being apart, she was never going to get a chance to see her mum's face again.

Mags sounded hurried. 'I'm sorry, I can't really explain on the phone. She's asking for Zoe, but I didn't have her number, so—'

Zoe's heart jolted. 'I'm here, Mags.'

'Thank God. She wants you to help her.'

'Are you sure?'

'Yes.' Mags's voice was definite. Clear. 'You need to come. Right now. You need to come and get her out of here.'

Married quarters, Queensbury Barracks, Wiltshire
Birthday present: you don't care about presents, you
   just love the wrapping paper
Favourite music: 'Twinkle, Twinkle'

15th June, 1985

Darling Zo-bear,
   So. You made it to one. Thank God for that. There
were times when I wondered if you would.
   Right from the beginning, nothing's gone according
to plan. The birth wasn't exactly the cheesecloth-and-
tea-light scenario I'd imagined. I thought Alistair would
be holding my hand and looking manly and helping me
breathe through the INSANE pain, but – of course – he
was away on exercise when you decided to arrive, so
he had to leg it here in the back of a truck and only
arrived the day after I first got to hold you in my arms.
I wasn't even due for another month, and I was about
thirty minutes away from giving birth in the loo at work
when my poor nervous manager Roger offered to
drive me to the hospital in his ancient Ford Fiesta. We
made it just as your head was starting to appear, and
the first words you heard were 'Bugger me' as he fell
to the floor in a dead faint.
   So, not the most glamorous start. But I didn't care.
Because there you were. You had two eyes and ten
toes and red fuzz all over your head, and you were
perfect. Just perfect. It was only the two of us for
ages, as Alistair was sent away so much. God, I

missed him – I hate the endless cycle of sending parcels/writing letters/hoping it's not me who gets the dreaded visit about the sniper or the injury – but with you here it was so much better. We were happy, the two of us. Well, the four of us if you count my boobs, which were pretty much all you were interested in at the beginning. For the first few weeks it was total chaos. No shipshape and Alistair fashion (your daddy is a fan of rearranging the contents of the fridge into very straight lines. I know. We'll train him). Instead, it was all muslins and nappies and Wagon Wheels and Heinz ravioli and peas every day for my tea. The beige army paint was peeling off the living room walls, but so what? I didn't give a flying one about anything except you.

My mum visited occasionally – whenever she could get away from the hectic demands of having her hair done every other bloody day – and told me I wasn't changing your nappies properly, or that you were too small or too fussy or too red in the face. Sod her. I dutifully clicked the camera shutter the one time she held you per visit, inwardly cheering you on if you chose that moment to belch in her face. When she left, I just cuddled you closer, flicked two fingers at her back and locked the door behind her. Good riddance.

When you hit three months, Alistair was based here for a while. He couldn't believe how amazing you were. You'd curl up on his chest and sleep all the sleep you'd so valiantly resisted when you were alone with me. You'd clasp his big thumb in yours, calloused from weeks spent stripping rifles or crouching in bushes or whatever mad shit he gets up to leading his boys. You'd gaze up at him, and whatever was in your eyes, he couldn't get enough. He wanted to smother you in kisses. To lift you high in the air. To dandle you in the sunlight in our crappy strip of a garden as the trucks rumbled down the road outside.

I spent hours watching him with you. It made me love both of you more. Sometimes I'd stare at you and him and my heart would hurt with how much you meant to me. Like when you squeeze all the water out of a sponge and all that's left is your fist aching and the gristle scratching your fingers. I love you both that much. That hard. My family.

At night, Alistair was less helpful. Or rather, he was better at sleeping than I am. You would hiccup and scream and grimace the night away, your arms gesturing wildly at me like an actor doing a really over-the-top audition for a TV soap. He slept on. I still bloody woke up even on the miracle nights when you actually kept your eyes closed till 5. I had to check you were still breathing. Still with us. In the mornings I looked about five hundred years old. You both looked adorable. Your daddy chucked you under the chin and went off to work to tell all his mates how angelic his daughter was. I had yet another Nescafé and got on with the day.

Once, I took you into my old office at the travel agency. No. I don't know why either. My boobs leaked, I had porridge in my hair and all my old colleagues looked at me like I was from Mars as you screamed your way through our 'lovely afternoon out'. At one point I was breastfeeding in the back office when poor Roger came in. As if he hadn't seen enough of me already. He looked like he'd swallowed a printer cartridge. I got the giggles and then you puked on the photocopier. Don't think I'll be going back there again.

But I won't miss them – they might say Alistair's too serious for me, but I know they're all just jealous. It was *me* he picked that night. Me he wanted to dance with to the mind-numbing strains of that terrible wedding band as they murdered every hit ABBA has ever had. I remember their faces – Mel and Tiff and the rest – green with envy. There I was in Alistair's arms, looking up at those cheekbones and that thick dark hair and thanking the Lord that for once I was about to kiss a man whose idea of whisking me off my feet wasn't just force-feeding me a pint of cider. His hands were on my back. His body was close to mine. The world was in its proper place.

That hasn't changed. I love him so much. And he loves me – it's there in every glance and every embrace. He calls me his queen of chaos, smiling indulgently as I leave a trail of clothes and shoes and make-up brushes around our bedroom. He is besotted with us both. His girls. He loves it when you smile at him and pull up against his hands and toddle forward towards whichever toy you want. He loves making sandcastles or constructing elaborate banana towers for your breakfast. You are his golden girl and those Sunday afternoons when we're all just being ourselves in the garden are golden times. They're so short. So sweet. He's deploying next week. Northern Ireland again. Four and a half months. It's a long time. So many weeks of people wanting to kill him and only barbed wire and guns to hold them back.

It terrifies me. But at least I have you. Beautiful, beautiful you. You smile and gurgle and grin. We have a routine now. Feeding (you). Sleeping (you). Throwing things around (you). Pointing at things (you). Cleaning, cooking, wiping, soothing, washing, clearing, picking up (me). Falling asleep on the sofa at half eight with a beer in my hand (me).

Sometimes, when you finally close your eyes, I stand in your room, unable to tear myself away. I listen to the hush of your breath, see your tiny hands opening and closing as you dream, and I think of how far we've come. I breathe you in, savouring every last piece of you. I can't get enough.

Before you, I didn't really like babies. I'd hold them for a minute and then claim I needed the loo and pass them on. But now? I'm hungry for you. I do everything I can for you. I wrap you up warm. I brush your teeny teeth. I file your nails when you're sleeping so you can't scratch your face. And you reward me. You do. You blink at me with those wonderful catlike eyes, and you smile, and I can see that your heart is full of me. I can't wait for the day when you will say 'Mum'. When you will say 'I love you'.

God knows, I love you too.

Happy first birthday.

Mum x

Two

Z oe couldn't believe what she had done.

She stared out of the window of the cab, ignoring the curious glances of the driver as the London traffic refused to help her speed to her mum's side. She examined the wheels of the bus next to them as they stopped at yet more red lights, before raising her eyes and seeing that they were just across the road from a church. It was 2 p.m. Prime wedding timing. Sure enough, the bells were ringing out in joyful celebration of a marriage that presumably would actually go ahead.

Zoe couldn't tear her eyes from the scene, watching the smartly dressed men in morning dress laughing together on the wide stone steps. Women in frocks and fascinators clutched minuscule bags as they made their way to the entrance in elegant high heels.

She fingered the heavy folds of her dress. Her friends were waiting for her right now. Her dad. Jamie. She had let him down. She had let everyone down. For years she had tried to run from this feeling, yet here it was again. Shame.

Mercifully the cab pulled away just as the bride's long white car drew up alongside the church. Zoe's heart ached as she thought of the music she and Jamie had chosen together back in April for her walk down the aisle. A Debussy prelude. They had sat together in their tiny kitchen, listening to the intricate swell of the piano, and she had known with her whole heart how much she wanted to marry him. She had smiled at him and held his hand, and they had both stared into a future that felt like it belonged only to them.

Then it had all changed. And when the call had come today, an inexplicable instinct had told her she needed to leave. It had all seemed to add up. All those dreams of her mum. All the fights with Jamie. The seething sense of uncertainty. Mags's voice had felt like a sign. But sitting here now, that moment of conviction had well and truly disappeared. All that was left was shock and disbelief. She should have explained to Jamie what she had been feeling, and why. Why she was running.

Lily would already have told them all. The expression in her sister's eyes when Zoe had left the hotel room would stay with her for ever. Her gentle sister, looking at her with absolute dismay. Zoe couldn't blame her. Especially when Lily was the one who had to tell Dad that the wedding was off. Lily had even offered to go and help Mum herself. She had clung to Zoe's arm and said that getting married was the most important thing – that Zoe had to stay.

But Zoe hadn't listened. In that one moment, there had been clarity as opposed to doubt. She knew what she had to do. Mum needed her help.

Now it seemed a moment of madness. And yet something wouldn't let her turn back. She drummed her fingers on her thigh, then reached over and turned her phone off before settling back in her seat. Her almighty hair didn't want to play ball, and instead devoted itself to impaling her on the headrest.

'You all right, love?' The cabbie caught her eye in the mirror.

'I'm fine.' She untangled herself and pointedly stared out of the window, folding her arms to discourage further conversation. She would have enough explaining to do later. No need to start now.

Soon they were moving more quickly, and the central London sheen was off the streets. She could see a newsagent's with half its sign hanging off, a mattress leaning against a wall, a dog rubbing itself against a battered postbox. A group of sun-reddened men sauntered along with cans of beer in their hands. The breeze on her face was hot and sticky. She thought back to the scented luxury of the suite she had been in only thirty minutes before. It already felt part of a different life.

And then she saw her.

She leant forward and asked the driver to stop, and he drew to a halt next to the spot where Mags was leaning against a railing. It had been so long since they had seen each other, and yet she looked exactly the same. Still in jeans and Adidas with short dark hair and that triangular gold pendant around her neck.

'Zoe!' She was already talking as Zoe paid the driver with her emergency twenty and opened the door to try to get out of the cab. It wasn't an easy manoeuvre, given the dress situation. She swung her legs round and staggered on to the pavement. Mags put her hand to her mouth. 'Oh my God. I didn't realise it was your . . .'

Her words petered out as she surveyed Zoe's outfit. A small puppy with straggly fur came up and surveyed it too. He started to raise his hind leg, until Zoe gave him her hardest stare and he wisely chose to run away.

Mags's mouth was hanging open. 'You got married today?'

'Not yet, no.' Zoe closed the cab door.

'What?'

'It doesn't matter.'

Mags frowned. 'And you didn't even invite Gina to your wedding?'

Now really wasn't the time to get into this.

'No. I didn't. Now let's get inside.' She started to pull Mags along, conscious of the stares and nudges from passers-by.

'But . . .' Mags was tapping her hand repetitively against her jeans and chewing frantically on a piece of gum that periodically appeared between her teeth. This was not the Mags that Zoe remembered. She had always been calm, lying back in a deckchair or a sofa with a glass of wine in her hand. Nothing wound her up. She hadn't even batted an eyelid when her son Johnny had accidentally set fire to the kitchen. Now she was disrupted. Jerky. Her speech was staccato, each word fighting to be the first out of her mouth.

'Oh God, this is such a nightmare.' She put her hand to her forehead and came to a halt. Zoe reluctantly stopped too, as a piercing wolf whistle came from across the street.

Zoe focused on Mags. 'Just tell me what happened.'

'Gina got a bit confused, and—'

'Well she's not a child, is she? Surely she can look after herself?'

Mags shook her head. 'God, it really has been a long time since you saw her, hasn't it?' She planted her hands on her hips.

'So?'

Mags continued. 'We were having coffee together and then she headed to Sainsbury's, while I did a couple of errands. Then by the time I got there the police had come and she was shouting at them to get off her – that she hadn't done anything – and then they arrested her and

24

bundled her in the back of a van.' Her mouth worked and Zoe could see tears forming. 'They handcuffed her, Zoe.' The lines in her forehead bit deep. 'I mean, Gina. For God's sake. For all her gob, there's no way she'd ever hurt anybody.'

Zoe swallowed. 'What had she done?'

'They said she'd stolen some food. The store detective caught her as she went out, and called the police in.'

'Are you kidding me? That's why she's here?' Zoe looked around, just to check the world was still turning and this wasn't some kind of incredibly vivid pre-wedding nightmare.

No such luck.

Right. So this was real. Bloody Mum. So much for the call being a sign. Mags had made it sound like she was in real need, but all the time she'd just got a bit peckish in Sainsbury's and hadn't bothered to pay. 'Has this happened before, Mags?'

'God, no!' Mags looked so horrified that Zoe believed her. 'I know it's been a while, but surely you know your mum a bit better than that?'

Zoe knew her mum was capable of anything.

However, she was here now. Might as well get on with it.

'How is she, anyway?' Zoe heard a flapping noise as they started to climb the wide steps towards the big brown building. She looked down to see that a crisp packet had attached itself to the tip of her shoe. She waved her foot around a couple of times, and then tried to reach down to pull it off. Her dress continued its campaign of quiet sabotage and refused to let her get further than waist height. As she straightened up again, she heard a siren screeching behind her.

'I don't know. They won't let me in.' Mags kept pace with her as Zoe did her best to sprint up the steps. Despite everything, the thought of her mum behind bars made her nauseous. She passed a woman who smelt strongly of bins and came to brown double doors with 'Kennington Police Station' stamped across them in intimidatingly large letters. She gulped and then tilted her chin high as she pushed through. She knew she was the right person to get her mum out. And she was in the mood for a fight.

As the doors banged shut behind them, Zoe was moving so fast, she bumped into a huge wall of a man with an improbably tiny rucksack over his right shoulder. It reminded her of the one Jamie wore to go running, and she had to rapidly block an image of him waiting for her next to the stand of flowers in the conservatory.

She needed to focus.

'Excuse me, excuse me.' She edged round the man only to see that there was a queue. She cursed under her breath. A sunny Saturday in central London. Tourists out admiring the sights. Of course the crime rate was soaring.

She had to get to the front.

She turned to Mags. 'Look, why don't you sit down over there? I'm sure they'll let me through, and you might as well make yourself comfortable while you wait.'

'I'm not sure they will.' Mags hovered as if there was more to say. 'I think you might need to—'

'It'll be fine.' Zoe cut the conversation off by turning back to stare at the tiny rucksack. She heard the squeak of Mags's trainers as she turned and went to sit down. Good. Zoe wasn't in the mood for talking. She looked at the rucksack again. A tiny thread was hanging from the corner and she had to fight back an urge to pull it off.

She was twitching with adrenalin.

'Excuse me.' She tapped the man on the shoulder. He didn't turn round.

'Excuse . . .' She noticed the white cords of his earphones and reached up and pulled one out of his ear. 'Hello. I was just—'

'What the FUCK do you think you're doing?' He moved quite fast for such a big man. And his eyes were really terrifying, now she could see them.

Shit.

Oh well. It wasn't as if she had anything to lose. And at least she had his attention now.

'Look, my mum's in a cell back there.' She indicated the 'Custody Suite' sign on the double doors in the corner. 'I really need to get to the front, so I was wondering if . . .' His expression was not exactly encouraging, but she had to carry on. 'I was hoping I could go in front of you?'

'Fuck off.' He turned round, and she could see the ripple of muscle along his back as he tucked the earphones back into his ears.

'Right.' She looked at the black marks on the lino and wondered how to persuade him. She felt a beat of hope as he turned round again.

He ran a meaty hand over his sparse brown beard as he spoke. 'And you look like a total dick in that dress.'

Excellent. Rage pulsed through Zoe as he turned his back again. She looked at the clock on the wall. She should be going into the reception now, the wedding ring snug on her finger. But instead she was trapped here with this charmer and a room full of people who clearly thought she was a little overdressed.

She turned to the woman behind her, hoping for sympathy. Instead she was treated to ten minutes of pouting and loud complaints about the person who had crashed into the

27

woman's car. After five minutes, Zoe established that said person was in fact a bollard. After seven she had worked out that the woman herself was responsible for the impact.

The final straw was when the woman was re-enacting the collision in such dramatic detail that she stood on Zoe's dress, resulting in the kind of ripping sound that strikes fear into women the world over. Zoe looked behind her to see that her expensive marital underwear was now being shared with all the occupants of the police station, including the drunk teenager leaning against a far wall, who had his head on one side in open-mouthed admiration.

She was just trying to work out how to pull her dress together when – of course – she reached the front of the queue. She grasped the material with one hand while attempting to look authoritative.

'Hello.' She tried her most charming smile.

The policeman behind the glass looked entirely unimpressed.

'Yes?' He stared at her with eyes that had definitely seen it all. 'What do you want?'

She felt the hole in her dress gape open again and desperately pulled it together. The policeman brushed one of the black epaulettes on his shoulders, and Zoe saw a cloud of white specks fall towards the floor.

His voice was gruff. 'Is it a husband you're after, love?'

'No.' She drew herself up in an attempt at dignity. 'I'm looking for my mum. Gina Whittaker. She's been taken through for questioning, apparently.'

'Oh yeah?' He tapped on his keyboard. 'And what's *she* wearing? A ball gown?'

He found his own joke hilarious and burst into wheezy laughter that appeared to last several lifetimes. Zoe fought back her impatience as a man with a shaved head and tattoos right up to his eyeballs grunted on the bench by her side.

'Look, can you just let me through, please?'

As she waited, she looked over her shoulder and surveyed the room again. In the corner, she saw a woman muttering determinedly about resisting the system, holding up two bandaged wrists defiantly as her grey hair fell around her pinched face. Two men leant against a wall, discussing Sheffield Wednesday's current form and whether the manager was an idiot or a genius. A man with disorderly blond hair moaned incessantly about bureaucracy as he filled in a long white form that was resting on his knee. It wasn't surprising that the policeman in front of her was desperate for amusement of any kind. She would be too.

The policeman was tapping on a tired-looking keyboard and peering at the screen.

'Gina . . .?' He looked at her enquiringly.

'Gina Whittaker.' Zoe had a growing urge to scream, and the smell of the man beside her wasn't helping.

'She's not listed on here.' He drummed ponderous fingers on his chin.

'She must be. She was arrested earlier this afternoon.'

'Wasn't she at your bash, then?' He was visibly surprised.

'No.' She knew she sounded defensive. She was too used to missing out on those seminal mother–daughter experiences she kept reading about in magazines. Spas. Shopping trips. Getting ready for the wedding together. That look of joy and understanding between them as they emerged together to the applause of the entire family.

They had never been like that. The last shopping experience they had shared was buying Tampax when she was thirteen. Her mum had been exhausted as usual, so their time together during this rite of passage had consisted of her mum throwing the box into the shopping basket and then asking her if she wanted fish fingers or chicken nuggets for tea.

She must concentrate. She leant towards the glass. 'I need to see her.'

The man tapped on his keyboard again. With one finger.

She was never going to get to her mum.

It was so clammy in here, her palms were sweating. 'Have you found her yet?'

She thought she could hear the computer groaning.

'Yep. Got her.' He nodded.

Zoe's stomach tightened. 'And?'

'She's being questioned at the moment.'

'And can I see her?'

He frowned. 'Who did you say you were?'

'Her daughter.'

'Oh. Yes. Of course.' He looked at her suspiciously and she snapped.

'Look, it's my bloody wedding day. Do you think I'm faking a relationship with her for the sheer bloody fun of it? Do you really think I wanted to mosey down to a police station just at the moment I'm supposed to be saying "I do"?'

'OK, love.' He looked utterly unconcerned. She was probably a kitten compared to most of the people he saw in here. 'Don't get your tiara in a twist.'

Zoe was seething with frustration. 'Can I see my mum, please?'

'Well, here's the thing.'

'What?'

'No, you can't see her. You need to wait here until she's been questioned and they've decided what to do with her.' He looked behind her. 'Next.'

Sod that. 'But I *need* to see her.'

Any amusement on his face had long since gone. 'You can't. Solicitors only.'

Her heart leapt. 'I am a solicitor.'

'Really?' He raised an eyebrow. 'Show me your ID.'

Damn. Even if she had been a solicitor, there was no way she would have chosen to squeeze her ID into her tiny satin bag.

She tried to bluff it out. 'I don't have it with me.'

He shook his head. 'Nice try. Next.'

Behind the double doors, Zoe could hear a dull banging. Then shouting and swearing.

Her mum was in there. Probably scared. And all alone.

She tried again. 'Please? You don't understand, I have to—'

'No.'

'But—'

'No! Now move, please.'

Her whole body drooped as she realised she wasn't going to win. She turned and went over to sit next to Mags on one of the plastic benches that ran around the edge of the room. Her train was brilliantly designed to pick up every single fleck of dust and grime on the floor. There were plenty to choose from. The teenager eyed her suggestively as she went past, and she resolutely clasped the material that was falling apart behind her.

He grunted. 'Can I have your number, darling?'

Oh GOD.

As she sat down, Mags's hand was warm on her arm. 'You did your best. We'll just have to wait it out.' She delved into the bag looped over her shoulder. 'Do you want this?' She brought out a safety pin.

'Yes please.' Zoe swallowed her embarrassment and

shifted forward as Mags pinned the dress in place. She needed to get through that door. She wasn't used to failing, and this was twice in one day. It brought back those awful summer days from long ago. The slam of metal into her body. The words she'd tried so hard to forget but which had been stamped across her dreams for weeks. His words. Every morning they had taunted her on the tube as she headed to the office. Every evening they had been her soundtrack as she ran home.

Here in this sterile pit of a room, her wedding felt unreal. But those words rang true.

The minutes ticked by as Zoe and Mags sat side by side. Zoe's knee was constantly jiggling, as she had endless visions of her mum being ruthlessly interrogated by evil officers with Tasers or truncheons. Mags got two teas and a Crunchie from the machine. Zoe couldn't touch them.

And then, just when Zoe was going to combust, the door to the custody suite opened and there she was. Mum. Zoe's heart flooded with long-forgotten memories. Seeing that face at the school gate when all she wanted was home. Reaching for that hand and genuinely believing it could make everything better.

Her mum's head was bowed, and the same red hair hung down her back. The familiar brown eyes gleamed. The tiny scar still ran along her lip where next door's dog had attacked her when Zoe was three. Seeing her face dissolved the present and took Zoe back to childhood dens and scribbles stuck to the fridge and wonky biscuits baked on rainy afternoons.

It took her a second to realise what was different.

Her mum had no make-up on. But that wasn't it.

Her mum was wearing glasses. But that wasn't what had changed.

No.

It was the look on her face.

Without even knowing it, Zoe had braced herself for the expression of disappointment that was all she could remember from those last, looming encounters with her mum. But now she was smiling. That wide, warm smile Zoe remembered from childhood knee scrapes or bad days at school or doing the hokey cokey in the bathroom before bed.

The smile from before. The smile from the past.

Before everything was broken.

Married quarters, Rhine Garrison
Present: a big toy monkey
Favourite music: 'The Alphabet Song'

15th June, 1986

Darling Zo-bear,

So. Two today. You celebrated by pulling Alistair's toy
aeroplane (sorry, his model De Havilland Mosquito – he
hates it when I call it a toy) off its table in the corner
and smashing it into a thousand pieces. Of course it was
an accident. And of course he knew that, and so he kept
trying to smile and say it was fine, while obsessively
hunting down every last piece of wing and every single
screw from every bloody corner of the living room. You
can read him like a book, and your eyes were so wide
as you watched him, as if they held all the tears the
world has ever cried. I told him not to be an idiot, and
that didn't go down well, and the atmosphere was 100
per cent morgue until you walked over to him and put
your tiny hand on his shoulder. I flinched, wondering if
he would push it away, but then he turned and hugged
you as if he would never let you go. He even had a tear
in his eye. I've never seen that before.

What you don't know is that we lost Bean a couple
of weeks ago. We want so desperately to give you a
brother or a sister, but it wasn't as quick as the first
time, and then . . . this. I didn't know how to tell him.
He was so bloody happy when I got pregnant, and I
hate letting him down.

34

I was with Mags when it happened, and thank God she was there. She lives next door with Alistair's best friend Richard and has a little boy called Johnny. You two were making some kind of lethal den in the kitchen out of chairs and a load of tea towels when I went to the loo and saw the blood. I just sat there panicking and crying and Mags brought me a cup of tea with about fifty sugars in it and stroked my back and kept talking to me until I felt a bit better and we went to the hospital. Turns out she'd lost a baby too, years ago. She knew what I meant when I said I hated my body – that I felt like it had betrayed me. The next day you toddled around waving your little spade as I planted a sycamore tree in the garden. A place to remember Bean. To imagine who our baby might have become.

When I did tell Alistair, I couldn't stop apologising. He was so kind and did that thing where he pulls me into a huge bear hug so I can't see his face. He's more about action than words. No wonder he joined the army. He kissed my hair and squeezed me so tight, then turned and poured me an enormous glass of wine while he got a beer from the fridge. He talked about next time. He talked about trying again. And he held me – at least till the next morning, when he went off on exercise again. I wanted him to be there to look after me, but I knew that he couldn't. I'm so proud of him. My soldier.

This is your birthday letter and listen to me! Banging on. I'm going to give you a whole book of these letters when you're twenty-one, so you can laugh at what a nutter I was and what a miracle it is you made it to adulthood without some kind of serious mental condition. You can treasure it for ever, or shove it into the bottom of your wardrobe with your old bras and pictures of ex-boyfriends who you'd quite like to kill. Up to you.

Anyway, for now I'll get back to the point and write about what you've been up to, birthday girl. Over the past year we've become closer than ever. It's my hand you wanted to hold as you learnt to walk and my lap you want to sit on when you're tired. You can't get enough of me. You stroke my hair and snuggle into my neck and tell me the names of your army of friends. Foxy (the fox). Donkey (the donkey). You can see a trend here. They are fed and watered and bathed and pushed dangerously high on the swings in the park. One day Johnny tried to steal Bunny and you screamed and fought and pulled his hair till he gave it back. There's no arguing with you. Alistair thinks I should encourage you to be less aggressive – I think you're perfect. God knows you'll need to stand up for yourself in this crazy world of ours.

We moved over here to the German base last month. Our little semi on the patch has narrow stairs and peeling paint in the most depressing shade of magnolia in the world, but you love it. Your grin was so wide when we first came through the checkpoint that you even made the soldiers on duty smile as they relentlessly checked our papers. You love the endless bread and the cheese and the smell of dark German coffee in my mug. This place is surrounded by barbed wire, but to you it's just one big playground.

You stand blowing kisses at the window, waving bye bye to Daddy as he goes off on whatever tour it is this time, and your favourite thing in the world is twirling round and round the grey street lamps until you're dizzy and then jumping off the chunky kerbstones into the road. You want me to take you to the huge sheds at the end of the base by the perimeter fence, next to the Ministry of Defence signs telling us that SERVICE DOGS ARE ON PATROL. You could spend hours watching the armoured vehicles and the tanks coming in and out on exercises – you love the clanking rumble as they approach, while I just want to put my hands over my ears and sing bad pop songs till they're gone. I am never, ever letting you join the army. If you ever decide to obey me on anything, please choose that.

And how else do you fill your busy toddler days? You love feeding yourself – as long as someone is watching admiringly – and you love sorting the washing into mad piles and opening and shutting all the drawers we have. You 'cook' things in the oven. Play-Doh. Flannels. My keys. My bras. You overwater my plants and bustle around all the time, and you've already worked out that you love sugar. And peas. And stealing my hair clips.

You copy me. Most of the time I love it, but last week I was sad about Bean and I cried and then I heard you cry too. I made damn sure to paint a smile on after that. I didn't want you sharing my grief. It's not your pain. You haven't failed. Only me.

Sometimes I look at you and I'm terrified. You're so joyful and full of wonder and energy. Where will I go wrong? What mistakes will I make?

But then the sun shines and Mags sticks her head over the fence and we decide yet again to have tea together. She puts on the sausages and her favourite Spandau Ballet album and we pour beer and squash and the four of us have a messy, ketchuppy picnic in the garden, and I don't care about anything but the cord that ties us together. One to the other. Mum to daughter.

I will never let you down. That's a promise.

All my love,
Mum x

Three

'Did I lose the . . .' Zoe's mum dipped her teaspoon into the bowl on the table until it was heaped high with sugar. She transferred it carefully across and tipped it into her mug of tea, then tapped her spoon against the rim with evident pleasure, a gesture that reminded Zoe of teatimes on the army base spent discussing whether *Bagpuss* was better than *Button Moon*.

She realised her mum had tailed off again and tried to prompt her. 'Lose the what, Mum?'

The spoon was on its way back to the bowl again. 'Did I . . .' Her mum's eyes dimmed, and she tucked a loose strand of hair behind her ears. It was greying at the roots now, finally losing the coppery sheen that Zoe had brushed and plaited with such fervour when she was a little girl. 'Did I lose the thing that meant I could come to your wedding?'

Zoe stared at her, puzzled. In her experience, her mum had never had a problem locating the words she needed to get her message across.

Mags leant forward. 'You mean the invitation?' She frowned at Zoe. 'No. You didn't lose it, Gina. Did she, Zoe?'

Zoe folded her arms defensively. She didn't deserve blame from Mags. Not after what Mum had done all those years ago.

'So that means that . . .' Her mum stopped again as she worked it out. 'Oh.'

Zoe ignored her stab of guilt as she saw the disappointment on Mum's face. She wasn't going to apologise. No way.

'Well, as it turns out, you didn't miss much.' She drained the last of her black coffee. As she put the cup on the table, she looked down at her wedding dress. At the beads. The bodice. The hope sewn into every single stitch.

Jamie. She knew she had to see him, but she dreaded what he might say. His hurt. His anger. She knew she deserved it all. She knew it was time to face him, though, and reached for her phone, stopping only when she noticed that her mum was heaping yet more sugar into her mug. Her fingers looked pale and fragile without her wedding band or her engagement ring.

Zoe put a hand out to stop her. Her mum's skin felt so cold. 'Mum, that's your fifth. Maybe that's enough sugar, unless you're actively trying to get diabetes?'

'I like it sweet.' She dropped the sugar in and stirred. Zoe saw how her hands were shaking as she lifted the mug to her lips. She sipped and grimaced as she spat the tea back out.

'Bloody hell, that's disgusting.' Her voice was so loud that even the people on the furthest table turned around.

'Mum. Keep your voice down.' Zoe smiled apologetically at the owner of the café, who was rearranging the sandwiches in the wheezing cool cabinet in the corner. The woman smiled back, unconcerned. She had probably heard worse. Being located next to a police station couldn't exactly be conducive to the peaceful consumption of muffins and cappuccinos.

'More milk. That's what I need.' Her mum poured the entire contents of a small jug into her mug and the liquid swirled white as she stirred.

Next to her Mags picked at the remains of an egg salad sandwich. It was neon yellow and was doing its best to make Zoe feel even sicker than she did already. Bits of watercress fell on to the plate as Mags took a bite, and the pungent smell of the egg made Zoe want to gag. Once upon a time, conversation had flowed so easily between the three of them as Zoe played or drew while the two mums had a glass of wine and made tea. Now all she could hear was the silence.

She looked out of the window, seeing a figure in a tight blue suit standing at the top of the steps of the police station next door, crushing a cigarette beneath his heel. The custody sergeant. The man who had officially released her mum under caution. He was tilting his face towards the sun and rubbing his fingers through the beginnings of a salt-and-pepper beard. She remembered how he had lowered his bushy eyebrows when she had taken him aside and asked him if her mum had confessed. How he had pinched the bridge of his nose as he told her that her mother claimed she couldn't remember what she had done. Then he had asked Zoe a question that she didn't want to answer. A question that had made the whispering fear on the edge of her consciousness become real.

She drummed her fingers on her empty mug. It was 4.30. The wedding breakfast should be starting now. And somehow she had made the decision to be here instead, drinking bad coffee in her wedding dress with two women who were effectively total strangers. Guilt skewered her again. She must have hurt him so badly.

41

She leant forward and put her elbows on the table. It felt sticky, so she rapidly sat up straight again. It was time to get some answers.

'So why did you do it, Mum?' The custody sergeant had told Zoe in no uncertain terms that her mother had been lucky to get off with a caution, especially given the way she had resisted the officers at the scene when they had tried to get her into the police van.

Angry as she was, Zoe still couldn't bear to think about it. Her mum fighting the police while Saturday shoppers picked up their burgers and their beers. Her mum caged and handcuffed in the back of a van. Alone.

'Mum?'

For a second her mum looked her in the eye, then her eyes swivelled away. 'God, that woman has a huge arse.'

'Be quiet, Mum! You can't go around saying things like that.' Zoe looked round to see if the woman concerned had heard.

Her mum tutted loudly. 'Why? She can't hear me.'

Said woman was about three feet away, and definitely had heard if the reddening skin on her neck was anything to go by. Zoe stared at her mum, trying to get her to focus.

'Mum. We need to talk about today. About what you did. Why did you take the food?'

Her mum's eyes slid towards the window. 'I didn't mean to. It was an accident. And they shouted at me. They all ganged up on me.'

She had never been good at owning up to things. Zoe of all people should know that.

She leant her head to the side to block her mum's view. 'Why did you take those chicken legs?' Even as she said the words, she was aware of how ridiculous they sounded. Because that was the cause of the afternoon's drama. A half-eaten pack of chicken legs and some Wagon Wheels.

It wasn't exactly a good reason to miss her own wedding.

Her mum just shifted her head the other way, then took a sip of her tea, smiling as she reached out and gently stroked Zoe's cheek. Her hand was covered in scrawled notes in a rainbow of colours. That, at least, hadn't changed. Zoe remembered the way her dad had left pads of clean white paper ostentatiously throughout the house, trying to encourage Mum to use them. He wrote neatly ordered lists in tidy capital letters. Mum just scribbled on her skin.

The caress took Zoe back to the days when her mum had been the start of every day. The footsteps beside her on every walk home.

She shivered. The past was stalking her again. She jerked away from her mum's hand and sat tall against the back of the chair. She needed familiar territory. Fighting. Arguing.

Her mum spoke first. 'It's so lovely to see you, Zoe.'

Zoe looked at her as if for clarification, remembering all the anger that had gone before. But her mum was staring out of the window again, humming a tune beneath her breath. 'Golden Slumbers'. The lullaby she had sung every night as she tucked Zoe into bed. Zoe remembered the cool pillow beneath her cheek and the glow of the landing light underneath the door.

She blinked, losing her train of thought entirely. She was in flux. Outside, the world carried on. Cars on the road. Sirens. Birds perching on telegraph poles. Once upon a time she had felt certain and strong. Now nothing felt right. Nothing felt true.

'I'm off for a wee.' Her mum stood up, and Zoe could see how her dress flapped loosely around her body. Her black leggings were wrinkled, and one of her white plimsolls was undone.

'It's that way.' Zoe pointed towards the sign at the back of the café, but then her mum surprised her by swooping down and enveloping her in a hug that had been ten years coming. Zoe could feel the birdlike beat of her heart, and she was five again, delirious with chickenpox. Every time she'd cried out, her mum had always been there. Cool hands on her forehead. Low voice reading *The Secret Garden* as the itching, sweaty hours ticked by.

'My golden girl.' Gina released Zoe and looked around. 'I need a wee.'

'Yes. You said.'

'Where's the loo?'

'That way.' Zoe pointed again. Mum really was having an off day.

As her mum ambled towards the loos, Zoe thought back to the last time they'd met. Ten years before. She could still remember the scrape of the chair against the floorboards as she'd stood up. The fury in every inch of her being. The squeak of the door on its hinges. The click of her own high heels as she strode away.

The memory faded away, and once again she was in a café on her wedding day with a woman who stole things and told people they were too fat. Judging by the giggles and snorts from the assembled audience, they were certainly attracting attention. She felt self-conscious and uncomfortable, and was increasingly in need of gin.

She turned angrily to Mags.

'Why the hell did you get me here?'

44

'Given the circumstances . . .' Mags gestured at her wedding dress, 'why the hell did you come?' She looked at Zoe, arching an eyebrow in a way that Zoe remembered as being distinctly dangerous. She didn't care. She was spoiling for a fight.

Mags wiped her mouth with her paper napkin and then pushed her plate tidily out of the way. She turned to Zoe, her mouth pressed into a reproving line.

'Why do you think I got you here, my girl?'

'I don't know.' She bristled. 'And I'm not your girl.'

'That's right. Pick on the least important thing to object to. Just like you always did.' Mags put her hand to her neck and moved her head from side to side. 'You haven't changed a bit.'

Zoe was rigid with indignation. She could practically feel every pulse of blood round her body. 'Mags, you have no idea whether or not I've changed. And I'm telling you that I have.' She felt a beat of pride. 'I've got my own business. Good friends. A man I love.'

'Not enough to actually marry him, apparently.' Mags dabbed her mouth again with infuriating cool. 'And I haven't seen you rushing to pick up the phone to the poor guy.'

Guilt prickled again, but Zoe wasn't going to let Mags see it. 'Oh come on. I've been here, haven't I?'

'Yes. Having a coffee.' Mags's voice was loaded with sarcasm. 'I'm sure he'll totally understand when you finally deign to catch up with him.'

Zoe felt heat coursing through her. 'Mags, you told me to come.'

'But I didn't know, did I?' Mags balled up her paper napkin. 'And if I had, you can bet your life I wouldn't have asked. And another thing. I should have known, Zoe, because Gina should have told me. She should have dragged me out shopping to help her buy a new dress. You should have invited her. Your own mum. I can't believe you left her out.'

No. That wasn't fair. Zoe inhaled, trying to master her rampaging emotions. She hated feeling out of control. She would need to go on a very long run when this was over. Sweat it out. Push through it.

'We haven't talked for years. Somehow having her watch me saying "I do" didn't feel right.' She knew she sounded harsh. 'Why should I reach out when she's the one in the wrong?'

Mags shook her head and the trio of silver skull earrings she had always worn in her left ear shone in the sunlight. 'Well, that's debatable.'

'No it's not.'

'And anyway, you didn't want to give her a chance? You know, see how she was doing after all this time?'

Zoe felt sweat trickle down her neck. 'Lily lets me know how she is.'

'And that's enough, is it?' Mags frowned. 'God, the things I could tell you about your mum, Zoe. About what she's been through.'

'I don't want to know.' Zoe's mouth was dry and tight.

'No.' Mags stared at her, infinite disappointment stamped across her face. 'I don't suppose you do.'

The slope of Mags's shoulders told Zoe that the conversation was over. 'OK.'

Mags stared at the table. 'OK.' Before Zoe could relax, she looked up again. 'What did that custody sergeant ask you?'

'What do you mean?'

'He asked you a question. At the end.' Mags pointed towards the police station.

'Oh. It was nothing.' Zoe pulled her phone out of her bag but still couldn't bring herself to switch it on.

'Zoe.' There was steel in Mags's voice.

'He just asked me if she'd ever had any mental health problems.' Zoe shook her head dismissively. 'I'm sure it's nothing.'

'Are you?' She could feel Mags's eyes boring into her. 'Are you really?'

'Yes.' Zoe stood up, desperate to escape. 'She's just having a bad day. Look, I need some air. I'll be outside, OK?'

She moved towards the door and was turning the handle when she saw her mum coming out of the toilet. She looked so small and lost. Zoe watched as she gazed around, blinking in the bright light. She could see the confusion dimming her expression, and then her relief as her eyes finally settled on her daughter. She walked over and stood in front of Zoe, the sun highlighting the deep lines on her face.

Zoe stiffened as her mum's hand crept into hers. Her fingers were warm and trusting, and Zoe had no choice but to hold on. Her mum's voice was tiny. 'It's so good to see you.'

Her bowed head brought tears to Zoe's eyes. Her mum never admitted defeat. Never.

The chin rose again and the brown eyes searched hers. 'Things haven't been right, you see.'

Zoe could see. All at once she could see only too well. The set of Mags's shoulders. The endless spoons of sugar. The repetition. Zoe stood still, holding her mum's hand, feeling a tingle on her skin as the pieces slotted into place. She squeezed the familiar fingers, and pulled her mum into a hug, trying to hold tight enough to make up for all the years apart.

Then she looked out of the window and saw him.

Jamie.

Just as he turned and walked away.

Married quarters, Rhine Garrison
Present: a toy keyboard. I'm already regretting it.
Favourite music: whatever you thump out on the above
   – no obvious tunes yet . . .

15th June, 1987

Darling Zo-bear,

   So. Three today. And so grown up! This morning you
put a whole packet of butterfly clips in your hair and
refused to let me remove even one. You're currently
wearing the fairy wings I made you last Christmas
(thank God for coat hangers), and your Victoria Plum
pyjamas. You call yourself 'the Furry Princess' (and yes,
I know what you really mean), and the paddling pool is
your kingdom. Only the truly loved are allowed in. Me.
Alistair. And your little sister, Lily. One month old – so
small and precious and miracle of miracles actually
HERE.

   When I turned my back today, you picked her up
and held her on your lap in the pool. You'd picked half
my daisies and they were floating on top of the water
– you were trying to make some kind of magic grotto
for her, I think. Fortunately there wasn't much water in
the pool yet, but still, you thought she'd be delighted
– and then of course she cried. She does that a lot. I
fished her out and dried her off as the sun glowed on
her pale skin, and you stood pouting in the water. One
of your wings was soggy and your whole body sagged.
You haven't worked out how to love her yet. You're too

49

bangy and splashy and *big* for her. I know you'll get there, though. You have the biggest heart. Last night I saw you creeping into her room and kissing your fingers and placing them gently on her head as she wheezed her way into a rare hour of sleep. My heart was so full, I nearly cried. Then I tripped over your toy dog and swore instead.

Anyway, today I called you to me as I tried to calm Lily, but you turned on your heel and set about trying to dig to Australia with your tiny yellow spade. There was no distracting you. Not till the cake came, anyway. But then Lily miraculously slept for an hour or two and we toasted each other in squash, and Johnny and Mags gave you a plastic sword for your birthday (yikes) and you waved it around with absolute glee. We danced to Starship and you laughed and threw yourself at me, and as I held you and whirled you around, it was your smile and my smile against the blue, and it felt like it would last for ever.

You love Lily, and you want to help so much. During that first week you tried to change nappies and dress her, but she was too little and too weak and she has horrible reflux, so eventually you gave up and tried to look after me instead. I've never drunk so many cups of stone-cold tea. Eventually you got bored and I spent my days encrusted in puke and nappy cream while you ate fish fingers by yourself out of my Honey Monster bowl, or went out to the base playground with Mags and Johnny and the rest of the gang.

You miss your daddy too when he's away. You keep his picture in your room, and you take it down every bedtime and religiously kiss him goodnight. I wish I had the energy to miss him. All I do instead is fear for him at 3 a.m. when I'm shoving a boob in Lily's mouth in a desperate attempt to get her to sleep. I can't think about what might happen to him. I have to block it out.

I had no idea how lonely this would be when I met him. He loves the army. I know that. It's his other family – the one that stands shoulder to shoulder with him in the face of all the danger I can't bear thinking about. He *is* the army. Yet he's still my Alistair. The man who can juggle jars of marmalade and patiently show you how to kick a ball, and who can put the world right simply by taking my hand.

Despite how much being a soldier means to him – and how much it defines him – sometimes, when he's about to leave and he's packing up his endless piles of kit, I want to throw myself on him and hold him so he can't ever leave us again. When we met, I thought he'd be away for a few weeks at most every now and then. I didn't realise it would be months and months, and how much plans would change and tours of duty would extend.

When he's away, he's reduced to blueys through the letter box and occasional conversations. I get so excited about his calls, but then all we get is ten minutes in which the pressure to say everything in the world is so much that I just end up babbling on about the bloody weather or how I've just managed to make some really shit cupcakes. He doesn't say much – doesn't want to scare me, I expect. And I don't get to say what really matters until the final seconds, when I blurt out how much I love him, and normally the phone cuts us off before he can reply.

At night sometimes I think of him in Belfast

surrounded by bombs and guns and I feel so bloody
scared I want to go over there and pull him out. Or
move us there like he wanted. If I hadn't been so
unbelievably pregnant, I would have packed us up and
gone when he deployed a couple of months ago. But it
was too risky. The doctors wouldn't let me. So now I
have to wait and be patient, and sometimes I can't stop
crying and I get into bed with you and inhale the soft,
beautiful sleepiness of you until my pulse slows and I
can breathe again.

But we still have our good times, us girls. Some days
you help me in the garden, pulling up weeds or
planting potatoes or gathering sticks and leaves for
one of our bonfires. Some days I actually have a
personality and am not just a walking bag of bones and
milk and tiredness who can't wait for her evening G&T.
We go out and explore the countryside. We have
picnics and we paddle in freezing rivers and we climb
hills and plant flags made out of sticks and leaves on
the top.

Lily comes with us. She has dimples. Skinny little
legs. Strawberry-blonde hair. A quiet little cry, as if she
doesn't really expect anyone to hear. She is too placid.
Too weak.

But she has you. Her big sister, ready to protect her
against the world with your sticks and your toy bow
and arrow and all the love you have in your heart. Last
week you squeezed Lily's fingers and kissed me and
the world was perfect. I am so proud of you, birthday
girl, and so in love with your tangled coppery hair, your
sticky fingers and your wiggly toes. I love your curiosity, your imagination, and the way you sing yourself
to sleep with endless rounds of 'The Lion Sleeps

Tonight'. And I love the way you look after us – asking your daddy whether he's having enough milk to drink at 'the war'. Checking that I've eaten all my greens. Making sure Lily has an extra blanket whenever she leaves the house.

Alistair says he'll be home soon. He'd bloody better be. I'm getting too used to dinner for one.

I love you.

Mum x

Four

Z oe burst out of the café.
   'Jamie!'

He didn't stop.

'Jamie!' She scooped her skirt over one arm so she could move at faster-than-aisle speed. An old man at the bus stop watched her with evident amusement. Three kids on scooters pointed and laughed. She really couldn't blame them. She must be even more entertaining now she was chasing a man in morning dress.

He was getting away.

Sod it. She kicked off her shoes and started to sprint, her feet slapping against the warm concrete. Then a big red bus rumbled between them down a side road, and when it had passed she couldn't see him. The blond hair. The dark coat. Gone.

She came to a halt, still searching. Still hoping.

Nothing.

The sky was still blue. The smell of cut grass and diesel was still in her nostrils. But all her tomorrows with him were gone.

She staggered over to a low wall and sat down. She leant forward and stared at the pavement – at the lines and squares that had probably witnessed hundreds of dramas just like hers. She thought of him dragging her back into bed every morning after her run. Of his slow smile as he put his favourite tunes on and the way his fingers tapped against his coffee mug as they started to play. Of his forehead resting against hers just after he had proposed.

'Zoe.'

She raised her head so fast her neck clicked.

'Jamie.' She rose to her feet and reached for him.

He stepped back.

Fair enough. She deserved that. 'I'm so sorry.' She gazed at the flush on his cheeks. The blue eyes that had never been so cold.

'Jamie?' Her heart was hanging on this moment.

At last he spoke. 'I came to see if you were OK.' His voice chilled her. 'And there you were, having coffee in a café as if this was just any old Saturday.'

'It's not what it looked like—'

'You didn't even call me.' He looked right at her, and she could see the hurt blazing across his face. Hurt that she alone had caused.

She reached for his hand again and gripped it tight. His fingers were lifeless in hers for a second before he pulled away. Deep down, panic started to whirl. He had made her feel safe. Now all that was about to be stripped away, leaving her alone and vulnerable again.

'Look, I—'

He didn't let her finish.

'Why didn't you come and find me? Talk to me?' The pain on his face made her catch her breath. 'How could you just leave like that?'

The guilt was acid in her stomach.

She reached for the words that might keep him here at her side.

'I love you, Jamie.'

'Funny way of showing it.' He shoved his hands in his pockets and scuffed the pavement with his shoe.

'I'm sorry. I know I should have come and found you. But the call sounded so urgent.'

'And marrying me wasn't?' He flung his arms wide. 'I mean, all those months of planning and choosing and updating that bloody wedding spreadsheet every night and then you just turn around and piss off before the ceremony's even started?' He shook his head. 'I mean, I only wanted a beach and a barbecue, but I put up with all your mad *Hello!* magazine shit, and then you leave me hanging?'

She had never seen him this angry. This man who smiled first thing in the morning and last thing at night.

He started wrestling with his tie. 'Got to get this damn thing off.' He yanked it and the knot pulled even tighter.

'Let me help.' She put out her hand.

'NO.'

'OK, OK.' She sat down on the wall again. The concrete grazed the tops of her thighs. The safety pin must be losing its grip. What a day. She dropped her head and rested it on her hands.

When she looked up again, Jamie had flung his tie to the floor and was undoing the top button of his shirt with evident relief.

'Thank God for that.' He took off his morning coat and threw it next to her on the wall. At least that meant he was staying a bit longer. Every second mattered.

Time to try again. She reached out and touched the coat, still warm from his body. 'I'm so sorry.' He was pacing up and down now, gaining speed all the time. Normally his default walking pace was 'amble'.

She stood back up and planted herself directly in front of him. 'I knew she needed me, Jamie.'

He stopped. 'And I didn't?'

There was no going back now. 'Of course you did, but she was in a police station and she was asking for me, and I know it sounds mad but – I just left.'

His face didn't change. 'But you hate her, Zo. You haven't talked to her in years, and then suddenly you're legging it away from your wedding and trying to save her?' Frustration was stamped across his face. 'It makes absolutely no sense.'

She knew. Oh God, she knew.

She was flustered now. She hated this feeling of being in the wrong. It made her want to fight. 'Look, sometimes these things happen.'

Not what she'd meant to say at all. It got the treatment it deserved. 'Really?' Jamie looked incredulous. 'Because in all the weddings we've been to over the years, I haven't seen it happen even once. Kate and Jonathan? Both ended up with rings on their fingers. Tim and Nij? Yep. They made it down the aisle. And Lucy and Emma? Them too.' His mouth had a new hardness to it. 'So somehow I'm still not convinced.' He walked over and picked up his coat. 'I think there's something else going on here. Something you won't bloody talk about.' He took a few paces away from her as a van zoomed past belching black fumes.

She stepped towards him. 'Look. I love you, Jamie. More than anything. But I had to come here. Please believe me.'

He shook his head. 'Not good enough.' She was horrified to see that he had tears in his eyes. 'There I was waiting for you to come through the door and make me the happiest man alive, and you didn't come, and then I stopped believing you would – I *knew* something was wrong when I saw you upstairs – and when Lily came and told me I just crumpled, right there in front of all your dad's army mates and everyone I've ever met. Thank God Russ was there. He got me out and poured beers down my throat and kept me in the pub till I'd got myself together enough to come here.' She hated the despair on his face.

'I'm so sorry.' She felt heavy and stupid. Of course she should have put him first. Then they'd be cutting the cake now rather than standing here on a street corner dressed in clothes that increasingly felt like they belonged in a farce. 'But I love you. So much.' She knew the words were losing impact every time she uttered them. But she had nothing else. She couldn't begin to explain. She would have to go right back to the beginning – to the face and the voice that she had been running from all these years. She shuddered at the thought.

Jamie rubbed his hands over his eyes. He looked exhausted. Normally she'd pour him a beer and play his favourite Daft Punk album until he smiled. But now she feared she would never be able to cheer him up again.

He frowned. 'Look, I can't be around you right now, Zoe. OK?'

'OK.' She nodded. She had no choice.

He stared at the block of flats across the road, speaking as if she wasn't there. 'I need to get out of here.'

Another siren shrieked along the road. 'Me too.'

Before, they would have taken each other's hands. Now their arms swung awkwardly at their sides. Separate.

She had to know what was coming next. So she could start the long, hard process of adjusting.

'Where are you going to go, Jamie?'

He shrugged. 'Back to the pub. Russ is waiting with a big bottle of whisky.'

'Right.' She nodded. 'Makes sense.' He started walking and she followed him. 'And then?'

'Well, I'm hardly going to come home, am I?' His lips twisted bitterly. 'I'll stay at his place for a bit. Might even go on our honeymoon. I've got the time off work, so why not? Russ'll come with me. He can ogle all the waitresses and embarrass himself while I drink shots by the pool.'

I don't want you to. I'll miss you. She opened her mouth to speak, but he got there first.

'And look, Zoe.' He stopped then, so she did too. 'When I get back, you need to be straight with me. Because either there's something you're not telling me, or you don't love me. It's one of the two.'

She started to protest, but he shook his head.

'You walked out on our *wedding*.' His voice cracked. 'I gave you a chance to talk, but you didn't take it, and then you just left me and ran away. And so all I can think is maybe I'm not the guy for you. Or maybe there's something else going on.' His voice was low and urgent. 'And if there is, I want to hear it.'

'I . . .' She tried to find the bravery she needed to say the words she had suppressed for such a long time.

It wasn't there.

'I'm sorry.' It was the best she could do.

'Me too.' His face was full of regret. 'I thought we were more than this. I really did. But right now I need to leave, because even looking at you is too much. Because in all your years of working too hard and being late to meet me because you had to make one last bloody call, and refusing to ever miss a gym session or cleaning the bathroom at one a.m., you have NEVER . . .' He took a breath. 'You have never made me feel like I don't matter.'

She blinked back her tears and reached for him one last

time. But he swerved to avoid her and dashed across the road, narrowly missing a red car with music booming from its speakers.

She stared after him, feeling the infinite space opening up around her. So. That was it. No arm around her shoulders. No one there when she got home. Just her.

You'd think she'd be used to it now. Before Jamie, she'd had enough practice. But she felt like hell, standing on the street in her gaping wedding dress, watching the man she loved walk away.

She turned and rubbed a hand over her aching brow as she stumbled back the way she had come. Back to her shoes, which miraculously were still there on the pavement. Back to the café where her mum and Mags were talking on the step. Mum was gesticulating wildly and Mags seemed to be trying to calm her.

Then she heard something else.

'Where is she?' She knew that shout.

'Dad?' She turned, and there he was across the road. Dignified. Resplendent. So far, so wedding day. He looked absolutely furious as he waited at the traffic lights, next to a group of kids pretending they were old enough to smoke.

Not so wedding day.

She clenched her fists and prepared to stand her ground. She deserved his rage. She was ready for this.

And then she saw that she wasn't the target. He was aiming elsewhere. She followed his glare and knew that he was on a mission. Target: Mum. ETA: one minute if the lights ever changed. She saw the frown lines on his forehead as he locked on. The widening of her mum's eyes as she saw him.

It was all too familiar. The pattern of their childhood playing itself out right here next to the café and the Lick'n

Chicken shop. Scenes flashed through Zoe's head. Her mum burning the dinner for the CO and his wife. Her dad shouting. Her mum giving as good as she got. Dad about to leave for Northern Ireland and her mum not having his kit washed on time. Slammed doors and angry words. She remembered stroking Lily's hair, singing lullabies to try to drown out the noise.

Mags had seen him too and was trying to get Gina away. Zoe walked across to them.

'Mum?'

'Zo-bear.' The name sparked distant memories. Cuddles before bedtime. Prodding Christmas presents in the small hours.

'Mum. What train do you need to get?'

'The train home.' Her mum looked back at her dad. She was trembling. He was close now. Zoe swallowed and stepped in front of her as her dad strode onwards. A woman next to them shouted obscenities into her mobile phone, and in front of them a man pushed a buggy containing two very small and dissatisfied children.

Now her dad was right in front of them. Tall. Immaculate. Absolutely furious.

Over her shoulder, Zoe could see her mum looking at him with fearful eyes. Zoe couldn't blame her. There was a reason that the British Army had trusted him to lead men into battle.

'Dad, this is my fault.'

He ignored her and spoke only to his ex-wife. 'What the hell were you thinking, Gina?' His voice had lost none of its authority. 'Your wedding vows may not have meant much to you, but surely even you can understand how important today is for Zoe. For our family.'

Zoe intervened. 'Dad, please. She didn't even know—'

As ever, there was no stopping him. Once the anger erupted, it needed to run its course.

'No, Zoe.' He held up a hand. 'Your mother has managed to ruin your wedding, and I'm not going to let her get away with it.'

She heard a sound from behind her.

'What, Mum?'

'He always shouts at me.' Her mum jabbed a finger towards him. 'Doesn't he? Why does he always shout at me?'

She was ducking low behind Zoe now. Mags folded her arms protectively and gunned Alistair down with her stare. It had no effect.

Zoe squared her shoulders. 'Dad, you need to stop this right now.'

'Why?' His stare was bracing, to say the least. She'd felt warmer atmospheres when she'd gone to Prague last December and spent the entire time wishing she'd invested in thermal underwear.

She stood her ground. 'Dad, this isn't her fault.'

It's mine, she wanted to scream. *MINE.*

He looked at her in disbelief. 'Why are you defending her?'

Zoe put a hand on his arm. 'I can't talk about it here. OK? Just . . . believe me. Please?'

He didn't listen. He was too full of rage. 'Well I don't know what we're going to do now. All that organisation. All that preparation. And now what?'

'I don't know, Dad.'

'Why did you leave, Zoe?' His face was confused. 'Seriously. Why? Why didn't you follow the plan?'

Once she started trying to answer that, it would never end. She would talk and talk and talk until everything was out there and her dad stopped shouting at her mum and started shouting at her.

She tried distraction instead. 'Dad, there's no point talking about this now. Is there any way you could head back to the hotel and see what we can do about all the food and drink?' He needed action. A target.

He shook his head impatiently. 'You can do it, can't you?'

'I need to look after Mum.'

'Look after her?' He was outraged. 'She doesn't need looking after. She's not ill; she's a criminal.'

'It's complicated.'

'No, it's not.'

'Please, Dad? I'll call later, but I have to get her home now.' She realised she had absolutely no idea what her mum's address was, and felt a surge of shame.

'Lily's at the hotel. It's fine.' He didn't move.

She tried again. 'You know Lily hates that kind of thing. And it would be a shame for all that champagne to go to waste, wouldn't it?'

That got him moving, but not before he turned and aimed a parting shot at Gina. 'This isn't over, you know. I can't believe you're selfish enough to ruin your own daughter's wedding. Just because you weren't invited. You always were vindictive, but this takes the bloody piss.'

'Dad!' Zoe stepped towards him, but he had already turned away and was hailing a cab. She didn't envy the driver – they were in for a particularly loud journey.

'Can we go home now?' Her mum's voice was quiet. Too quiet.

'Of course we can.' Zoe took her arm. Once these arms had protected her. From bumping her head. From wasps and bees.

Now it was Zoe's turn. No matter what had happened, she owed her mum that much.

'Mags, can you lead the way?'

'Sure.' Mags nodded. 'Thanks, Zoe.'

'Where are we going again?' Her mum squeezed her arm.

'Home, Mum.'

Silence for a second.

'Where's that?'

'Good question.' Zoe shook her head. 'Good question, Mum.'

And the three of them walked on into the dusty sunlight of the evening.

Legion Barracks, Wiltshire
Present: Little Grey Rabbit books
Favourite music: Disney. Anything by Disney.

15th June, 1988

Darling Zo-bear,

FOUR TODAY. We went to the beach to celebrate.
No party this year, as we've only just got back from
Germany and haven't really met anyone yet. But you
had a plan. You stood on a chair last night, watering
the cress in the yoghurt pots on the windowsill. You
were dressed in your princess outfit (aka a purple
tablecloth, a tinfoil crown and a pair of gold sandals
with crazy high heels that I used to wear back when I
could stay awake past *EastEnders*), and announced that
for your birthday you wanted to go to the seaside.
Your daddy unglued himself from the six o'clock news,
took one look at your excited little face and said yes.

Of course the wind was blustering round the pebble-
dash this morning, and nature even threw in some rain
for good measure. Alistair asked you if you were sure
you still wanted to go, in that 'sensible' voice of his –
the same one he uses when asking me to tidy up the
kitchen – but of course you said yes and so we packed
up the car, and then of COURSE he was called away to
sort out some trouble in the barracks. That bloody CO
he works for is a total tyrant. Thirty-eight days off a
year Alistair's meant to have. We're in June already and
I think he's had about five.

Anyway. Your birthday. It was 8.15 in the morning and off we went on our merry way, once I'd found the car keys in the oven, of course. You said they needed to be hot for the car to work. Loving your logic there. So there we were, the three of us, in clapped-out Norma the Nissan with a whole lot of jam sandwiches and Wham bars, jolting our way through the English countryside. It's so bloody wonderful being back home. I hadn't realised how much I love those rolling green fields and scenic sheep that the brochures at the travel agency used to bang on about. Norma seemed at risk of imminent breakdown most of the way there, and Lily took the trouble to be sick about five times, but eventually we arrived. Lovely sandy beach, sadly entirely soaked by the relentless rain.

Most kids would have thrown a tantrum or refused to get out of the car, but not you. I strapped Lily on to my back in her waterproof coat – she's still light as a feather despite all my attempts to fatten her up – and took your hand, and you felt so warm and sure, and out we went into the soggy joys of one of England's finest summer days. You had on your pink polka-dot wellies and your biggest smile, and your hair whooshed around your face as you sang 'The Bare Necessities' into the wind.

We ran around like mad people, writing our names in the sand before big waves washed the letters away, cackling and laughing and doing forward rolls and making sand angels. Lily slept against me as I watched you cartwheel and dash your way through your fourth birthday, mouth wide, eyes alive, every last inch of you sheer unadulterated joy. When the rain had penetrated through to our pants, we got the trusty old windbreak

out of the car, in all its ragged red glory, and pegged it
into the sand before eating our picnic.

Our sandwiches were more sand than jam, but you
said they were a pirate's feast and insisted I ate every
last bite on pain of walking the plank (an old stick lying
next to us on the beach). So I did. We toasted your evil
pirate crew in lemonade, then we walked along until
we found an ice-cream shop and we sat down and had
an almighty sundae, with vanilla and chocolate and that
Ice Magic sauce you love so much. I had a tea and
burnt my tongue like I always do, and you gave me a
big dollop of your vanilla to cool me down.

Lily started shrieking halfway through, but we carried
on. This was your day. But she got louder and louder
until the shopkeeper pointedly held his hands over his
ears and we left, giggly and shaky with sugar and
excitement, and headed back to the car. Somehow
Norma managed to start, and somehow she kept
going, and we sang the theme tune from *The Wombles*
and laughed, and Lily slept again – her birthday present
to you, I think.

When we got home, Alistair was back and he
whisked you off for toasted marshmallows and football
and stories before bed, while I unpacked the car and
wondered if my bra would ever be dry again. Lily sat in
her chair and watched me, eyes clear and untroubled
for once. I wrote my first letter to her when she
turned one. So much of it was about how much I love
watching the two of you together. My girls. My life.

Later, Alistair and I sat and talked about the future. I
asked him about when he thought he might leave the
army, and it was the right time and he didn't get tetchy
and he told me how hard it would be to leave his

100,000-man team, all fighting for the same cause. I said how tough it is without him and how much he's missing out on – first teeth, first smiles, the endless adventure of your imagination as it grows. He didn't like that and we nearly had a row, but then he held me close and said it wouldn't be too long. Two years, maybe three. I hugged the idea to myself – my own special heartbeat of hope. We miss him so much. Every night while he's away you creep into my bed, as Lily slumbers in her cot. The three of us blink in the morning sunlight as another day starts. Another day without him.

But we're so lucky. I know that really. And so – thank you, my beautiful girl. Thank you for a perfect day. For howling into the rain with me. For singing 'Heigh-Ho' with me and not telling me how out of tune I am. For taking me in your special spaceship to the moon and for keeping my days full of adventure and bouncing on the bed. For loving me with your whole heart.

And of course, I love you too. I love every hair on your head and every fold of your knee and that gorgeous soft patch just beneath your chin where I bury my nose and exhale ever so gently. And you laugh and you laugh and you laugh.

You are amazing.

Mum x

Five

Three days later, Zoe braved reading through the WhatsApp messages on her phone.

Ten minutes after the ceremony was due to start, her colleague Bruno had sent: Have you been abducted by aliens? WHERE ARE YOU? Your dad is going crazy.

Zoe scrolled on. Here was Mandy, her oldest friend from university. Shit. Just heard J's in the Maldives with Russ. Are you OK? Zoe swallowed. So Jamie had done it. He hadn't been in touch since walking away from her on Saturday. Sixty-two hours and thirteen minutes ago, to be precise. And yes, she was counting. Zoe gripped her tea as if it was a lifebuoy. Here was another. You can run but you can't hide. I'm coming round.

She leant back against the cushions. At least there was some small comfort. Mandy would never find her here at her mum's flat. Last night Lily had come over too, and they had slept on the sofa cushions on the floor, cuddling together just as they had when they were children. Her sister hadn't asked any questions but Zoe could feel her watching. Waiting.

Zoe deleted all her messages, still unable to explain what had happened, and stretched her arms over her head. 'Is Mum still asleep?'

'Yes.' Lily swooshed water into the mug she had in her hand. 'We'll have to get her up for work soon. She

69

normally leaves at eight. I'll take her with me when I go.'

'Is her job still going OK, then?' She thought of her mum's confusion when they had got her back here on Saturday, and wondered how she was managing to carry on working as a PA. Organising meetings. Remembering what papers were needed. What calls to make.

'As far as I know, it's going fine.' Lily turned off the tap. 'Are you going into work today, Zo?'

'No.' Zoe shook her head decisively.

'Not ready yet?'

'No. That's not it. I just feel like working from here.'

'Are you tired? I heard you tossing and turning. Are you missing Jamie too much? It must be so hard when—'

'I'm fine, Lily, really.' Zoe could handle anything except sympathy. She didn't want to talk about how much she missed him. How much she had cried and cursed the choice she had made that afternoon. How bleak the world looked without him and how she knew – deep in her heart – that he was never, ever coming back.

It was easier here. Easier to forget. That first night she had got home, still in her dress, to find the entire place full of balloons. All Jamie's work, of course. She had imagined his face as he squeezed the balloons through the front door – the grin as he anticipated her surprise and excitement as they arrived back from the wedding to pick up their honeymoon bags. There was a card on the mantelpiece. *To my beautiful bride.* Inside, a simple star design and one sweet sentence. *So, I got you over the threshold. Can't wait to see what happens next, J.* And that was the moment her mask had fallen. In their empty flat, covered in silk and sweat, she had lain down on the sofa and howled.

The next morning, she had got up after sleepless night

number one, packed a bag and headed back to her mum's. She didn't really know why. No one had invited her. There wasn't even a bed to sleep in. But it was somewhere else to be. Somewhere to try to forget.

'Jamie and I will be fine, Lil. We just need some time apart.' She smiled reassuringly at her sister. 'It'll all be OK.'

'That's good.' Lily put the mug down on the drainer. Zoe caught the doubt on her face and felt irritation flare.

'Stop worrying about me, Lil.'

'What do you mean?' Her sister blinked at her, twirling a short strand of hair around her finger.

Zoe finished the last of her tea. 'I can see you. Wondering if I'm going to lose it and hide under my duvet for a year.'

'No, I—'

'Well I'm not. OK?'

'But I don't really understand.' Lily reached down and scratched her ankle.

'What don't you understand?'

'Why you're staying here.'

Zoe didn't want to answer that. Instead she did what she did best. She turned things around. 'Well there's something *I* don't really understand either.'

'What's that?' Lily was mashing the frayed ends of her baggy pink jumper between thumb and fingers.

'Why you didn't tell me about Mum earlier. About how confused she is.'

Lily folded her arms defensively, but Zoe kept going.

'You never told me how bad things are. If you had said something earlier, I could have done something to help.'

Lily leant against the sink. 'Zo, she's always been a bit vague.'

'A bit vague?' Zoe grimaced in frustration. 'I think it's

71

more than that. She couldn't even remember how to do up her zip yesterday.'

Lily shrugged. 'So? Sometimes I can't get that right when I've had a few drinks. It doesn't mean anything. Look . . .' She pointed at the windowsill. 'All her plants are still fed and watered. That basil plant looks like it's about to take over the world.'

'Yes, but she can do that in her sleep. It doesn't prove anything. And what about the fact that she was keeping the sugar in the fridge and the butter in the oven when I got here?'

Lily opened her mouth to reply. Zoe kept talking.

'Or the fact that her entire diet seems to consist of meringues and Weetabix? No wonder she's so bloody pale.'

Lily looked at the floor and Zoe sensed victory. 'And then there's her room. That entire wall chock-full of pictures. Of me. Of you. Even of Dad. Some of them have labels on them, Lil. It's like she's trying to remember everything – trying to lock her memories into her head. I've been googling, and it says that—'

'Zoe.' Lily cut her off. 'They're pictures of the people she loves. What's wrong with that?'

'Including Dad?' Zoe shook her head. 'That doesn't make sense. It seems to me that—'

'What, Zo? What does it seem like to you? You never see her. You never talk to her. Or about her. You didn't even want her at your wedding.'

Zoe defended herself. 'So? That doesn't mean I don't care.'

The look Lily gave her could best be described as sceptical. 'Whenever I mentioned her, you got really shitty. Even when I just told you stuff in passing.' Her silver earrings caught the light as she talked. 'You know, like when I told you she'd got a new job. You didn't give a flying one.'

Zoe tapped the table with her finger. 'That's not the point. You should have told me about . . .' She gestured to the huge pile of boxes of Sainsbury's meringues on the sideboard. 'This.'

As ever, Lily stepped back from the brink. 'I'm sorry, Zo.' Her eyes were huge. 'But I wasn't deliberately not telling you. The fact is, I didn't really know how bad she was till Saturday. Most of the time she seemed OK. She goes to work and shops and watches action films on a Friday night just like she's always done. Every now and then she got a word wrong, or couldn't remember someone's name, but mainly I thought she was all right. So don't be angry with me. Please.'

She was looking around the tiny kitchen as if hoping to locate a trapdoor.

Zoe relented. 'I'm not angry.'

'That's just how Dad says it when he's *really* angry.' Lily chewed on her lip.

Zoe struggled to appear calm. This situation wasn't Lily's fault. She knew that. She got up from her seat, pushing the small table forward so she could get out and give her sister a hug. As she did so, the black tea caddy balancing on the edge wobbled and fell to the floor with a clang. Bits of paper scattered across the dull blue squares of lino in a wobbly arc.

Zoe reached down to pick them up. She stuffed a handful back into the caddy without looking. Then another. Then she looked down and spotted that the scraps were covered in her mum's scrawling handwriting. The first one she read was a recipe for apple crumble. The next covered how to fix the grumbling boiler in the corner. One was

Lily's contact details – email and phone. Despite herself, Zoe found herself looking for her own details, even though she knew they wouldn't be there. There were gaps opening up all around her. Gaps where the love should be.

'What are you doing?'

She started guiltily as her mum entered the room and picked up the cat bowl.

She recovered herself quickly. 'Nothing. These fell out, so I'm just putting them back.'

'I'll do it.' Wisps of hair tangled around her mum's face as she reached down and swept up the rest. She stuffed them into the caddy and put the lid on, slamming it down with the palm of her hand. Her slippers made a squelching sound as she headed for the cupboard, and Zoe wondered when the floor had last been cleaned. Her mum pulled out a tin of cat food and emptied it into the bowl.

'Murgatroyd!' She put the bowl down on the floor. Zoe still couldn't believe how big he was. Folds of fat ringed his face and body, and he was so heavy, his legs looked like they were struggling to bear his weight. Once he'd been capable of skewering sparrows from a standing start – now, even yawning looked like too much effort.

Zoe sat back down and looked at her mum, who was wearing the same stripy green dressing gown she'd always worn, and the hedgehog slippers Zoe had bought her when she was eleven. Anxiety knifed her heart. Mum could make crumble in her sleep – it had once been a Sunday-afternoon ritual, like trying and failing to do the quick crossword and arguing over what to watch on TV. Yet now she was writing herself reminders.

She must know her memory was failing.

Her mum made a beeline for the kettle, flicking the

switch and getting out a cream teapot with the Highland Toffee logo emblazoned on the side. Zoe remembered the way her teeth would get stuck in the sticky sweetness as they shared a bar on their way home from swimming. The smell of chlorine and sugar in the car. The day one of her mum's fillings had popped out as the toffee pulled away, and their mad scrabbling around the floor of the Nissan as they tried to find it.

Zoe had forgotten how much fun they'd had.

Lily gently turned the kettle off. 'Let's just put some water in here, OK?' She picked it up and carried it to the tap.

Gina's head snapped round. 'There was enough in there, you know. For one cup.'

Lily's voice was calm. 'Well I'd like one too, OK?'

Gina responded by opening a cupboard. Closing it. Opening a drawer. Banging it shut. It was as if she was a newcomer trying to find the cups in a friend's kitchen.

Lily put the kettle back on its stand and switched it on. 'What do you want for breakfast, Mum?'

'Weetabix.'

Zoe couldn't help smiling. In some ways, everything had changed. In other ways, nothing at all.

'Why don't I get it for you?' Lily picked a bowl off the dryer.

'I can do it myself.'

'OK.' Lily handed the bowl over and Gina put Weetabix and milk in and came to the table. She sat opposite Zoe without making eye contact. For a minute there was just the clang of spoon against bowl.

Then her mum looked at her and she felt the old kick of resentment.

'How's work?'

Hardly a conversational hand grenade.

'Good. I run my own company now.' Zoe didn't want to think about the mountain of unanswered emails in her inbox.

'I knew that.' Frustration flickered across her mum's face. 'Are you enjoying it?'

'Yes. We've got a lot of projects on the go.' God, she sounded like a bad marketing brochure. 'It's great.'

Her mum chewed thoughtfully. 'Same old Zoe, then?'

'What do you mean?'

'Saying one thing, meaning another.'

Zoe crossed her legs. Uncrossed them. 'What do you mean?'

'Doesn't matter.'

Her mum put the final spoonful of Weetabix into her mouth, and then picked up the bowl and slurped the milk.

'Mum.'

'What?' She wiped the milk from her upper lip with the back of her hand.

'That's gross.' Zoe turned her head away, only to see an enormous spider's web stretching down from the cupboard above her. She grabbed a tissue and reached up to wipe it away.

'Bloody hell, you've got a bit finicky, haven't you?' Her mum pushed her chair back. 'I remember when you used to spend your whole life grubbing around in the dirt, trying to dig your way out of the . . . out of the . . .'

Zoe looked meaningfully at Lily.

Gina clicked her fingers. 'Out of the place with the flowers.'

'The garden, Mum? Is that what you mean?'

Gina's eyes flashed. 'Of course it is. Stupid question.'

'OK, OK.' Zoe looked at the stain in the middle of the

kitchen table. It was a depressing shade of brown. No amount of Dettol had got it off yesterday.

She looked through to the hallway, with its worn beige carpet. It was even worse. A large patch of mould was quietly taking over the ceiling above the door.

She realised her mum had been talking to her. 'What?'

'What are you doing here?'

She had forgotten how penetrating her mum's stare could be.

'I . . .' She saw Lily communing with the floor again and knew just how uncomfortable she was feeling. She tried again. 'After what happened, I thought I should . . .'

'When?' Her mum looked as blank as the shopping list hanging from the fridge.

'Saturday. When . . .'

'When what?'

Everything in the room diminished to the confusion on her mum's face. To the total lack of comprehension in her eyes.

'When you . . .'

Her mum threw her head back in the raucous laughter Zoe hadn't known she'd missed until now. 'Just messing with you. You mean our little trip to the police station, don't you?'

Zoe was totally wrong-footed. 'Yes. I wanted to see . . .'

'If I'm a bloody nutter?'

'No.'

'Oh, but your face says yes!' Gina turned to Lily. 'Doesn't it? She thinks I'm off my rocker!' She cackled again. 'Well, no need to worry, Zo-bear. I just got a bit confused. Just like you at that birthday party when you mixed up the clues in the treasure hunt and threw a massive screamer in the kitchen.'

Zoe thought back to that day. The sun beating down. Snoopy party bags containing Wham bars and party poppers. Wearing silly hats and running through the sprinkler to a backing track of Kajagoogoo and Spandau Ballet. She heard a miaow and looked down to see Murgatroyd, whiskers thick with cat food, about to bed down on her socks. She leant down to pet him, glad of an excuse to look away, her brain still struggling to accept what she was feeling.

Because her mum's gaze – now so soft – made her feel like she was coming home.

Years of convincing herself she didn't need the woman in front of her. Years of fury and regret, still there no matter how hard she tried to bury them.

She buried her confusion, running her hands over the thick ginger fur. Murgatroyd gave a deep, throaty purr.

Her mum's knees clicked as she joined Zoe by the extremely happy cat.

'He's such a softie, aren't you, Murgy?' She patted his head and he smiled the smile of a cat who had arrived in feline heaven. 'Shall we feed you?'

Lily was now by Zoe's side, and Zoe felt her flinch as the words sank in.

'Come on, let's get you some breakfast.' Their mum walked to the cupboard she had walked to ten minutes before. Opened it. Got out a tin of cat food. Emptied it into the bowl.

It was now very clear why Murgatroyd had put on a few pounds.

He ambled over to the bowl and started eating.

Zoe waited for her mum to laugh. To tell them she was joking. To make it all OK.

Nothing.

Zoe put her arm round Lily and squeezed her tight. Lily leant into her, and Zoe felt a wave of love so overwhelming she couldn't bear to let her go. Here was one person she could hold on to. One person she was never going to let down.

Lily looked at her, amused. 'Are you crying, Zo?'

'No. Just something in my eye.' Zoe shook her head vigorously.

'Of course.' Lily grinned. 'Because you never cry, do you?'

'Never.' Zoe decided to gloss over the last couple of days.

'She used to cry.' Their mum threw the tin into the rubbish bin. 'That awful man made her cry. Didn't he?'

Zoe froze.

Because she knew her mum didn't mean Jamie. No. She was referring to someone else.

Someone she had never been able to forget.

Legion Barracks, Wiltshire
Present: Lego tank set (your dad's idea). I think you
    were more excited by the free jelly key ring you got
    in the box of cornflakes.
Favourite music: still on the Disney kick (make it
    STOP!)

15th June, 1989

Darling Zo-bear, aged FIVE (no days, no minutes, just
exactly five, it's important we're clear about that).

You stood up for Lily today, birthday girl. She'd just
puked on your daddy's uniform and he was doing all
his usual pre-shouting manoeuvres – pacing around and
exhaling loudly through his nostrils like a hungry horse
– and you stood in front of him, all of forty-two inches
tall, put your hands on your hips and told him he
should stop and that she was only little and she didn't
mean to. I loved you for that, just as I loved you for
grabbing his hands and making him dance you round
the kitchen to the Happy Birthday song. You got him
smiling and laughing, and it was as if you weren't five,
more like twenty-five, with years and years of all the
wisdom I don't seem to have in your veins.

Alistair lost Richard, you see. The man who loved
beers and rugby and who drew brilliant cartoons on
any available surface. The man who had been his
closest friend ever since Richard lent him some socks
in the freezing Wales countryside and they realised
they both supported Wasps.

He died at the end of last summer. A helicopter crash on a routine exercise. Alistair hasn't been the same since. He can't sit still. He can't take a day off. He has forgotten how to smile. He shouts at us when we leave things in the wrong place, or take too long to get ready to go out. You stand there and stare at him, your face an indignant question mark, your hands on your hips. He doesn't see you. He doesn't seem to see any of us at the moment.

He can't stop thinking that he should have somehow known about the faulty engine and stopped Richard getting into that cockpit. Sometimes when we're sitting at the kitchen table when you're both asleep, I see him answering my questions or chewing absently on his food and I know that he isn't really with me at all. He's back there on that day reliving their last mug of tea together and wondering if he can somehow change the truth.

It was just a horrible accident but now there's a hole in all of our lives. Mags has lost her husband. Johnny has lost his dad. And Alistair has a cut so deep I don't know how to help him heal it. We fight more. We talk less. Every day his heart is disappearing, frozen beneath the words and gestures that get him through the day.

I miss Richard too. Of course I do. His rumbling laugh. His way of pulling Mags towards him and nuzzling her hair, and the rightness of the two of them sitting on our sofa in our living room as we all tucked into a Chinese takeaway. The turn of his head as he made plans with Alistair about the company they would set up together when they left the army.

All that is gone now. And all that remains is a sad

group of people who desperately miss him. You kept asking when he was coming back – I didn't know what to say. And you noticed that Alistair had less patience and time for you than before Uncle Richard disappeared. You miss Mags and Johnny too now they've gone back to her parents' place to try and piece themselves back together again. I write every week. No replies yet, but I'll keep trying. I bloody love that girl.

Anyway, your birthday. You had a party – eight kids came, plus a couple of stray puppies, so it was all a bit feral. When things showed signs of going quiet, I threw around more strawberries from the garden, and created the world's least challenging treasure hunt (vintage clues like *I live in the cupboard and you have me with chips* – I'm not made for being creative under pressure). The mums had wine and Salt 'n' Shake crisps and too many jelly babies from the big bowl in the living room, and we all tried not to talk about how much we missed Mags.

Alistair told you at the party that he was going to leave the army soon. He's been thinking about it since Richard died – but of course not talking about it, except occasional mentions when we're watching TV or digging the vegetable patch. He's an expert at putting on a brave face, he really is. You were so excited that you ran around in circles for ages, screaming and giggling, and Alistair and I just stood there, his arm round my waist, Lily clinging on to my leg, the three of us watching you until you dived on to the sofa with your legs waving in the air. It was perfect. The best time we'd had together since the news. The four of us together and loving each other. A family.

So what have you been up to this year? You've
started telling me what to do, that's for sure. You're all
'no, it's this way', and 'no, *I'll* make the lunch', and
frankly, it's great having some help, so I just let you get
on with it. The Brigadier's wife looked like she'd swallowed a tea bag when she saw you pouring the coffee
out with your teeny-tiny hands, but I just gave her
another Bourbon biscuit and she shut right up. I'm
getting better at army rules, but mumming is one thing
I won't take advice on. I have to do this my way. You
grow cress in cups on the windowsill. You march
around the garden giving me orders, watering the
roses and singing to your sunflowers to help them
grow quicker.

But most of all you spend hours and hours playing
with Lily. And when I watch you two together, I know
I'm doing OK. Red hair next to strawberry blonde on
the pillow, curled around each other in your bed. You
start off by yourselves, but during the night, she wakes
up and comes in and snuggles down next to her big
sister. Sometimes I creep in and sit on the carpet, just
to absorb the two of you. The peace. The love.

When I look ahead, I can't wait to see what's in store.
I think of you as you carefully brush Lily's hair before
bed. She sits there so quietly as you smooth out each
strand, your tongue sticking out between your teeth, a
little furrow between your eyebrows. You care so much.
Your heart is so big that you are going to do amazing
things. Huge things. World-changing things.

I can't wait to see what they are.

All my love,
Mum x

Six

'**W**hat on earth are you doing here?'

'And good morning to you too, Bruno.' Zoe put her bag down, enjoying the clean sweep of the desk after the confused clutter of her mum's flat. After a week off, it was good to be back. It was time to get on.

Bruno rose elegantly from his chair and poured her a mug of the thick black coffee he kept constantly bubbling on the machine his ex-boyfriend had brought over from Italy. He carried the mug across and put it on the floor by the big leather sofa in the corner.

The sofa had been the scene of many key moments since Zoe had started her web development company, Zapp Digital, three years before, using every last penny of her savings to rent this office in a unit in Shoreditch. She dreamt of doing things better than her employers ever had, and her first move had been to lure Bruno here, and to keep talking until he agreed to come and work for her. She had carried on for so long that he had thrown himself back against the patterned orange cushions and raised his arms in supplication. 'OK, OK! But only if you make me a director.'

'Technical director?'

'Done.' They shook hands, and since then the sofa had become the site of coffee breaks and cash-flow crises and of celebrations that began with two mugs and a bottle

84

and ended in the karaoke bar down the road duetting on 'Billie Jean'. Their first client. Their first award. The sofa had celebrated them all.

Bruno eyed her meaningfully as he carried his mug over too and placed it next to hers. He sank down into the creaking leather.

He wanted a chat.

She didn't.

'Thanks for the coffee.' She hung her denim jacket on the peg by the door and then picked up her mug and walked over to her desk. She sat tentatively on her swivel chair, wondering whether it was going to spontaneously collapse as it had several times before. One day she would have the cash to replace the furniture she'd bought second-hand from a shop over the road. The reasons it had been so cheap were now abundantly clear. Random squeaking. Castors that didn't move.

But today her chair behaved. It clearly knew what kind of mood she was in, and that she would merrily hurl it out of the window if it dared to cross her. She sighed and switched on her Mac, hoping to lose herself in the flicker of the screen.

She thought of Jamie in the Maldives. Jamie on a sunlounger. Jamie meeting lithe girls in bikinis who lured him off for cocktails and bloody beach volleyball every night.

NO. Work.

She was about to log in when a tanned hand reached out to stop her.

'Stop right there,' Bruno's voice admonished her. 'No working yet. You're meant to be on honeymoon, for God's sake. Do you know how worried I've been? I've been calling you ever since the un-wedding, and you haven't answered once.'

'I texted you.' She swallowed a mouthful of coffee. It was so strong she could feel her blood pressure rising.

'Yes. That.' His voice dropped sardonically as he swiped his phone until he found it. 'Am OK. Don't worry.'

'What's wrong with that?' She logged in.

'It's a bit minimal, isn't it?'

'It covered everything.' She stared resolutely at her screen. 'Besides, it's true. I *am* fine. Look at me.' She met his gaze. 'Hair washed, clothes on, teeth brushed. Nothing to see here.'

'Really?' His eyebrow arched upwards and he searched her face.

'Yes.' She felt exposed, and so turned her head away and stared at the red and cream brickwork underneath the window, avoiding his piercing stare.

He slid into the seat across from her and pushed his huge white screen to one side so he could see her face. 'So are you going to tell me what happened?'

She wondered if ignoring him would make him leave her alone.

No.

He took a pen from the pot in front of him and rolled it between his fingers. 'Come on. Spill. I don't get dressed up in tails for just anyone, you know.'

'Bruno, you once wore your tails to an all-you-can-eat Chinese.'

He flushed, but remained focused. 'Stop trying to distract me, boss. I know your tricks, remember?' He got up again and came and stood by her side. 'Now, whatever you say, I know you must be feeling shit, so are you going to let me give you a hug or not?'

'Not.' Zoe was horrified to find tears in her eyes.

'Oh yes you are.' He held his hands wide.

'No!'

'Come to Bruno.'

'No.' Zoe couldn't help smiling as she reached up and put a hand over his mouth. 'Stop talking.'

He shook himself free, then lifted Zoe from her seat. He was much stronger than he looked. He wrapped his warm arms around her and she felt herself unfurling.

His voice vibrated through her. 'I just want to help, you know. You put your whole heart into planning that wedding.'

She would not cry. 'Look, my mum got ill and I had to leave, all right? It's going to be fine. I'm OK.' She pulled away and sat down, clicking her inbox open. Apparently she had received over five hundred emails since she had skipped off to get married. In the past, work had always helped her to keep going. Had been her reason for waking up and for failing to ever get to bed before midnight. Time to try its medicinal powers again. She opened the first mail.

Bruno pushed her screen to the side.

'But you're not OK, are you?' He sat on her desk and crossed his legs. Skinny jeans today, with bright red socks. 'I saw how hard you worked. Staying here late frantically making wedding favours. Doing the table planning. Working out who would click with who and who might get a snog in and who wouldn't be offended by your creaky old Aunt Miriam with her "SEND THEM ALL HOME" views on immigration. You *can't* be OK about this.'

He was right.

Nothing was OK. She missed Jamie so much she just wanted to stay in bed all day and sleep. She missed him

87

so much she regularly googled flights to the Maldives in the hope of going out there and winning him round. But then she remembered the hurt on his face and knew there was no point.

Bruno brushed a speck of dirt off his Converse. 'I remember when you met him, you know.'

'I—'

He ignored her. 'When we were working at skiparty.com and he came in to fix my computer. You were hungover to the back teeth and then suddenly you perked up and disappeared into the bathroom to fix your hair.'

'No I didn't!'

He held up a finger. 'Don't be coy.'

She felt her cheeks burn. 'I'm not!'

'And you kept sitting there pretending you were really bored by him. Playing hard to get. But actually you were like a bee on honey. You kept popping up at my desk with "urgent" things to discuss, you know, like that totally empty green file that you claimed was some kind of international crisis.'

Zoe knew he was right. Normally the arrival of a guy from IT was entirely unexciting, but that day it had been different. Something about the glint in his eyes. The red T-shirt clinging to his chest. The baggy-jeaned saunter.

Bruno interrupted her trip down memory lane. 'You even pretended your computer was broken. Just so he'd talk to you.'

She shook her head. 'Doesn't sound like me.'

'Exactly.' Bruno stood up. 'It was love at first sight.'

She tapped the edge of her keyboard with the tip of her finger, remembering how her pulse had risen when she had spied him waiting outside the office. The sweet tang of his aftershave. The casual way he'd asked her to come for a drink at the pub round the corner. After years of saying no to dates without a second thought, she knew he was the one to say yes to.

They had never looked back. Until that night in May. Until the past had caught up with her.

She realised a tear was sliding down her cheek and wiped it furiously away. More came in its place. Bruno grabbed a tissue and handed it to her as she tried to force the emotions back down. This wasn't what she did. She coped. She carried on.

The phone rang, and without thinking, she reached her hand out.

Bruno dived for it too. 'I can get it!'

She had already picked up. 'Hello, Zoe speaking, how can I help you?'

She listened as a client bemoaned the fact that the mobile app they had developed for his plumbing business wasn't working. Zoe gathered strength with every word. She knew what to do. She knew how to help.

She calmed him down and set out a plan, emailing the relevant developer as she did so. 'So, we'll look into it for you and get it sorted as soon as we can.'

'OK, great.'

'Is there anything else I can help you with?'

'No thanks.' He sounded thoroughly mollified. 'Oh. No. Wait a minute. One more thing.'

'Yes?'

'I just wanted to say congratulations. How's married life treating you?'

Time to end the call. 'Great, thanks. Speak soon.' She hung up, wondering how many more times that question was going to torment her.

Bruno was shaking his head. 'I have no idea how you do that.'

'What do you mean?'

'There you were at DEFCON 1, and suddenly you pull that out of the bag. What a performance.'

'It's what I do.'

'I wish I could do it too. But clients make me panic and talk too much.' He sighed. 'Maybe one day I'll figure it out. When I grow up.'

'You're fine, Bruno.'

'I don't know about that.' He began to pace. 'My pitch to that coffee company was terrible.'

'Not terrible.'

'Come on, Zo.' He grimaced. 'They were laughing. And definitely not *with* me.'

She remembered only too well. That was one contract they hadn't won. She had done all the pitching since then.

Time to change the subject. 'There is one thing you could do to help.'

'Name it.'

'I'm going to have to send all the presents back.' Presents she and Jamie should have opened together. The Bose speakers. The New York cityscape mugs she loved. The portable table tennis net and bats he had added on when she wasn't looking. She looked at Bruno with an absolute sense of gloom. 'Every last one of them. They all arrived at our flat yesterday and my dad is already stressing me out about it. I know he's right, and I feel so bad after all the money he spent on the wedding.' She sighed. 'But he keeps saying that the proper thing to do is to write a card with each returned gift. I mean, what am I meant to say? *Dear X, soz about the lack of wedding vows, maybe next time?*'

Bruno shook his head. 'God, your dad is a bit much, sometimes.'

'Yeah.'

'I'll help you with the presents.'

'Are you sure?' He nodded, and she reached out and squeezed his hand. 'Thank you so much.'

'Pleasure.' He moved away and sat back down. 'I'll bring round wine and Frazzles and we can get them all sent back where they belong.'

She frowned. 'I'm not very good company, you know.'

'Oh, I know.' He raised his eyebrows. 'Two years of sharing an office, and you think I haven't noticed *that*?'

She laughed. 'OK, OK. Yes. Please come round. Please help me with my sad pile of presents.'

'Excellent! How's Friday?'

'Great.' She didn't have to think about it. Didn't have to consult her diary. She had nothing planned apart from cleaning the grouting and early runs for one.

She looked at her friend as he pulled his keyboard towards him. They had first met at a holiday start-up a few years before, and their friendship had gone from strength to strength. Nights at the pub. Sunday cinema. Jamie used to joke that Bruno was her other boyfriend. Zoe would reply that Bruno's actual boyfriend might have something to say about that.

The boyfriend was long gone now. And Bruno was here and was trying his hardest to be her friend. She sighed. Everywhere else she looked, other people weren't there. Lily was off on a health and safety course, and her dad was doing his best, but she knew he was struggling. He had missed their Sunday run for the past two weeks, and his texts were concise, to say the least. Sorry. Can't make it today. Have to meet the boys from the regiment. Boys, indeed.

The majority of them were in their sixties, with second wives and medication to take every morning.

She missed him. She missed the person she used to be in his eyes.

'Earth to Zoe!' Bruno leant over and tapped her on the forehead. 'We are conversing here.'

'What?'

'You know. Exchanging words. Thoughts. *Feelings?*'

'Oh. Yes.' She looked out of the window and saw a mum holding on to her little boy, who seemed hell-bent on trying to scale a postbox. Zoe felt a pulse of longing, and instinctively curved her hands over her stomach.

Bruno was still watching her, his brown eyes kind. 'Are you OK? To work today? Really?'

For a second she felt her world tremble. She was light and fragile – dust on the wind. Then she resolutely pressed her lips together.

'I'm OK.' She clicked open her first message. 'Ready to work. I hope you are too?'

Bruno emitted a theatrical groan. 'Slave driver.' He adjusted his screen and started to type.

Zoe forced herself to focus. Cash flow was problematic, so she went through her spreadsheet of overdue payments, reissuing each invoice with a red banner at the top. At this rate they'd be out of money before too long, and she didn't have any savings left to keep them afloat. But no matter how hard she tried, her mind refused to settle on the task in front of her. Instead she just found herself staring at the screen-saver picture of her and Jamie at an Everything Everything gig last year. Gazing at his face, his smile, his joy.

She came to with a start and checked the time. Only twenty minutes had passed. She started to review her pitch for a contract they were in the running for. Normally she could lose herself in the images and the words as she tried to work out how best to get their message across. But not today.

It was such a relief when the phone rang.

She glanced at the screen and saw that it was her mum. She had typed her number into her mum's phone when she'd finally headed home at the weekend, and stuck it on her fridge for good measure. And by her bed.

She felt a jolt of nerves as she wondered what was wrong, and then picked up.

'Hi, Mum. How—'

She didn't get to finish her sentence. 'Mr Ames is going to rob me.'

It was 10 a.m. Broad daylight. Zoe thought it was highly unlikely that Mum's gentle next-door neighbour would choose this as the ideal time to commit a robbery. But the fear in Gina's voice was real, and she felt a pulse of something primal. Something protective.

'Are you sure?' Zoe had met Mr Ames the week before. He was small and wrinkled and was currently on crutches. Hardly ideal for an aspiring criminal.

'He's looking through the window now.' Her mum's voice rose. 'I don't trust him. You need to come and help me.'

'But I'm miles away, Mum. In Shoreditch. At work.' Zoe found herself wondering why her mum wasn't at work too.

'He's heading towards the house.' Her mum's voice rose higher. 'You have to help me.'

'It's just . . . I don't really know what I can do . . .'

'He's got a knife!' Zoe could hear the clatter of a dropped plate at the other end of the line.

'What?'

There was a scream. Then silence.

'Mum?'

Nothing.

'Mum?'

Zoe leapt to her feet.

Silence.

Then she heard a muffled rustle. 'Oh no. It was just his paper.'

Zoe exhaled in relief. Too soon.

'He's coming in. Oh God.' Her mum was practically sobbing. 'What am I going to do? Please can you come? Please?'

'Of course, Mum.' Zoe pulled on her jacket, tucking the phone against her ear. 'Don't worry. I'm coming. OK? Just lock the door and stay where you are till I get there.'

'I don't know where my keys are.'

'Well just flick the latch up, then.'

'The what?'

Oh God. 'The thing on the door that clicks.' Zoe waited. 'Can you find it?'

'Yes.'

Zoe grabbed her bag. 'You'll be fine, Mum. I promise.'

Empty words. By the time Zoe got there, Gina might have set the flat on fire. Mr Ames was the least of Zoe's worries.

'I'll see you soon.'

Well, as soon as time and public transport would allow. She hung up.

Bruno had leapt to his feet. 'What's going on? Can I help?'

'No thanks.' She couldn't talk about her mum. Not yet. 'I just need to leave for a bit. I'm sorry.'

'Do you want me to come with you?'
'Thanks.' She smiled at him. 'But it's OK.'
In reality, it was anything but.

Southern Rhine Garrison, Germany
Present: a tutu. Your dad nearly killed me. You love it.
   You wear it everywhere, even into the swimming
   pool when I wasn't looking.
Favourite music: someone gave you a Pac-Man album.
   Come back, Disney, all is forgiven.

15th June, 1990

Darling Zo-bear,
   So. Today he did it. He didn't wrap it up in pink
paper and tie it with a silver bow, but he did it. He
resigned from the army. Major Alistair Whittaker is
about to be a thirty-five-year-old civilian. Hallelujah.
Happy sixth birthday, golden girl.
   He told you over breakfast. You were having your
usual meal – Dairylea with Marmite on toast. It's the
latest in your strange range of breakfast specials,
following hot on the heels of tinned peaches sprinkled
with digestives, and peanut butter spread on a banana
and drizzled in honey. We were all so excited. No more
starting again. No more new sets of keys, or army
magnolia, or another desperate hunt for the kettle
when we arrive in yet another semi on another army
base. No more bloody waiting for him to come home.
The distance between us widens each time, and sometimes as the transports pull up I worry that we'll never
truly be a partnership again.
   As for you and Lily, you've both moved so many
times, you've become obsessed with your stuff. You

have a purple box – Lily's is yellow. Yours contains your diary (an old exercise book, basically outlining what food you've eaten and who you've played with – aka The Important Stuff), your monkey (grey, moth-eared, I live in terror of losing him because THE WORLD WOULD END), your favourite pyjamas (bloody Care Bears) and your favourite books – currently *The Famous Five* and *The Magic Faraway Tree*. Whenever we move, you cling to your box, chin lifted, face determined, and insist that it's on your lap in the car as we judder off to our latest new home. Fingers crossed, only one more move to go now. Hallelujah.

You've had an amazing year, birthday girl. You have become friends with the girls at the garrison school – who confusingly all seem to be called Sarah. You ran home after the first week and asked me to promise that we would never ever leave here. I wish I could have said yes. Seeing you so happy makes me want to shove Madonna on the stereo and dance until I do myself an injury. You were lonely back in England. I love seeing you and the Sarahs together – playing hospitals, playing hide-and-seek, playing – inevitably – soldiers. Lily plays quietly by herself in the corner – laying her toys out and putting them tenderly to bed – but you always make sure you include her eventually, and her face lights up as she comes across and acts as your patient or your baby. I love you for keeping her close.

You're not going to like it when you work out that your dad leaving the army means that you're going to be leaving the Sarahs behind. No more climbing trees together, pushing each other high on the swings or bustling around the garden playing house in the shabby old tent Alistair got from the mess. No more notes passed round the classroom. No more watching *Sesame Street* together after school. I only hope there are more Sarahs to be found wherever we land once Alistair is free, and that we get to grow some roots at last. God knows we need some. I'd love to have a friend I could build real history with, beyond baking drives and walks in the park.

So. Your birthday present is that we can be a family. Not three girls waiting for their man to come home. I've tried my best, but you need your dad around. And he needs you too. He still misses Richard. He still likes his whisky a little too much. He has other friends, but they're not the same, and some days he forgets to smile until he sees you after school. We are both so tired and scratchy, and you soften us when we get shouty over stupid things like who's going to empty the bins this week. He still calls me his Queen of Chaos, but with less of a smile, more of a sigh. You remind us that there are good things in the world. Exciting things. You're so full of life.

Sometimes when he's hunched over the kitchen table, thinking about whatever exercise he has to coordinate next, you go to him and just lean your head on his shoulder. Then and only then does he snap out of his working brain and smile and offer to play castles or football or whatever madness you're suggesting this time. Lily clings to his shoulders as he kicks the ball, while you do your best to flatten him into the grass, laughing as he groans melodramatically when your determined little head butts against his legs. Lily squeals with nerves as he teeters, but he would never let her fall. He puts her down carefully, kissing her pale forehead, and she sits and makes daisy chains while you two rough-and-tumble on the grass.

You know what he needs. You're so wise. At night I still go into your room and watch you – feeling so proud as you lie in your favourite starfish position, splayed happily across the bed beneath that wretched Pac-Man duvet you made me get you for Christmas.

Tonight, as I was staring at you, I realised that your dad and I have never lived together properly before. Two or three months at a time – that's our record. I wondered how it would be. How long it would take to feel normal.

But then you shifted in your sleep and a little smile lifted the corners of your mouth and you burrowed deeper into the pillows so only your long hair showed above the duvet. I wondered if you were remembering your birthday breakfast with your dad. Or the My Little Pony cake. Or your present from the Sarahs – a Spiderman comic and a football to replace the one you kicked over the perimeter fence last week.

And suddenly I couldn't wait for us to be a proper family, no matter what it's like. Alistair. Me. You. Lily. Together at last.

I love you.

Mum x

Seven

'I really don't know why we're here.'

Zoe rubbed her eyes. Her brain had logged out and she had absolutely no ability to keep her eyes open. Her mum's calls hadn't ended with the non-existent threat from Mr Ames. Oh no. There had been a day or two of peace, and then Zoe's phone had rung at 2 a.m. Her mum was frightened and didn't want to be on her own. Zoe had calmed her down and gone back to sleep. Two hours later, the phone rang again. This time it was the police. Gina had apparently just turned up at Mitcham police station, saying she couldn't find her way home. Zoe had got up and headed over there by cab, only for her mum to ask her what on earth she was doing there.

At her desk that morning, Zoe had nursed her fifth coffee and decided that it was time to overcome her mum's resistance and get her to a doctor. Lily's boss wouldn't let her out during office hours unless the building was on fire, so that was that. Zoe had to do it alone.

Her mum had moaned the entire way here about how there was nothing wrong with her at all, and with classic timing she did indeed appear to be in complete control of her faculties today. 'I don't want anyone poking around.' Her mouth was set in a firm line. 'And I don't know why you're sticking your nose in anyway. It's not like you normally take an interest.'

'Mum, can you just give it a rest for a second?' Zoe looked round the packed waiting room. Above them the digital board beeped up names that were never her mum's. Two kids were fighting over an alphabet book in the far corner, while in the opposite row a family of five all seemed to have matching rashes across their cheeks. Behind her Zoe could hear the receptionist managing to maintain an admirable calm in the face of people demanding prescriptions or letters NOW, or asking 'just to see the doctor, love' when it was extremely clear that all the GPs were locked in their consulting rooms being very busy indeed.

Her mum sighed. 'I can't believe I'm missing work for this.' She waved an arm round the room, then turned and gave Zoe an unexpected smile. 'I mean, we could have gone to a spa instead.'

Zoe giggled. The idea of her mum being forced to sit still for even an hour was entertaining. She had always been restless but now she never stopped moving. Her foot was kicking the chair in front of her and her fingers tapped against her jeans. 'Yes. I suppose we could.'

Her mum folded her arms. 'We could have got facials. I love a nice mud pack.'

Zoe raised an eyebrow. 'I think things have moved on a bit since your day, Mum. It's all organic Chinese clay and light therapy nowadays.'

'I know.' Her mum wagged her finger. 'I'm only fifty-six, Zo. You can't write me off just yet.'

Her certainty made Zoe's heart beat faster. She only hoped her mum was right.

'What are you looking so thoughtful about?'

'Nothing.' Zoe forced a smile. 'It's just . . . good to see you. That's all.'

'You daft cow.' Her mum patted Zoe's leg. 'Here we are, surrounded by illness, and you start saying you're enjoying yourself.' She flicked a strand of hair out of her eyes. 'You're bloody mad.'

Her name beeped on to the screen.

'Let's go.' Zoe leapt to her feet.

'OK, if you really want me to.' Her mum got up reluctantly, muttering under her breath. 'But I'm only going in there to prove to you once and for all that there's nothing wrong with me.'

Zoe nodded and inwardly crossed her fingers.

Please let her gut be wrong. Let it be a urinary tract infection. Anything but what Google had told her. Please.

They walked through the glass doors and along a pale blue corridor to Room 5. Zoe was about to knock, but her mum just barged straight in, planting herself on a green chair in front of the doctor's desk.

'Hello.'

'Hello.' Dr Okoye blinked benignly behind his glasses. 'How are you, Mrs . . .?'

'See?' Gina pointed at him as Zoe sat down next to her. 'He doesn't even know who I am. How's he meant to find out what's wrong with me?'

Zoe flushed. 'Mum. He can hear you, you know.'

'Yes, I can.' The doctor seemed immune to Gina's comments as he read the screen in front of him. 'Mrs Whittaker.' He leant back in his creaking chair and steepled his fingers together. 'How can I help you today?'

Silence.

Come on, Mum. Zoe could almost hear her own pulse in the quiet of the room. She looked around to distract herself, seeing an A4 sheet of phone numbers on the pinboard listing local care homes, pharmacies and refuges.

A couple of framed pictures of the jungle hung on the far wall. A box of muesli sat on the top shelf next to a pack of chocolate digestives.

The room waited, immune to yet another patient's future hanging in the balance.

Then her mum leant forward.

'My daughter's got thrush.'

Zoe whipped her head round. 'Mum!' She looked back at Dr Okoye, who seemed a bit bemused to be meeting a thirty-something woman still being accompanied by her mum to GP appointments.

Zoe spoke fast, flushing with embarrassment. 'I'm sorry. I haven't got thrush, I promise. I'm a hundred per cent OK . . .' She realised this sentence wasn't going anywhere good. 'Down there.' She crossed her legs uncomfortably. 'We're really here about my mum.'

He narrowed his eyes. 'Are you sure?'

'Totally sure. Yes.' She nodded, just in case any more emphasis was required. 'I'm all clear.'

'I see.' He scratched his head, and Zoe noticed that he had potent taste in aftershave.

'So how can I help you?' He looked at her mum, who stuck her chin out stubbornly.

'You can't.'

Oh God. Zoe intervened again. 'She's a bit confused.' Understatement of the century, but she had to start somewhere.

He frowned. 'A bit confused?'

Gina shook her head indignantly. 'I'm not confused. Zoe has thrush. She gets very embarrassed about these things.'

'Mum!' Zoe was so tired, she couldn't keep the sharpness out of her voice.

'I'm just trying to help.' Her mum adopted her righteously indignant pose. Face tilted up at an angle. Mouth firm. Shoulders squared. All these years apart and it hadn't changed at all.

Zoe needed to take control. And fast. 'Look, she keeps calling me telling me she sees burglars, and she wanders around sometimes in the night.'

Gina's expression was one of pure betrayal.

Zoe felt her guilt increasing with every word. 'I'm sorry, Mum, but it's true.'

'I'm fine.' Her mum spoke through gritted teeth.

'Mum!' Zoe looked at her reproachfully. 'Last week you thought the postman was going to kill you. You've known him for years.'

She turned to Dr Okoye. 'He just wanted to give her a gas bill and a leaflet about delivery changes.' She had to convince him to help. 'I'm really worried about her.'

The doctor nodded, reading the notes on his screen.

'Mum?'

Her mum wasn't listening. She was staring at the ceiling and humming. Soft notes. The tune she had hummed to soothe Zoe and Lily when they were upset. She'd take them on to her lap and sway back and forth, rubbing their backs until they were calm. Then she'd tell them a story. Hearing the words 'once upon a time' still took Zoe back to that bubble of comfort where dragons could be slain and your mum's hand on your forehead could put a distorted day to rights.

She kept trying. 'Mum, please.'

Gina looked at her and gave an almost imperceptible nod.

'I might have been a little bit forgetful.'

Dr Okoye started typing. 'What kind of things are you forgetting?'

Her mum's voice was soft. 'Words sometimes . . . aren't there. Things, too. And the other week I came out of my office and . . . I didn't know where I was.'

Zoe hadn't known this. The fear on her mum's face made her want to cry.

'And I'm really tired all the time.'

Not surprising, given her night-time antics.

Then her chin was up again. 'But most of the time I'm fine. Nothing wrong with me at all.'

The doctor nodded. 'Now, just let me take a full history. Are you a smoker?'

Zoe sat back as her mum answered questions about alcohol units and diet and all the other things that no one ever wanted to think about until they found themselves in front of a GP.

'Thank you very much, Mrs Whittaker.' Dr Okoye ran a hand over his beard. 'Sometimes when people are having difficulties with their memory, they may find themselves doing things like leaving the gas on or forgetting to lock the door . . .'

'Not me.' Her mum shook her head.

'But you do leave the house at night?'

'Sometimes. But only when I need to.'

He nodded. 'I now need to ask you a few questions that may seem a little odd.'

Her mum sighed. 'If you must.'

'Can you tell me what day it is?'

'Monday.'

'And what month?'

Her mum rolled her eyes. 'August. Obviously.'

He opened his mouth but she spoke first. 'Do you want

the year, too? 2015.' She indicated Zoe. 'And her middle name is Agnes. After Alistair's mum. Terrible name, I know. I wish we'd gone for Scarlett like I wanted.'

Zoe blinked.

Her mum crossed her legs. 'Is there anything else, or can we go now?'

Dr Okoye watched her keenly. 'Can you tell me where we are?'

'In hell.'

'Mum!' Zoe frowned at her. 'You can't talk like that when he's trying to—'

'It's OK.' Dr Okoye held up a hand. 'If you could just answer the question, Mrs Whittaker?'

'For God's sake. We're in a GP surgery, aren't we?'

'And what floor are we on?'

'First.' Her mum shook her head. 'No. Ground.'

Zoe felt relief start to flower inside her. Maybe all her worrying had been for nothing. Maybe Mum was fine. Maybe she was just a bit vague, as Lily had said.

The doctor carried on. 'And can you remember the following address for me: 29 Hamilton Street, London E1.'

'Why?'

'Just humour me, Mrs Whittaker.'

Her mum gave the slightest of nods.

'Thank you.' He coughed. 'Could you just count backwards from 100 in sevens, please?'

Her mum gave him the impatient look Zoe remembered from childhood when she had dropped a plate on the floor or when she and Lily had been fighting over the last sweet in the tin or whether to watch *Neighbours* or *Home and Away*.

'100. 93. 87. 80. 74. 65.'

A pause. Zoe could hardly bear to look at her.

'60. 53. 45.'

Shit. Shit. Shit.

Gina shrugged. 'That's enough of that.' Dr Okoye tapped a note on his keyboard as she smiled triumphantly at Zoe. 'See? I told you there was nothing wrong.'

Zoe couldn't smile back.

'Just a few more questions now. Who is the current prime minister?'

Gina's eyes flickered with entirely undisguised impatience.

'That man with the cheeks.' She clicked her fingers. Once. Twice. 'Oh no. It's not Tony Blair. It's that other one.' Zoe saw her looking hopefully at the doctor.

Dr Okoye remained silent.

'Oh. You know. With the brown hair and that wife . . .'

He relented. 'David Cameron – was that who you were thinking of?'

'Yes! That's him.' Her mum sniffed. 'Never liked him.'

Zoe was starting to feel sick. This was real. She felt an urge to get her phone out. To make a list. To break this nightmare down into a series of bullet points she could tick off.

Deep down, she knew that no list would help her with this. Nothing could.

'And can you tell me the date the Second World War started?'

Her mum barely hesitated. '1939. And it ended in 1945. And we were fighting Germany, just in case you were about to ask.'

'Thank you. Just one more now. Could you tell me the address I gave you just now?'

Her mum stared at the wall. 'It was in London.'

'Yes.'

'Something Street?' She grimaced. 'Who needs to remember a silly address anyway? That's what we've got phones for.'

Dr Okoye smiled and made a note.

Zoe felt her mum's hand on hers. 'See? I did pretty well there. I knew there was nothing wrong with me.'

'Sure.' Zoe's heart twisted as she wondered how many times she would have to lie. 'Well done.'

Gina nodded. 'Told you so.'

But Zoe could see how tightly she was gripping her handbag. The flicker of nerves on her face.

Zoe turned to Dr Okoye, awaiting his verdict.

He looked at her mum. 'Mrs Whittaker, obviously this is a very basic test, but the results, along with the history that you and your daughter have given me, make me think there's enough here to warrant looking into this a bit more.'

All the light had gone from her mum's face.

'Now, it's quite common for people to come to the doctor about this kind of thing, and it isn't possible to say immediately exactly what's going on, but I'll request blood and urine tests that we'll do here, and also a CT scan of your head at the hospital, and I'll refer you to the local memory clinic for further review. The doctors there will have the blood and scan results and they can examine you in more depth.'

Her mum was on her feet, fiddling with her cardigan, her hands shaking.

'No thank you. I don't think there's any need.'

Dr Okoye shifted in his seat. 'I just think that—'

'No.' Her mum's voice was absolute. 'I'm not going.'

Zoe leant towards him. 'Thank you. We really appreciate your help.'

Her mum let loose a snort that implied she didn't appreciate it at all. She was shaking so much she couldn't even get her cardigan on. She shook Zoe off when she tried to help and stalked out, leaving her handbag sitting on her chair.

Zoe rubbed her hands over her face. 'I'm sorry about that.'

'Not a problem.' She wondered how many people he had to break bad news to in his average day. He leant towards her. 'It might be an idea for you to have a look at the Age UK website – there are lots of ideas on there.'

'OK.' Zoe nodded, fears crowding into her brain. Mum lost in a train station. Mum letting strangers into her flat. In all the years of anger, she had assumed somehow that her mum would always be there. Always be OK. Now the future was fragmenting right before her eyes. 'Thanks for the advice.'

'No problem.' He passed her a small plastic bottle. 'This is to drop off a urine sample. You can book her in for blood tests at the front desk, and she will get letters about the CT scan and memory clinic appointment soon. There's a waiting time of two to three months, so if you have any concerns or questions in the meantime, feel free to come and see me again. There's lots of support available, so please do let us know if we can help in any way.'

Zoe smiled gratefully. It sounded like help might be just what they needed.

She picked up her mum's bag and walked out in a daze. Gina was leaning on a red-brick wall outside the surgery, face upturned to the morning sun. Zoe adjusted to the rumble and chatter of the outside world, wondering if this was how life would be now. Checking for things left behind. Always keeping an eye.

As they walked back to the road, she remembered the tidy-up song they had sung together during her mum's sporadic attempts to keep the household mess under control before Alistair came home on leave. Lily in her bouncy chair on the floor. Zoe and her mum parading around the house pretending they were on inspection. Picking up piles of toys and books and the sheets they had used to make houses when the rain poured down outside. Her stomach tightened as she thought of her mum dancing round the kitchen retrieving bits of jigsaw from underneath the table.

Everything had been so simple back then.

'What are you thinking about?'

Her mum's voice called her back to the present. Back to the messy, lonely confusion of now. A now with her mum wandering the darkened streets asking squad cars to take her home. She wished she had someone to call. Jamie. Not an option. Dad. She always called him for advice, but she knew this would simply enrage him.

'Nothing, Mum.' She put an arm around the thin shoulders.

'Shall we have a cuppa before we go back to work, Zo-bear?'

Zoe thought of her busy inbox. 'Sorry. I need to get back to work.'

'Please?'

Zoe saw the need on her mum's face. She could work late tonight. 'That would be great.'

So the two of them walked down the street together as if they hadn't a care in the world. Two ordinary women leading ordinary lives. A mother with her daughter, going for a nice cup of tea and a cake.

Only Zoe knew how precious each moment was. Only she knew how soon these times might end.

Her mum still thought they had forever.

OUR OWN HOUSE, Kent. OK, it's rented, but still . . .
Present: Rockin' Robot cassette player
Favourite music: ABBA. As sung by you. On the above.

15th June, 1993

Darling Zoe,

Damn. Somehow two birthdays have escaped me, and now you have reached the very Big Girl age of NINE. Happy birthday, golden girl. The last couple of years have sped by and I never sat down to put pen to paper – too shattered trying to navigate the pick 'n' mix highs of last year's cinema trip (*The Little Mermaid*) and the horror of unwinding your ABBA tape from the machine when it jammed during musical chairs the year before.

So, now you're nine, you choose your own clothes, and today you were in a pink T-shirt and tiny denim shorts that have aged your dad by about ten years. He hates the fact that you are growing up, and God knows he notices, because he's still away so much that you are a whole new person every time he puts his bag down and brings out the presents for you and Lily. I get sick of you two asking me where he is now. I never really know – Warrington, Edinburgh, Cambridge. He never takes a breath. And as you girls curl up together in your room, I go downstairs to yet another night of *EastEnders* and wine for one.

I never thought I'd say this, but at times I miss the base. I miss knowing everybody and popping out to

gossip over the garden fence, and the talk of letters
and calls and birthday parcels. Now it's just me in
Tesco trying to stop Lily touching yet another lethal
object she's taken a shine to (her current favourite is
razors), while having to send you off to get the things
we need.

I don't miss the danger, though. I would never, ever
miss that.

Anyway, when he got back yesterday from Ipswich
or whatever place he was 'sourcing customers' this
time, you started performing the routine from *Fame*.
You twirled around and shook your body in a way that
will have you causing mayhem in nightclubs as soon as
you can pass for eighteen, with Lily providing sterling
support on the toy tambourine she got for Christmas.
He watched you and said all the right things but then
sent me one of his finest dagger stares. Great. We were
already off on the wrong foot and he hadn't even
kissed me hello yet. Normally we at least have sex
before we have our 'Alistair's home at last' row. Not this
time. Last night, after the shouting was over, I was lying
right next to him, yet he'd never felt further away. Then
I went to the loo and thought I heard whispering from
your room. I'd assumed you were asleep, but you must
have heard the whole thing. I'm so sorry, golden girl.

I get so cross with him and I've never been one to
hold my tongue. I thought things would be easier once
he left the army. I thought he'd be around more. I had
visions of family roasts and trips to the bowling alley.
But no – now he's become a soldier without a uniform,
waging his own war, trying to gain territory from every
single one of his competitors. He wants his company,
Redhouse (some old school name or something), to

rule the world, and as founder and CEO he's the man who is going to make it happen, one security contract at a time. It's too much for one man, but he's never going to admit that. He just works harder and sleeps less. Cash-flow charts on the kitchen table at 2 a.m. – that's how we're living now.

Richard was always meant to be in charge of the money – years ago that was their plan as they chatted around the kitchen table about a future out of uniform. But now it's just Alistair, and he's trying so hard to make it work. For us, but also for Richard. I understand that and I'm proud of him. I just find it hard to tell him, because when we moved here, I thought I'd have his warmth beside me as I turned over in bed. Nope. Instead I've got intermittent phone calls and debt. All our savings are in the company, and it's not making money yet, so now I'm back to work. Two children, a house to run and a full-time job. No wonder I'm on ten coffees a day.

And you know what I hate most? I hate how grown up you have to be, golden girl. I want you to be making friendship bracelets and putting on puppet shows and wearing trainers that flash whenever you take a step. Instead of which you make spaghetti bolognese and babysit Lily, and you know how to relight the boiler in the kitchen when it goes on the blink. Lily adores you – she just trails round the house after you, and you're so sweet with her, not even protesting when she follows you into the loo. You do everything together. Homework. Monopoly. Playing in the garden. I only wish I had time to join in. And then I come back and I'm tired and you argue with me and I find myself snapping – shouting sometimes – and I

wonder how I got here. This isn't the kind of mum I
ever thought I'd be.

You're disappearing into yourself. We still see
Johnny and Mags sometimes, when they come down
for the weekend, but at school you don't seem to be
making friends. The other day I arrived late to pick
you up (bloody boss), and I could see you in the
playground, pushing your way towards the far corner,
where Lily was surrounded by a group of kids, all
elbows and teeth. They were forcing her back towards
the wall and I started running too, but you were
quicker than me and you stood in front of her and
stared every single one of those kids down. No
wonder Lily adores you.

I talked to the school, of course. Lily's form teacher
says she's just a bit quiet and never plays with the
other kids. And your teacher says you spend a lot of
time with her – that you don't seem that interested in
anyone else. But I know you're looking out for her. I've
seen you play and chatter with the Sarahs or Johnny
and I know how much you love it. I want to fix it. I
want you both to be the centre of the crowd. You
shouldn't have to protect her. That's my job.

But when I asked you about it, you just shook your
head. 'We're fine, Mum. Nothing to worry about.' The
forced smile on your face broke my heart.

So there you have it. You are your own person now.
You don't need your mum to put a plaster on when
you cut yourself, or wipe your mouth after meals, or
read you to sleep. You have your own plans now. Your
own ideas. I still know what colours you like, and what
your favourite meal is, and the way you like me to plait
your hair, but I can't read you any more. You hide

behind your games or your books. I remember how
close we used to be. How we laughed and finished
each other's sentences and pulled faces at exactly the
same time. I remember your hand in mine. Your
biscuity fingers weaving an endless cat's cradle round
my wrist.

Golden times. Now sometimes I feel like I've lost
you. If I had time, I would fix it. If I had a husband who
was here, I would leave Lily with him and take you out,
just the two of us. But Alistair is away and I have to
work as a secretary to the grumpiest accountant on
the planet, and somehow our chats have been whittled
away to 'Do you want beans with that?' or 'Yes, it *is*
time you had a bath. Get in there. Now.'

So all I can do is write this letter and say how much
I love you. Remind you that you will always be my Zoe.
My golden girl. One day we'll be two peas in a pod
again, I promise. I'll make it happen. Soon.

All my love,
Mum x

Eight

'Earth to Lily.'

Lily didn't move her gaze from a little girl colouring a picture of a horse on the next table. She carefully chose a purple crayon and started on his tail, a half-eaten toastie cooling on a plate beside her. The tip of her tongue stuck out as she bent over her task, while her mum chatted to a friend and gently rocked a pram in which all that could be seen was a tiny pink hat.

Zoe looked away, pierced with a sadness that was all too familiar.

She sighed and focused back on her sister. 'Lil?'

Lily jumped. 'What?'

Zoe waved. 'Hello. We're meant to be having a drink here?'

'Well you were on your phone again, so I was just having a look around.' Lily smiled at the girl. The brown eyes lifted for a second and a grin spread shyly across the little face.

Zoe stared uncomfortably at her gin and tonic. 'Come on, Lil.'

She glanced up to see her sister looking straight at her. 'Sorry. You know what I'm like. Can't resist the little ones.'

'I know.' Zoe was keen to change the subject. 'When's your business course start, anyway?'

'January.' Lily stirred her spritzer with a straw. 'But I'm

not sure about it. It feels like I might have left it a bit late, and work's going OK anyway.' The girl's mother took her hand as they weaved their way between the tables towards the exit. Lily waved goodbye and the tiny hand waved back.

Zoe dipped a piece of bread in oil and popped it into her mouth. 'But you've always hated that job. And you're only twenty-eight. You're hardly past it. When I was your age, I—'

'Started your own company. I know.' Lily sighed. 'Just like Dad did after the army.' She shrugged. 'What have I been doing with my life?'

Zoe shook her head. 'That's not what I meant, Lil.'

Lily sipped her drink. 'I know. But I'm happy as I am. Really. I'm not sure I want to do a course.'

'But you keep saying how crap it is managing that office.'

Two bright spots burnt in Lily's cheeks. 'OK, OK. But Gary says that—'

'Gary?' Zoe frowned. 'Are you two in touch again?'

Lily looked down at her lap.

Her silence spoke volumes. Zoe felt a familiar rush of frustration. 'Oh no, Lil. You're not, are you? After what he did? I just don't know how you can even speak to him.' She remembered Lily's tear-stained face when Gary had told her he was breaking up with her. Her fourteen-day residence on their sofa. The endless tissues and Wispa wrappers.

She couldn't believe her sister could even think about forgiving him.

'Zoe, don't freak out. We just met for coffee.' Lily pulled her bra strap up her shoulder and wiggled her blue top back into place.

'Why? He was *vile* to you.' Zoe straightened the coaster in front of her.

'It wasn't all him.' Lily wouldn't meet her eyes. 'Look, I know you don't like him, but you don't really know him, do you?'

'I spent Christmas with him at Dad's. I think that's enough, don't you? I mean, you do remember the way he kept disappearing upstairs during dinner to play Halo?'

'He was nervous.'

'Why?'

Lily muttered something under her breath.

'Lil?'

Her sister sighed. 'Maybe it was you and Dad making him feel inadequate.'

'What?' Zoe folded her arms. 'I don't think that's fair.'

'I know you didn't mean to.' Lily put a conciliatory hand on Zoe's arm. 'But you two can be a bit intimidating sometimes. Sitting there talking about your strategies and visions and stuff.'

'We didn't.'

'Yes you did.' Lily frowned. 'It's what you two do. And I don't mind, but whenever he saw you, Gary always got nervous. He said you seemed so controlled. So calm.' She grinned. 'And I know you're just some doofus who once stayed up late to tape a Boyzone gig off Radio 1, but you made him feel a bit shy.'

'Shy? He never stopped talking.' Zoe thought back to last Christmas. Dad pouring drinks. His wife Wendy serving up the biggest turkey Zoe had ever seen. And Gary talking. Banging on about house prices or shares or how to mini-mise VAT.

'Well, he wanted to impress you.'

Zoe felt a beat of recognition, but she pushed it away.

Lily chewed on her straw. 'I mean, even Jamie ended up playing Halo in the end, didn't he?'

'No.' Zoe knew she sounded too sharp. 'Well, only right at the end. And just to keep Gary company.'

'Sure.' Lily didn't push her. 'Whatever you say.' There was a slight flintiness to her tone. Unusual. The Gary influence. Zoe pictured him – broad shoulders, brown hair, bright jumpers, *The Times* under his arm. Jamie had always got on well with him, but that was only because they both loved *Game of Thrones*. And because Jamie gave everyone the benefit of the doubt.

She sighed. She spent every day trying not to notice Jamie's absence, and every day it seemed to be getting harder. No amount of working or running or trying to figure out what to do about her mum was making the lack of him feel any less raw. He should be back by now, but she had no idea where he was. He hadn't called. He hadn't texted or emailed or DM'd. His Facebook account was ominously silent. For all she knew, he was still out there in the Maldives, staying on in the sun to wait tables or run the kids' club or fix computers or something. She had seen how hurt he was. She knew how far he might run to try to forget her.

This morning she had found herself staring at his toothbrush in its Cool Dude mug and wanting to cry. She had dug her nails into her palms to stop herself, and then shut it away in the back of the bathroom cabinet.

She sighed. Normally on a Friday night he would be leaning back in his chair, smiling up at her as she shrugged off her jacket. He was always the first to arrive at any party. Always the last to leave. He would hold out his arms when she ran in muttering about overdue emails and investment updates, and she would nestle on his knee and exhale and their evening together would begin.

He made her want to stay out longer. To ask one more

question. To hear one last song. The night she had told him how different their future was going to be, she had asked him how he would cope. With the nights in. With having to plan ahead. With not being able to live life on a whim and a prayer. And he had cuddled her and kissed her and told her that nothing mattered more than this. That nothing ever could.

It wasn't only Jamie she had lost.

'Zo?'

She realised Lily was talking.

'What?' She finished the last of her gin and tonic, fiercely trying to force the memories out of her head. To lock them away. To move on.

Around them the café was getting ready for the evening ahead. Staff were dimming the lights and cleaning glasses behind the bar. The daytime mums and children were disappearing, to be replaced by people with work bags and suits and copies of the *Evening Standard* under their arms.

Lily repeated her question. 'When's Mum's memory clinic appointment again?'

'It's next month.'

'OK.' Lily nodded. 'So she still hasn't been given a diagnosis?'

'Not yet.' Zoe stopped the waiter as he came to put a tea light on the table between them, and ordered another round. She was going to need more alcohol if they were going to talk about this. 'We need to decide what we're going to do, Lil.'

'What do you mean?'

The fairy lights on the bar glowed. A couple near the window leant in to each other, his fingers weaving in and out of hers. It was date o'clock. And here were Zoe and

Lily, talking about their mum losing her memory. That just about summed things up right now.

Their drinks arrived and Zoe took a huge glug of her gin and tonic. It made her feel calmer. Stronger.

'We need to make a plan.'

'Why?'

'Because she's ill, Lily. She can't carry on living by herself.'

'But that's what she wants.'

Zoe felt frustration prickling through her veins. 'That doesn't matter. It's too risky. And the phone calls are getting worse. She had me up three times last night.'

'I know. I get them too, you know. Maybe she just needs something to help her sleep.'

'It's more than that. She keeps forgetting how to use the kettle. And if I ask her, she denies it. Says she just forgot to switch it on.' Zoe could see the clench of her mum's jaw as she said it. Her fists balled up inside her dressing gown.

'Thank God she doesn't have a car.' Zoe thought back to the things that had occurred to her in the shower that morning, while trying to simultaneously clean the tiles and wash the conditioner out of her hair. 'I've started making a list of things we need to do.'

Lily crossed her legs. 'But if she hasn't even been diagnosed yet, then maybe it's not what we think. Not dementia, I mean.'

Zoe tapped the table with her fingers, feeling an old resentment at always having to be the sensible one. 'You weren't there, Lily. At the GP. You didn't see her.'

'That's not fair.' Lily's brown eyes flashed. 'You know I couldn't get out of work.'

Zoe held up her hands. 'I—'

'And I know you're suddenly spending all your time with her since Jamie went, and it's great that you're trying to help.' Lily's silver charm bracelet gleamed as she spread her hands wide. 'But it still doesn't make sense to me. Why have you suddenly forgiven her? You said you *hated* her. I mean, ten years, Zo. That's a hell of a long time to freeze someone out.'

'I know.' Zoe swallowed. 'And I haven't forgiven her.' It was true. She could still remember the stinging anger as she realised what Gina had planned. The sense of betrayal as she realised that yet again her mum didn't care about her thoughts. Her feelings. 'It's just different now.'

'Why?'

Because she knew they didn't have forever.

'Because she's ill.'

'She might be.' Lily shook her head. 'We still don't know for sure.' She chewed a mouthful of bread.

'*I* know she is.' This was one thing Zoe was absolutely sure about. 'How many examples do you need? Sure, some days she's OK, but she forgot to take her slippers off when she went to work the other day. She keeps losing her keys. She—'

'Loads of people lose their keys.' Lily checked her watch. 'And if she's still working, she must be OK, mustn't she?'

'Yes, but for how much longer?' Zoe's worry was tightening her chest, bringing her words out in staccato bursts. 'We have to think about what we're going to do. Where she's going to live. Who's going to look after her.'

Lily held up her hand. 'I think you're getting ahead of yourself.'

Zoe needed to make her sister understand. 'No, I'm not.'

'We need to wait and see.'

Zoe sighed. Around them the evening buzzed and chattered its way into full swing. The couple were kissing now, the man's hands stroking the girl's dark hair. Behind them male voices argued about Mourinho or Wenger. Then the opening chords of a James Bond theme played over the speakers, and Lily downed the rest of her drink decisively.

She picked up her bag. 'Sorry, I've got to go.'

'What? But we haven't decided anything.'

'I'll call you.' Her sister knocked the table as she stood up. She straightened again.

'But . . .'

'It's too soon.'

Zoe pushed on. 'We need to plan ahead.'

'We can't.' Lily was moving away. 'That's the whole point. We can't solve this. We just have to work it out as we go along. And I know that probably doesn't fit very well with whatever five-year plan you're working on right now, but that's just how it is, OK?'

'Why are you so angry with me?'

Lily glanced at the ceiling. 'Because you always assume you can do things better than me. That *you* have to sort everything out. And all the time you fail to notice that I've got a job and I'm paying my rent and living my life and keeping an eye on Mum and . . .' She exhaled, leaning close so Zoe could hear her above Adele. 'Not all of us *think* as much as you, Zoe. Some of us just do things. I mean, you practically have to fill out a spreadsheet before you choose what restaurant to go to on a Friday night. Doesn't it ever get too much?'

Yes. Oh yes.

But Zoe wasn't going to admit that.

She opened her mouth, but Lily was still talking. 'I'm worried and I'm scared too. But you just have to let me do this my way.'

Zoe opened her mouth to answer, but her sister had already gone.

She stared at the slice of lemon in her glass and felt the emptiness of the evening settling on her shoulders. She thought about walking home to the dark flat, lit only by the glow of her laptop as she put in yet more hours on the investor presentation she was doing next week. More cash for quicker expansion. Yes. That was what she should do.

It was better than sitting here communing with her drink. Keep things moving. That was what her dad always said.

'Surprise!'

She turned round.

'Bruno!' She had truly never been so delighted to see him.

He waved his arms with the kind of extravagance normally associated with a musical finale. 'Look who I've brought with me?'

'Oh my God, Mandy!' Zoe flung her arms round her best friend and clung on.

'Uh-oh.' Mandy detached herself and held Zoe at arm's length. 'Has there been some drinking on an empty stomach going on here?'

'Yes,' Zoe admitted. 'I've had some bread, though.'

'I see.' Mandy put her red bag down on the table and shrugged off her leather jacket. 'Well, we'll have to do something about that.' She marched off to the bar, easing her way effortlessly past a group of girls arguing over whether to have mojitos or sambuca. Within seconds she had the attention of the barman, who was soon reaching for a spirit bottle and starting to pour.

Zoe turned back to Bruno. 'How did you know I was here?'

He snorted. 'You are aware we have a shared Google office calendar, aren't you?'

She smiled. 'Oh yeah.'

He sat down and looked around approvingly. 'I mean, obviously you're the only one who uses it, but it's quite handy for keeping tabs on you. Just a little light stalking every now and then. You know.'

Zoe squeezed his shoulder. 'Well thank God you found me.'

He narrowed his eyes. 'Did you and Lily have a fight? It looked like it through the window.'

'You were snooping?'

'No.' He pointed at Mandy. 'I was waiting for her to arrive.' He grinned. 'And doing a bit of snooping on the side.'

'I knew it.' Zoe ran a hand through her hair. 'And no. Not a fight. Just a discussion.'

'Whatever you say.' He flicked a crumb off his cords. 'But it looked like a fight to me.'

She felt the truth of his words, but the kindness in his eyes somehow made her feel better. He reached over and kissed her on the cheek. 'It'll be OK. I promise.'

'Here we are. Emergency cocktail. And food.' Mandy put down a tray containing a bowl of peanuts and three drinks so luridly yellow, Zoe could already feel a hangover start to form. She picked up one of the tall glasses. Looked at it. Then downed it in one.

'Bloody hell.' Mandy flicked her long dark curls over

her shoulder. 'Looks like we're playing catch-up, Bruno. Get to it.' She lifted her own glass.

'On it.' Bruno finished his in seconds and stood up and headed over to get more drinks. Zoe felt the world get a little more fuzzy. A little less sore.

She could do this all night.

Mandy cupped her chin in her hand. 'So how are you, babe?'

'I'm OK.' Zoe reached for another nut.

'Really?' Mandy arched her eyebrows. 'Because the Zoe I know doesn't normally drink cocktails on an empty stomach.'

'I've had some bread. And some peanuts.' Zoe popped a handful in her mouth.

'Yes. And there's the next sign.' Mandy looked at her sternly. 'Eating foods high in salt and sugar. Straight out of the Zoe-Whittaker-off-the-rails textbook.'

'I'm not that predictable, am I?'

Mandy shook her head. 'Babe, you have gone running every day at six a.m. for YOUR ENTIRE LIFE. Yes. You are that predictable.'

'Oh.' Zoe hated feeling like the boring one. Mandy was a graphic designer and was all zumba and vintage pop-ups and impulse. They had met in the uni bar on their first night in halls, giggling as they were both chatted up by a balding maths student with a black umbrella tucked into the belt hook of his jeans. Neither of them could remember his name, but they'd be grateful to him for ever. Years of Sunday roasts and overcompetitive pub-quizzing. Of sweaty yoga and takeaways. Years of cheering each other through first jobs and bad dates and sharing a damp flat on Tooting High Road.

'Here we are.' Bruno put a cocktail jug and a wine cooler down. 'Didn't see any point in taking things slowly.'

'Great.' Zoe started to pour. 'So, what made you two come along and find me?'

She saw them looking at each other. Saw the worry in their eyes.

She put the jug down.

'What? What is it?'

The locket round Mandy's neck glinted gold in the candlelight. She reached for the jug and aimed it at Zoe's glass.

'Let's just fill this up.'

Zoe put her hand over the top. 'No.' She felt a chill creeping through her. 'No. Just tell me.'

'OK.' Mandy watched her carefully. 'Jamie's back.'

'Really?' Zoe swallowed. 'When? Today? Because he probably hasn't had time to—'

Her friend shook her head. 'He's been back for a week. He's staying with Russ.'

'Oh.' Zoe's spirits sank as she searched for an explanation that wasn't there.

A whole week.

He had said he wanted to talk to her when he got back. That he wanted to understand.

Maybe he'd changed his mind.

She raised her head and pushed her glass forward.

'Fill me up, please.'

Bruno didn't need telling twice.

Zoe watched the liquid arcing into her glass. She could cry. She could scream. But right now, the only thing she wanted to do was drink.

She looked sternly at her companions. 'No sympathy, OK?' She pointed a warning finger at them. 'You know I hate that.'

'OK.' Mandy held up her hands.

'Agreed.' Bruno nodded. 'But can I do some really bad dancing instead?'

'Absolutely.' Zoe nodded vigorously. 'The worse the better.'

She lifted her glass and swallowed.

'Here, please.' Bruno leant forward to speak to the cab driver. 'That one there. The red-brick one.'

Zoe peered at the quiet street, indignation bubbling inside her. 'This isn't Russ's place.'

'No.' Mandy put a hand on her arm.

'I said I wanted to go and find Jamie.'

'Now's not the right time, Zo.'

'But I want to see him.'

Mandy shook her head. 'Just sober up first, OK?'

'But—'

'Zo. Believe me. You reek of tequila and your mascara's run. This is not the way to win him back.'

Somewhere deep down she knew her friend was right.

'OK, OK.' She felt around for her bag. And her phone. And her jacket. She thought she had thrown them all into the cab, but now she couldn't work out where they were.

'Here you go.' Mandy was holding them out to her. 'I kept track. It felt like my turn, for once. You've got me home enough times.'

'Thank you.' Zoe tried to hug her, but only succeeded in banging her on the head with her elbow. 'Sorry.'

'That's OK.'

Bruno had his face glued to the window. 'Who's that?'

'Who?' Zoe stood up straight and knocked her head on the roof. 'Ouch.'

She peered into the darkness. The council really should

fix that street light. She would write an email. Right now.

Then she saw it. A figure sitting on the doorstep outside the flat.

She squealed. 'Oh my God. It's him. It has to be.'

She could see a hoodie. Jeans.

Jamie must have forgiven her.

She was flooded with sweet relief and grappled with the door.

Mandy put a hand out to stop her. 'Zo. I'm not sure it's him. I . . .'

Zoe didn't listen. She got out, stumbling over her own feet in anticipation of feeling his arms around her. She clattered across the edge of the road and on to the pavement. Houses stood dark and quiet all around her. Watching. Waiting.

She tottered closer to her own front door, feeling the biggest smile of her life crossing her face.

Then she stopped.

Those trainers weren't his.

And she'd never seen that bag before.

And she could see a very portly cat.

It wasn't Jamie. It was Mum.

Excitement became concern. Giddiness became nausea. Zoe walked forward, suddenly feeling very sober indeed. 'Mum?'

'There you are.' Her mum stood up and stretched her arms above her head. 'About time too. You need to get me a key, you know.'

'What are you doing here? Are you OK?'

'Yes. Of course I am.' Her mum stared at her, a rucksack in one hand and a carrier bag in the other. 'I just wanted to see you.'

'OK.' Zoe fumbled for her keys and opened the front

door. 'But it's two in the morning. Couldn't it have waited?' She felt a pang of fear at the thought of all the things that might have happened to her mum on the way over here.

'I had to come.' Something in Gina's voice made Zoe reach out for her and draw her into a hug. Her face was freezing against Zoe's cheek.

'What happened?' Zoe switched on the hall light and closed the front door behind them.

She turned and caught something in her mum's expression. A fragility. A fear.

'What is it?'

'The boss called me in today.' Her mum's voice was all breath and panic. 'He told me I needed to take some time off. He said I'd made too many mistakes recently. That maybe I needed a rest. And he told me some of the stuff I'd done – meetings with the wrong people and things – but I couldn't remember any of them.' Her face held for a second and then dissolved. 'What's happening to me, Zoe? What's happening?'

Zoe stood there, her mum sobbing into her shoulder, desperate to comfort her, yet not knowing what on earth she could say.

OUR OWN HOUSE, IT'S A MIRACLE, Longford,
Wiltshire
Present: a guitar. I'm already regretting it. If you play
   those three chords again, I will scream.
Favourite music: Boyz II Men. God help me.

15th June, 1996

Dear Zoe,
   So, another three years and you're TWELVE. It's no
wonder my last two letters to you barely got started.
As soon as I had us set up and started to recognise a
face or two, Alistair would spot a new opportunity and
off we'd go again. Finally, I put my foot down. We are
staying here.
   Home is now a three-up, three-down grey stone
house with a ramshackle garden, and an overwhelming
smell of cat. I scrubbed the carpets and the curtains
until my hands were red and sore, but it made no
bloody difference at all. The previous owner died in the
living room, which is how Alistair picked up the place
so cheap. For the first three months here, whenever I
went into the corner shop, people would ask me how I
felt about Mrs Nicholls, crowding around as they
wondered whether I ever felt her spirit in the house.
   Helpful.
   Of course you picked up on it, and you got really
scared and started refusing to sit on the sofa with me
and Lily when we were watching David Attenborough
on telly. Instead you went off to your room – well,

your oversized cupboard, really – and got on with some of the mysterious things that apparently twelve-year-olds do. One day I finally got around to doing the washing and walked in there to put some clean clothes on your bed, only to see that you'd covered the walls with pictures of half naked members of Take That and your beloved Boyz II Men.

I just stood there with your T-shirts in my hands and thought, shit, things have moved on. I remember the old you. Your beaming face as you gave me a 'pillow' (aka a hardback book) as I lay beside your bed on the nights when you couldn't sleep. Your grin as you handed me the damp fur ball that was Monkey to keep me warm. Your tiny fingers exploring the rings on my fingers.

All that is long gone. You don't talk to me any more unless we're having one of our many rows. Sometimes you look at me as if you despise me, or as if I disappoint you so much you would prefer it if I didn't exist. You eat your food. You take Lily out to play football or go swimming. You do your chores. But you're not happy. I used to know that if I held you, I could make everything better. Now I have no magic left.

We moved here bang in the middle of the school year, so you went off to senior school at the worst possible time. That first day. I'll never forget it. You came home and sat on the back step with your purple box on your knees, and you told your dad, with great determination, that it was only four years till you could leave and set up your own business like him. I wanted to weep. But of course I didn't have time. We may have a mortgage now, but financially things are still at the precarious end of the scale, and my middle name might as well be 'overtime'.

Anyway, the only time you seem happier is when your dad is here. He's with us for a couple of weeks or so a month now, and he's hiring more people to work for him, which he says is a good sign. I'll believe it when I see the cash in our bank account rather than in his head.

His new company HQ is in Chippenham, and eventually he plans to work there full time and travel a lot less. But for now you still get really excited every time he's due home. You and Lily run around baking enormous biscuits full of peanut butter or chocolate chips, and you ram one into his mouth pretty much as soon as he walks in the door.

He likes setting you challenges and you always say yes. Long runs. Better results. Crazy winter swims together in freezing seas whenever we're at his parents' house for Christmas. You try so hard to please him.

You're different when he's gone. Quieter. More withdrawn. You sit in your room looking at the boys on your wall and trying to get your hair to do that thing that Angel's does in *Home and Away*. You don't seem to call anyone or see anyone except Lily. Your form teacher says there's nothing to worry about, but she doesn't know you like I do. She hasn't seen you screeching songs into a hairbrush at 7.30 in the morning. You're living life on mute and I have no idea why.

I want to help. Sometimes you hover at the edge of the kitchen when I'm scrabbling together some tea. I try to talk to you then, but it takes too long to get going, and then my boss will call saying I've lost a file (it's always his fault), or Lily will appear and the moment is gone and your face settles back into its normal expression of resignation. And I know I have to make this conversation happen, but I have two girls and a job and a husband who doesn't seem to want to touch me any more, and before I know it, another week or month has gone by and you're even further away from me.

For your birthday today we got *Chariots of Fire* out on video and watched it – just you, me and Dad. You were glued, but even as you sat there in between us, you kept sneaking little looks at us out of the corner of your eye, as if checking that we really were all sitting there together. I wonder how much you've overheard. Me questioning him about nights spent away. His angry denials. But that never stops me. I'm so bloody angry. I keep going, asking him where he was. Who he was with. Why he said the name 'Sally' in his sleep last Saturday.

Receipts don't lie. But I'm starting to think Alistair can.

I'm so glad you had a happy day, golden girl. One day I hope every day is that happy for you. I know it will be.

All my love, birthday girl,
Mum x

Nine

Zoe had spent more time than she would like to admit imagining seeing Jamie again.

She had emailed him the morning after her mum had arrived, and when he didn't answer, she had followed up with two visits to Russ's flat, only to be greeted by a front door that steadfastly refused to open.

She had made sure she looked immaculate on both occasions – her hair half up in one of the loose ponytails he loved and a thin layer of blusher on her cheeks. She had even put on the green dress she had worn on their first proper date, watching *Drive* at Somerset House.

She had wanted to wow him. But no. Life had other plans.

'I can't find it, Mum. Are you sure you put it under here?' She was underneath the sofa in her flat, groping around trying to find the remote. Her running gear was sticky with sweat from her morning 5k, and her hair was desperately in need of a wash. Since her mum's arrival last week, she had been too afraid to let her leave again, and her Saturday so far had largely been spent looking for things that didn't seem to be there.

'Yes.' Her mum's foot tapped impatiently on the floor, next to a trail of mugs, biscuit crumbs and orange peel. 'I dropped it next to the . . .'

Zoe began the increasingly familiar guessing game.

'The table?'

'No. The . . .'

Zoe was so far under now that she couldn't see daylight any more. She encountered an enormous dust ball and sneezed. 'The curtain?'

'No. The . . . Oh, hello. Have you come to help?'

Zoe swore under her breath. Her mum had quite enough going on without talking to imaginary friends too.

'Are you looking for this?'

Zoe instinctively tried to sit up, and succeeded in hitting her head on the sofa springs. She knew that voice.

'Shit.' Her head was so sore she had tears in her eyes. She started to reverse out of her prone position, aware that Jamie must have a prime view of the mud caked on her calves. As she wiggled backwards, she tried desperately to fix her hair, before realising it was a lost cause. She sat back on her haunches and looked at him.

He looked ridiculously good. Tanned. Hair bleached blonder. White T-shirt over jeans. She stood up and caught a glimpse of herself in the mirror over the fireplace. She looked like she had just survived a hurricane.

Perfect.

'Hi.' She wiped her cheek and a large piece of fluff fell to the floor. Her skin itched with awkwardness. 'How are you?' Everything in her wanted to run to him, but she forced herself to stand still. Straight. Separate.

'OK, thanks.' He shoved his hands in his pockets. 'You?'

'Yeah.' She stepped on one of her mum's mugs and staggered, banging her leg against the coffee table. Her voice was higher than usual as she rubbed the sore spot. 'I'm good.'

He fiddled with the change in his pocket. 'And this must be your mum?'

'Yes.' She leapt into action. 'Mum. This is Jamie. My . . .' She realised she didn't know what he was any more.

Her mum had no such qualms. 'Your fiancé, of course.'

Zoe winced as Jamie looked meaningfully in her direction. She didn't know how to communicate 'my mum's got memory loss' via the medium of mime, so she just kept quiet. She could explain later.

Gina held out a hand and smiled. 'So lovely to meet you.' For a woman in checked pyjamas and earmuffs, she exuded an amazing amount of dignity. 'Are you back now, then? From your holiday?'

'Yes.' His voice was gruff as he shook her hand.

'Good.' She sank back into the cushions. 'You need to stop her working so hard.'

Oh God.

'She's always at it. Never stops. It's not healthy. She was up with the lark this morning, tapping away before her run.'

'Mum . . .'

Jamie cut in. 'I know, Mrs Whittaker. But she's very hard to persuade.'

'Gina. Call me Gina.' Her mum looked positively girlish. She patted the space next to her. 'Come and sit here . . .' She tailed off and confusion crossed her face. She had clearly forgotten his name.

Zoe helped her out. 'Jamie.'

'I know that.' Her mum's voice was sharp. 'Come and sit down.'

Jamie looked at Zoe and hesitated.

Her mum patted the space again, and the floral scrunchie holding her hair back dropped to an even more dismal angle.

'Come on. David Attenborough's on telly soon.'

Jamie sat down, looking somewhat puzzled. Her mum's social antennae were disintegrating rapidly. Zoe went to the purple armchair by the window and plumped a cushion with rather more violence than normal. She set it straight and exhaled in the vain hope that it would make her feel more relaxed. 'Jamie and I need to talk now, Mum.'

'No you don't.' Her mum pulled a fig out of the bag that lay on her lap. 'Not while David's on.' She chewed happily.

'Yes we do.'

Her mum dug for another fig. 'Well, if you must.' Her right leg emerged from her blanket, and Zoe averted her eyes from the varicose veins and the splay of dark brown hairs sprouting from her thigh. She was about to get up again. Just when Zoe had managed to get her to keep still.

'What do you need, Mum? I can get it.' Her mum's wandering was driving her mad. She appeared in rooms, moved things and disappeared again, leaving Zoe trapped in a permanent game of hide and seek. Scissors. Notebooks. Zoe's phone. Nothing was safe.

'I want Murgy.'

That cat. He was making himself exceedingly at home. His favourite spot was the kitchen table. He liked making a nest for himself on top of the newspapers and stretching out in the sun.

'I'll just go and get him.'

'And my glasses. I need them too.'

Aha. An easy one. 'They're on your head, Mum.' Zoe adjusted the vase on the mantelpiece and picked up a plate covered with crumbs.

'Oh yes.' Her mum located the glasses and put them on, then tucked herself under the blanket again. 'Why are you always tidying things?'

Zoe looked around the room, enjoying the increasingly rare feeling of everything being firmly in its place. The black vase full of gerberas. The small statue of an owl from Jamie's trip to India the year before.

'I like it tidy.'

'Why?' Her mum frowned.

'It's just the way I am.' Zoe was acutely conscious of Jamie's gaze. When she was little, her mum had been all about chaos, adept at navigating her way through a constant trail of washing that was just about to go in the machine, dirty plates and cutlery, and the toolbox that was constantly open as she tried to fix the various things always going wrong around the house. Zoe liked calm. Control.

Her mum turned to Jamie. 'Zoe used to be so messy, I could barely find the . . . the thing you sleep in.' She clicked her fingers. 'The thing in her room. When she was sixteen, she—'

Zoe felt a kick of adrenalin as Gina veered towards things that were best left unsaid. 'Yes, well, things change, Mum.' Luckily Murgatroyd chose that moment to walk in and leap on to her mum's lap, turning round and round until he found a suitably comfortable position.

Zoe picked up the remote and prayed for David Attenborough. The screen flickered into life. First up was a group of glossy American teenagers running across a beach. Zoe switched channels. Next a news anchorman stared into the camera and intoned about the latest terrorist threat to the UK. She flicked again. And there he was. The calm backing track to her youth. The man she was sure her mum would have run away with given half a chance.

'I love this one.' Her mum smiled. 'It's where the bison get slaughtered by the lions.'

'Oh. Nice.' Zoe looked at Jamie to see that he was smiling too. Their eyes connected and she could feel heat rise inside her. Then he dropped his gaze and the moment was gone.

Her mouth was dry. 'Would you like a coffee?'

'Sure.' He stood up and stretched, and she could see the tanned flesh of his stomach as his T-shirt rode up. If only she could touch it. Last night, after finally getting her mum into the spare bed, she had found herself watching *Match of the Day* just to try to make herself feel that he was near.

She led the way down the corridor, past the picture of them both on the Millennium Bridge just after Jamie proposed, and went into the kitchen and flicked the kettle on. They had bought it together when they had first signed the contract to rent this flat eighteen months before. A kettle, a bed and hearts full of hope. It had all seemed so easy.

'Wow. Your herbs are looking a bit better than they used to.'

Zoe grinned at the pots on the windowsill. 'Mum. She's got green fingers. She brought them back from the dead.'

'You're telling me.' Jamie's eyes flicked around the walls. 'Sorry I haven't been round before. Len from next door told me he'd seen you a couple of times.'

'It's fine.' She folded her arms. Unfolded them. Leant against the worktop in an utterly unsuccessful attempt to appear casual.

He rested his hand on the back of a kitchen chair. 'I needed more time.'

'I see.' She forced herself to keep standing tall.

'So I thought I'd come and pick up some stuff, if that's OK? My holiday T-shirts are getting a bit repetitive.'

'OK.' She would NOT cry. 'But you'd still like a quick coffee, wouldn't you?'

'Um . . .'

'Please?'

He slid reluctantly into a seat. 'If you want.'

She did want. She would quite happily have parked a JCB across the doorway if it would make him stay.

He looked around, seeming ill at ease in the kitchen in which he had spent so many hours. Drinking. Reading. Singing as he danced around to his favourite tunes, while making enough chilli to feed the two of them for a month.

His eyes flicked towards her and then away. 'Your mum seems nice. Not at all what I was expecting.'

She filled the kettle.

'What did you think she'd be like?'

'I dunno.' He fiddled with the keys in the middle of the table. Her heart ached as she watched his long fingers and the light brush of blond hair on the back of his hands. 'You never talked about her, so I guess I was expecting some kind of monster. Someone worth hating that much.' She could hear the question underlying his words.

There were so many things she hadn't told him.

She turned her face away and made two coffees, and a cup of tea with extra sugar for her mum.

'Why's she staying here, anyway?'

'I'm just helping her out for a bit.' Zoe gave him a mug. 'She's been here for a couple of weeks now.'

She could see the questions on his face.

'I'll just take this to her. Then we can talk.' She wondered wildly if she could fit in a shower on the way back.

No time. She was too scared he would disappear.

In the living room, her mum had fallen asleep, head resting on Murgatroyd's back. Zoe gently put the mug of tea down on the table next to her and stood watching for a moment. Her mum's face was so gentle in sleep. Her lines softened and blurred. Zoe remembered games of hide-and-seek when Mum would cram herself into the laundry basket, only emerging when both her daughters had become convinced she had been taken away by fairies. After years of suppressing them, she was starting to enjoy those memories. Thinking about her childhood was like the sweet discomfort of rubbing arnica into a fresh bruise.

She turned and went back into the kitchen and sat down opposite Jamie. She blew on her coffee and watched the steam rising.

She didn't know how to begin.

She looked at the set of his mouth, and knew he wasn't going to make it easy for her.

'This is a bit different from our last Saturday together, isn't it?'

He looked up, his face flinty. 'What, the wedding day?'

'No, the one before that.'

He drummed his fingers on his mug. 'I don't remember.'

He was deleting the good times. She couldn't blame him for that. 'We read the papers in bed in the morning.' She could almost feel the warmth of him now, as he'd kissed her on the shoulder and got up to make them tea. 'Then we went up to Covent Garden. Saw that amazing singer in the piazza and had burritos and beers with Mandy and some of her mates.'

His lips were still set in a straight line. 'And then we had a fight. Again.'

'Yeah. But then there was that sunset. As we walked back over Hungerford Bridge. Do you remember?'

'Not really.' He was staring into his mug.

143

'And then you gave me a piggyback to the tube because I'd broken my heel.'

'Yes.' At last he looked at her, and she felt a tremor of hope again.

He shook his head. 'Funny how standing alone at the end of an aisle can block all of that out, isn't it?'

Her optimism dwindled again.

'Jamie, please, you said you wanted to talk when you got back. And I'm ready. I am. Whatever you want to know, I—'

He frowned. 'No, Zoe.'

'But you were right. I'm so sorry. I shouldn't have—'

'No.'

She stopped.

He was drinking his coffee so fast, he must be burning his tongue.

'You know, it hurt me too, Zo.'

'What did?'

'Losing the baby.' He stared into his mug. 'I don't think you ever understood that. It felt like the whole thing was about you. And I get that. Of course. It was your body. But it affected me too.'

She was shaking now.

The blood. The familiar ache of loss. During those first few weeks as May seeped into June, when the loss was so stingingly real, she had spent hours wondering what their baby would have become. Boy or girl. Big or small. Blond or redhead. If only they had been given the chance to find out.

It had been too raw to talk about. Too painful to share.

Jamie carried on. 'And you wouldn't talk about it with me. You just picked yourself up and carried on – running, swimming, working, doing anything you could to stop yourself thinking about it. You never let me in. And if you marry someone, you need to trust them enough to be open.'

'But I can. I could. It was just that—'

He wasn't listening. 'I thought about it all the time, out there on my romantic honeymoon with Russ and his roving eye.' He gave a mirthless laugh. 'Going on stunning boat trips with him chatting up the girls serving our drinks. Or sitting in bars and watching him trying to convince everyone we weren't gay.'

Despite everything, Zoe felt her lips twitch.

'I bet he hated that.'

'Yeah.' Jamie's mouth curved upwards. 'And every now and then I *might* have stroked his arm, or leant towards him, just to keep myself entertained.'

For a second he looked young again. Unburdened.

'Until he "playfully" punched me and nearly broke my arm.' He nodded. 'That taught me that particular lesson.'

'Ouch.' She reached out across the table. She wanted to tell him the whole story. 'Look, I'm sorry I didn't talk to you when it happened, but there was a reason. And I want to tell you. Please.'

He held up a hand to stop her. His shoulders were hunched.

'You don't have to any more. If you wanted to say something, you should have said it before.'

'But—'

Anger was etched across his face. 'Do you remember the night I proposed?'

'Of course I do.' A pop-up cinema in a car park. A tangle of fairy lights. *Eternal Sunshine of the Spotless Mind* on the big screen. Cocktails. His knee against hers as he turned and asked the question she had been hoping for ever since they met.

'And do you remember what we did afterwards?'

'Yes.' She wondered where he was heading. 'We went to the Millennium Bridge and listened to that busker with the accordion and the dog.'

'Exactly.' He ran a hand through his hair. 'And I told you then, didn't I, that I'd always be totally honest with you?'

Her stomach dropped. 'Yes.'

'And you promised the same.'

Shame stung her. 'Yes.'

'I told you then. About what happened with my sister.'

'Yes, but—'

'About how I let her get in my dad's car with me and drove her home when I was six pints down.'

'Jamie . . .'

His eyes were distant and dark. 'She was thirteen, Zoe. You know how ashamed I am of that. You must do. Even though we only grazed a wall, and even though the police didn't catch me, I'll never forget my dad standing there when we got back. His face when he saw the dents in the car and realised I was drunk. The way he dragged me into his study and shouted that he expected more of me.' He shuddered. 'I told you everything about that. Something I've never told anyone.'

'I know.' She reached again for his hand, but he pulled it away.

'I waited, Zo. I waited for you to talk to me. To tell me your secrets. But you just hugged me and kissed me and told me you loved me, and I was stupid enough to believe that you were as honest as you seemed. That you didn't have any skeletons.' He drained his coffee. 'But then you left me standing there at our wedding, and I knew there was more to you.'

'And I can tell you about it.'

'No.'

'But you're here. I'm here.'

He put his mug down. 'But there's a problem now, Zoe.'

'What do you mean?'

'I'm starting to think you did the right thing. Running away in your wedding dress.'

Her breath caught in her throat at these words from the man she wanted to spend the rest of her life with.

'I think it's just as well you stood me up. Because I can't trust you.'

'Jamie . . .'

He stood up.

'Please listen, Jamie.'

'I'm sorry.' He rested his hands on the back of the chair. 'I really am.'

She felt an age-old punch of resentment. 'I'm sorry I didn't talk to you. But it's hard to be honest when your life hasn't always been clean and straightforward and neat. It's—'

'I can't believe you're trying to justify keeping things from me.'

'I'm not. I'm trying to explain.'

He shook his head. 'Russ told me I shouldn't bother coming.'

'Well maybe you should have listened to him.' She was veering close to the edge now. He looked at her as if she was a stranger in a police line-up. No emotion. No trace of love.

'I'll get my stuff then.'

'Fine.' She could feel herself receding. The armour clicking back into place. Trying to tell the truth was just too painful.

She fought back her tears. They weren't for him to see. She pulled her laptop towards her and focused on the screen as he went into the bedroom. She wanted to go and beg, but she didn't. She wouldn't. Instead she answered emails and worked on a pitch until the packing was over and the front door was shut behind him.

Then she pushed the laptop away, and in the privacy of her kitchen, where no one else could see, she put her head down and wept.

Our house, Longford
Birthday present: Topshop vouchers
Favourite song: anything with screeching guitars

15th June, 1997

Dear Zoe,
   Thirteen. Bloody hell, how did that happen? Looking
at you all hunched up on the sofa after our Pizza Hut
birthday tea, I can see the woman you're going to
become. You have curves now. Hips. Long auburn hair
that you wash about ten times a day and wear flicked to
one side so your head looks like it's being drawn downwards by an invisible anchor. You pull the fringe down to
cover the spots that are starting to appear on your
hairline. You're pale. You don't want to climb or play
football any more. You just want to sit and eat crisps.
   It's like a flashback to me when I was younger. I
don't tell you that, of course. You're reaching that age
when the thought of being in any way like me fills you
with utter horror and sends you screaming to the
chemist to buy some product to obliterate my gene
pool. Spot cream. Hair dye. Sun-In. It's all happening on
the bathroom shelf.
   There's no child left in you now. You like sitting in
your room listening to music while you and Lily paint
each other's nails. You lie on the sofa watching *TFI
Friday* or *Brookside* or that totally annoying
programme with Matthew Kelly on ITV. Or, when
you're even more hormonal than usual, you get into

149

your dad's precious Audi, putting your hands on the wheel as if you're about to drive it away.

God knows why you're allowed to even breathe on it. In the six months since it arrived, I've barely been allowed to open one of its hallowed doors. I call it the love of his life. I'm not sure he understands that I'm not joking. Communication isn't exactly our strong point nowadays – we're more into grunts and sarcastic sound bites than actual words that mean anything. I can't forgive him. I don't care if he's not with her any more, or if it was only a few times. I can't just move on like he wants me to, however many flowers he buys me or however many times he takes me out for posh dinners I am too choked to eat. It hurts too bloody much.

I do my best to keep up appearances for your and Lily's sake, but I know you're not fooled, my sharp-eyed daughter. Sometimes I catch you watching as we navigate another meal of small talk and evasion and I know you can see everything that's missing. Touching. Eye contact. Genuine affection rather than a grunt and a dash out of the door.

Luckily we have friendly neighbours now to paper over the cracks – a couple of accountants called Simon and Anne. They like their beers and don't have kids yet, so they actually have the energy to stay up past ten. Alistair gets on like a house on fire with Simon, so they come round all the time for Sunday roasts or for pasta and wine in the evenings. Time goes quicker with them around. Alistair smiles. I remember how to laugh. Simon advises Alistair about the firm's accounts, while Anne and I chat about work and life and why we both love Madonna.

Simon is handy, too. He helps me out when something inevitably breaks down as soon as Alistair's left
on a business trip. It was the washing machine first
– he had it fixed in ten minutes flat and then stayed for
tea, like he has a few times lately when Anne's away
working. He helped me plant an apple tree last week,
and mend the shed the week before. He's six foot two,
with dark blond hair, and frankly the fact that he's
always mowing the lawn with his top off isn't making
the summer pass any slower. Sometimes I take my
time over the washing-up or the cooking just so I can
gaze. He has this smile when he looks up and catches
me staring. So mischievous. Like we're in a secret club
of two and we've just found a magnum of champagne.
It always makes me blush, but I keep smiling back and
time slows and then I'm called away to work or to take
you somewhere and the rest of the day sits lighter on
my shoulders somehow.

The other day you walked into the kitchen and
caught me looking at him. Next thing I knew you were
staring too. The expression on your face sparked
memories of Judy Blume's *Forever* and that scene in
Dirty Dancing where Baby puts the watermelon down
and dances the samba with Johnny Castle. My instinct
was to reach out and pull the blind down. To shut you
in. Protect you. God knows, I know where that kind of
thing leads. You're swept off your feet aged only
twenty-four, and then you get pregnant and you're
married, and fourteen years later your bed is cold at
night and you realise your husband never holds your
hand any more.

But saying any of that just leads to another row, so
instead I got you to take the washing upstairs. I think

you knew what I was doing, but you let me think I'd got away with it and went and sat in front of your mirror learning how to put on eyeliner, or something. If I ever try to say anything to Alistair about how I'm worried about you, he just shakes his head like I'm the problem. He tells me I drink too much (like he can talk), and I should help you more. 'What?' I say. 'When? In the three seconds between emptying the washing machine and taking Lily to Brownies?' And he looks at me with that bloody patronising expression and says, 'If you think she's lost her way, then maybe you can help her fix it. Girls need their mums.'

I want to punch him, but Mags tells me that wouldn't be a good move. She's living in Oxford now, and it's a total godsend having her close again. Her new husband Dominic makes looms or something. He works in a shed in their garden and never goes off anywhere dangerous, and she's so happy she's practically flying whenever we meet. She looks at me with reborn eyes and says that things will get better for me and Alistair. That underneath all this we're solid. That we are meant for each other, despite Sally the alarm consultant from Bedford (it feels better if I describe her like that).

I think she's wrong, but I keep carrying on. I snap at you when you fiddle with the food on your plate or tell me how naff my trainers are, but I keep the meals coming and taking you to school and trudging onwards hoping I'll feel like me again one day. You and I argue. Alistair and I argue. And so it goes on. And last night when I got home I just felt like crying, so I went out on the back step and had a fag and a glass of wine to calm myself.

And then Simon was outside and it was too late to

hide and he pushed his way through the gap in the fence we've never fixed and he just sat with me and let me cry. Then, when I'd had enough, he talked about telly and how he hates Michael Flatley and how much he loves the Stone Roses until I was quiet again. And I was right next to him and my head was leaning on his shoulder and I could have left it there for ever. His hand rested over mine and I could barely breathe with wondering what was going to happen next.

Nothing, as it turned out (damn you, phone). But he gave me the strength I needed to get through the rest of it. Lily moaning when we couldn't find her bloody dog (stuffed; approximate age 103). You spending about a year in the bathroom when I really needed the loo. Same old same old. Simon listened to me. I'd forgotten what that feels like.

So. There it is. You are officially thirteen. I'm looking forward to you liking me again in about five years' time. But only if I get rid of these trainers.

I love you, golden girl.

Mum x

Ten

'I can't believe I'm missing work for this.' Gina looked suspiciously around the car park. 'You know I hate hospitals.'

'This shouldn't take too long, Mum.' Zoe tried to keep her voice calm. 'And you're off work at the moment anyway, aren't you?'

This was met with a beat of silence.

'I knew that.' Her mum fiddled with her seat belt.

Mags piped up from the back. 'What? You didn't tell me that, Gina.'

Zoe unclipped her own seat belt and turned round, widening her eyes meaningfully at Mags. She hated having to lie but she couldn't cope with her mum being any more upset than she already was. Not today. 'She's just using up a bit of leave, aren't you, Mum?'

'That's right.' Her mum swore under her breath as she tried to unclip herself.

Zoe reached out to help.

'I can do it.' Gina kept going.

'OK, Mum.' Zoe put the ticket on the dashboard. It had cost her about as much as a new pair of running shorts, but she still felt lucky to have squeezed the car into the only available space in this grinding mass of near misses and bad temper. She looked up and saw gunmetal skies. In front of the car a woman in a bright pink coat was leading a hunched man towards the yellow facade of the outpatient building. He tried to make a break for it just as a car reached the two of them, and Zoe held her breath as it screeched to a halt inches away. The woman guided the man onwards, looking admirably calm. She was clearly used to this kind of thing.

Zoe wondered if she would become used to it too.

Her mum fiddled some more, her fingers clumsy. She swore under her breath. Zoe looked pleadingly at Mags, who reached forward and clicked the belt loose.

'Right, Gina.' Mags opened her door. 'Let's get in there.'

She climbed out and went round to the passenger door. Zoe turned to Lily, who was sitting in the back, too agitated to drive her own car. 'Thank God Mags came with us.'

'I know.' Lily nodded. 'She's the only one who can get away with telling Mum what to do.'

Or not. Gina was sitting firm. 'I don't want to.'

'The quicker we get in there, the quicker it'll be over.' Mags held the door wide. Gina closed her hand around her bag, as if about to use it as a weapon. Then she sighed.

'Well, only to prove you lot wrong, OK?'

'OK.'

As Mags wrestled Gina out, Zoe felt a hand on her shoulder.

Lily spoke in a whisper. 'I'm scared.'

Zoe managed a smile. 'Let's just see what they say, OK?'

Their mum was still protesting as Zoe locked the car. 'This is a waste of everyone's time.'

'Maybe.' Zoe put her keys in her bag. 'But we need to talk to someone about your test results.' She looked sternly at her mum, wishing she didn't feel like such a bully. 'Ready?'

'If I have to be.'

They trooped through the bitter wind towards the doors. When they got there, Gina hesitated. Fear replaced defiance and she visibly paled.

Zoe stepped forward and took her hand.

Her mum patted it. 'Will you help me, Zo? In there?'

'Of course.' She squeezed the thin fingers.

'I just need to do my lipstick.'

Zoe sighed and checked her watch. Five minutes till their appointment. Of *course* now was the time Mum would want to do her make-up.

She shifted impatiently. 'We haven't got long.'

Gina had already pulled her mirror out of her bag and was applying red lipstick in the long, steady stroke Zoe remembered so well from childhood. Upper lip. Lower lip, then a final pout and pat.

'I'm ready now.'

'Good.'

Mags stepped forward. 'Come on, you old tart. Let's get in there.' She slapped Gina on the bum.

Gina rolled her eyes. 'That's the only thing that'll shut you all up, isn't it?'

'Damn right.'

Zoe led her inside, flanked by Lily and Mags. The reception area in front of them was predictably unmanned, and an enormous map on the wall to their right showed a confusing mass of lines and arrows that were presumably intended to help them find their way to their destination.

Zoe's phone buzzed and she answered the call while scanning the map.

'Are you going to make it back in time, Zo?' It was Bruno's voice. Hurried. Anxious.

'No, but I'll dial in.' She pulled her mum's hospital letter out of her bag to see if it provided any more clues as to the location of the memory clinic. She found a map on the back. 'Don't worry. There's plenty of time.'

'But you normally lead investor updates.'

'I know.' Zoe sighed. 'I'll be on the call. I promise.' She turned the map upside down to see if it tallied any better with the instructions written on the letter.

It didn't.

'It's this way.' Her mum launched herself against the flow of people heading towards the exit.

'Mum, I . . .'

Her mum didn't hesitate. 'Come on.'

'Bye, Bruno. Speak soon.'

Zoe joined Lily and Mags in sprinting along behind her mum, who was proceeding at her normal warp speed. Her chin stuck out at its most righteous angle, and Zoe knew that the tilt of her head meant that her dial was set to battleaxe. She remembered it well. From playground fights in which Lily had come off worst and Gina had waded in to try to save her. From times when she had been short on cash and had been forced to take food back to the shelves with the whole supermarket queue watching. From that afternoon many years ago. The end of the end.

No. Not that. Not now. Zoe increased her pace and caught up her. 'Are you sure we're going the right way, Mum?'

'Yes.' Her mum had always had a better sense of geography than her. Years of driving along random roads to find the latest army camp, as Dad inevitably got held up, with two girls curled up on the back seat pretending they didn't miss the home they had just left.

Her mum confidently rounded a corner, only for them to come face to face with some yellow waste bins.

'Mum?'

Gina stood in silence. 'But . . .'

'It's OK.' Zoe took her arm, only to have her hand thrown off. 'It's my fault for putting the map the wrong way up.' She tried to laugh, but the anguish on her mum's face shocked her.

Gina was muttering to herself now. 'I know it was here. I was sure it was this way.' She walked back along the corridor, pushing on random doors, the three of them trotting behind her.

'Mum.'

Her mum didn't stop.

'MUM.'

Gina turned.

'I think it's this way.' Zoe indicated a corridor on their left. 'Shall we try it?'

Gina opened her mouth. Closed it. 'OK.'

It was her meekness that cut Zoe to the core.

At the door to the memory clinic, her mum turned to her. 'It's like when we went to Woolacombe when you were both little, isn't it? When I went the wrong way and you were the one who found the ice cream shop?'

'Exactly.'

'I used to love it there.' Her mum smiled in reminiscence. 'In Woolacombe. Being on the beach. It was the one time I'd feel like the best mum I could be. Space. Sunlight. Sea.'

Mags pushed open the door. 'Come on. In we go.'

Gina didn't move. 'I loved it when you were little.'

Zoe's chest was too tight. Her heart too full.

Mags took control. 'Come on, Gina. No more messing about. Time to go in.'

'If I have to.'

158

Zoe saw the nervousness on her mum's face. She stood beside her. 'Just trust me, Mum, OK?'

Her mum nodded. 'OK.'

She held out her hand and Zoe took it. They walked forward into a peaceful waiting room and the chaos of the hospital seemed far behind them.

It was only when they got to the reception desk that Zoe realised she was the one leading her mum. Their role reversal was complete.

Dr Jones leant back in her chair. 'Thank you, Gina, for sharing what's happened to you so far, and the worries you have about the future.'

Zoe sat next to her mum, staring at the whiteboard behind the doctor's head. This was it. The moment she had been dreading. She kept her hand steady on her mum's arm, wishing she had Jamie on her other side, his hand in hers. She missed his calm strength. His kindness.

But no. She had to do this by herself. She thought of Lily and Mags, sitting outside in the waiting room surrounded by leaflets about the disease they all hoped Mum didn't have.

The doctor pushed her big black glasses higher up her nose. Her gold earrings swayed beneath the choppy line of her bob. Zoe could feel her mum trembling, so she squeezed her hand harder. She had to be comforting. Reassuring.

Dr Jones's smile was kind. 'You were referred to me because you had concerns about your memory, and we've spent the past hour talking about your experiences, and doing a few tests to see if anything has changed since you saw your GP.'

'Yes. And?' Her mum sounded defiant, and Zoe felt a

growing admiration for her bravery in the face of all this. She had seen Gina's consternation when she had tried to draw the hands on a clock face to show ten past five. She had drawn them at ten to five, and had stared and blinked and scratched her head, knowing something was wrong but unable to see what it was. Zoe had been itching to step in. To help her save face. She had sat on her hands and stared out of the window, feeling any remaining hope seeping away.

Dr Jones crossed her legs, laying her hands neatly on her knee. 'And I know that you said earlier that you wanted me to label the problem if I found one. Is that still the case?'

'Of course.' Her mum sat up straighter, as if bracing herself.

Dr Jones nodded. 'Well, given the test results, and after talking to you and your daughter, it seems that your memory isn't as good as it could be.' Her expression was concerned. Serious. 'And it's not because you're getting older, Gina. I'm afraid it's because you've got early-onset Alzheimer's disease.'

Zoe closed her eyes. However much she had expected it, hearing the words still made her want to hunch over and scream. To beat her fists. To blame someone.

She didn't dare look at her mum.

It physically hurt. The truth.

Dr Jones flicked her eyes down to the notes spread across the desk in front of her. 'Now, I know that's very hard to hear, and I'd like to try to help you live your life in the way you want to. I want you to be as independent as you can.'

Gina was staring out of the window, as if wishing she could fly away. Zoe leant forward.

'So what's next? What happens now?'

Dr Jones's face was sympathetic. 'I'm going to prescribe Aricept, which can delay progression of the disease. It can have side effects, but you can monitor that with your GP and the dementia nurse.'

There it was again. Hope. 'Can it halt it altogether?'

'No.' Dr Jones's voice was final. 'I'm afraid not. But it can give patients more time. And there are other things you can do. We have hundreds of patients living with their dementia. There are coping strategies. Staying active. Eating well. Being sociable – staying connected to family and friends. Looking after yourself.'

'This is total rubbish.' Zoe's mum shook her head. 'There's no way I've got that . . .' Predictably, she lost the word she needed. 'That thing she says I've got.' She jabbed a finger accusingly at Dr Jones.

Zoe glanced apologetically at the doctor. 'She's trying to help you, Mum.'

'No.' Her mum shook her head decisively. 'She's not.'

'But Mum—'

'No.' Gina stood up. 'She's wrong. This isn't happening.' A tear rolled down her cheek. 'This isn't . . . me.' She scraped the chair out of her way. 'It can't be true.' She put her hand to her mouth to hold back a sob.

Zoe stood up and tried to put her arms round her mum. 'We'll help you. We will.'

'I don't need help.' Her mum kept moving. 'I'm absolutely fine. Never better.'

She was at the door now, and Zoe followed her, throwing a question over her shoulder to Dr Jones. 'What happens now? Do we see you again?'

Dr Jones nodded. 'We'll review Gina here in six months and retest her to see how things are. I know it's very hard.

But it's not the end. There really is a lot you can do.' She held out the prescription and a pile of leaflets.

Zoe took them while her mum wrestled with the door handle.

'Our dementia nurse will be in touch. And there's a number you can call if you need support.'

'Thanks.' Her mum had the door open now and had stormed into the waiting room. Zoe wondered how many patients reacted like her. How many refused to believe their diagnosis. She couldn't blame them. It was a life sentence. A world that would shrink and squeeze until there was no room for a future.

The door closed behind her and she breathed hard. The shock of Dr Jones's words had left her pulse racing. Alzheimer's disease. Mags and Lily got up from their chairs, their expressions showing that they had read Zoe's face. That they knew.

Zoe gave Lily a fierce hug and then turned round to see that her mum had disappeared.

'Shit.' She started scanning the room. No red lipstick. No orange coat.

'Mags, can you stay with Lil?'

'Of course.' Mags took her sister by the arm and sat her down again, folding her in her arms as she started to cry.

Zoe turned and ran. Past the little kitchen, where two members of staff were having a cup of tea. Past the toilets. Past the bottle of alcohol gel and the buzzer and out through the door.

Where was she?

Zoe was frantically pressing the button for the lift when she saw her. She was leaning against the wall in an uncharacteristic slump, eyes vacant, as a very pregnant woman was wheeled past in a chair. Zoe swallowed. Her mum's chin was no longer tilted upwards. Now her face was aimed squarely at the pale grey floor, her mouth slack, and under the neon lights, Zoe could see a nightmarish vision of the future. No welcoming smile. Nobody home.

She walked over, wishing she had the words to make it better.

'It's not true, is it?' Her mum looked at her, eyes wide and vulnerable. 'What that doctor said? Doctor . . .' She clicked her fingers. 'Bugger, I can't remember the name.'

'Dr Jones.'

'Yes. Her. It isn't true.' The grief on her face told Zoe that she knew it was.

She tried to distract her. 'Why don't we go back to the car, Mum?'

Her mum was revving up again. 'I mean, I found my way here. Didn't I?' Again she looked to Zoe for reassurance.

Zoe wanted to give it. But she couldn't.

Her mum's eyes flashed. 'Well I think it's all bullshit.' She bristled and pulled her handbag higher up her shoulder. 'I'm perfectly capable of looking after myself. I don't need medicine. I don't have any . . .' She searched for the word. 'Any problems. I just need everybody to leave me alone and let me live.' She turned on her heel. 'And I'm off to drive myself home.'

No she bloody wasn't. Besides, Zoe had the car keys.

Gina strode off determinedly, and Zoe was about to give chase when her phone rang. She fished it out of her bag. Bruno. Shit.

'Tell me you're dialling in.' His voice was urgent.

'I can't.' She started to move. God, her mum was fast. 'I'm sorry.'

'Oh bloody hell, Zo.' She could hear the panic in his voice.

'I know. Things just took a bit longer than I thought, and now Mum's really upset. You'll do a brilliant job, Bruno.'

'Stop trying to butter me up.'

'I'm not.' She realised it was true. 'You'll be fine. Just talk them through the figures. OK?' A huffing sigh. 'Zoe, we . . .' He stopped, but she knew what he must be thinking. She knew she needed to do more. To be the old Zoe, who always had the drive and the ideas to keep her company growing. 'Well, I'll do my best, OK?'

He hung up. Zoe stared at the phone for a second, wondering if her world would ever right itself. Whether she'd ever feel under control again. In here, with her mum and the news and all these people hurrying around her, she felt weak. Lost.

Shit. Mum. She couldn't see her. She started to sweat as she ran back towards what she thought was the hospital exit. She got lost in winding corridors, saw lifts she was sure she had been to before, and at one point thought she had made it only to find herself back outside the door to Clinic C. She exhaled to calm her rising hysteria and then tried again. Back into the crowds. Past the café. Past the bench where a little old lady surrounded by carrier bags appeared to have taken root.

And there it was. The car park. Zoe ran out, sniffing the petrol-fumed air, and headed straight to the car.

Her mum wasn't there.

She turned around and scanned the car park. Nothing.

Then she heard it. Crying. And there her mum was. Hair cascading round her face as she sat hunched over on a bench, her forehead pressed against her hands and her shoulders heaving.

'Mum?' Zoe sat down next to her.

Her mum ignored her.

'Mum?'

She looked up. Red eyes. Exhaustion in every line on her face.

'I don't understand what's happening.' Her lower lip trembled, and now Zoe wanted to cry too. 'Why did you bring me here?'

Zoe put an arm round her shoulders and pulled her close.

Her mum rested her head on Zoe's shoulder. Zoe's suit slowly dampened as Gina cried. Grey silk became black. Zoe kept still and stroked her mum's back.

'I'm scared.' Her mum was howling now.

'Me too, Mum. Me too.'

'What's going to happen to me? You'll look after me, won't you? You're not still angry with me?'

Zoe shook her head. 'It doesn't matter now.' And she found it was true. There was no time for resentment now.

'Can I stay with you, Zo-bear? Please? Will you look after me?'

'Of course.'

She ignored the needling voice telling her this couldn't work. That she couldn't cope with the business and her mum, with her wandering and her night waking and her habit of leaving the front door wide open at all hours of the day and night.

'I can trust you, can't I?'

'Of course you can, Mum.' She had to do this. She had to make up for all the years apart.

'You won't put me into a home, will you?'

'No, of course not. I'll look after you, I promise.'

'Thank you. I never want to leave you.'

Zoe hugged her more tightly and sat watching cars search for non-existent spaces, wondering what would happen. Where they were all heading next.

Maybe it was better not to know.

Our house, Longford
Birthday present: Our Price vouchers
Music: Stone Roses. Over. And over. And over.

15th June, 1998

Dear Zo,

So. Fourteen. And the party spirit is back, because it seems you had a little celebration planned for yourself this year. I came home after another day in halitosis hell with Dr Chambers, trying to make the pitiful practice repairs budget extend so we can all actually sit on chairs, to find you were once again out without telling me.

I went into your room. For a small space, you cram in a lot of mess. There was crap everywhere. Magazines and lipsticks littered across your bed, a new set of youthful male six-packs on the wall, used cotton wool pads, a box of Tampax, and some bloody tiny lace pants. When the hell did you buy those? And what with? I'd like you in pants up to your belly button till you're thirty if you don't mind. I hate you growing up. I miss laughing with you. I can't even remember the last time you smiled.

Anyway. There I was. In your room. Trying to work out where you were. And then I saw it. Not your diary, before you start swearing at me. I found that a couple of months ago and haven't read it. I remember how much I wanted to kill my mum when she read mine.

Aloud. To my dad. It had boys in it. Thanks, Mum. Just bloody perfect.

Anyway, back to my story. I reached up to your top shelf – the one with the French set texts you never read – and there it was. Cool glass. A metallic lid. Shit.

You had Sainsbury's vodka on your top shelf.

At least it hadn't been opened yet. Every cloud and all that.

I was about to throw it out of the window when I thought better of it. Instead I twisted the top off and had a slug before taking it downstairs and putting it in the back of the kitchen cupboard. God knows I needed it.

I wandered the local sights until I found you. Park. Corner shop. Bus stop. And there you were. All alone with a Marlboro Red and the saddest face I've ever seen. You saw me and you practically coughed up a lung in shock, and dropped your fag amongst the crisp packets and sweet wrappers at your feet. You were busy preparing a defiant look, but I was in no mood to shout at you. Because you know what? It wasn't the smoking that shocked me. It was your total isolation. No friends to share your covert puffs. No one to giggle with as you ripped off the cellophane.

Worry started gnawing away at me, and I sat down next to you on the thin plastic seat and saw the red grooves around your bitten nails and opened my mouth to say a thousand things. Nothing came out, though. It was your birthday, for God's sake. It was meant to be a happy day. And I didn't want another massive row. We're getting too good at those. Homework. What's for tea. We can turn anything into a fight. So I told you that your dad was coming home specially to share your birthday cake, and we were taking you out for supper, and that we should get back smartish to meet him.

But you didn't get up. Instead you leant away from me and asked me in the tiniest voice why he was coming home when I didn't want him there, and why I kept pretending it was all OK when I just shouted at him and made him miserable.

The accusation on your face – I'll never forget it. We had never felt further apart. You were probably thinking about how I was ruining Alistair's life, while I was thinking about how he was ruining mine. Of how much he has hurt me.

So we sat in silence, next to the quietest road in the world, while the ducks quacked on the pond across the green, and I tried to work out if it was worth explaining my side of the story. But most of all I kept glancing at the hunch of your shoulders and that beautiful face hiding beneath your hair, and I missed you.

I wondered where I'd gone wrong. Whether I should have thrown in the towel ages ago when things got harder and Alistair and I stopped reaching for each other at the end of a day. The cracks that started when Richard died and that have only got bigger as I tried and failed and tried and failed to get close to Alistair again.

You shifted on your seat. 'I hate all the fighting, Mum.'

I had run out of lies. 'I know.' I pulled you to me and you didn't resist and I stroked your long red hair and I loved you with all my heart.

'Are you going to split up?'

I tried to think of an answer that wasn't a lie.

'I don't know.'

A bee buzzed into the bus shelter and circled around a Mini Cheddars packet on the floor.

'Will you try to make it work, Mum?'

I thought of telling the truth – that I could try till kingdom come but it would be no good. But I had to try to reassure you. 'Of course, golden girl. Of course.'

And you pulled away and arched an eyebrow and just said, 'Golden girl? Why are you calling me *that*?'

I could almost feel the sting, and I drew you close again, grabbing each precious second before you remembered you were a teenager and walked away. And as I sat there breathing you in, I realised how far life has brought you. How my memories aren't yours. How you are living your own story and parts of me are already edited out. The names I called you. Your sprinting feet ahead of mine on a thousand adventures in the park. It made me want to bottle the softness of your hair on my cheek and lock it away in my heart for ever.

We never made it out in the end – Alistair got back too late – but Simon and Anne stopped fighting for a night (we can hear it through the walls, every evening when she gets home) and came round and helped us to make it feel like some kind of a party. You sat next to Simon and talked about bands I'd never heard of, and you laughed and there was colour in your cheeks and I was so bloody grateful to him. He gave you a CD and you ran straight over to the stereo and put it on, and for once your dad unglued himself from his work and actually focused on us.

It was such a relief to put our hatchets down for an hour and sit round a table and feel faintly like a family. Lily giggled and glowed – summer always lights her up.

She'd made you a mix tape and decorated the case
with flowers and hearts and all the strange sayings you
two have dreamt up together over the years. Alistair
and Simon were full of plans for the company –
Simon's the new accountant there and is helping them
to land some big contract up north that'll really turn
things around. About bloody time.

Anyway, you stayed chatting to Simon on the back
steps for a while after tea, as I was clearing up with
Alistair. I kept looking at the man washing up beside
me – father, businessman, and still a soldier through
and through. I didn't tell him about the vodka or the
fags – I would never tell him your secrets. Instead I
sounded like the wife he wants. The perfect one who
makes casseroles and is welded to a can of Pledge.
Once you were in bed, Anne went home. Alistair got a
work call and Simon chatted to me as I made coffee
and poured a big slug of whisky into each mug. It turns
out he and Anne are on the rocks – she's moving out
as soon as she can get a new place.

He seemed sad, so I changed the subject and asked
what you and he had talked about. He said you were
having a tough time at school, and it opened the
floodgates and soon I was telling him all about the old
you – the girl with the world-stopping smile – and he
let me talk on and on, and then he said he was always
here to help if we needed him. And I started crying –
all the tears I didn't cry in that bus stop. The tears for
the daughter I had lost.

Then he said I was a great mum for caring so much,
but I said that's just nature – what any mum would do
for her kid. I was nothing special. He said I shouldn't be
so humble, and that I was a brilliant mum, and

somehow we were really close and he rested his hand on my arm. Next thing I knew I was leaning towards him and planting a kiss on his mouth.

So soft. So perfect.

But then he pulled away, eyes wide with embarrassment, and I knew he didn't want me and I hated myself. Suddenly I was just a tired woman drinking whisky in a messy kitchen, full of pointless hope about something that would never happen. I excused myself and ran to the loo, and when I came back, Alistair was there and Simon had just headed out of the door.

Oh God, the shame. My cheeks are still burning. I went out and dug up the veg patch for an hour in the dark, and even that didn't help. Every time I think life can't get any worse, I come up with a new way to humiliate myself. I can't bear the thought of seeing him again. Should have thought of that before I threw myself at him. I really thought he was interested. Talk about misreading the signs.

So. There we are. Not exactly a vintage birthday, my girl. But you know what? Here – on paper – I can say it. You can disappear as many times as you like. Blame me as much as you like. Hell, you can even slam doors or scream if you want. But I will still love you. I will still try to help you. I'm messy and deluded, but I will always fight like hell for you.

Because that's what mums do, isn't it? Or this one, anyway.

All my love,
Mum x

Eleven

'I feel like I should have a gin in my hand.' Bruno flicked a crumb off the sleeve of his checked shirt and watched her sympathetically.

'It's OK, really.' Zoe stared at the sandwich in front of her and attempted to feel in some way excited by it. Her body felt light and fluttery, but the only thing she had managed to eat so far was a tiny packet of raisins her mum had randomly brought home from the supermarket. Sun-Maid. Memories of lunch boxes past.

'This is your fifth coffee, and you didn't run in this morning.' Bruno raised his eyebrows. 'It's officially the apocalypse. Your poor mum. Poor you.'

'It was worse for Mum. She nearly set fire to her dressing gown.' Zoe remembered the fear in those familiar brown eyes as she had run in and grabbed the electric kettle off the gas hob last night. Fear. And shame.

'And she's not going back to work?'

'No.' She picked out a piece of cheese from her sandwich. 'They've been really kind, but she simply can't remember things well enough.' She nibbled the cheese cautiously, but it made her feel sick, so she put it down and sipped her black coffee instead. 'But she's upset.'

It wasn't as if her mum was her only problem. There were more. Things she couldn't talk about. Since Gina's diagnosis last month, she had endured a constant programme

173

of memories playing on repeat in her head. All the scenes she had been avoiding jostled relentlessly for space – each one stark and spotlit in savage neon.

The hospital bed. The silence in the car. A door slamming in her face. Her mum's tears on her shoulder. Lying wide-eyed on the bathroom floor as the future she and Jamie had dreamt of had disappeared.

Once she had been so good at shaking herself free of the past and carrying on. She would go for a run. Work on a pitch. Cuddle up with Jamie and lose herself. But now, with Mum there all the time, she felt like it was going to suffocate her.

Tears pricked her eyes and she blinked them away fiercely.

'Look, Bruno, we really need to win this pitch, OK? I need some good news.'

'You're telling me.' His hand snaked across the table and picked at a particularly plump piece of ham.

Zoe pushed the sandwich towards him. 'Have it.' She sighed. 'Have it all.'

'No.' He blinked. 'You're the one who force-feeds me whenever I'm down.'

'I'm fine.' If she said it enough times, it might come true.

'If you say so. But you're turning into a Twiglet. Look at you. It's amazing you have the strength to lift that cup.'

'That's total crap.' She finished her coffee, looking out at the mass of Londoners marching purposefully along the street outside. Red buses rumbled past, with brave cyclists weaving their way in and out of the cars and vans. Horns beeped. Engines roared.

She looked away. 'How about you, Bruno? How are things with you?'

He shrugged. 'Nothing to tell.'

'Oh come on. A hot date. Some right swiping. Anything.'

His attempt to look dignified was slightly marred by the fact that he was losing the fight to open his popcorn bar. Zoe reached out and took it from him, ripping the plastic open with her teeth.

'There you go. Now spill.'

He split the bar and held half out to her. 'Have some. Please?'

'OK.' She forced herself to take a bite. She needed the energy; the pitch started in fifteen minutes' time. inlovewithlife.com had been started by two old office mates who had used the death of a much-loved colleague as a catalyst to develop a site that celebrated the fun in life. They were expanding fast, and now they wanted somebody to develop a mobile app. Zoe knew that she and Bruno were exactly the right fit. They needed new business and this was top of her list.

Bruno dabbed his mouth with a napkin. 'Well, if you really want gossip, I could tell you about Michael, I suppose.'

'Is he the guy you went on a date with last week?'

'Yep.' Bruno crinkled the wrapper between his fingers and dropped it on the plate. 'He's married to the gym, so he's *hot*. Brad Pitt with shades of Poldark, if you can imagine that.'

'Wow.'

'Exactly.' Bruno nodded. 'Anyway, he likes horror films, and wearing shorts when it's freezing cold. Oh, and he lives in Los Angeles and comes over here for work every month or so.'

'I see.' She picked up her phone to check the time. 'Well, you love a tormented long-distance relationship, don't you?' She smiled. 'I can't remember the last time you went out with someone who was actually based in this country.'

'Bullshit.' Bruno shook his head indignantly. 'There was Maximus.'

Zoe rolled her eyes. 'Well the name should have been a giveaway there. Didn't he hate it when you shortened it to Max?'

'He did.' Bruno grinned. 'So of course I did it all the time.'

Zoe was thinking about her mum again. Things weren't getting any better. Zoe kept waiting for the Aricept to take effect, but it had, if anything, made things worse. The side effects were proving particularly unpleasant, especially as her mum kept forgetting to flush the loo.

Meanwhile, everywhere she looked, more questions arose. How to keep her mum safe. How to keep her stimulated. How to help her set up systems to cope with the things in life that had once been so simple – making tea, cooking. Gina had been so proud of herself the other day when Zoe had called her at lunchtime, saying she was going to make roast chicken and apple crumble for dinner.

Zoe's hopes hadn't been high, and when she had arrived home, she had found her mum swearing at the oven. 'It doesn't work, Zoe. You must get a new one.' Then she had stormed off to her room, leaving Zoe staring at the uncooked chicken before quietly switching the oven on herself.

'Zoe?'

She realised Bruno was talking to her. She gulped more coffee and tried to get her game face on.

'Are you sure you're OK to pitch?' He was peering at her as he put his empty coffee cup on the silver tray.

'Yes. Of course.' She thought of her mum wandering

round the flat, and suddenly wondered if she had remembered to hide the matches.

Her phone vibrated.

'Because I'll give it a try if you want. I've been practising.'

'It's OK.' She couldn't keep the irritation out of her voice. 'I'm absolutely fine.'

The text read: Locked out.

Obviously this was one of the days her mum could remember how to use her phone. Zoe picked up the tray and walked over and slid the remains of their lunch into the bin. She found the number she wanted and dialled.

'Mags?'

'Hiya.' She could hear an engine starting in the background.

'Sorry to bother you, but Mum's locked herself out and I can't get back to sort her out. Can you help?'

A horn beeped at the other end of the line. 'I'm sorry, I can't. I'm just waiting for my niece to finish her driving test.'

Shit. Zoe pushed open the glass door so she was out in the hustle and buzz of lunchtime London. She strode off in the direction of the nearest traffic lights.

'Zoe?'

Zoe knew what Mags was going to say. It was what she had been saying ever since the memory clinic.

'You know we need to do something, don't you? You can't go on like this.'

'Yes I can.' Zoe dug her nails into her palm. 'I just need to figure out how to—'

'It's not what she needs, Zoe. Being alone in your house all day. She would be happier if she could see people. Socialise.'

177

Zoe felt a pulse of frustration. 'Mags, I can't talk about this now. I have to find someone to go and help her. Let's speak later, OK?'

As she hung up, her head was aching. Too much juggling. Too many worries about options that were getting narrower all the time.

'Zoe? It's that way.' Bruno was running after her, pointing in the opposite direction.

'Shit.' She turned on her heel, sweat warming her skin as she dialled another number.

'Lily?'

'Hi, Zo.' Her sister sounded light. Happy.

'Can you get round to mine? Mum's locked herself out.' She was about to step into the road, but Bruno pulled her back. A millisecond later, a bus passed.

'Shit, Zoe.' She could see the shock in his eyes. 'Be careful.'

The world was whirling past her. Outside the house, her mum might do anything. She could decide to wander down to the park. Accidentally steal something from the corner shop. Try to go back to her own flat. End up in an alleyway with her bag stolen and no memory of how she had got there.

And it would all be Zoe's fault.

'Sorry, Zo.' Lily spoke fast. 'I can't help out this time. I'm minuting a board meeting soon, and I can't get out of it.'

'OK. It's fine.' Zoe's jaw was so tense it hurt. There was no answer. No solution. 'I'll figure something out.'

'Are you sure? You know I can—'

'Look, I've got to go.'

Zoe hung up. Shit, shit, shit. She looked around. She saw a woman with a Selfridges bag going into Pret. A man in a dark blue suit shouting into his mobile. The fruit seller on the corner handing over a brown paper bag of apples to a man dressed as a clown.

There were millions of people in this city, and yet there was nobody who could help.

'Zoe?' Bruno put his hand on her arm. 'Are you sure you're ready for this pitch?'

She whirled around. 'What do you mean?'

He steered her past a lamp post. 'I mean that you're not concentrating. Normally you're running figures beforehand. Going over the details. But you're trying to sort out your mum – of course you are – and I'm just worried that—'

'That what? That I can't cope?'

'No.' She prickled at the sympathy in his voice. 'I just think you're going through a lot, Zo.'

The frustration of the past few weeks was starting to ignite. She should take a breath and calm down, just as she had so many times before. She needed to focus. Needed to get the next hour right.

The problem was that part of her didn't want to be calm. Part of her wanted to do all the screaming that she had been holding back for so long.

She took a step towards him. 'Bruno, I can't believe you're saying this. You know I'll be fine.'

'I've just never seen you like this.' They reached the building and she saw the words *inlovewithlife.com* on a sign at the top of the stone steps.

'I can handle it, OK?' She marched up and pressed the buzzer. The door opened and they walked into a high-ceilinged marble vestibule. The November sunlight filtered down from a skylight above them as they signed in at a small desk in the corner.

Zoe clipped her ID tag on and headed for the lift.

'What floor were they again?' She was still wondering who could go and help Mum. If only Mandy was here, rather than luxuriating in a spa in Greece. She had helped out a few times and was a big hit with her mum. Zoe had come back two weeks ago to find the two of them giving each other a makeover. It was safe to say that Mandy had come off worse.

And then she had an idea. She hated it. But it was the only option she had.

She pressed the button to call the lift and dialled.

'So as you can see, Hayley, we really have a lot to offer in terms of helping you to grow your business.'

Bruno was grimacing at her. She must talk to him about managing his facial expression.

She moved to the next slide. 'Here you can see the impact our apps have had on the business of cuppacakes.com, which has a customer base that . . .'

Thoughts of her mum wouldn't leave her alone. Where she might be. What if she had found the Oddbins on the high road? There was no telling the trouble she might get into with alcohol in her system. Zoe could see her now, tucking into a bottle of wine and then wandering up to a total stranger thinking they were her best friend.

There was danger everywhere if you didn't know who to trust.

She suddenly realised that the two women behind the table were staring at her expectantly. She seemed to have stopped talking. Shit. She was trying so hard to concentrate, but her mind refused to stay in the room.

Come on, Zoe. She fought to regain her train of thought.

'We can drive sales and increase efficiency through optimising your app to be user-friendly, maximising . . .'

Or her mum might go to a train station. That would be worse. She could hop on a train and end up in Scotland, with only a handbag and a cash card she couldn't remember the PIN for.

Concentrate. '. . . maximising conversion rates to meet your business ambitions.'

Time for the big finish. 'We promise to give you the individual attention you need to make lovinglife the biggest player in the industry.'

Next to her, Bruno seemed to be having some kind of attack.

Nearly there now. Then she could check her phone.

'We will work closely with you both . . .' She tried to smile at her audience but felt she might only have succeeded in looking like a vampire ready to attack. 'With you, Hayley, and you, Amanda, to make your app an industry leader. Thank you.'

She was used to a vague sense of triumph in the air when she finished a pitch.

Today it was more of a funereal vibe.

'Any questions?' She looked at the dark-haired women in front of her. One tall and sleek in black, the other smaller, with a chunky blue bracelet around her wrist. She had no idea which one was which. But she could see that they both looked decidedly unimpressed.

The one with the bracelet coughed and laced her hands together.

'Just for the record, Zoe.' Her voice oozed sarcasm. 'My name is Emma, not Amanda.'

'Oh.' Zoe thought she saw her phone light up. Adrenalin jolted her. 'I'm so sorry, I—'

'And our company,' Emma continued, 'is called inlove-withlife, not lovinglife. I would have thought you might have known that, seeing as you're so keen to work with us.'

'Yes. Of course.' Zoe felt embarrassment stain her cheeks red. The temperature had risen to a million degrees. She normally didn't get things wrong. She was reliable. Accurate. She did her research and it showed.

Hayley sipped her water. 'I have to say we're disappointed. We'd heard such great things about Zapp Digital and the service you provide.'

Zoe fought back. 'And I assure you that all those things are true. I promise you that if—'

Hayley shook her head. 'I'm sorry. We need people we can rely on. If you get our company name wrong now, who knows what you might do next?'

Zoe winced.

Hayley stood up. 'Thank you for coming in, but it's a no.'

Zoe tried one more time. 'Please? Let us show you what we can do. I promise you won't regret it.'

'I'm sorry.' Emma's voice was final. 'But you're not even concentrating. I can see you looking at your phone. And we had some great pitches from other firms.'

'No, I—'

'Thank you for coming in.'

Zoe felt a rush of pure frustration as Bruno started gathering up their things.

'Well, we'll leave these anyway.' She put down two glossy files containing all their ideas. She'd been working on them till two that morning. What a waste. 'Just in case they're useful.'

Hayley looked at them as if they had recently been extracted from landfill. 'Thank you.'

'You're welcome.' Zoe smiled again. It made her cheeks ache. 'And do get in touch if you have any questions.'

She picked up her bag and her phone. No missed calls. No messages. Maybe her plea hadn't got through and Mum was still wandering around out there.

She walked to the lift and hit the button. Nothing happened. She hit it again. Then again.

'Zoe.' Bruno's eyes were wide. 'Stop it!'

She dropped her arm to her side.

'What happened in there?'

'Nothing. It's fine.' She didn't need rebukes from him. Not now. 'They were a tough crowd.' She couldn't handle admitting she had failed. 'We couldn't have done any better.'

Bruno wrinkled his nose. 'Zo, you got their names wrong. And you missed out half the slides. You never do that.'

'So?' She shrugged, full of a wild desire to scream. 'It was just unlucky.'

'It wasn't unlucky. And we'd done so much work.' She hated the disappointment on his face.

She snapped back. 'Well, I'm sorry if I've let you down.'

'Zoe.' She saw the shock on his face. 'That's not what I meant. But . . .' She could see him weighing his words. 'But are you sure you don't need to take time off? Your mum's diagnosis was such a shock, I . . .'

She shook her head. 'I can't, Bruno. It's my company. Don't you get that? There are only the two of us and we need more business or we'll run out of cash. You're flat out on the technical side, so I have to be here to keep the clients happy and win new contracts.' Her breath was coming fast now. 'I don't have time to relax. I really don't.'

'But I can help.' He frowned. 'Can't I? I thought we were a team.'

The lift pinged open and they both got in. They stood in silence as it descended, Zoe glaring at the doors, as if they were to blame for all her problems.

She cast a sideways glance at her colleague. He was watching her. 'Zoe, I've never seen you like this. It's not like you.'

She knew. She had spent a lifetime making sure no one ever saw her like this again.

'I'm OK.'

'Let me help, Zo.'

'How are you going to do that? Unless you can find a cure for Alzheimer's. Or invent a time machine so I can go back to July and actually make it to my wedding.'

He leant back against the wall, folding his arms across his chest. 'You're impossible, Zoe.'

'Thanks.'

'I'm your friend. You should trust me.'

'I don't have time! Don't you get it?' Her heart was pounding. 'I can't wait around for anyone else to fix things. I have to do it myself.' She was shaking. 'Do you know what my life is like right now? Let me tell you. I spend my evenings watching David Attenborough documentaries to keep my mum quiet – I never want to see another antelope EVER again – and then, when I finally get to sleep, she keeps waking me up to tell me it's morning. Three times last night and then when the actual morning comes she's sound asleep and I have to go to the office and try to get some work done.'

The lift doors opened and she strode out. Bruno was close behind her and he reached out and held on to her arm.

She tried to shake him off. 'Let me go.'

'Zoe.' He looked her straight in the eyes and she felt

horribly exposed. 'Yes, things are shit. But everyone has problems. You know that. So why can't you just talk to me?'

So many answers. So many secrets. So many fears. If she started talking, she might never stop. About how lonely she was without Jamie. How since Mum moved in she didn't want to open the front door each night and see what chaos the day had brought. How tired she was of keeping her feet moving and her mouth speaking and of carrying the weight of the past on her shoulders.

But no. Never admit defeat. That was her motto. Her salvation.

'I'll sort things out, Bruno. I promise.' She started walking towards the exit. 'But right now I have to go and check on Mum.'

He lifted his arms in frustration and let them drop again to his sides. She could feel his eyes on her back as she walked away.

When she finally reached her street, her head was full of apocalyptic visions of what might have happened to her mum. Mugging. Gina lying spreadeagled on the floor. Her brain even threw in a flood for good measure.

She turned her key in the lock, surprised to hear music coming from the kitchen.

'Hi, Zoe.' Her mum stuck her head out into the hall. She hadn't looked this animated in weeks. 'Jamie found all the music!'

Thank God. So he had got her message. Zoe exhaled at last as she walked down the corridor. Once it had been so natural to find him here. The sweet end of every day. Delicious smells would meet her at the front door and have her running down the corridor to see what he had cooked up this time. His arms would close around her and she would lean into him and feel herself unwind.

There he was, their iPad in his hand as music blasted from the speakers.

'Hi.' He glanced at her and then away.

'Hello.' She wondered whether to kiss him on the cheek. No. Too impersonal. 'Thank you for coming over.' She put her bag on the floor and sank into a chair. 'I'm so sorry I had to call you.'

'No worries.' He gave her a fleeting smile. 'The joy of being freelance.' He was wearing the purple T-shirt she had got him from a street stall in Amsterdam. He grinned at her mum. 'And we've had fun, haven't we, Gina?'

'We have.' Gina was shimmying round the table to 'The Sun Always Shines on TV', merry as a teenager after her first encounter with a pint of cider. 'I love this band.'

'A-ha.' Jamie nodded. 'They had the odd good song, it has to be said.'

'What?' Zoe started to take off her shoes. 'I didn't know you had an eighties streak.'

'I have some secrets, you know.' He appeared to be about to say something more, but then pressed his lips together and stopped. She felt a thud of pure sadness. Not seeing him at all was better than this awkwardness. Communicating in stops and starts like two strangers making conversation at a bus stop. This wasn't who they were meant to be.

She couldn't stand it. 'Jamie, I . . .'

'Yes?'

Zoe glanced at her mum, who appeared fully absorbed in dancing with a chair.

'Can we chat? Things ended so weirdly last time.'

'Come on, Zoe. Dance!' Gina grabbed her by the arm.

'Not now, Mum.' Zoe gently shook her off. 'Can we talk, Jamie?'

'OK.' He kissed her mum on the cheek. 'You take care, Gina.' He laughed as Zoe led him into the hall. 'She tried a forward roll in the living room. Terrible.'

Zoe went into the living room and sat down on the sofa. He didn't join her, choosing to stand near the door as if poised to run away.

So nothing had changed. This really was how things were now.

She hunched forward. 'Where did you find her?'

'She was curled up on the doorstep.' He shrugged. 'She seemed quite happy.'

'Thank God.' Zoe nodded. 'I was so worried. Thank you for coming.'

'You tried everyone else first, right?'

She smiled sheepishly. 'Of course. I didn't know if I could . . . if it was OK to get in touch.'

She saw only kindness on his face. Nothing more. 'Well, I'm my own boss, so if I can help, I will. I could come round once a week. Keep her company. Be her DJ for the afternoon. How would that be?'

Her spirits lifted. It would be amazing. She could be there too, and maybe they could talk and rebuild and—

'That way you can have a more relaxing day at the office. Without having to worry.'

The breath went out of her. 'Great. Thanks.'

She looked at the man who should have been the father of her child. Who would have put a ring on her finger and been at her side for life.

He wasn't even looking at her. 'Just so she doesn't get lonely.'

She bit her lip. 'Sure. Thanks.'

'No worries.' He could have been talking to a colleague. 'Oh. By the way . . .'

'Yes?' Despite herself, she was flooded with hope.

'She kept mentioning some guy. From way back.'

'What?' She was on her feet in seconds.

'And a clinic? She kept talking about that.'

Zoe froze. The door slamming. The shouting. Strangers staring at her on the street.

She had tried so hard to get away from what she had been.

'Zo? Are you OK?'

'I . . .' It would be such a relief to tell him.

'Michael Jackson!' Her mum appeared next to Jamie. 'It's Michael Jackson. Let's dance!' She raised her arms and twirled around.

It was safe to say the moment had gone. In another minute Jamie had headed out of the front door and Zoe was back in the kitchen, listening to the music of her childhood.

She wondered how on earth everything had gone so wrong.

And how on earth she was meant to put it right.

Our house, Longford
Present: the coat you said you wanted, ohh, FIVE
    THOUSAND TIMES
Music: Oasis

15th June, 1999

Zoe, Zoe, Zoe,
   I'm so angry I can't sleep. I'm pacing the living room,
past all the crap, and I'm realising how little it matters
that there are CDs and mugs all over the place when
it's 2 a.m. and pitch black outside and you stumbled in
an hour ago in tears, your new birthday mascara
running down your cheeks. For a second I thought the
worst – thought that tomorrow I could be one of those
mums you see on news conferences on the telly. Pale.
Tearful. Desperate to find someone to blame.
   But no. Instead it seems this boy you had a crush on
– Charlie – just buggered off with another girl and left
you at some random party in the next village and you
had no credit, and there was no pay phone, so you had
to walk all the way home by yourself. I'm shaking as I
think about it. Cars passing you as you walked along
the darkened road. Who could have been in them and
what damage they could have done.
   Bloody hell, what a lucky escape. No wonder my
mum screamed at me when I used to stagger back
home in the small hours with cigarette breath and
grass stains on my jeans. It wasn't anger – it was pure
bloody terror.

189

When you missed your curfew, I kept going into your room and the bed was cold and your lipstick was still open on the chest of drawers, just as you left it when you hurried out with such excitement. I smoothed your duvet and folded up some clothes, but mainly I sat at the kitchen table, staring at the picture of you and Lily on the windowsill. At last Alistair is making enough money to get you the present you wanted, and your new coat was still there where you had left it on a kitchen chair, after deciding reluctantly that it was too warm to wear tonight. I remembered your face when you opened it and stroked the fake fur as if it was gold. Your smile. So beautiful.

It's long forgotten now. You were crying in great juddering sobs when you got in, and I was so bloody angry with Charlie for disappearing without you, I just wanted to punch the world. You shouldn't be so alone. Not you. Not my talented, big-hearted daughter. Then – thank God – your dad and Simon came in from a client night out and sat either side of you on the sofa, telling stupid stories and feeding you marshmallows, and gradually your shoulders relaxed and the weeping stopped. And Simon told you how beautiful you were and God, I was so grateful to him for trying to help that I thanked him in the kitchen, when we were topping up the biscuit plate. And he shrugged and said we'd looked after him so well during his divorce, he was just returning the favour.

And tonight his eyes were so blue and I remembered that awful night when I tried to kiss him, and how kind he'd been afterwards, and I felt that old embarrassment reappear and he seemed to know because he just whispered in my ear, 'Don't worry about it, Gina. All forgotten.' Then he went back to the sofa and put on *Chariots of Fire* – still your favourite – and the four of us watched until you fell asleep leaning against the sofa cushion and finally the night was over. You looked so young as Alistair carried you upstairs in his arms, your red hair trailing downwards, your skin so pale against his black shirt.

And from now on? I'm looking out for you. I'm not letting people hurt you again. No way. I don't care if I embarrass you. I don't care if you hate me – I'm going to help. I'm still your mum. Live with it. That's the deal.

I love you.

Mum x

Twelve

'Well, that was a wonderful meal as usual.' Zoe's dad dabbed his mouth with his deep red napkin. He looked up at the owner of the Steamhouse and smiled. 'Thank you, Jim.'

'My pleasure, Alistair.' Jim's blue eyes gleamed with delight. 'Anything for my old CO.'

'You're very kind.' Alistair put his napkin down by his extremely clean plate. 'Did you enjoy yours, girls?'

Lily nodded. 'I don't think I'll be able to fit any more food in before Christmas.'

'Exactly.' Zoe patted her happy stomach. 'It was delicious, Jim.' She was relieved to see her dad looking at her the way he always had. Interested. Proud. He had been overseas working so much that she hadn't really seen him since that awful Saturday.

She shouldn't have worried. Judging by his conversation so far, he laid the blame for the wedding fiasco entirely at his ex-wife's door. Zoe had rapidly changed the subject as soon as he brought it up. She was used to keeping things from him, but this was different. This time she knew she was the one to blame. She was the one who had chosen to leave.

Explaining that, however, would have meant telling him about her mum moving in and her diagnosis, and Zoe didn't want to talk about that today. She wanted to relax. To have a whole afternoon of not thinking about reality.

'More wine?' Her dad's wife Wendy held out a bottle of red.

'Yes please.' Zoe nodded gratefully.

Wendy poured. 'You look tired, Zoe. Are you OK?'

Zoe opened her mouth to reply.

'OK? Of course she's OK.' Alistair looked at Zoe approvingly. 'She's a toughie, aren't you, Zoe?'

Zoe took a large mouthful of wine and nodded.

Her dad smiled. 'Zoe always knew how to handle herself. You don't win a digital start-up of the year award without having a core of steel, do you?'

Zoe flushed. He had a framed picture of her receiving the award from a Google exec on the wall in his study, and every single visitor was duly taken in to see it.

He was so proud of her.

She had such a long way to fall.

Wendy stroked his arm. 'Anyone for coffee?' She beamed at Jim. 'Could I have a cappuccino, please?'

'Of course.' Jim nodded. 'You're sure you don't want any more food?'

'No room.' Wendy shook her head regretfully. 'Or I definitely would.'

Jim flushed with pleasure. For a six-foot-four ex-soldier, he took a childlike delight in all things foodie. Zoe had first met him when she was five and he and his wife had welcomed them round for Sunday lunch. There were six courses. When he left the army, absolutely nobody was surprised when he opened a restaurant.

The four of them came here every year in late November. A pre-Christmas treat. Zoe checked her phone discreetly under the table, only to see her battery was flat. Damn.

Mum must have switched the charger off at the plug again. This was one of a new range of random habits, including growing petunias in the bath and attempting to light a fire in Zoe's grate. The chimney had been blocked off for ten years. Luckily Zoe had got there before the smoke alarm went off.

She felt a twinge of anxiety.

Lily put her hand on Zoe's arm, keeping her voice low. 'How's Mum?'

'She's watching Formula One with Mags, so hopefully she's OK.'

'Gary says that—' Lily stopped.

Zoe crossed her legs. 'What does Gary say?'

'Nothing.' Lily fiddled with her glass.

'How often are you seeing him now?'

'Not that much.' Two pink spots appeared on Lily's cheeks.

'Lily?'

She shook her head. 'It's not a big deal, Zo.'

'If you say so.'

There was steel in Lily's eyes. 'He's a good friend.'

'Are you sure?'

Lily sighed. 'I wouldn't expect you to get it.'

Zoe felt the kick of being misunderstood. 'I'm just looking out for you.'

'Well maybe you don't need to.' Lily turned away, making it very clear that the conversation was over.

Zoe felt a pulse of frustration. Jamie would have known what to say. How to help. She sipped more wine, trying not to think about last year. He had been sitting next to her, charming Wendy, making Dad laugh and eating his own bodyweight in steak. She remembered catching his eye halfway through the meal, both of them hugging their secret close before he had tapped on his glass and announced that they had just got engaged.

Stop it, she whispered to herself. *Stop it.*

'Would you like some chocolates with your coffee?' Jim had come back to collect more plates. He always insisted on serving them himself, despite having an expert raft of waiting staff weaving in and out of the wooden tables throughout the lunchtime rush.

'Yes please.' Zoe was flagging. All caffeine was welcome.

'Any more drama from your mum recently?' Alistair's gaze was trained on Zoe and Lily.

'I don't know.' Zoe tried out a casual shrug.

She felt Lily nudge her.

'I mean, when I last saw her, she—'

Alistair frowned. 'You've seen her again?'

'Yes.'

'I see.' His mouth smiled but his eyes didn't join in. 'Has she been spending more time at the police station, then?'

This time Lily jabbed Zoe so hard it hurt.

'Ow. What?'

Lily leant forward. There was a new steeliness to her face. 'I'm tired of this, Zo. We need to tell him.'

'Tell me what?'

'There's something you need to know.'

'Stop, Lil.' Now was not the moment for this.

Deep down she knew she would never feel like it was the right moment.

Alistair poured milk into his coffee and picked up one of the crispy thin ginger wafers that always made Zoe wish she had eaten less of her main course. He watched Lily intently as she started to speak. Started to tell him why Gina had been arrested. Why . . .

Lily had only said a few words when she stopped, her gaze caught by something near the entrance.

Zoe exhaled in relief. Reprieve.

Then she noticed that her dad and Wendy were looking the same way. There was someone behind her. Someone quite surprising, judging by their expressions.

Suspicion prickled across her skin.

Oh no.

She turned her head so fast it made her dizzy.

And there she was. Mum.

In her pyjamas. The checked ones with the tea stain on the knee. At least her coat was covering the egg stain on the collar.

Zoe didn't dare look at her dad.

'Over here, Mum.' She stood up and waved.

Her mum spotted her and beamed. Her red wellies slapped across the floor, the sound exaggerated by the sudden silence that greeted her entrance. Eyes followed her progress towards them as Mags ran into the restaurant behind her, breathing heavily. 'I'm so sorry, Zoe. We were on the sofa watching TV and then she wanted to find you and she got so upset I couldn't calm her down.'

Zoe shook her head. 'It's OK.'

It wasn't. She risked a glance at her dad. His face was apocalyptic.

Her mum looked only at Zoe. 'We came in a . . .' The pause extended. Seconds passed.

Zoe rescued her. 'In a cab.'

Her mum was still searching. 'In a special car.' She twirled her hair around her finger in an increasingly familiar gesture, as necks craned towards her from every corner of the restaurant. 'The driver was very friendly. It was a . . .'

Zoe could see the frustration on her face.

'It was a cab, Mum.'

'Yes. A cab.' Her mum nodded. 'I knew that.'

The buzz and chatter began again as the other diners lost interest and returned to their meals. Zoe gently took her mum by the arm and settled her in a chair. Her mum wriggled out of her coat, leaving the egg stain to shine forth. Alistair looked away in disgust.

Zoe waved at Jim, who rapidly brought over two more chairs for her and Mags. She thanked him and took as long as she possibly could to sit down.

There. That had killed a few seconds.

Not enough, though. Not nearly enough.

She found herself stroking the handle of her coffee cup, as though she was expecting a genie to appear.

If only. It would take more than three wishes to get them out of this mess.

'Hello, Alistair.' Gina picked up a ginger thin and crunched it enthusiastically. She looked at Wendy. 'And great to see you again . . .'

Zoe's dad growled in reply. 'You know perfectly well what her name is.'

Gina licked a crumb off her finger. 'Yes. It's . . .'

Zoe stepped in again. 'It's Wendy.'

'Of course.' Gina nodded. 'Of course. You married again.'

'You know I did.' He was drinking his coffee fast. Downing it. Keen to escape.

'How are you, Gina?' Wendy reached her hand across the table. 'It's good to see you.'

Gina stared at it for a second before taking it and pumping it up and down.

She turned to Zoe. 'I came to find you. You weren't at home.'

'No, Mum.'

'Home?' Alistair leant forward, back ramrod straight.

'Yes.' Zoe nodded. 'Mum's living with me now.'

He blinked, and his eyes pierced Zoe's fragile facade. 'Pardon?'

She met his eye. She would not be ashamed. Not about this.

'We're roomies.' Gina leant over and helped herself to a lump of sugar from the bowl. She popped it into her mouth and crunched.

Zoe looked at Lily. Lily looked at Zoe. Under the table they reached out and held each other's hands.

'Why?' Alistair looked only at Zoe. She remembered now why she had always tried to please him. He was so damn scary when she didn't.

'Mum . . .' She hated talking about her mum when she was right there. 'I thought she might be lonely.'

Gina appeared to be enjoying herself. 'I wasn't lonely. You were.'

'Mum, that's not—'

'She begged me to move in.' Her mum was back on the ginger thins. Mags tried to move the plate away, but she had already got three in her hand.

'Dad, I didn't. I . . .'

But she saw that he was raising his arm to ask for the bill.

She felt a surge of frustration.

'Dad? Don't be angry with me.'

'I'm not angry.' He put his coffee cup down. 'Just disappointed.'

Zoe could feel the chill wind blowing across the table.

'First the wedding and now this, Zoe.'

So he hadn't forgiven her. He had just blocked out what she'd done.

She wanted him to look her in the eye. 'Now what, Dad?'

She could see Wendy's hand on his arm. See her trying to calm him. But it didn't matter. Zoe knew where this conversation would end. Her dad's world was black or white. In or out.

He didn't answer.

'Dad? She's my mum and—'

'Your mum. Yes.' He squared his shoulders and she saw the anger that had begun so many years before. Still there. Still burning. 'It seems to me that since she reappeared, you've been getting more and more out of control.'

'Dad . . .' She wanted him to look at her with his old affection.

Gina crunched another sugar lump. 'You never did understand her.'

He turned on her. 'I beg your pardon?'

Gina folded her arms. 'You were never there to see her. To see us all. You don't know the half of it.'

Zoe gulped her wine. She could feel the past at her shoulder. Those eyes. Those hands. The love that only she had believed in.

'What can we do?' Lily whispered in her ear. These fights were memories nobody wanted to relive. The worst kind of nostalgia. Round upon round of accusation. Dad was a workaholic. Mum was a lush with a roving eye.

And so on and so on, every time Dad was home, until it had been a relief when they had finally split up. Especially for Zoe. Finally she could stop pretending. Stop talking to the woman who had ruined her life. Stop talking to her mum.

She realised she was digging her nails into her palm.

Alistair's face was a gauntlet.

Zoe tried to stop him. He could attack her, but not her mum. Not now. 'Dad, this is meant to be a celebration.'

'Exactly.' Wendy smiled at Jim as he brought the bill and laid it on the table, next to a plate of dark marbled chocolates.

Alistair nodded thanks to his old comrade. 'You don't need to protect her, Zoe. I seem to remember that Gina is more than capable of looking after herself.'

Not any more.

But Zoe had no time to explain. Her mum's fists were clenched under the table. A vein throbbed in her neck. Her hair was falling out of its bun, and Zoe saw with a pang that she had a splodge of Weetabix just behind her ear. 'Yes. I can stand up for myself, Zo-bear.'

'I thought so.' The sneer in her dad's voice broke Zoe's heart. 'You always did talk a good game.' He raised his fingers in mocking quotation marks. '"I'm such a great mum. Look at me singing songs and building dens. I'm such a great wife. I'm so supportive." Until—'

'Alistair, that's enough.' Wendy shook her head.

Gina's face froze. 'I was! Or I was trying to be. I wanted to . . .'

She stopped. Her face was desperate as she searched for another word that had betrayed her by disappearing when she needed it most.

Zoe waited, squeezing Lily's hand in hers, feeling the sweat begin to prickle beneath her dress.

'Wanted to what, Gina?' Her dad's voice had risen.

Gina picked up a spoon. Put it down. She started pleating the corner of the tablecloth between restless fingers.

'Gone quiet now, have you?' Alistair rolled his eyes. 'You always talked too much.'

'No I didn't.' Gina was breathing fast. Her eyes couldn't

rest on anything or anyone. 'I never told you about Simon. What he did. I never told you anything about that.'

Zoe closed her eyes. That name. The name she had doodled in a hundred notebooks. The name that had made her heart soar. God, she had been so stupid. Thinking she could hide from this. Thinking her dad would never find out.

'Simon? What's Simon got to do with anything?' Her dad's voice was thick with indignation.

Gina's cheeks were flushed. 'Simon was a liar.'

'No.' Alistair shook his head. 'No. You're the liar, Gina. You're the one who tried to seduce him one night in the kitchen when the girls were asleep upstairs.'

'Dad.' Zoe spoke without thinking. 'We don't need to talk about this.'

She felt Lily turn and stare at her. 'You knew about this?'

'Yes.' Zoe nodded. 'But it isn't important.'

'Well, it might have been nice if you'd told me.' Lily pulled her hand away.

Gina was speaking. 'It was one kiss, Alistair. Wasn't it?' She looked at Zoe for confirmation. 'I can't remember.'

'Oh can't you?' Alistair threw his hands in the air. 'How convenient.'

Zoe had to stop this. 'Dad, please.'

Gina raised her voice. 'You're a fine one to talk, Alistair. You weren't exactly . . .' She petered out. 'Damn it. You weren't exactly . . .'

He didn't let her finish. In all the clamour, Zoe didn't have time to wonder why. 'Oh my God, are you drunk?' Alistair was speaking in a distorted hiss. 'You really haven't changed a bit, have you?'

Zoe could see how hard her mum was fighting to stand

up to him. Despite the horror of the situation, she felt a beat of pride.

'Simon was a shit,' Gina brushed the ginger crumbs from her fingers. 'You were just too blind to see it.'

Zoe knew what was coming.

'Mum, I—'

'No, Zo-bear.' Her mum held up a hand, and Zoe could see the thread dangling from her pyjama sleeve. 'No.'

'Mum?' She needed Gina to remember. To remember that this was their secret. That no one else needed to know.

'He ruined everything.'

'Don't you dare talk about him like that.' Zoe could see a vein standing out on her dad's neck. 'Simon was my friend.'

'Yeah. What a great friend.' Gina laughed disparagingly.

'How dare you!'

She stared him down. Only Zoe could see the tapping of one leg against the other under the table.

'Mum? Maybe we should go now. I can—'

Alistair shook his head. 'Zoe, don't get in the middle of this.'

Wendy was quietly paying the bill so that poor Jim could stop hovering and exit this minefield of a conversation. Mags seemed to be attempting to disappear under the table. And Lily was leaning away from Zoe, arms folded and face ablaze with hurt.

Gina pointed at Zoe. 'I was protecting her.'

'What's Zoe got to do with it?'

Zoe shrank back in her seat. She couldn't stop this now. Gina leant forward, her voice crystal clear.

'I found them in bed together. Simon and Zoe. That's what he was really like. That bastard you called your friend.'

Zoe froze, eyes closed. There they were. The words she had been dreading for fifteen years.

She wondered if the world would stop turning.

No.

Alistair shook his head. 'Simon would never have done that. She was only a child.'

Gina was pleating again, her fingers moving faster and faster. 'That was the point, Alistair. That was the whole point. Did you really think he ran away because I kept chasing him? He could have just stopped coming round.' She reached for more sugar. 'There was way more going on. You were just too blind to see it.'

Zoe reluctantly met her dad's eyes. She saw disbelief. Consternation.

'Zoe? Is this true?'

She realised that she could carry on running. Hiding.

Or she could set herself free.

She felt her mum trembling next to her.

'Yes,' she said.

He gaped at her. She could feel Lily's eyes searching her face.

It was like having a layer of skin ripped off.

'I loved him.' She thought of the nights spent dreaming about his touch. 'And I thought he loved me.'

'No. None of this can be true. He would have told me.' Her dad looked physically winded. '*You* would have told me, Zoe.'

All she could do was shake her head.

She had expected rage. Shouting. Tempests.

But no. He just looked old. Diminished.

She tried to explain. 'I was so unhappy, Dad. So lonely. He . . . talked to me. And—'

Her dad held up his hand. 'I don't want to hear it.'

He couldn't look at her. And he didn't even know the whole story. Gina had stopped half-way through. There was more. There was worse to come.

'You never said anything to me.' Lily was staring at her as if she didn't know her at all.

'I didn't know how, Lil.'

Her mum threw an arm round Zoe's shoulders. 'I tried to protect you, Zo-bear. Didn't I?' The confusion on her face brought tears to Zoe's eyes. 'Did I? Did I do that?'

'You tried.' For the first time Zoe understood how hard it must have been.

Wendy shot Zoe a sympathetic smile. She was the only one. Lily and her dad were both looking anywhere but at her.

This was going to be so lonely.

She turned to Gina. 'Shall I get you home, Mum?'

Zoe blinked back tears. 'Right. Well.' She stood up. She felt deadened. Tired. 'I'm so very sorry, everyone. I really am. I'm sorry to disappoint you.'

Lily remained still, staring at her hands.

How could they forgive her when she couldn't forgive herself?

Her mum stood by her side.

'Come on, Zo-bear. Let's go home.'

'OK, Mum.'

But Alistair wasn't finished yet.

'No, Gina.' His normally smooth voice came out in breathy spurts. He shook his head. 'You can't just turn up. Ruin our lunch together. Bugger off.'

Gina stood tall. 'That's what you did, Alistair. Over and over again during all our years together. And you never thanked me for anything. Not once . . .'

His face was drawn. Shuttered. 'I shouldn't have needed to.'

Gina shook her head. 'Thought so.'

She took Zoe's hand and the two of them made their way outside. The sun was shining. The buses stopped and started. The cars beeped.

Zoe leant over and whispered in her mum's ear. 'Thank you. Thank you for not telling them everything.'

Gina squeezed her hand. 'That's what mums are for, Lily.'

Zoe watched her, hoping she'd correct herself. And she knew then.

She knew how quickly time was running out.

Our house, Longford

15th June, 2000

Zoe,

This afternoon. What I saw. I don't know how to
begin. I don't even know what to think. I can't eat. I
can't drink. I can only sit here in the dark and think of
ways to kill him.

It all started so well. The sun was shining and I had a
message from you at work saying your GCSE English
had gone well. I came home early with food in my bag
ready to make your birthday tea, and Alistair and Lily
were on their way. I wanted everything to be perfect
this year. I wanted our faces united in that rosy family
glow you get once in a blue moon – when everyone's
happy and no one's lost their briefcase or their homework and we all just eat and share and laugh and have
the time to remember what a treat that is.

I had made a cake. It hadn't collapsed. I took this as
a sign that maybe, just maybe, we were finally turning
a corner. Alistair and I were doing a bit better – fewer
rows, at least. So I opened our front door full of
expectation and shut it quietly behind me, drinking in
the peace.

I put the bags down and then realised I could hear
something upstairs. A creaking sound. Great. That was
all I needed. A bloody burglar to come and ruin our
evening. I wasn't scared – I was just furious. So I
picked up the tennis racquet you absolutely never use

206

and crept up the stairs with it. I avoided the patch of wood at the top that always bloody squeaks and I stood and listened. Our bedroom. That was where it was coming from. I dashed across and pushed open the door, and then it happened.

I can't bear to think about it. I really really can't. I saw your legs. Your hair flung across the pillow. Your face curving up into the tanned skin of his neck. Your bitten nails digging into his broad shoulders as you urged him on.

I saw your childhood going up in smoke, that's what I saw.

Then you turned your head and noticed me. Your eyes widened. You started trying to push him off you but he was too carried away – it makes me sick to the stomach to think about the state he was in, to be honest. He didn't want to stop but you kept saying his name, *Simon, Simon*, shouting it, until finally he came to a halt, breathing heavily, and you pointed frantically at me. His head turned. His mouth fell open.

The mists descended and I couldn't see or hear or think. I knew I was talking. I knew I should take a breath, get some control, but I couldn't stop myself.

'How dare you?' I was walking towards the two of you, but I was looking only at him.

He started scrambling to get under the sheets. To hide that betraying, evil lump of a body. 'Gina, I—'

'Don't you bloody Gina me.' I was right beside you both now. I wanted to punch, to scratch, to damage.

'Mum?' You tried to talk but I cut you off. I'd deal with you later.

He finally managed to cover himself, sitting up against the pillows. *My* bloody pillows.

The rage was blurring my vision, let alone my mind.
'How dare you do this to her? She's just a child.'

Your voice. 'No, I'm not, Mum. I'm sixteen. And we
waited. This was our first time.'

I turned on you, seeing the defiance in your smile.
The coy sideways glance at this man we had thought
to be our friend. Failure and fury whirled through me.
'Oh, and that makes it OK, does it?'

You were unperturbed. Calm. Like you were the
mother and me the child. 'We love each other, Mum.
We're going to be together.'

'Not on my watch.'

You shook your head. 'Don't, Mum. Please.'

'Don't what?' I curled my fists, enraged by your
sheer bloody front. You, who I'd nursed. You, who I'd
fed, clothed, worried about every single bloody day of
your life.

What the hell had it all been for?

Your voice was clear as crystal. 'Don't be jealous.
Simon told me, you know.' You brazenly took his hand
beneath the sheets. 'He told me you tried to kiss him.'

How dare he?

I could feel the blood pumping round my body,
faster and faster. 'You think I'm jealous?'

'Durr.' Your eye roll enraged me.

I stood over you, really close, feeling a savage
satisfaction when I saw the challenge in your eyes turn
to fear.

'You stupid little cow.'

You opened your mouth, but I didn't even let you
catch a breath.

'You fell for it, didn't you? His bullshit.' I glowered at
her. 'I thought you were supposed to have a brain. He

doesn't love you. What could he ever see in you? You're a child. Just another shag, another notch on the bedpost. That's all.' I knew that the anger was coming out all wrong – firing at the wrong target – but I couldn't stop. 'And it breaks my heart that you're too stupid to see when you're being used. You're such a fucking cliché.'

Your face went white. I could see you dwindling right in front of me.

I put my hand to my mouth. And as you stared down at the duvet and tried not to cry, I knew I had to come up with something to make it better. This was his fault. I knew that. Me and my big bloody mouth.

And then we heard it.

The key in the door. A cheery chorus of 'Hello, birthday girl!'

Alistair and Lily had come home.

We all froze. You, naked as the day you were born. Him, our sheets furled around his body. Me with a tennis racquet in my hand, wondering if I should aim it at my own stupid, thoughtless cannonball of a head.

'Dad. Shit.' Your face crumpled. I had to do something. I had to protect you.

'Simon, get your damn boxers on.' My jaw was so tense I thought it would crack. He stood up and I turned to you, but you kept looking down and wouldn't meet my eye.

'Zoe, I—'

'No, Mum.' You shook your head and I didn't have time to argue. Not with the other two downstairs. Instead I rushed around the room picking up your scattered school uniform and throwing it under the bed, while all the time my mind ran a relentless inventory. How many times Simon had come over in the past year. How often he'd looked at you. How often I'd found you bent over the stereo together or laughing out on the back step.

How the hell hadn't I noticed?

Simon balled up his clothes and looked at me. 'What now?'

I was half tempted to let him sweat. To let Alistair open the door and see just what his 'friend' had done. But then I looked at you. So scared. All grown up and so damn angry with me, and yet still my little girl.

No. Not yet. I could tell Alistair later.

I pointed at the window. 'Get out.'

'But . . .'

Alistair was nearly at the top of the stairs. I took a step forward, speaking in some kind of distorted hiss.

'No bloody buts. Get OUT.'

He didn't need telling again.

'Simon!'

The desperation in your voice made me want to throw him on to the concrete below.

He didn't answer, busy fiddling with the catch.

'Call me. I love you.'

There it was. Your heart on the line. And he didn't even answer.

He finally got the window open and clambered on to the sill.

You looked like you were going to reach for him, but I ordered you to stay in bed and pull the sheet up as high as it would go and pretend to be ill. Alistair wouldn't look close enough to realise what was really going on. He never did.

The bedroom door opened just as Simon disappeared through the window. I heard a muffled cry and a thud and very much hoped he'd done himself a serious injury.

Later, as *EastEnders* came on, I locked myself in the bathroom and sat on the loo seat and tried to work out what to do. 1. Maim Simon and force him to move away. 2. Help you to mend your broken heart. 3. Somehow prevent you from screwing up the rest of your life.

Simple.

The temptation to go for Option 1 and simply head over there and strangle him was overwhelming. So up I got. I cut through the fence at the back, just as I always have, only every blade of grass seemed to be laughing at me and every stone of his bloody patio seemed to be paving another layer of rage into my heart.

'What do you want?' He was in the kitchen with a glass of whisky in his hand. He looked at me warily.

I couldn't even speak. All I could hear was white noise as I stared at him. His face. I had trusted this face. I walked through the open French window, feeling the tiles cold beneath my feet. I pushed it shut behind me.

'I'm sorry.' He snuck a look behind him, as if hoping for rescue. 'I should never have let it get this far. But Zoe started sending me notes and—'

I couldn't believe how low he was stooping. 'You what?'

'Notes.' He was warming to his theme. 'And she kept popping round to borrow CDs.' He shrugged, as if none of this was his fault. 'That kind of thing.'

'Don't you bloody dare blame her.' I was shaking.

'You're the one who's meant to know what's right and what's wrong. You're Alistair's friend, for God's sake. You work with him.'

'So?' He stood squarely on both feet but I could see the way his fingers were tapping against his leg. I folded my arms tightly across my chest as I realised how entangled he was in our lives. Work. Leisure. He was at the heart of everything.

My hands were itching to slap him and I walked up close to his smug, lying face and was pleased to see a flicker of panic. 'Simon. Let's just get one thing clear. This is your fault. And you are never, EVER going to see my daughter again. Got it?' I pointed my finger right in his face. 'Stay away from her, you shit.' Such an inadequate word for so much rage. 'I haven't told Alistair yet, and—'

'And you never will.' He took a gulp of whisky.

I took a second to catch up. 'What?'

'If you tell him, I'll just show him the pictures.'

The shock took the wind out of me.

'The pictures?'

He got some ice from the freezer and casually added it to his glass. 'Yeah. She took a couple of Polaroids and gave them to me.'

No.

'I've got them upstairs.'

I couldn't believe it. You weren't that stupid. No way. Not my girl.

'I don't believe you.'

He shook his head. 'You can see them if you like. Not sure you'd like them, though.'

Graphic images swirled through my brain. Dark. Burning.

And then I remembered. My camera. The way it had mysteriously disappeared a few weeks ago. So *that* was where it had gone.

And there it was. The moment my heart snapped in two.

I clenched my fists. How could you, Zoe? Who *were* you? Where had my golden girl gone?

Behind me I heard the French window sliding open, but I couldn't turn to look. I couldn't do anything but howl all my hatred into his face. 'For fuck's sake, Simon! You should have stopped her. She's just a lonely kid who doesn't know any better and you were meant to be the adult. You were meant to be our friend. Instead you let her take disgusting pictures of herself and throw herself at you and you've broken her . . .'

I ran out of words and put my hand to my forehead and bent over, my stomach knifing me with disgust and horror.

The thought of it. You. Beautiful, fresh-faced you. Setting up the camera. Taking off whatever you took off. Lying down on the bed and pouting as the shutter clicked.

I couldn't bear it.

And then I heard a sob behind me and I turned, and there you were and your whole face was a scream.

'Zoe. Oh God.' I tried to remember what I had said. Disgusting pictures. Lonely kid.

You turned and ran. I yelled after you – 'STOP! I didn't mean it!' – but you'd already disappeared. All that was left was this room and this mess and this bastard excuse for a man.

Tears were blinding me.

Simon took another sip. His calm enraged me. 'Look, I promise I'll do my best to avoid her. I've got some business trips coming up anyway. OK? And I don't want to tell Alistair anything – you know that. We do work together, after all.'

I stood there, shaking, trying to see how to make things better with you. Trying to see how to mend this. And then I looked back at him, and I swear, Zoe, if there'd been a weapon, I would have used it.

'Besides.' He ran a hand through his hair. 'It's Zoe I'm worried about.'

That was it. I hit him. Straight across the face.

God, it felt good.

'Give me the pictures.'

'I can't do that.' He put a hand to his cheek. 'Then I won't have—'

'Anything to blackmail me with?' I held out my hand and took a step forward. 'You'll just have to trust me, won't you? Because I'm not taking no for an answer. And I won't tell Alistair, not yet – though not for your sake. For hers.'

He stared into his glass for a minute, then turned, and I heard his footsteps on the stairs. The fridge still hummed. The smell of barbecue wafted in through the window. Life went on around us.

I didn't move until he came back.

He handed the photos over.

'Is that all of them?'

'Yes.'

'OK.' I scrunched them in my hand and turned to leave.

He coughed. 'You know, you can be as angry as you like, but maybe you need to think about why she kept coming over. She says I'm the only person she can really talk to. The only person she can trust. Without me, she's got no one.'

I pointed a shaking finger in his face. 'Stay away from her.' I turned and stalked towards the door. 'Or I will kill you.'

On the way home, I got out my lighter and burnt those bloody pictures, dropping the ash on to the charred remains of yesterday's bonfire. Good fucking riddance.

When I got back, I tried to talk to you. You didn't want to listen. I tried and I tried, but all I got back was your dead-eyed stare and your door in my face. The final time you pulled me into your room and spoke in a vicious whisper so the others wouldn't hear, spilling out all the things you can never take back. The words that will haunt me in the small hours.

You said you could never forgive me for trying to split the pair of you up. That you were really in love. That I was wrong and that you would prove it. I tried to answer – to explain that the man you loved tried to blackmail me – but you were on a roll. I was a jealous old cow for saying the pictures were disgusting. I was always too busy, I drank too much, I shouted all the time.

Then the finale. You said you wished I wasn't your mum.

That stopped me in my tracks and got me going downstairs and reaching for the gin. I drank one. Then two. Then I went outside and looked at the stars. They were nearly as bright as your eyes when you told me that you loved him. I cradled the glass in my hands and I knew I'd totally and utterly failed. If you're deluded enough to think you two are going to be together for ever, then that one's on me. My doing. My fault.

Happy birthday? You must be joking.

Mum

Thirteen

'Come on, Zo. You can do this.' Mandy stared at her sternly.

Zoe groaned. 'You're such a nightmare.'

'I believe you mean I'm such a wonderful friend.' Mandy tapped the toe of her boot on the ground. 'One who has your best interests at heart.'

'Can't I do it tomorrow?'

'No.' Mandy pointed at her sodden umbrella. 'Because if you do wait till then, I'll have to come back here tomorrow. And frankly, I have an actual life to live. Your mum's ill. You need to fix this. So go.' She shoved Zoe in the direction of her sister's front door. 'And don't you dare turn round and leg it when you think I'm not looking.' She pointed two fingers to her eyes and then at Zoe. 'I'm watching you.'

'OK, OK.' Zoe clutched the brown paper bag to her chest and walked up the steps. She looked round to see Mandy watching her, face stern.

She took a deep breath and knocked.

'Lily.' Zoe hoped her sister wouldn't slam the door in her face. 'How are you?'

'Oh. You know. Peachy.' Lily stood on the doorstep, arms folded.

'I brought muffins.' Zoe held out the brown paper bag. It was so wet, it was starting to disintegrate. Damp crumbs were already sticking to her fingers.

'Great.' Lily's voice didn't sound as if it was great. She sounded as if Zoe had brought her an arsenic gateau.

'Can I come in?' Rain was pouring down in torrents, and Zoe's beige mac was dark with water. Her umbrella had been defeated by the gale about five minutes into her trip, and her hair was in mournful rats' tails down her back. Her grey handbag was dripping on to the stone step, the rose stitched into the handle drooping sadly towards the ground.

Lily stood back to let her in.

'Thank you.' Zoe kissed her on the cheek. Her sister's skin felt cold as ice.

Lily's sheep slippers slapped against the floorboards as she walked towards the kitchen. 'Gary's here.'

'That's nice.' Zoe hoped she sounded convincing.

'Isn't it?' Lily pushed open a wooden door. Classical music was playing on the radio, and across the gap between the kitchen windows Zoe could see a man in blue boxer shorts in the next flat, pouring himself a coffee. She put her bag down and took off her coat.

'Where shall I hang this?'

Lily shrugged and climbed on to a yellow stool by the tiny breakfast bar. Her green polka-dot pyjamas reminded Zoe of the gym bag her sister had carried in primary school. She had hated the plain green material, so their mum had sewn her name on it in bold polka-dot letters. Lily had loved it so much, she started sleeping with it under her pillow. She had called it her magic bag, and pretended to pull out rabbits or talking dolls or homework that had miraculously been finished.

'Why are you smiling?' Lily spooned porridge into her mouth.

'Doesn't matter.' Zoe hung her coat up on the window

fastener. A steady drip-drip began on to the bare floor-boards below. She looked up to see Lily watching her.

'You're dying to get a bucket, aren't you?'

'No.' Zoe saw the suspicious glint in Lily's stare. 'I was just remembering your polka-dot bag when we were little.'

'What bag?' Lily took a sip of tea.

Zoe opened her mouth to reply and then shook her head. 'Doesn't matter.'

'Oh.' Lily put her mug down. 'You can make yourself tea if you want some.'

'Thanks.' Zoe walked over and clicked the switch on the kettle. She opened a cupboard and took out a Cluedo mug. Lily had made her play game after game when they were little. Wet Sunday afternoons with Colonel Mustard and co. She pulled a tea bag out of the canister and popped it into the mug.

'Would Gary like one?'

Lily's eyebrows disappeared into her fringe. 'Wow, you really are feeling guilty.'

'No.' Zoe poured in boiling water. 'It just seemed polite to ask.'

Lily snorted. 'Since when have you been polite to Gary?'

Zoe glanced at her sister over her shoulder, before finding the milk in the fridge and pouring it in. She waited. She had a feeling she knew what was coming.

'So.' Lily put her head on one side.

'What?' Zoe turned to face her.

Lily pretended to think, tapping her spoon against her teeth. 'Oh. I don't know. I thought maybe you'd have something to say about lying to me for fifteen years.'

So there it was.

Zoe blew on the top of her tea.

'Look, Lil. I'm—'

Lily scraped her spoon across her bowl. The sound made Zoe wince.

'Lil?'

Lily looked her dead in the eyes. 'How could you not tell me?'

Zoe couldn't hold her stare. She hated the shame that bubbled through her even at the thought of what had happened. She had been running from it for so long. Her mum's face at the bedroom door. Her lashing words. Simon gone without a word, and then the way he had looked at her when she had finally tracked him down. The woman draped around his neck. The pain of realising that her mum had been right about him. Hating her for that. And for so much more. Tears falling as the hope – so sure, so certain – that Simon was going to be there beside her for ever collapsed. And then the shame – the never-ending shame – of being stupid enough to believe that he had ever loved her.

'I don't know what to say, Lil.'

'Well that makes a change.' Lily licked her spoon and clattered it back into the bowl. 'Normally you're so good at sharing what you think.'

'I . . .'

Lily crossed her legs. And then her arms, just in case the crossed legs weren't enough of a hint. 'How could you not tell me?'

Zoe put her mug down and gripped the sideboard behind her. 'I didn't know how.'

She opened her mouth to try to describe that summer. Another day at school with no one to talk to. Always an empty seat next to her in class. The sighs as people were forced to partner her in chemistry experiments. The feeling that she would never ever fit in. And then that disastrous fifteenth birthday when Charlie had made a £20 bet that he would take her out and get off with her, and she had been so excited, and then afterwards he and his mates had just laughed at her and left her at the party. The tears as she'd walked the long road home all by herself, wondering what was wrong with her. Wishing she knew how to put it right.

And then Simon had been there. Telling her she was beautiful.

God, she hated how pathetic it sounded.

Lily rolled her eyes. 'Now's the time, Zoe. Now's the moment when you explain what happened.'

Zoe bit her lip and stared at the floor. She had given presentations to clients and conferences, but she couldn't think how to begin now. She couldn't work out how to strip away her layers of protection and leave herself open to what people might think.

She raised her head. 'I loved him, Lily.' She felt a sob threatening to explode from her throat.

'But he was Dad's friend. And he was ancient.' Lily's short hair stuck upwards as she sat up straighter.

'Yes.' Zoe nodded, for the first time feeling the pinch of her sister's pain. 'But I was lonely. And he was so kind to me.'

Lily snorted. 'He was kind to me too, but—'

'It was different for me.'

'Why?'

Zoe took a deep breath. 'I didn't have anyone else. You had friends at school by then. I didn't.'

'But you had me.'

'I know.' Zoe smiled tentatively. It wasn't reciprocated. 'But I wanted friends of my own.' She hated how much admitting that still hurt. 'I was always different. Bloody red hair, for starters.' She tried to laugh but didn't even convince herself.

Lily shook her head. 'You always said you love standing out.'

'Yes. I know that's what I said, and I do, but . . .' Zoe wondered why she never felt sure of anything any more. Why everything she said nowadays felt so confusing and unclear. She wanted to go back – back to striding confidently onwards, ticking achievements off along the way, safe in her cocoon of aspiration.

But apparently life didn't work like that.

'Was that another lie, then?' Lily slumped down on one elbow. 'That you liked standing out when all the time you were just as much of a mess as the rest of us?' She pushed her bowl out of the way and rested both elbows on the breakfast bar, dropping her chin until it was resting in her hands. She looked so sad. 'God, I always believed you, didn't I? I really thought you were perfect. I've spent so many nights wondering what you would do, or what you'd say, or wishing that I knew how to convince people like you can. I can barely convince myself, most of the time. And now I find that all along you were the reason Mum and Dad split up.'

'That's not fair.'

'Why not?' Lily's eyes flashed. 'Mum protected you. Simon buggered off. Dad was furious and bloody miserable. And all along it was your fault.'

'I was so young, Lil. And Mum and Dad started fighting years before Simon and I got started. In fact I can't really remember a time when they didn't.'

'Don't make excuses.' Zoe could see tears in Lily's eyes. 'And what I really don't get is that you rewarded Mum by bloody ignoring her? For ten years? She asked about you all the time, Zo.'

Zoe blinked. 'You never told me that.'

'So I kept a secret too.' Lily threw her arms wide. 'What a surprise. Dad's probably got a few as well, tucked away somewhere.' A tremor crossed her face and Zoe walked over to put her arm round her, but was pushed away. 'God, this is such a bloody mess.'

'Yes.' Zoe had nothing else to say. 'Yes, it is.' She reached for her normal supply of fixes and ideas. Nothing. She pulled out a stool and climbed up facing her sister, grabbing the bar as it wobbled dangerously under her fingers.

She looked down. 'Do you want me to put something underneath to balance it?'

'No, I don't!' Lily shook her head despairingly. 'I can do it myself.'

'OK, OK.' Zoe nodded. 'Have you heard from Dad?'

Lily stood up and put her bowl in the sink. 'Nope.'

'Oh.' Zoe nodded. 'He hasn't been in touch with me since the lunch. No emails. No calls.'

'Well of course he hasn't. You're the apple of his eye and he's just realised he let his friend take advantage of you right under his nose. He'll be going through hell.'

'He'll probably be calling him out for a duel.'

'Don't joke.' Lily shoved her hands deep in her pockets. Zoe stared at her neighbour. He was currently spreading about half a pound of butter on his toast. Zoe's stomach rumbled. 'Simon had better get a bodyguard. If Dad unleashes his army contacts, Simon is screwed.'

Zoe closed her eyes as she remembered him. Simon. The man she had once loved so fiercely she had actually written him poetry. She cringed at the thought. He must have thought she was such a fool. Simon, with his tan and his smile and his incredible ease. He could make her feel better simply by catching her eye across a room. And he always made sure he did. Turning up with chocolate when she was meant to be revising. Always sitting too close. Always replying with such charm when she started leaving notes under his door. Making her mix tapes. Inviting her for walks. Just the two of them.

She felt Lily looking at her. 'Would you ever want to see him again?'

'Simon?' Zoe knew the answer to this one. 'No.'

'Why? I mean, you say you loved him.'

'Yeah.' Zoe nodded. 'I did. Until I went to see him after . . .' She still hadn't told Lily the rest of the story. The most painful part. 'I went to find him, you see. To ask him if he'd be with me for ever.' She exhaled. 'Only there was another woman with him. Mum had told me about her, but I didn't believe her, and I never told her I had seen her too. I never told her I went to find him. I felt too stupid and ashamed. And then when I told him he asked me if . . .'

'Told him what?'

Zoe's knuckles were white around her mug. 'Told him about the baby. He asked if it was his. It was the first thing he said. Before I could say a word.'

'Oh my God. You got pregnant.'

'Yeah.' Zoe stared into her tea. 'I was so fucking stupid.'

'No. He was such a bastard.'

Zoe knew she'd been to blame too. All these years she'd known it, way down deep in the recesses of her heart.

'Yeah. So that's why I don't want to see him. I already know he's a total shit.'

She could still feel the shuddering sickness of discovery.

Lily sighed. 'Shit.'

'Yep.' Zoe felt very tired. 'So now you know everything.'

'No I don't.' She saw her sister straighten in front of her. 'What happened to the baby? Did you get an . . .?'

Zoe shook her head. 'No. I didn't.' She steeled herself to say the words. 'I wanted to keep it but I . . .' She gulped, still hating to speak her failure out loud. 'I lost the baby. Just before I saw Simon and he asked me if it was his. I lost it.'

'Oh my God, Zo.' Her sister came round to her, curving her arm around Zoe's shoulder. 'I'm so sorry.'

'Me too. And then it happened again. With Jamie. I lost another baby.' She thought of the blood and the pain and wondered if she could ever make herself feel whole again. 'And it ruined everything.'

'So that's why.' Lily was murmuring as if to herself. 'That's why you left the wedding.'

'I'm so sorry, Lil. I should have told you. I know that.'

Her sister pulled her closer. Zoe nestled in, needing the warmth. The understanding. It took her a long time to sit up straight and wipe her tears away.

'So there you have it, Lil. The whole sorry disaster of a story. Nothing left to tell now.'

Lily's eyes were bright with sympathy.

Zoe finished her tea. Pieces were slotting into place. Biting back the fear as she got her first business loan. Staying up till 5 a.m. revising for exams. Spending the whole of her first date with Jamie telling herself she wasn't going to let him get close to her. She remembered staring in the toilet mirror after an hour, warning herself of the danger – muttering that she shouldn't lose focus at this stage in her career, that she didn't need anyone, that she was better off by herself.

Then she had gone back outside and had another drink and he had asked her what her *Desert Island Discs* choices would be, and she had got stuck on six, and he had laughed and called her a Radio 4 junkie and said that he'd need to do something about that. His blond hair shining in the lights. His finger tapping the air in time as Ryan Adams sang his version of 'Wonderwall'. His assumption that she would be a part of his future. Somehow by the end of that evening her hand had been holding his and she had agreed to see him the next night.

And so it had carried on. He was never bothered by her attempts to say it wasn't forever. If she worked late, he turned up with strawberries and very strong coffee and played his guitar on the sofa until she was done. He had all the faith that she lacked. All the optimism that had been broken by Simon.

But then she had miscarried and the bubble of Jamie was broken. His love couldn't protect her. She could see it now. Simon and the miscarriage were still with her. Every single day. She was still running.

She pulled herself back into the present to find tears running down her cheeks again. She turned away.

Lily put a hand on her shoulder, and Zoe clasped it in hers.

'Are you OK, sis?' Lily scanned her face.

'Yeah.' Zoe nodded. 'I'll get there.' She blew her nose. 'Might have a muffin though.'

'Good plan.' Lily pulled one out of the bag and got a plate from the cupboard. 'Dig in.'

'Can I come in?' Gary appeared at the door in a red towelling dressing gown and flip-flops. The dressing gown might have fitted him when he was fifteen, but it was really struggling to cope now that he had got himself a desk job and become rather fond of beer.

'Hi, Zoe.' He had grown a beard. It suited him. He looked younger. More comfortable in his own skin.

'Gary.' She could feel Lily's eyes on her as she smiled

at him. Sod it. She couldn't get much else right, but she could do this. She walked across and kissed him on both cheeks. 'It's great to see you.'

'Oh. You too.' He flushed with surprise. Zoe couldn't blame him. She knew she hadn't exactly been friendly the last time they had met. 'Sorry I'm not more . . . dressed.' He looked at Lily. 'I can't find my clothes. They must have got lost when . . .'

A sizzling look passed between them. Zoe turned and stared out of the window. The neighbour really did enjoy his toast. What these two had got up to last night was yet another thing she didn't really want to think about. After a minute, she looked round to see they were in each other's arms. His head was resting on hers. The smile on his face. The peace on hers.

Despite his bare legs, the polka dots and his ridiculous dressing gown, they looked beautiful.

Zoe pressed her forehead against the window pane as the door opened again and Lily went out.

Gary clicked the kettle behind her. 'How many slices has our neighbour had today, then?' His voice was nervous. Eager to please.

'I think he's on his fourth.'

'He's just getting started, then.'

'Really?' Zoe exhaled.

'Yes.' Gary wasn't quite meeting her eye. He was busying himself with bowls and spoons. 'He had eight the other day. It's quite hard to look away sometimes.' He got some Shreddies out of the cupboard and held up the packet. 'Would you like some?'

'No thanks.'

'Toast?' He dangled the packet of bread in his other hand.

'Er . . . no.' Zoe stepped backwards. 'I've had a bit of muffin.'

'Bagel?' There was a manic determination in his eyes.

'I'm good.' Zoe held up her hands. 'But thank you.'

'Oh.' His shoulders sagged. 'How about more tea, though?'

Zoe couldn't say no any more. 'Sure. That would be great.'

'Brilliant!' He beamed. 'Sugar? Milk?'

'Just milk, please.' She averted her eyes from his hairy legs. 'How's work going?'

'Oh, good, good.' He nodded. 'I mean, not covered in glory like you, but . . . you know. I'm doing OK.'

Zoe thought of the botched presentation and Zapp Digital's total failure to meet new business targets for the quarter and winced.

'I'm glad to hear it.' She smiled. 'There's a lot to be said for doing OK.'

He handed her another mug of tea. It was too dark and she'd seen him put sugar in it, but she took it nonetheless and sipped and predictably burnt her tongue.

'And Lily's really excited about her new job.'

Zoe put the mug down. 'What new job?'

He tipped Shreddies into his bowl. 'You know. At the nursery.'

'What?'

'Oh shit.' He flushed and poured in milk. 'I wasn't meant to tell you.'

Zoe felt a beat of concern. 'Tell me what?'

'Tell you that I'm doing it. At last.' Lily came back in T-shirt and jeans, with a hoodie in her hands. Gary mouthed an apology to her and disappeared with his bowl.

'Doing what?'

'Going to work with kids.'

Zoe stared at her. 'Really?'

'Yes.' Lily had her hands on her hips. Her face was ready for a fight. 'And don't you try and stop me.'

'I—'

'Because things with Mum, well . . . life is short and I don't want to bugger about any more.'

'I know what you mean.'

'Don't pretend you think this is a good idea.'

'But Lil—'

'Doing this, I'll laugh every day. I'll sleep well at night. And that's pretty damn precious, isn't it? I'm twenty-eight. Mum's fifty-six now. I want to enjoy whatever time I have. Not sit in an office or a business school pretending I care about spreadsheets.'

Zoe nodded. 'I'm happy for you. Honestly. I don't know why you don't believe me.'

Lily was still going. 'All my life I've done so much to please you and dad. Ooh, you could study maths at A level, Lily, it would put you in a great position for college; no, Lily, you shouldn't have a gap year because you won't get into the job market as soon.'

Zoe watched her helplessly. 'I'm sorry if you think we pressurised you.' The pressure she put on herself was worse than anything she ever passed on to her sister. The voice in her head. Commenting. Criticising. She wouldn't wish it on her worst enemy.

'So I know you want me to do this course, but I just want to do what I love.'

'I'm so sorry, Lil.' Zoe looked at the floor. 'I never meant to make you feel like that.'

'Well, you did.' Lily put her hoodie on and zipped it up.

Zoe walked across the room to give her a hug.

And then she saw them.

Brochures. On the side by the door. Glossy blues and purples. Fairfield View. Green Hills.

'What are these?'

Lily turned and her face fell. 'Just . . .'

'They're care homes, aren't they?'

'Yes.' Lily put her hand out to protect them, but Zoe was too quick.

'Why have you got these? Do you want to lock her away, Lil?'

Confusion clouded her sister's face and then was replaced by something new. Conviction. She stood, hands calm at her sides.

'I ordered them off the internet. Just thought I'd have a look. Just in case. Mags said—'

'Mags?' Zoe felt a shot of pure sadness. 'It's not her decision.'

'No.' Lily shook her head. 'And it's not yours either.'

'Yes it—'

'It's ours,' Lily said simply.

'And Mum's!'

'Of course.' Lily was the calm one now. Zoe was the one who couldn't keep still. She fiddled with the brochures, looking at them with absolute hatred.

The brochures didn't care how she felt. They just lay there, smooth and shining, proudly displaying meaningless slogans like 'Supportive care focused on living well' and 'Individual care for individuals'. Ouch. Zoe flicked through the pictures and saw sunny tables with floral mugs and people far older than Mum posed in frozen happiness. Wide doors. Huge windows. Grey-haired people gathered round a piano.

God, she loathed them all.

Mum would loathe them more.

'Lily, you shouldn't have done this. Mum will be fine where she is. With me.' After all the years apart, this was the one thing she could give her mum. Time together. Love.

'Zoe, she keeps trying to get out.'

'I know.' Zoe's neighbours were getting a bit testy, to say the least. 'But I can sort it. I'll put in another movement alarm. More locks. Something.'

Lily put a hand on her arm. 'Zoe, you're not making sense. You need to live too.'

'And I am!'

Lily shook her head. 'You haven't slept in weeks. Bruno said you—'

'Bruno?' Zoe ran a hand through her hair. Talking about the past. People worrying about her. This wasn't who she wanted to be. 'Is everyone ganging up on me?'

'No.' Lily's voice was suddenly gentle. 'We're trying to help.'

'It doesn't feel like it. How could you do this to Mum? She asked me never to put her in a home. She made me promise to look after her.'

'But that's the thing, Zo. She doesn't know what she's saying half the time.'

Zoe thought of her mum that morning, hugging her and calling her 'golden girl'.

She had to mean it. Zoe needed it to be real.

'Lily, we can't do this.'

Lily shook her head. Zoe had to make her see.

'I'm just trying to help her, you know? And maybe the Aricept will start working. The consultant said everyone's different. It progresses at a different rate in each case.'

'I know.' Lily took an apple from the red bowl on the side. 'But she can't stay with you for ever.'

'Why not?'

'Because you have a life, Zoe.' Lily shook her head. 'A life and a job.'

'But . . .'

'No buts, Zo.' Lily looked at her, and Zoe saw a new-found steel. 'She can't live there much longer. And she can't go home by herself. You know I'm right. We have to look at our options.'

Zoe fought back. 'But she's happy there. She's much gentler.' She shuddered as she thought of the screaming matches she and Mum used to have when she was younger.

Lily flushed. 'Well, you last lived together when you were a teenager. That might explain it. If we get her in to sheltered accommodation now, she can—'

'Get her in?' Zoe shook her head. 'No. She's our mum. We need to look after her, not dump her somewhere she won't know anyone and she won't have her things. Where she won't have us.' She was so tired of fighting all the time. 'I can manage this, Lily. I can keep things on track.'

'Zo, don't you get it? There is no track. It's chaos. Her memory is going to get worse. And . . .'

Zoe couldn't accept it. 'And what?'

'And for once you have to see that you're not in control.'

Zoe put her mug down on the breakfast bar. 'Lily, I've watched Mum over the past few months. I know she's getting worse. I see the way she gets four mugs out of the cupboard when she's making one cup of tea. I notice that the water's cold or she forgets the tea bag and just drinks sugary water. I was there when she was diagnosed. I get what's happening to her, OK?'

Lily was silent.

A wild fever gripped Zoe. 'But I don't accept that I'm

doing the wrong thing by keeping her with me. It's what she wants.'

'She doesn't know what she wants.'

'She does.'

Lily sighed. 'Zoe, you don't have to do this just because you feel guilty.'

'What?' Zoe looked at her sister, wondering how they had grown so far apart. 'That's not why I'm doing this.'

'It is.' Lily nodded. 'You just can't see it.'

'Yeah, well, you just can't see that what you're suggesting is like chucking her in the bin. Bye, Mum. Thanks for raising us. Now just piss off and rot in a bed where no one gives a shit about you. Did you see that documentary on Channel 4? The one about the abuse at that care home? Do you really want to put Mum in that situation?' Lily turned pale, and Zoe knew that she was saying the wrong things to the wrong person, but she couldn't stop. 'I can't believe you would do that to her.'

Lily was crying now.

'That's so unfair.'

The door opened and Gary came back in, mercifully free of the dressing gown. He took one look at the two of them and held out his arms. Lily ran to him, and he curved his face towards her and kissed her tears away.

Zoe felt a bolt of loneliness so fierce she wanted to slide down to the floor and curl up until the world had left her alone. But no. That wasn't how she did things. Instead, she wrenched her coat away from the window catch and threw it on. She picked up her bag and rammed it over her shoulder. Then – finally – she picked up the brochures and threw them into the bin.

'Don't you dare talk to me about this ever again.'

She stormed out of the front door and into the street,

resisting the urge to turn. Resisting the urge to throw her arms around Lily and burst into tears.

When she got home, she went straight to her bedroom, determined to get her trainers on and go for a few laps of the park before Mum came back with Mags. She pulled on a T-shirt and shorts and found her headphones, but then hesitated at the door of the spare room – which was now indisputably her mum's. Flowery pants on the bed. A box on the chest of drawers containing hairbrush and face cream, neatly labelled *Morning*. A huge pile of library books covering the bedside table, even though her mum couldn't ever remember what had happened from one chapter to the next.

A piece of paper caught her eye. It was headlined in bright colours: *To Zoe and Lily. Things to remember once I can't.* She unfolded it and scanned the top few lines. *How I like my eggs. Why I hate avocado. Things I'm scared of. Songs to sing at my funeral.*

She couldn't read any more. No more crying. Not today. She put it down on the bed and went outside for her run.

Mags's house, Oxford
Birthday present: like you'd take anything from me
Favourite song: God knows

15th June, 2001

Dear Zoe,

So here's my side of the story. Maybe one day you'll
read it and hate me a little bit less. I have to hope that.

Today you turn seventeen. I wonder what you're
doing and what presents you'll get. Mine was returned
with a label in your incredibly neat writing, my name
underlined against the white. I sat and stared at the
parcel until Mags quietly took it away and hid it
upstairs, and then she sat with me and poured some
wine and held my hand as I talked about that party
when you were little – the one where the dogs stole
the balloons and everyone got high on Sherbet Dip
Dabs. The old days. Such a sweet place to hide.

You blame me for everything. That's the simple truth.
But I was only trying to help.

A few weeks after your last terrible birthday, I heard
you puking one morning and I knew – just knew – you
were pregnant. You didn't deny it. Simon had been
away for weeks on business trips and holidays, but that
didn't stop you dreaming. Oh no. As soon as he was
back you would be together. You stuck your chin out
as you told me that the two of you would make it
work despite me. Despite me trying to keep you apart.

I guessed straight away. I guessed he hadn't answered

235

your messages and that he had no intention of making a go of anything. So I cornered you whenever I could, trying desperately to persuade you to do the sensible thing and go to a clinic to talk about your options. I tried to make you see how great your life could be out there in the big wide world – that being lonely at school didn't mean being lonely for ever.

You snarled and said that was wrong. That I didn't understand. That I was just a jealous old cow who didn't want you to be happy.

I made the appointment anyway. I pretended we were going to the dentist right up until the moment we got there. And when you saw the sign as we turned in, you looked at me like I was some kind of witch. You reached for the door handle and I grabbed you and the car was still moving and you were trying to open the door and I kept holding on and we ended up scraping against a big posh Volvo and then I stalled.

You were still fighting to escape and you got the door open and your feet were on the ground and I leant over and grabbed you again and pulled you back and then you fell towards me, hitting your face and your body against the door and the seat. Then Lady Volvo came out and started yelling at me, and I yelled back, and I was trying to get out and check you were OK but then she started calling the police and by the time I'd finished with her you were long gone.

I drove home, and on the way back, just to make the day even worse, I saw Simon letting another woman into his house. Tousled black hair. Red nails. Tight leather dress. It made me fume. I went and banged on his door so I could shout at him, but he didn't answer. I went round the back instead. I nearly broke the

window, I was hammering so hard. He's always been a
bloody coward.

I was so angry I could barely see as I stumbled back
to our house. Your bedroom door was shut and I could
hear Guns N' Roses pounding from your stereo. So I
went downstairs and made you some tea. I took a
breath. I knew I had to get this conversation right. I had
to get you to understand what he really was.

But when I eventually brought you the tea, you were
crumpled on your bed, clutching your stomach as if
desperate to keep something inside. My whole heart
froze. I knew that feeling. I hated the world for making
you go through, it too. You turned your face away and
told me to leave you alone, but there was no way that
was going to happen. Not once I'd seen the blood.

I drove you to the hospital, and all the way there
you pressed your face to the window and refused to
even acknowledge I existed. When we got there, you
told the doctors you didn't want me with you, and they
looked at me as if I was the scum of the earth. I sat
there with people vomiting and having nosebleeds all
around me, and waited. My heart was breaking for you,
and I was remembering Bean and how the world
stopped spinning and how for a while all I saw were
mums and babies and the happy, sticky cuddles that
Bean would never have. You never forget them. And I
was so sad for you, golden girl.

When they finally called me through, the doctors
said what they needed to say – that it was probably
stress, that sometimes nature just makes the decision
for you, that it happens a lot in the first twelve weeks.
I nodded and knew that none of that would make any
difference to you. It never did for me. I still wonder if

it was something I did. If I was the reason Bean didn't make it.

You were frantic. Your sobs will stay with me for ever. So rasping and sad. I'd have done anything to make things better, but when I sat down at your side, you looked at me with the coldest eyes and said that I must be happy now. That this was my fault. That I'd pushed you deliberately into the door of the car. That this was all part of some kind of plan to ruin your life.

But I would never hurt you, golden girl. I wish you knew that.

I'm so sorry we fought. I'm so sorry you fell. And if it was my fault, I will spend a lifetime trying and failing to forgive myself.

All I wanted was for you to have a chance at life.

I reached out to touch your hair, but you shoved my hand away. So we stayed there until you slept, and then I laid my head on the pillow next to yours and put my arm round you. In your sleep you didn't fight me. You just nestled closer as I held you and stared at the wall and whispered all the love and sorrow that was in my heart.

When we got home later, Alistair didn't listen to my made-up story of where we'd been. He grabbed me and pulled me into our bedroom, telling me how Simon had come round and said he was leaving. Alistair had asked why. Simon had demurred. Alistair had pushed him and Simon had told him some cock-and-bull story about how I had been coming on to him for months and he needed to 'do the right thing' (HA!) and leave before things got out of hand. I opened my mouth to defend myself. I wanted to throw this right back in Alistair's face. After all, he'd done it too. And he'd probably gone a whole lot further than a tiny kiss in a kitchen.

But then I thought of you in the hospital. Pale. Broken. And I knew this was the perfect cover story. Simon was gone. He would never have the balls to come back. This would set you free.

So I admitted it. I admitted it all. Why not? Our marriage was over anyway.

Alistair stormed off and I was left to break it to you that Simon had left. Bloody hell. Your face. You asked me if I'd made him go.

I said no. You didn't believe me.

I told you then about the woman with the black hair, trying to get you to see the truth of him. But you just swore in disgust and started frantically packing a bag. You were so upset and still so weak, and I kept trying to stop you, but you screamed at me and ran out of the door and into the night. I found out later that you'd gone to the bus station and headed to Oxford. That you'd wandered the streets for a night looking for him, till you ended up at Mags's house and she brought you home. You said you never found him. The bastard didn't even have the courage to face you. I wish I was surprised.

When you got back, Mags made tea while you sat on the sofa, with the weight of the world on your shoulders, and we all agreed never to tell your dad about any of it – there was no point him finding out now. Alistair wouldn't talk to me except in a shout, and pretty soon we were well over the finishing line. I couldn't hold it in any more. All the rage I couldn't vent at Simon was fired at Alistair instead, and we both just gave up. The arguments escalated and sliced through what was left of our marriage, eventually leading to the divorce papers that arrived this morning in their crisp brown envelope. A life together reduced to clauses and provisions and assets. What a waste. I should feel sadder about that, but instead I'm just sitting here crying for you.

Yeah, I know. 'Tragic', as you would say, with a roll of those beautiful eyes.

But it's your seventeenth birthday and I'm not there. I won't be able to embarrass you with my kisses. I won't see the expectation on your face as you open your first present. You both live with Alistair in London now – you couldn't get far enough away from me, and Lily has always followed your lead. Her face the day we all moved out. Clinging to her yellow box and staring at me with all the pain the world has ever felt written on her face. She needs to go and babysit the kids next door and play netball in her team and keep the familiar pattern of her days. She needs the four of us together, and we have failed her.

I always knew I'd lose you both one day, but I'd imagined happier scenarios. The first daffodils of spring in the aisles. A packed church. The open arms of men who were worthy of you both. Or perhaps an overflowing car pulling up to university halls, where you'd join the chattering throngs of bright-eyed students wearing jeans and trainers and wondering where the rest of their lives would take them.

I miss you both so much. I miss the furrow on Lily's brow as she spreads half a tub of margarine on her bread and then adds peanut butter and honey. I miss the clothes hanging off the banisters. The two of you watching soaps on the sofa, legs pulled up underneath you, red and blonde hair against the cushions. I miss the thump of your feet on the stairs. The rhythm and the breath of you.

And now I'm curled up on Mags's sofa, wondering how on earth I ended up as the villain when all I was doing was trying to protect you. He took your lonely loving heart and he made you believe in him, when you should have believed in me. And in yourself.

I miss you.

Mum x

Fourteen

'Zoe.'

'Jamie!' She stood there with her keys in her hand, staring at him.

He dug his hands deep into the pockets of his hoodie. 'How was your day?'

Terrible. It had been terrible. Angry clients. Missed deadlines. Before, she would have put in more hours – now, because of Mum, she couldn't and despite all her confident talk to Bruno, she knew her company was suffering. What she didn't know was what on earth she could do about it.

'OK, thanks.' She summoned a smile. 'How about you? Were you saving the world of IT today?'

'Yeah.' He nodded. 'An insurance company in the City. An employee had a password that was his exact name.' He rolled his eyes. 'Amazingly, he got hacked and downloaded a virus that meant everyone in the firm shut down in three minutes.' He grinned. 'But I saved the day.' He bent a fist to his forehead. 'Like the super-hero I am.'

She twisted her keys in her fingers. 'I bet they lifted you on their shoulders and praised you to the skies.'

'Yeah.' His lips curved upwards. 'Something like that. I mean . . .'

God, she wished she could hug him.

'. . . they made me a cup of tea and gave me a biscuit. So that's not a bad result, is it?'

'A biscuit?' She was so tired she was shaking. 'Yeah. Much better than being praised to the skies. WAY better.'

She felt faint and sat down suddenly on the wall outside the flat. She leant forward and looked resolutely at the path while black dots fizzed in front of her eyes.

'Are you OK, Zo?'

She breathed carefully. In. Out. 'Yes.'

He sat down on his haunches and looked up into her face. 'You're very pale. Can I get you something? Water?'

'No.' She felt steadier and stood up. 'I'd better . . . go in. You know. Mum.'

'She's asleep.'

'Oh.' She felt a smattering of rain on her face. 'So you've been inside?'

'Yes.' He gestured behind him and she saw a big bag lying on the ground. 'I thought I should pick up some more stuff. Russ is going away for a few months, so I can properly move into his place now.'

No. Please, no. It was too final. She didn't have the strength for this.

'OK.' It took everything in her not to crack. 'Makes sense, I suppose.'

She tried to sound cheerful. Upbeat. Her normal self. 'Well, I'll go in then.'

'Zoe?' He reached out a hand. 'Why don't we go for a drink?'

She wasn't sure she could bear it.

'I don't know . . .' She moved towards the door.

'Please?' He held his hands wide. 'For old times' sake?'

She thought of the empty wardrobe where his clothes no longer hung. The CDs that wouldn't be lining the sitting room wall. The big blue parka that wouldn't ever hang on the pegs in the hall again.

And she said yes.

She pushed her way back from the bar, seeing Jamie as if for the first time. The fingers tapping out a rhythm on the dark wood of the table. The easy lean of his shoulders against the wall behind him. Bright blue eyes above his green T-shirt.

'Here you go.' She pushed his pint across the table and sat down, lifting her own glass to her lips.

'Wow, you're on a mission there.'

She put the glass down. Half the drink had somehow disappeared.

'Sorry.' She flushed. 'This is pretty weird, isn't it?'

He nodded as 'Saturday Night' by Whigfield bounced out of the speakers. She remembered the last time they had heard it. A random pub on the South Bank full of weekend hysteria on Jamie's birthday. There had been laughter. Shrieks. Jamie dragging her on to the floor as they both made abortive attempts to remember Whigfield's dance routine.

It felt like another life.

Jamie sipped his pint. 'So, what's been happening, Zo?'

She had no idea where to start. The terrible lunch. Her dad's expression. The hurt on Lily's face. Her mum.

She looked into his open, honest face.

'Come on, Zo.'

She hesitated. 'It's nothing, really.'

'It didn't look like that when you nearly fainted back there.'

She half laughed. 'Didn't my brave face convince you?'

'No.' He shook his head decisively. 'Not any more.'

'Damn.' She played with her straw as one of the bar staff came over and placed a tea light in front of them, smiling at them in what he clearly hoped was a romance-inducing way.

It was a bit late for that.

'Is it your mum?'

She thought of the brochures. Of waking to find Mum at her bedside at 3 a.m. asking if they could go out for breakfast.

She sighed, lacing her fingers round her glass. 'Yes. It's Mum.' No. She would tell him. 'But it's more than that.'

The sympathy on his face made her want to grab hold of him and never let go.

'Dad's furious with me.'

'No.' Jamie shook his head. 'Not possible. Not his angel child.'

'Yes.' She nodded. 'And he's right.'

'What?' He leant forward. 'I don't believe you.'

'No?' She crossed her legs. 'Well, let me tell you what they found out the other week, and then let's see what you think.'

'OK.' He raised an eyebrow. 'Prove me wrong.'

'When I was younger, I fell in love.'

'That's hardly against the law.'

'With my dad's best friend.'

'Oh.'

'It didn't turn out well.'

'No. I guess not.' Jamie frowned. 'How old was this guy?'

'He was thirty-two.' She could hear how wrong it sounded, but at the time she had been so lost in him that she hadn't been able to understand it. Only her mum had seen clearly. Only her mum had tried to help.

Jamie frowned. 'And you were how old?'

'Nearly sixteen, when it started.' Zoe sipped her drink again.

'God.' He took a long swallow of beer and wiped his mouth with the back of his hand. 'That's some friend your dad had there.'

'But—'

'I mean, that's illegal. No wonder your dad's bloody furious.'

'Yes.' It was strangely liberating. Telling the truth.

So she carried on. She told him about the fighting between Mum and Dad. About how things had started with Simon.

'Shit.'

'But there's more, Jamie. And I need to tell you because it's why . . . it's why I fell to pieces when we lost Teeny.' His face softened as she used their name for the child they had lost. 'Because . . .' Adrenalin made her skin tingle. 'Because I got pregnant back then, too.'

'What?' Jamie put his pint down.

'It was awful. Mum found out about everything, and she took me to a clinic without telling me where we were going.'

Jamie's hand was over hers. It gave her the strength to finish.

'I was so angry with her, Jamie. I was so bloody angry. All I wanted was him. All I could see was him. And she was trying to stop us being together. To stop me having the baby of the man I loved.' She took a breath. 'When we drove up, I started opening the door of the car before she'd even stopped. She kept pulling me back and she nearly crashed and . . .' Now that she was finally telling someone, she couldn't stop. 'And I just knew I had to get out and protect our child, and that's what I was trying to do. Then she crashed.'

'No.' He squeezed her fingers.

'Only into a parked car. But this woman came out and shouted at us and Mum just kept pulling me, like she owned me.'

She took a shaky breath. 'I finally got the door open and I was nearly free and I was going to run and find Simon and get my happy ending, and then she reached over again and grabbed my hand and I wrenched it away.' She wished she could remember this without reliving it too, but she had to carry on. 'I fell. I fell hard. I blamed her, but now I know it was me and my stupid new wedge heels that I thought were so fucking cool.' She closed her eyes, feeling the impact. The slam of her stomach into the door. The drag of her body as it fell to the ground.

'No.' Jamie's voice seemed very far away.

Zoe nodded, tears streaming down her face. 'I ran home and I lay down and prayed that I hadn't fucked everything up. But somehow I knew I had.' A tear dripped into her wine glass. 'And I was right.' She looked up at him, knowing he was one of the few people who would understand.

'So that's why you've been so angry with your mum.'

'Yes.' Her world had narrowed to the tears on her face and the memory of that night. 'It was easier to blame her. I couldn't forgive her for knowing better than me.'

He held on to her hand.

'And I carried on, like you're meant to.' She sniffed. 'I started again. Sorted myself out. Got my exams. Moved here. I never stopped. I knew that if I stood still it would swallow me. And eventually I met you and it was magic.' His face didn't change. 'And I wanted to tell you but I knew you wanted kids and part of me worried about whether or not I could give you that. Whether it would happen again. And I couldn't bear to lose you.'

If only he would say something.

'And then I got pregnant and we were so happy it made me feel like I was flying. I believed in happy endings. At last. But then it happened again. And I knew it was my fault this time. My body. Because I'd done all the right things. Folic acid. Eating my greens. Going paraben-free.' She sighed. 'No falls this time. And yet it still happened. So it had to be my fault, right? Two out of two. A one hundred per cent failure rate.'

'Zoe, don't be so hard on yourself.'

'Why not?' She shrugged. 'I'd been so hard on Mum. That day in May when I saw the blood, I knew I'd been wrong. And I was so ashamed of how I'd treated her that when she rang on our wedding day, I had to go to her.' She got a tissue out of her bag and dabbed her nose. 'And now Lily wants to move her into a home and I can't bear to think how much time I've wasted. She deserved so much more. She was trying to protect me.'

'I wish you'd told me.'

'Me too.'

He hit the table gently with his hand. 'Why didn't you say anything?'

Zoe shook her head. 'I was scared you'd love me less.' She was talking as if to herself. 'Just like Dad. I was scared he'd hate me if he ever found out about Simon. And . . .' she sighed, 'it turned out I was right.'

'No, Zoe. You're not.'

A pointless flicker of hope. 'What do you mean?'

'People love people despite what they've done.'

'Do they?' She watched him. 'I think that only happens in movies.'

'Did you really think I'd blame you for losing Teeny?'
He looked incredulous. 'Don't you know me at all?'

'Yes.' Zoe reached out but the table had never seemed
so wide. 'And believe me, I wish I'd told you.' She had
nearly finished her wine. 'But how could you forgive me?
I can't. Never.'

He was rubbing his temples with his hands.

Zoe finished her drink. A headache was beginning to
bite. She saw them now. All the mistakes she had made.
All the pain she had put people through. Mum. Jamie.
Even Dad and Lily.

Jamie had nearly finished his pint now. There was no
way he'd be staying for another.

'What are you going to do about Lily wanting your
mum to go into a home?'

That was the one thing Zoe was sure about. 'I'll talk
her out of it.'

'Are you sure?'

His question surprised her. He was the kind of guy who
would spend half an hour encouraging a spider on to a
piece of paper and then throw it out of the window, rather
than killing it in ten seconds flat. 'Yes, I'm sure. I don't
want her in one of those places.'

'What places?'

'The ones where people dribble in chairs and don't get
taken to the loo in time and where—'

'They're not all like that, Zo.'

'Mum doesn't want to move.'

'And do you think she's the best judge?'

She stared at him.

'My granny had Alzheimer's.'

'I remember.'

'And it was a nightmare for my mum. She wouldn't

249

give up her car until she'd driven it into a tree. All her neighbours told my mum she was a total cow to put Granny into care, but none of them came and visited once she'd really lost her marbles. But she was so much happier in that home. Like she was free from all the responsibility of living by herself.'

His granny wasn't Gina. Zoe shook her head. 'Well, each case is different, isn't it?'

'Sure.' He shrugged. 'But it's worth thinking about. You're doing an amazing thing looking after her, but it must be so hard.'

Not as hard as losing him.

He put his glass down. He was going.

No surprise there then.

She was full of a wild desperation. This might be the last time she saw him. She had to try.

'Jamie. Do you think we could ever . . .' Her eyes held his. She saw hurt and knew that she had caused it. And then he reached out and put his hand over hers. She didn't speak. She didn't breathe. She was clinging to this moment, trying to spin it out into a lifetime. But the threads were too thin. The tension was too great. All that would be left soon were ragged remnants of goodbyes.

'I don't know, Zo.'

He held her soul in his hands. As she stared at him, she could feel herself being peeled away, layer by layer. Down beneath the freshly washed hair. Beneath the sleek business suit and the calm voice that had pitched to big corporate clients.

Beneath all that she was Zo-bear. Running scared.

'I need you, Jamie.'

She had said it.

After the pre-Jamie years of loneliness and sleeping at

her desk, being with him had felt like being understood. At last. But he had seen through her now.

'I'm sorry, Zo. I think it might be too late for us.' He shook his head.

One last try. 'No. It's not.' She reached out for his hand but didn't quite have the courage to take it. 'I know things are messy. And half the time we're not sure about anything. But . . .'

She stared at him. *Come on. Say it. SAY IT.*

'I love you, Jamie.'

There. That was the best she could do. She felt a buzz of triumph. Whatever he said, or did, at least she had tried.

He stared at her as 'Come on Eileen' started to play. Around them, hundreds of people carried on living hundreds of lives that were entirely unrelated to the two of them. Lives with friends and families and problems and jobs and hobbies and one or two drinks too many on a Saturday night.

Jamie's face was wide open.

'I wish I could believe you, Zoe. But I just . . .' He stopped. 'I just don't know.'

She had played her final card. Just the goodbyes left now.

He heaved his bag on to his shoulder. 'My mates are in a bar just up the road. I'd better go and join them.'

'Sure.' In films, goodbye scenes always seemed to be tear-soaked, complete with violins and a cute animal to make sure the audience cried. In reality, it was all about staring into an empty wine glass with bad music in the background while the man you loved walked away.

'Will you be OK?'

'Yes.' She nodded.

'And listen. You will have kids one day and you will be

251

an amazing mum.' He bent down towards her, and some ridiculous part of her thought he might kiss her. 'I know it.'

She couldn't speak.

He picked up the hoodie that had been lying by his side.

'Goodbye, Zoe.' He raised a hand and dropped it.

'See you.' She had nothing left.

He gave her an awkward pat on the head, picked up his bag and left.

She sat staring after him long after he had gone.

So this was what goodbye felt like.

That night, she woke up to hear her mum screaming.

'Don't come in. NO.'

Adrenalin jolted through her and she leapt out of bed and ran down the hall to Gina's room. It was in pitch darkness, and Zoe blinked as she looked around wildly to see what was wrong. The window was closed and she could make out a figure on the bed.

'Mum?'

'He's tapping on the window.' Gina's voice was hoarse. Terrified. 'Don't let him come in.'

'Who is, Mum?' Zoe groped around for the light switch.

'The man from the bus stop.'

'Right.' Zoe's fumbling fingers finally found the switch, and the light dazzled her as it flooded through the room. 'Here we go. Let's see what we're dealing with.'

Gina squealed and pulled the sheet over her head.

Zoe opened the curtain, only to discover that her mum appeared to have stuck black cardboard all over the glass. She sighed and started trying to rip it off.

'Well this isn't the handiest for spotting intruders, is it?'

There was a loud ripping sound as she tore off a corner that seemed to be welded to the frame.

'No. Don't do that.' Her mum's eyes were wide. Fearful. 'I don't want him coming in.'

'But I have to move it to look outside.' Zoe continued pulling, only to find her mum's hands closing around the cardboard and holding her back. They tussled for a minute, until a thud from the upstairs flat told Zoe that perhaps her neighbours weren't enjoying this melodrama. She couldn't blame them. She wasn't enjoying it either.

'Mum, can you just let me do this, please?'

'No.'

'Well, tough.'

Finally all the cardboard came down, only for Zoe to see that there was a layer of paper behind it. Her mum had been thorough. So that was what she'd been spending all her time doing. If only Zoe had known, she'd have given her a paintbrush and got her to touch up the living room.

'See?' She tried to calm the terror on Gina's face. 'There's nobody there. Nobody at all.'

'But I heard him.' Gina peered anxiously out into the night. 'I'm sure I heard him.'

'Really?' Zoe was so tired, she knew her face alone would frighten off any burglar foolish enough to try to come in. 'I reckon it was just the foxes.'

'The foxes?' Gina frowned. 'I don't think so. I could hear talking. And breathing.'

'The neighbours?' Zoe pointed upstairs. 'Having sex?'

'NO.' Gina was shouting now, and her arms were flailing, and as Zoe reached out to calm her, one of her mum's hands slapped her across the cheek.

There was a beat of silence. Zoe stared at her mum. At

the unseeing eyes. The constant checking outside. The deep shadows.

'Did I hit you?' Gina reached out, but Zoe flinched away.

'It's fine, Mum.' Her cheek was burning. 'Nothing to worry about.'

'Good girl.' Her mum was mumbling now. 'My good girl.'

'It's all right, Mum.' She tucked Gina beneath the sheets and stroked her hair. 'I'll listen out in case he comes back. OK?'

Her mum's eyes rested on her face, and all Zoe could see were the hollows beneath her eyes and the pinched lines on her forehead. She looked so old. So tired. So much more drained than her fifty-six years should have allowed.

'Can I get you anything? Before you go back to sleep?'

'No.' Her mum's eyelids were fluttering. Nearly closed. Nearly peaceful.

Then she spoke again.

'Do you remember how you used to make lollies?'

'Ribena lollies?' Zoe nodded slowly, and knelt down on the floor at her mum's side, ignoring the scampering sound of a mouse under the floorboards. Murgatroyd didn't even wake from his contented slumber.

'Yeah.' Her mum smiled broadly. 'Any day it wasn't raining, you'd run in begging to make some. Even if it was only about five degrees outside, there you would be. All eager. Pulling the moulds out of the cupboard and finding the sticks, so that by the time you'd got everything together, I couldn't bear to say no to you.'

'I loved them.' Zoe grinned. 'I still love Ribena.'

'I used to find you wrapped around mugs of it when you'd had a rough day.'

'Yeah.' Zoe remembered the sweet steam as she curled her hands around her favourite mug. The *Jackie* one. She would inhale and close her eyes in an attempt to shut out whatever disappointments the day had brought.

'You're wonderful, Zoe.'

The words came out of nowhere into the silence of the night.

Zoe touched her stinging cheek and sat next to Gina, listening to her breathing get slower.

Wonderful. If only. But she knew that there was one thing she could get right. One thing she could work towards. She could make the most of every second they had left.

Shit flat, Morden
Birthday present: returned to sender
Favourite song: probably anything that involves the
    words 'I hate my mum'

15th June, 2002

Dear eighteen-year-old grown-up Zoe,
    They say absence makes the heart grow fonder. It
seems they were right. More and more often now I
dream about you. Sometimes I wake up and I'm sweaty
and my mouth is dry and the first thing that hits me is
the silence – no running taps or doors closing. There's
nobody here. Just a silence where your voice should
be. I hate to think about how grumpy and cross I used
to get about the noise you made. Now I ache for it.
    I always dream the same dream. Losing you in that
supermarket we used to go to in Germany – the
really big one with the endless aisles and all those
tempting dark shiny doors out to the bakery or the
place where they stored the meat. You used to love
pushing them open and pretending you were going to
go through to the forklifts and the cold and the
terrifying bread-slicing machines. Then I'd reach out
and take your hand as I paid and we'd go home and
the three of us would cuddle up in the big double bed
and spend the afternoon reading stories while you
tried to plait Lily's hair.
    Your absence is never far from my mind. Like a cut
on the tip of a finger, or a stone wedged in a shoe. I've

tried drinking too much. I've tried jogging too much.
I've tried everything. As if I could ever forget you.

So here's what I used to think would happen when
you turned eighteen. I imagined us both in a smart
restaurant. You a little gawky, not knowing how lovely
you are, tucking your fingers into the sleeves of your
T-shirt like you always do. Champagne. A discreet piano
in the background. Your slow smile as you taste your
food. Me beaming as you sit there across the table, so
proud of the woman you've become.

I wish I'd told you I loved you more often.

Lily tells me you're doing well now. She's here at
weekends, trying to bridge the distance between us,
crying and trying and failing to get past what happened
last year. She's shy and scared and stays in and
watches TV and sometimes she follows me round the
tiny kitchen as if she's afraid of letting me out of her
sight. I hope you're still looking out for her. God knows
she needs you more than ever now.

She says that your first round of A levels were a
write-off, but now you've promised Alistair to get your
head down and get to university. I know you can do it
if you try. Sometimes I send you letters telling you how
proud I am, but you never answer. Once I turned up
outside your school, but you glanced towards me and
away. I walked towards you, determined to have my
say, and by the time I got there, you'd disappeared into
the crowd. I was left standing there alone.

I wonder how you can live without me. I am trying
and failing to live without you. I work in a job I don't
like. I come home and pretend I want to eat, but I just
have a few mouthfuls and throw the rest away. If a
man tries to flirt with me, I move to another seat.

Sometimes I don't shower. Or brush my teeth. Lily brought me some pots and seeds but I can't even bring myself to take an interest in them. I just can't see the point. I don't care if things grow or if they die.

I don't miss Alistair. I'm used to him not being next to me. But you're a burning hole in my heart. I want you back. I want you telling me about what you're dreaming of or what you're going to do with your life. God, I'd even take you telling me you hate me right now. That fierce tilt of your head. That jab of your forefinger in my face.

I'd take that. And one day, I hope I will. But until then, until you're here and we're all singing 'Happy Birthday' and you're flushed and embarrassed and telling us to stop, I'll keep trying, golden girl. Inside, hope is burning.

Mum x

Fifteen

'Where are we going again?'

Zoe suppressed another yawn. This would be a lovely day out. It *would*.

'To Oxford, Mum. Remember? Like we used to when we went Christmas shopping when we were little.'

'Oh. Yes.' Her mum nodded. Her fingers never ceased fiddling with the strap of her handbag.

Zoe looked out at London in all its sleety glory. This wasn't quite the weather she had imagined when she had decided to do this. No blue skies. No fluffy clouds.

She put her hand over her mum's, trying to still the busy fingers.

For a second she managed it. Then they began again.

'Where are we going?'

Zoe exhaled, seeking the patience she needed. 'Oxford. We're just on the bus to Paddington station. Do you want me to write it down for you?'

'No, no.' Her mum looked offended. 'I can remember that, thank you very much.'

'OK.' Zoe looked out of the window again. A man was setting up a long row of paintings of London landmarks on the edge of the pavement. The London Eye at sunset. Big Ben backlit in swirling moody clouds. The Tower of London under a bright blue sky. All the places the tourists saw, while Londoners like Zoe just rushed on past. She

259

felt a twinge of guilt as she thought about Bruno back at the office.

But she needed this day. A special day. A perfect day. Just for her and Mum.

A baby started crying just behind them, and her mum flinched.

'God, that's loud.'

'It's just a baby, Mum.'

'Well it's a bloody loud baby.' She turned round and glared at the child's mother, who was wearing a blue coat and skinny jeans. Black hair stuck out from an orange bobble hat and a bag was slung over her shoulder. She was waving a toy in the baby's face. The wailing continued, and Zoe could see the girl darting glances around the bus. In the harsh winter sunlight coming through the window, her cheeks were flushed with embarrassment.

Zoe saw to her horror that her mum was opening her mouth to speak.

'Mum. Let her be.'

Gina had locked on. 'You could try feeding him. He's probably just hungry.'

The baby's mother received this with a tired glare.

Gina tucked a strand of hair behind her ear. 'Poor thing. She probably has no idea what she's doing.'

'Well I'm sure you just really helped her out, Mum.' Zoe mouthed an apology behind her mum's head, but the girl was too busy trying to get a bottle into her baby's mouth.

A woman in a headscarf and a blue coat turned round, tiny wire glasses perched on the end of her nose. 'That wasn't very kind.' She wagged her finger admonishingly. 'Having a go at her like that.'

'I was helping.'

Zoe's mum and her new adversary glared at each other.

Then her mum jumped as the word 'Victoria' resounded over the speakers. The bus reduced speed from its heady heights of fifteen miles per hour. Passengers in coats and scarves stood up and made their way to the back of the bus. The doors hissed open.

The woman jabbed a finger. 'I bet your baby cried too.'

'No.' Gina's knuckles were white around her bag. 'No. She never had a chance to cry. We lost her.'

Zoe stared at her. 'What?' Her mum was coming out with all sorts of things now, and Zoe was increasingly unsure as to what was real and what was not. 'Confabulating,' the dementia nurse called it – the brain filling the gaps left by the rampaging Alzheimer's with half-truths or outright fantasies.

Last night, comfortable on the sofa, her mum had told her some wonderful stories. Her and Alistair in their heyday. Parties. Dancing. Trips away in Norma the Nissan to B&Bs in remote villages where their dad always seemed to meet someone he knew from the army. She had talked about taking Zoe to football games where her dad was always the star. About the way his eyes had misted up when he had first seen Zoe, all wrapped up in a Sunny Holidays T-shirt that Gina had grabbed from work when she went into labour.

Happy tales of a life before reality knocked on the door. Zoe wanted to write them all down – to store them for ever before they disappeared like breath on a winter breeze.

And here on the bus was another story. 'Yes. Bean. I lost Bean.' Zoe couldn't take her eyes from her mum's face. There was truth there. Certainty.

The woman in front of them was silenced.

'I planted a tree.' A tremor passed over Gina's face. 'Somewhere in Germany, I think it was. Near Alistair's base.'

The woman nodded slowly. 'I bet it's a beautiful big tree now.' She gave a gentle smile before she turned away.

Gina's face was heavy. 'I miss Bean.'

'I know, Mum.' Zoe wished with her whole heart that her mum had told her about this before. That she had let Zoe know that she understood. It would have helped so much.

She felt the ache that was never far away. 'I know. I miss mine, too.'

Her mum turned to her, eyes wide. 'Oh yes. That summer. I remember. I hated watching it happen to you.'

'Yes.' Zoe bit her lip. 'But then it happened again.' Tears pricked her eyes. 'Two. I've lost two. And I don't know what I did wrong. Or if I'll ever have another chance.' Yet more tears were overtaking her now. With streets full of shoppers outside. Dance music from headphones behind them. Now. Now was the time she couldn't hold it all in any more.

'You didn't do anything wrong, Zo-bear.'

'I must have done.' Zoe felt pierced by failure.

'No.' Her mum hugged her closer. 'We can't help what happens.'

Zoe felt a comfort she couldn't have imagined possible.

Her mum sighed. 'It gets easier, Zo-bear. I promise. And you'll have more. I did. And God knows I'm so proud of you.'

Zoe's tears kept coming. The bus moved onwards and she rested into the crook of her mum's neck. Her mum's heart beat steadily on. She still smelt of Cussons Imperial Leather. And Zoe was once again a girl who was hurt and sad, and who truly believed her mum could kiss it better. However brief it might be, this one moment of love felt clear and true.

Then the bus slowed again and broke the spell. Zoe

wiped her eyes as a group of students piled on in matching yellow caps and rucksacks, apparently competing to see who could shout the loudest and carry the largest number of bags from the mysteriously popular M&M shop in Leicester Square. They milled around in the aisle next to her mum. The crying baby didn't stand a chance of being heard any more. No one did.

A student with a long plait running right down her back turned round and accidentally hit Zoe's mum with her rucksack. Zoe wiped her eyes, noticing the way Gina was turning inward. Switching off. Her mum, who had always loved running at life with a smile on her face.

It was another change. Another loss. The holes were opening up. The darkness was coming.

Her mum was being buried alive.

Zoe felt the space in the bus squeeze tight around them. It was too hot and too busy, and outside the windows, the street was crowded with shoppers who apparently had no jobs to go to and no places to be.

Her mum was bent over now.

'Mum?' Zoe put an arm on her shoulders, feeling the bones protruding through her coat. 'Are you OK?'

'Can we go home now? Please?' Her mum folded herself away from the students. Away from the noise. Seeking space and silence. 'I want to go home.'

Zoe could feel their perfect day disappearing into the petrol-fumed air. 'But we're going to Oxford. You love it there, remember? The colleges. The gardens. You used to spend hours on the high street, didn't you?'

Zoe realised she was speaking too loudly, trying to force the images back into her mum's mind.

'No. I don't remember.' Her mum's bottom lip was jutting out.

'Yes you do. Come on, Mum. Let's at least try to have a nice time.' The students were so noisy that Zoe's voice was now practically a shout.

And then she saw it with absolute clarity. The fear in her mum's eyes. How hemmed in she was. Noisy Italians on one side. Her own daughter on the other. Nowhere was safe for her. She was all alone in a world she no longer understood.

It must be terrifying.

Zoe ran a hand through her hair. Today had been too ambitious. Too much. Now there was only one thing to do. Get her mum home. Take her off the bus and back to where she needed to be. On the sofa with David Attenborough.

'OK.' She nodded. 'OK, Mum. We'll go home.' She reached up and pressed the button to stop the bus. Her mum practically leapt to her feet in her eagerness to get off. Guilt stung Zoe. She had made this happen. She had pushed her mum too far.

The bus braked suddenly and her mum fell forwards, straight into the woman with the wagging finger. Now all Zoe could see was how frail she was. How out of step with the world in all its loud, pulsating colour.

'I'm so sorry.' Zoe leant down to the woman. 'She's not well.'

'I can see that.' The woman's face softened for a second. 'I hope you get her home safe.'

'Me too.' The bus slowed again, and Zoe grabbed her mum's hand and held on to it for dear life.

'The door's this way.' She gently manoeuvred Gina out into the aisle, elbowing her way through the students, who were clustered around each other's phones, entirely missing the vivid London scenes outside. The cream columns of

Marble Arch rising proudly into the sky. Black cabs weaving in and out of the red London buses. They didn't notice a thing.

The doors opened, and Zoe held on to her mum for dear life as they pushed their way out. It seemed the whole world was on the bus today. An old man in a flat cap. A girl in a fake fur coat with her phone glued to her ear. A trio of gleaming children accompanied by two yawning adults who looked like they needed more coffee in their lives.

Zoe pushed on. She still had her mum's hand in hers as they stepped into the street. They both had their bags. So far so good.

But outside her mum got even more upset. A man with dark hair came up and tried to sell her a copy of *The Big Issue*, and she started shouting at him until he went away, muttering under his breath. Another man banged into her and didn't stop to apologise before marching away. The nearby fruit seller shouted out his offer of four oranges for a pound. The clamour of central London was everywhere and they were right in the middle of it all. Zoe's throat was tight and she could barely breathe, but she charged on, clinging to her mum's hand.

She just wanted to get them out of here.

But then the hand wasn't in hers any more. She turned round and saw that her mum had sunk down to the pavement.

Zoe went back and crouched down next to her, her coat scraping against chewing gum and receipts.

'Mum?'

'I want to go home.'

'I know.' South London had never felt further away. 'I know.' She rubbed her mum's back, the way her mum had once rubbed hers, trying to tune out the bustle around them. She was starting to understand why Mandy frequently referred to Oxford Street as hell on earth and absolutely refused to set foot here.

She looked around for a cab, but could see nothing through the sea of legs and bags. 'Mum? I'm going to get us a taxi.'

'Yes.' Her mum loved taxis. They were quiet. Safe.

Zoe rose to her feet. She had got today so wrong. Her mum would have preferred a cup of tea in the living room to all this madness. Zoe had wanted a perfect day so much, she had lost sight of what was best for her mum. Shame made her desperate.

She leant down. 'Or we could go to a café. Somewhere quiet. Mum?'

Her mum shook her head.

'No. Home.' She looked like she was about to cry.

'OK.' Zoe supported her to a tiny red plastic seat at a bus stop. 'Wait here, Mum.'

'I will.' Her mum looked around her with fearful eyes. A busker started playing a screeching electric guitar just outside the shoe shop behind them, and she turned and stared. She looked hopeless, as if she was lost in a maze with no exit and the sun about to set.

Zoe had done that to her.

'Don't move!' She pushed her way towards the road and saw a black cab with a yellow light on. Salvation. She held up her hand, only for some man with a briefcase to get in it first. She resisted the urge to run after him and hit him over the head, and instead scanned for more cabs. Nothing. Just buses choking out fumes and cars beeping and no one in the whole of the crowded hell of a street who actually wanted to help her.

And then there it was. A yellow light. She raised her hand. The cab stopped.

Hallelujah.

She turned back to where she had left her mum, heart lifting in triumph.

She wasn't there.

It was then, only then, that Zoe realised. She stood there with her hand on the handle of a cab she couldn't take. Her heart was pounding. Her breath was coming too fast. And her eyes were scanning. Looking for the grey hair. The green coat. For the wonderful brave woman she was proud to call her mum.

This was what the others had meant. Lily. Mags. That her mum wasn't safe.

Because anything could happen to her out here.

And whatever it was, it would be Zoe's fault.

Shit flat

15th June, 2005

Dear Zoe

I had such high hopes as I set off today. Visions of
finally putting things right and of the two of us
embracing over our crème brûlée and knowing we
would never be parted again. It's been four years since
we talked. I've seen you during that time, but I haven't
let you see me. I didn't have the courage, but then
Mags sat me down last month with shepherd's pie and
her firmest voice and told me in no uncertain terms
that it was time to at least try.

I admit it. I was nervous. My heart dropped as soon
as I saw you and the place you'd chosen. It was all
steel tables and teeny little slices of cake. The waitress
belonged on a catwalk with her minimal black dress
and endless legs, and just looking in the window made
me feel awkward and sweaty and wrong.

And there you were, just as Lily had promised. I
stood there for a moment, drinking you in. You don't
look like you any more. Your hair, for a start. It was
dyed a more vivid shade of red and scraped back
from your face into a perfect ponytail. You sat ramrod
straight – none of that slouching that I remember
from all those years around the kitchen table. And
your clothes! No more DMs and tattered jeans. No
more of those cotton bracelets that you used to
make for me once upon a long ago. Instead you were

in a purple dress sweeping low at the front. A silver chain was round your neck. You'd come out of your chrysalis. Twenty-one going on taking over the world. That's you.

I ached at the sight of you and I took a gulp of thick London air and went in, hungry for your smile.

'Hi.' No smile. OK. I'd have to work for it. Unfair, but I was determined to be patient today. You stood up as I closed the door behind me, putting me instantly on the back foot. It felt too formal – like I was a client and we were about to do a deal. I bumped into a chair as I walked towards you. It scraped loudly across the wooden floor and I reached out to catch it and ended up stumbling across to you and grabbing hold of your sleeve to balance myself. As I apologised and looked up, I saw something in your eyes dying, and knew how hard I'd have to fight to get through to you.

Your eyes flicked around the café, as if apologising to the one other customer in there, who had barely looked up from her magazine. You were embarrassed by me. By this woman in her polka-dot dress and her crazy heatwave hair who had come here to try to say she loved you.

I was determined, though.

'Zoe.' I reached out and pressed your fragile body to me, ignoring the resistance flooding from every single cell. 'It's so bloody good to see you.'

'Hi, Mum.' You were stiff and unyielding, then you pulled away and sat down in your chair, as if you felt safer with the table between us. So I sat down too, biting back memories of how close we used to be. The way you climbed all over me at bedtime and smothered me in milky kisses. The requests for one more story – anything for just one second more of me.

I tried again to get through. 'Happy birthday, Zo.'

'Thanks.' Your smile was so tight and I wondered if I could see tears in your eyes. With eyeliner that thick, there was no way you'd ever let them fall.

The waitress was hovering, so I ordered coffee and a sandwich. I needed something to give me the energy to get through to you.

At home as I washed my hair this morning, I dreamt of the anger and the hatred dissolving away in one glance as we first saw each other. But no. You had a veneer now. You were glossy and smooth and your heart was closed to me and I didn't know what to say to open it up again.

So I started small.

'How's college?'

A flicker of impatience crossed your face, then the mask was back. When did you learn to suppress things? From your dad, probably. The master of keeping calm and carrying on.

'It's uni, Mum. Not college. I'm doing economics and business.'

I am so bloody proud of you. Tears stung my eyes as I realised how much you had achieved. I took a breath to calm myself and stared at the dazzling white tiles on the wall behind you. I opened my mouth to congratulate you, but you spoke first.

'Why did you want to see me?'

'How can you ask that?' The words came out louder than I'd intended, and you scanned around again. My frustration was starting to smoulder. I didn't give a shit about keeping up appearances. I just wanted to see you. To connect to you.

My coffee arrived and I dived into it to gain a bit of time.

You sipped your tea and stared out of the window. You didn't ask about me. You didn't seem to care whether I was lonely or healthy or with anyone. How my job was going. You didn't ask anything at all.

Eventually you spoke. 'Look, Mum, I don't know what we can talk about, really.' Your cheeks were flushed. 'It's been so long and it's not like we got on that well even before . . .' You paused. 'Before what you did.'

'What are you talking about?' I hated how you had rewritten the past. 'We were close.'

'No we weren't, Mum.' Your chin was tilted forwards. You were so sure you were right. You picked up a sugar packet and twisted it between your fingers. Your nails were sculpted and shiny. 'We were never close. When I tried to talk to you about school or anything, you were never there.'

'I was working.'

'Sure. Working.' You put the packet down. 'You could have made time. If you wanted.'

It was as if Alistair was in front of me, lecturing me on how to be a better parent. Like he was one to talk.

I was just revving up to defend myself when my sandwich arrived. Two triangles of toastie and a measly handful of cress. I picked it up and tried to chew, but only succeeded in burning my tongue. I swore and reached for my tap water.

Despite yourself, I could see you starting to smile. 'You always do that, Mum.'

There. That was more like it.

'Yeah, well, patience isn't one of my virtues.'

'You don't say.' For the first time we really looked at each other, and the temperature rose several degrees.

I was flooded with hope. 'Look, Zoe, we haven't seen each other for years. Let's just try having a chat. How does that sound?'

'OK.' You sipped your tea.

'How's your dad?'

'You know.' You shrugged. 'Working too much. Building up the company overseas.'

'Still aiming at world domination, then?'

'You could say that.' You arched an eyebrow. 'And he's still colour-coordinating the contents of the fridge. Same old, same old.'

I laughed. You did too. God, it was such a relief.

I popped a piece of cress into my mouth, remembering growing it on our windowsill in Longford. 'And you? What are you getting up to? Are you seeing anyone?'

As soon as it came out, I knew it was the wrong thing to say.

Your face shut down.

'That's none of your business.'

'Zoe, I—'

You were taut but still under control. Your voice was low and even. 'You never get to ask that, Mum. Not after what you did.'

'But I wrote to you, Zoe. I explained.'

'I threw them away. I didn't want to read them.' The finality in your voice cut me to the quick.

'Zoe, what happened wasn't my fault. It was Simon who—'

Your eyes widened, and I knew I'd pierced your shell at last. Now all our cards were about to be on the table. I could make you see that I was only trying to help.

'You don't get to talk about him.' You were practically hissing. 'I loved him.' Your voice cracked. 'I loved him and I wanted to be with him and be a family until you decided that wasn't going to happen.'

'But he wasn't even . . .'

'No.' You shook your head. 'You sent him away. It was all your fault.'

So nothing had changed. I was still the enemy. The frustration made me sick.

'Why do you hate me, Zoe? After everything I've done for you?'

'STOP.' You were on your feet, shaking. The waitress was staring at us. The customer in the corner turned her chair away and pretended she was fascinated by the sugar bowl on her table. We were centre stage, in the heat of the spotlight.

You sat back down, but I could tell you wouldn't be there much longer. Soon you would walk out of the door and I wouldn't see you again. I had one moment to make things right. One moment to heal this.

I leant forward. 'Zoe, I was trying to help. Why can't you see that?'

Your voice was a distorted hiss. 'To help? Are you bloody kidding me?'

That was too much. Too harsh.

'That's not fair. You've always been so stubborn.'

'I'm stubborn?' You jabbed your finger in my face. 'You fucked up my life. Every day I try to get over it. Every day I try to move on from him and . . .' I know you can't say the words that come next. I never could either. If I talked about Bean, it made everything more real.

273

Your hospital bed loomed between us, but you fought on. '. . . and from what we lost.' Your eyes were so sad. All I wanted was to make it better.

You took a breath. 'And no, I'm not seeing anyone.' The sobs were coming, but you were forcing them down. 'I just can't think about anything like that. About *moving on.*' You made those little quotation marks in the air with your perfect nails and pulled your bag off your chair. 'And that's all thanks to you, *Mum.*' The word was a lash. 'If you hadn't stuck your nose in he wouldn't have gone away. You ruined everything.'

I was so shocked, I couldn't think of a single thing to say.

You stared at me, tears choking you. 'I think it's best if we don't try this again, don't you? If we don't pretend any more. Because seeing you just brings it all back, and it hurts so much, and I don't want . . .'

I waited.

You tried to breathe. 'I don't want to be this person any more. Your daughter. I can't do it. It needs to stop.' Tears ran down your cheeks and all I wanted to do was wipe them away.

'Don't be stupid, Zo-bear. You'll always be my daughter. I love you. We can—'

'No.' Your face snuffed out any hope I might have had. 'You can't call me that any more. Not ever again.' And you pulled your cardigan around you and turned away.

I grabbed your hand to pull you back but the look on your face made me drop it like it was red hot. I remembered that look from the day you fell. It'll be seared on my mind for ever.

So I had nothing left to fight with. And I just sat in my

horrible chair in the soulless café and listened to the clack of your heels as you marched away. I heard the door swinging open and then the dull thud as it shut.

And I knew that I had lost you.

I reached into my bag for the present I had bought you. The one I'd shown proudly round the office the day before, so bloody excited about seeing you at last.

A locket. One picture of you and one of Lily. My girls.

Then I threw it on the table and walked away.

Mum

Sixteen

There she was. Thank God. Zoe's heart felt like it was going to burst out of her body with sheer relief. Lily put an arm round Zoe's waist and pulled her close.

'Hello.' Her mum smiled the smile of a woman who had no idea that three people had just spent two panicked hours sweating their way through central London looking for her.

'Well done, Dad.' Zoe was so breathless, she struggled to speak. It was Dad who had worked it out. Zoe had got so desperate that she had called him at his office in Covent Garden. She hadn't spoken to him since that terrible lunch, but he must have heard the urgency in her voice, as he came straight out and started searching the shops. Then Lily arrived from work to cover buses. Zoe was on tubes.

It wasn't exactly the A-Team, but it was the best they could do.

Zoe had gone in and out of overheated stations, seeing glimpses of green coats wherever she looked, and realising quite how many people the staff must meet in a day. Photos of her mum on her phone yielded shrugs or maybes, as an endless stream of people bought tickets and jostled towards the barriers.

She had been about to call the police when she had got Dad's text to say they had found mum in the café on the fifth floor of John Lewis.

Now Zoe walked over and hugged her mum tight.

'Would you like some tea?' Her mum held up a white china teapot. There was no sign of her earlier distress. This corner of the café was quiet. Peaceful.

'That would be lovely.'

Zoe looked at their dad, wondering what he would say. He needed to play along.

He took his jacket off and loosened his tie. 'Yes please.' Zoe saw him taking covert glances at Gina. Examining the thin frame. The wild hair. She wondered if the penny was really dropping yet. She had explained on the phone, but it was different when you saw Gina in person.

She was grateful to him. He was the one who had remembered how much their mum loved John Lewis. How she would spend hours wandering through the haberdashery department admiring the beautiful materials on show, before taking herself to this café for a cup of tea and a cake on a white china plate so different to the colourful chaos of the crockery at home.

He sat down opposite his ex-wife, his back still erect even after years of working in an office. Zoe saw him as if through a stranger's eyes. The silver hair. The deep grooves around his mouth. The smile lines fanning out from his bright blue eyes.

Gina blinked serenely at the three of them as she started to pour. Zoe found herself holding her breath, as she did so often nowadays. She never knew what her mum would forget next. Gina worked her way methodically around the four cups on the table, and the three of them added milk and sugar.

Zoe picked up her cup and nearly spat the liquid out again.

The tea was stone cold.

She looked nervously at her dad, willing him not to say anything. But Alistair was looking at Gina, and Zoe could see him wondering where his ex-wife had gone. Asking himself what had happened to the red lipstick and the laugh that could make the world join in. She knew the shock of that loss and instinctively she reached out and took his hand.

'What are you doing?' Gina smiled. 'He can't eat his cake if you've got hold of his hand, can he?' Her expression was gently chiding. 'Which one would you like, Alistair?'

Zoe waited for his answer. It didn't matter if it was all a pretence. After the last couple of hours, what mattered was that her mum was calm. Happy.

On the next table, a couple stared ahead of them in stony silence, chewing miserably on two of the smallest salads Zoe had ever seen. The man wore a flat cap at a rakish angle while the woman had a fleck of cucumber buried in her navy scarf. Her lips were a perfect red bow. Zoe wondered whether they ever lifted into a smile.

Zoe's dad took a slice of chocolate cake. It was dark and moist and covered with a layer of icing thick enough to take out one of his fillings.

'Thanks, Gina.' He bit into it while Zoe and Lily eyed up the rest of the selection.

'Mum?' Zoe indicated the plate. 'What are you having?'

'You go first, Lily.' Gina dreamily sipped her very cold tea. 'It's your birthday, after all.'

'*I'm* Lily, Mum.'

Zoe shook her head at her sister. Lily blushed and reached out for a slice of sponge cake. 'Thanks, Mum. It looks great.'

'Yes.' Gina was watching shoppers travelling down the escalator that ran behind them. 'Mags helped me make it.'

Zoe's heart twisted as her eyes met Lily's across the table.

Gina looked around expectantly. 'Is she coming soon? Mags?'

Lily took a breath. 'I don't think so, Mum. It's just family today.'

'We should have got you candles.' Gina smiled at them as if they had never been apart. She happily surveyed the broken quartet, who had once all had the same phone number and the same front door and always had roast lamb on Sundays. At the four people who had once shared a TV and a bathroom but who were now scattered across London living new lives, only connected by email or phone or disaster – the ultimate social convenor. A family that wasn't real any more celebrating a birthday that didn't exist.

Zoe saw her sister discreetly wiping away a tear.

Only their mum seemed to be enjoying herself.

Zoe picked up a caramel tart and bit into it without enthusiasm. It was too sweet. Too damn celebratory for the way she was feeling inside.

She chewed. Swallowed. Wondered what on earth to say.

Gina sipped her tea. 'This is nice.'

'Yes.' Zoe took another bite and wondered if she was developing lockjaw.

Gina looked at her former husband. 'Are you working away again this week, Alistair?'

Zoe looked for the flare of irritation on her dad's face. Nothing.

He understood now that Gina was living in yesterdays.

Alistair calmly cut up his cake. 'Yes.' He managed a smile. 'I'm leaving tomorrow.' He put another piece in his mouth.

Well done, Dad.

'With Sally?'

'Who?' His jaws stopped stoically working their way through a cake he clearly didn't want. 'Do you mean Wendy?'

'No. Not her. Sally.'

Zoe and Lily swivelled towards him.

Lily got the question out first. 'Who's Sally?'

He flicked away a piece of chocolate cake that had landed on his tie. Gina sipped her tea. 'You know. Sally. The one you kept going to conferences with. Remember?'

Zoe watched him closely.

There was a creep of guilt on his face.

'Dad?'

'She doesn't know what she's talking about. Her memory's playing tricks.' He wouldn't meet Zoe's eye.

She felt a stab of frustration. 'Dad. Not now. Please. Don't pretend the memories she has left aren't real.'

'I don't know what you're trying to imply.'

'I'm not implying anything. You're the one with guilt written all over your face.'

'It was very brief. And it was a long time ago.'

'Wasn't everything?' Zoe wiped her mouth with a napkin. Then another thought struck her. Cold and raw.

'How could you have been so hard on her? About Simon?' She looked at this man who she had measured herself against for as long as she could remember. 'That's so unfair.' She pushed her plate away. 'Talk about double standards.' She thought of all the years of trying to please him. Trying to be the girl he wanted her to be.

It had all been a lie.

She felt Lily's fingers closing around hers. They shared

a look that told Zoe she had an ally again. Someone to talk to. Someone to trust.

Meanwhile, her dad seemed to be shrinking right in front of her. 'It was a very difficult time.'

'Don't make excuses, Dad.' Her anger was rising. All the things she couldn't fix, the years she couldn't get back, were bubbling out of her around this table in a café full of people who had come to buy toasters or hoovers or a set of sheets for their new bed.

She didn't care. She felt as if the pieces of her life had been sawn up into a jagged jigsaw puzzle with no picture and no hope of ever being solved.

'Tell us what happened, Dad.' Lily frowned and flicked a crumb away from her lip with a long purple nail.

He shook his head. Zoe had never seen him like this. He had always been a man who swept into rooms, hand outstretched. But now he looked diminished. Just a man in an expensive suit who had never really known how to forgive anyone, let alone himself.

She felt her mum's hand on her arm. 'Don't upset your-self, love.'

Her dad pushed his chair back and was standing up. The couple at the next table were looking more lively now. The Whittaker show was much better than attempting to have a conversation themselves. It was better than the telly.

Zoe looked up at the man who had carried her on his shoulders. Who had been the hero of her childhood stories.

'You can't go, Dad. Please.'

Lily joined in. 'Stay.'

He hesitated, drumming his fingers against the back of his chair.

'I'm sorry.' He coughed. 'I just can't . . . I can't bear to . . .' He glanced at Gina, and then turned and walked away. Another man in a suit merging into the crowds. Zoe kept hoping he would turn round, but that wasn't Major Alistair Whittaker's style. He didn't think twice. He didn't have regrets. He just marched on to whatever the next thing might be, holding his head high.

Just as Zoe had tried to do.

'Should I go after him?' She stared at her sister. 'I need to talk to him. To make him see.'

'Don't.'

Zoe raised her eyebrows in surprise. There was a new authority about her sister as she sat there calmly eating her cake.

'Let's stop this.' Lily put her hand on their mum's shoulder. 'Let's stop fighting about stuff that's already happened. I've had enough.' She exhaled. 'Everyone's made mistakes. And we have bigger things to think about.' She glanced towards their mum. 'Don't we?'

Zoe thought of the horror of the last few hours. Thought of her mum's world, diminished to a small flat and David Attenborough. That was what they needed to think about. 'Yes.'

'So let's figure those out. OK?'

'OK.' Zoe nodded. 'I'm going to start by finishing my cake.'

'Good idea.' Lily grinned.

Their mum was already way ahead of them.

After tea, Zoe was about to step on to the big escalator in the middle of the shop when she heard her phone ringing.

It was her dad.

She turned to her sister. 'Lily, can you go ahead with Mum? I'll catch you up.'

'Of course.'

She put the phone to her ear. 'Yes?'

'I'm sorry.' She could hear the tension in his voice. 'I couldn't stay.'

'Too embarrassed?'

'No. Yes. Partly.'

She let the silence build. She wasn't going to let him off the hook.

Eventually he spoke. 'Can I have a quick word?'

'OK.' She waited.

Nothing.

'Dad? You know you're meant to be the one talking?'

'Of course.' He coughed. 'I'm in the travel department. Can you come over?'

'If you want me to.'

She hung up and walked through the café towards the rows of suitcases and bags. Her dad was lurking in between the Antler cases and the Samsonites.

'What do you want?' She felt bitterness rising.

He lowered his head, and she saw how grey he had become. He was getting older too.

'I don't know what to say, Zoe.'

'About what?' She would make him say it. She would.

'About how I reacted. At the lunch. About today. About everything.'

'I see?'

'Good.' He dug his hands in his pockets and she heard the rattle of change.

This wasn't enough. Not after the way he'd looked at her. The judgement in his eyes. Turning on her and Gina when all the time he had been keeping his own secret.

'Anything else you'd like to say?' She was pushed sideways by a woman with a blue scarf and what appeared to be a serious shopping habit. Her dad steadied her, and in his touch was a thousand moments. Pulling her up out of the sandpit after another sandcastle triumph. Pushing her higher and higher on the swing. Handing her a chocolate bar as she revised for finals. Throwing a towel around her and warming her up after one of their crazy Christmas swimming expeditions.

His voice was low. 'I had no idea how bad Gina was.' His thick brows met in a frown and he stared at the ground.

'I would have told you. If you'd asked.'

'I know.'

She knew he was trying to reach out, but she wasn't ready to forgive him yet. He had made her feel so small. So ashamed.

He spoke into the silence. 'It must be very . . . hard. Gina being so ill.'

'Yeah.' Zoe bit her lip to stop the treacherous tears from falling. 'But we're doing OK.'

'Really?' His eyes crinkled into that familiar smile. 'Even I don't believe that. And I'm pretty stupid, apparently.'

'Yeah.' She kicked the floor with her boot. 'You are.'

'What are you going to do?' He glanced at her sideways and then looked away.

'We don't know yet.' Zoe felt stronger. She and Lily would handle it together. 'It depends what she wants. Whatever makes her feel safe. Whatever gives her the best life.'

He stared at the suitcase at his side.

'It's not fair, is it?'

'No.'

That at least they could agree on.

'Zoe? Thank God I've found you.' Lily was behind her. 'Sorry, but Mum didn't want to leave without you. She was getting worried.' They all turned and saw Gina approaching. Her hair fell around her face as she searched the room anxiously. She was so achingly familiar. The turn of her head. The collar of her coat up high. The black boots that looked distinctly similar to the ones she used to wear to dance round the garden when Zoe had barely been tall enough to reach her knee.

She was the past and the present and the past again. Their mum.

Zoe swallowed. 'I'd better go. We need to get home.'

He nodded. 'Of course. Off you go.'

And Zoe and Lily walked either side of their mum towards whatever was coming next.

Shit flat

15th June, 2006

Dear Zoe,

I dialled your number today and left a message. You ignored me. I can't say I'm surprised. So I'm just going to make sure I say it again. I miss you. I'm sorry about the way things have turned out. I was only trying to do the right thing.

Mags is on her way to take me out. Lily was here for breakfast. I have people looking out for me, which makes me lucky, I suppose. I hope you feel you're lucky too. I hope you're happy. And one day I hope you'll see sense and come and knock on my door.

I'll always be here, waiting, just in case you ever need me. I don't have a choice. This is for life.

Happy twenty-second birthday.

Love,
Mum x

Seventeen

'So, Bruno. What's the latest?'

Zoe sipped her coffee, wondering how many mugs it would take her to get going today. She had been up most of the night trying to work out what help they could get for Mum via the council. It was a labyrinthine business of attendance allowances and adult social care teams, of day care centres, extra care housing, means assessments and eligibility criteria. Zoe and Lily had sat together in the kitchen, laptops lighting their faces and a diminishing bottle of wine between them, managing to find out nothing more useful than the fact that Gina was too young to be eligible for any extra care council housing.

Every now and then one of them had walked down the corridor to check on Mum while she watched TV and slept on the sofa. It was her favourite place now. She lay underneath the red picnic blanket they had taken on so many childhood adventures, with cushions beneath her head and Monkey and Murgatroyd vying for position next to her. One of Monkey's eyes had fallen off, and his ears were pretty much eroded, but it was still him, and Mum liked having him at her side.

Zoe dragged her mind back to the office. On the way in this morning she had tried to use her front door key to get on the tube and she had narrowly avoided depositing her tax return in the bin rather than the postbox.

Still. She had made it here eventually. And Bruno's volcanic coffee would wake up her sleeping brain. Any minute now.

He finished typing and swivelled his chair round towards her. 'Simeon & Co. I think I sent you a summary?' He nibbled on a piece of the salt 'n sweet low-fat popcorn that had become his latest snacking obsession.

'You did.' Zoe nodded. Despite her tiredness, the work fog finally seemed to be clearing. 'Thank you.'

'No worries.' Bruno shrugged. 'A roller coaster of a read, I think you'll agree.'

Zoe smiled. 'Something like that. So, they're the bakers.'

'Yes.' Bruno nodded. 'Gluten-free, nut-free, but luckily not taste-free.' He indicated the brown paper bag to his left. 'They sent us over some samples yesterday, and I may have heroically managed to eat most of them. Just in the name of research, of course.' He pushed the bag towards her. 'Though I have saved one for you, if you fancy it.'

'Thanks.' Zoe was so busy trying to feed her mum up that she kept forgetting to eat herself. At their latest appointment, Dr Jones had told them how important diet was. And exercise. Walks. Swimming. Anything that made Mum's heart beat faster. Dr Jones made it sound so easy but it took Mum so long to find everything she needed to take out with her that frequently their expeditions turned into cups of tea in the kitchen.

Zoe pulled out the cookie and took a bite. Sweet. Gooey. Perfect.

'Oh, thank God.' She broke off another piece.

'What?'

'I might have a personality in here somewhere.'

'Hallelujah!' Bruno laughed. 'God bless Simeon & Co.'

'Amen to that.' She stretched her arms over her head. 'So are we meeting Simeon, or the and Co.?'

'We're meeting Nina Simeon herself, I think.' He peered at his screen. 'Yep. She's really excited about the visuals for their app, so we just need to be sure we make the overall package as appealing as we can.'

'OK.' Zoe finished the cookie and nodded. 'We've got a couple of hours. Let's get to work.'

'OK, boss.'

'And we'll split the pitch this time.'

He took a second to register what she had said. 'Pardon?'

'You heard me.' She smiled. 'We'll do it together.'

'Me?' A flush was spreading across his cheeks. 'Really?'

'Yes.' Zoe nodded. 'So get your arse over here and we can start dividing it up between us. We're a team, aren't we?'

He didn't need asking twice. He had pushed his chair round in seconds.

Zoe found the presentation and opened it up. 'God, you always smell so good. I should get you over to my side of the desk more often.'

'Flatterer.' He glanced at her sideways, looking suddenly suspicious. 'Why are you being so nice to me? Is this some kind of very late new year resolution?'

Zoe shrugged. 'Nah. It's that cookie. It had magical powers.'

'Of course.' Bruno tapped his pen on the table. 'After I'd eaten the rest of them, I donated my lunch money to that guy who's always outside the Wetherspoon's by the station.'

'You have lunch money?'

'Yes.' Bruno put the pen down. 'Why? Don't you?'

Zoe clicked open the first slide. 'Come on, Bruno. I colour-coordinate my sock drawer. Of *course* I have a lunch budget.'

'Wow. Self-mockery. Sharing presentations. What the hell's next?'

'I don't know.' Zoe frowned at the words on the screen. 'I'll probably marry Prince Harry and cause some kind of major royal scandal.'

Bruno's brown eyes gleamed. 'And I can say I knew you before, and share my outrageous tales of your lewd office antics.'

'Yeah.' Zoe sipped her coffee. 'Like how I organise my tea bags alphabetically. You'll make millions.'

'I can make stuff up.' Bruno sat back and put the tips of his fingers together. 'I used to get very high marks in creative writing at school.'

'I bet, J. K. Now stop chatting and calm down.' Zoe tapped him on the leg. 'Let's get on with it.'

'Just before we do.' His face was full of concern. 'Are you really OK, Zo? With all the stuff happening with your mum?'

A few months ago she would have said yes and brushed it off. Deployed her 'I'm fine' shield.

Not any more.

She thought of Lily. Of Mags. Of the team that was evolving. Team Mum. She felt a kernel of warmth deep inside her. 'Not OK, no. We're losing more of her every day. And now we have to decide what we're going to do next. Where she's going to live. The doctors recommend twenty-four-hour carers, or sheltered accommodation or a home.'

'Shit.'

'Yes. But . . .' she took a breath, 'and it's a big but . . . Lily and I are deciding what to do together. With Mum. And that feels good.'

'You're being so brave.'

'Nope.' She shook her head vigorously. 'I'm just figuring it out as I go along. And you and I need to make some decisions too.'

'About what?'

'About the business.'

'Are you sure now's the right time?'

'No.' She shrugged. 'But I know we need to think about it together. To work out if we want to expand or to pull back until our cash flow is a bit more secure.'

He squeezed the bridge of his nose with his fingers. 'How challenging is challenging?'

'Things are a bit tight.'

'OK.' He nodded. 'Can I say something?'

'Sure.'

'And please know that I am saying this with love.'

'What is it?'

'We have a presentation in two hours. Maybe we should focus on that?'

'Yes. Good point.'

She clicked back into the presentation.

'Now. Do you want to start?'

'Sure.'

The enthusiasm on his face gave her the boost she needed. She pushed her mum to the back of her mind and focused on the pitch.

They had just come out of the tube when she saw him. Bruno was panicking that he had forgotten to wear his lucky socks. Zoe was telling him he didn't need lucky socks. And there they were.

Jamie. And a blonde girl.

A very pretty blonde girl.

Oh GOD. Zoe pulled Bruno to one side and they hid

behind a tall oak tree. Traffic whizzed past them, with drivers looking at them curiously as Zoe wondered if she had a balaclava in her bag.

Damn her red hair. It wasn't exactly designed for blending in.

'What is it?' Bruno blinked at her, puzzled. 'Is this some kind of new lucky pre-presentation ritual? You're not about to give me a high-five, are you?'

'No.' Zoe hissed through the side of her mouth, even though she knew there was no way Jamie could hear them over the traffic. 'Look.' She jabbed a finger towards her ex. 'Over there.'

Bruno wrinkled his nose in puzzlement. 'What? The tree? It's lovely, but—'

'NO.' Zoe shook her head. 'Over there. By the big glass building. It's Jamie.'

Bruno peered round the trunk with all the subtlety of a can-can dancer taking to the stage.

'Bloody hell, Bruno. I think there might be someone in Canary Wharf who didn't spot you leaning out there.'

He looked at her, a furrow between his eyes. 'What's your plan here, Zo?'

'I don't know.' She wanted to pace, but the tree's width didn't exactly lend itself to that.

'We need to go. The pitch is in five minutes and they're not going to think this is a particularly good reason for being late. "I'm sorry, we had some urgent hiding to do."' He stroked his chin in mock thought. 'No. I can't see us thrashing the competition with that.'

'I know.' Blood was rushing to her head and she simply couldn't think about anything but the girl's snub nose, tilted so enticingly towards Jamie. 'I don't like this any more than you do.'

'Well how about playing it cool, then?'

'This from the man who once threw a cheeseburger in his ex's face because he dared to turn up at the same pub as you with another man.'

'All right, all right.' Bruno held up his hands. 'It was a difficult time for me. I wasn't making good decisions. Remember it was the same time I started wearing all those black polo necks and trying to write a play.'

'Exactly my point.' She looked at him with desperation as an old lady trundled past with a checked shopping trolley, huge green earphones attached to either side of her head and a smile playing across her lips.

That was the way to age. Not like Mum, scared of shadows and forgetting how to write her own name on a cheque.

Thinking of her mum enabled Zoe to get herself under control. Here she was, cowering behind a tree, because she was too scared to see the man she loved dating someone else. Her mum had to go through so much more.

She took a breath.

'Is she kissing him?'

Bruno looked confused. 'What, you mean you want me to look again?'

'Of course I do!'

'You do know that Jamie does actually know who I am? So there is a fairly large danger of him recognising me?'

'Yes.' Zoe pushed him round. 'But you can do this, Bruno. Come on. You've watched *Spooks*.'

'I hardly think that qualifies me—'

'Just do it!'

'Oh all right then.' He stuck his head round the trunk again. 'OH MY GOD.'

He whirled back round and nearly took her eye out with his elbow.

'What?'

He looked at her, clearly not sure how to communicate whatever he had seen.

'Nothing.'

She folded her arms. 'Bruno.'

'No, really it's—'

'BRUNO.'

He put a finger to his lips. 'What happened to whispering?'

She exhaled in frustration. 'Were they snogging? Oh God.' She felt her pulse spiral. 'They were, weren't they?'

'No.' He shook his head.

'Really?'

'Really.'

'Good. That's good.' She felt her heart rate return to normal.

'But . . .'

'But what?' She stared at him.

He looked at her as if she had her finger poised to press the nuclear button. 'Well, it looked like they were holding hands.'

'WHAT?' Zoe felt the world darken around her.

'Holding hands?' Bruno appeared to be about to demonstrate what he meant. 'You know. Like—'

'I know what it is, Bruno.' Zoe wondered if her heart might actually stop beating. 'I am familiar with the concept.'

'Good.' Bruno checked his watch again. 'We really have to go.'

'I just don't think I can . . .'

Bruno shook his head. 'Zoe. No. You have to come. I am not letting you screw this up.' He took her hand. 'Come with me. Now.'

'No.' She shook her head.

He put his other hand gently under her chin. 'Look. You've worked so hard, Zoe. You've looked after your mum. You've built up your own company. You should be so proud.'

'I—'

'And you are NOT fucking it up now.' He pulled hard at her hand and they were out from behind the tree, in full view of Jamie and the blonde. She couldn't bear to look at him. Couldn't bear to see her future caught in the spell of someone else's smile.

Bruno towed her relentlessly onwards.

'Casual,' he said out of the corner of his mouth. 'Let's go for casual.'

'Sure.' Her voice was squeezed and tiny. 'Casual.'

Jamie had his back to them, but Zoe could see that the two of them were holding hands. Great.

'Hi, Jamie.' Bruno beamed at the two of them, never letting go of Zoe's hand.

Jamie turned in surprise and pulled away rapidly from the girl. Zoe cast her a sideways glance. Predictably perfect in every way. Huge blue eyes. Pink dress with a silver scarf at her throat. Leggings and Converse. Wide smile.

Zoe hated her.

'Jamie, hi.' She tried to sound normal, even though her tongue appeared to have helpfully decided to pretend it was made of stone.

'Hi.' Jamie took a step away from the girl. Then another. Too late.

Zoe realised she had stopped moving, but Bruno tugged at her arm. 'Sorry, Jamie. Can't stop. We're in a hurry.'

Jamie managed to look her in the face.

'I need to talk to you, Zo.'

No. If there was one thing Zoe was sure of, it was that she didn't want to know what he had to say. *Zoe, I've met someone else. Zoe, she's amazing.*

Zoe, your whole life is over.

No. She looked at the girl, who was tactfully checking her phone. She probably knew who Zoe was. Knew she was the lunatic who ran out on her own wedding.

'Now's not a good time. We're just about to do a pitch.' She walked on. 'See you around.'

God, she hoped not. The two of them looked so right together. She feared the memory would be seared into her mind for ever

'Well done, Zo. Bloody heroic.' Bruno whisked her onwards until they were climbing the steps of the next building. 'Loved the "see you around".' He put his arm round her shoulders. 'I'm bloody proud of you.'

'Why?'

'For not weeping. Or punching him in the face.' Bruno took a deep breath and stood tall. 'Now come on, girl. Let's get ourselves a new client.'

Tears suddenly threatened to overwhelm her again. 'I don't know if I can do it, Bruno.'

'Honey.' He turned to her. 'Of course you can. We can do this together.'

'Are you sure?' She needed his support. Needed his reassurance.

'Yes.' He kissed her on the cheek and squeezed her arm. 'I am totally sure, Zoe Whittaker. And you should be too.'

She reached out and hugged him. 'Thank you.'

'My pleasure.' The door buzzed open and they were in a hall painted a delicate grey. Labelled pictures of spotlit cakes were on the walls. Chocolate. Ginger. Vanilla.

'Well, this is my kind of place.' Zoe steeled herself,

desperately seeking the calm she needed. She blocked out the image of Jamie standing outside. The girl's hand in his. Those blue eyes staring affectionately at his face.

She just thought about herself. And Bruno. And what they could do for Simeon & Co.

Together they started up the stairs.

Hours later, Bruno and Zoe emerged from the pub with Mandy.

'Are you sure you don't want to go to karaoke?' Mandy put her hands around their shoulders and attempted to drag them towards Poland Street.

'Yes.' Zoe nodded. 'I'm totally sure.'

'But it would do you goooooood.' Mandy practically had Zoe in a headlock. 'You know it would. You haven't had a night out in ages.'

'I think the wine has done me quite enough good, thanks.' Zoe lost her balance and Bruno reached out and grabbed her before she fell. She was losing count of his good deeds today. 'I need to get home. Mags is waiting for me with Mum.'

'I'll come with you, Mandy.' Bruno nodded. 'Seeing as you're twisting my arm.'

'YES!' Mandy's squawk of triumph scared a passer-by, who leapt into a doorway before picking up speed again. 'Let's do Blur. And A-ha. And Journey. And—'

Zoe leant towards Bruno and kissed him on the cheek. 'Well done today. I couldn't have done it without you.'

'Yes you could.'

'No.' She smiled. 'Without you I'd have still been standing behind that bloody tree.'

Then she turned and headed towards the tube, along streets full of revellers and pubs and people who didn't look like they had a care in the world. People holding hands. Groups talking about where they were heading next.

Zoe walked on, alone.

The girl's face haunted her every step of the way.

Cosy flat

15th June, 2007

Dear Zoe,

Your twenty-third birthday. What a day. I can barely
sit down. I've already watered my plants twice and am
currently running round the sitting room (I call it a
sitting room – it's more of a cupboard with cushions to
be honest), eating peanuts and toasting you in corner-
shop bubbles.

I am so proud of you.

I was there, you see. I saw you. Another face in the
crowd at the Royal Festival Hall, but one who had eyes
only for you. The polished wood. The tiers of seats full
of proud parents and brothers and aunties and grand-
parents. A room full of joy.

I was tucked away at the back, worried I wouldn't
be able to see you, but then I spotted you turning
your head to talk to the girl behind you, and God, I
nearly burst with pride. You were in your long black
gown and fur-lined hood, and you looked so
composed and at home. The world could have trusted
you with anything – delivering peace in the Middle
East or trying to turn around the England football
team, you know, little things like that – and you would
have delivered and still found time to cook a flawless
three-course lunch for ten.

Your hair was smooth and sleek down to your
shoulders and I knew how serious your eyes would be

– after all, I saw you on the starting line for the sack race at school. The gravitas with which you made your winning speech. As the ceremony started today, it was as if I was seeing all the ages of you, all the smiles and the frowns and the pigtails and the teenage hunch, combining magically in the beautiful young woman about to take her place on the stage.

I could see Alistair right down at the front with his new wife Wendy. She looked very neat with brown bobbed hair and a navy blazer. Lily looked over her shoulder at the beginning, nodding at me in satisfaction when she saw I was there. Her hand was being gripped by her boyfriend Damian. He never seems to let go. It's almost endearing until I remember what I overheard him saying to her about the size of her thighs the other night. She has no idea how much better she deserves.

But today both my girls were shining. And up there at the back of the big hall, watching as your name was called, surrounded by families in their best clothes and their broadest smiles, I felt something I haven't felt in a while. I felt grateful.

Even though we don't talk, at least I know that you're out there living and achieving all the things I never did. All the things I dreamt of for you. You were absolutely flying today. That's what matters.

Congratulations, Zoe Whittaker, BA Hons, MSc. I'm so bloody proud of you.

All my love,
Mum x

Eighteen

'Are you ready?'

Lily looked at Zoe and then gave the smallest nod in history.

'Yes.'

'Me too.' Zoe was also choosing not to tell the truth. She would never be ready. Not for this. Not for a tour of Woodleigh Place, a centre in Surrey offering specialist sheltered accommodation for people with dementia.

She steeled herself. 'Let's go in, shall we?'

They took each other's hands and walked up the wide stone steps towards the main house – a converted vicarage with a gabled roof and ivy growing up the walls and past the windows above them. Daffodils bloomed in the flower beds and a black cat wandered through the shrubs on the far right-hand side.

They reached thick glass front doors and rang the bell.

The doors slid open and started to close as soon as they had stepped through.

They walked towards another set of glass doors in front of them.

'Bloody hell. We're stuck.'

Lily put her hands against the glass. 'It's like bloody *Star Trek* in here.'

'Mum would hate this.' Zoe wondered how many residents ended up trapped in this glass prison. Trying to run.

She could imagine her mum now, eyes wild, face pressed against the glass as she sought the freedom she would never have again.

The lump in her throat grew bigger.

The second set of doors opened and they walked into a sunlit atrium that belonged in a big-budget TV drama.

'Wow.' Zoe craned her neck back. The ceiling soared above them and she could hear Mozart's clarinet concerto playing quietly over the speakers behind the welcome desk in the corner. It felt so calm. So peaceful. She grinned as she was assailed by a mental image of her mum asking to put on some of her eighties tunes and bopping around the pot plants and the beige armchairs, just like she did on her good days in the kitchen at home.

The good days were diminishing now. Zoe felt another clutch of failure.

Lily giggled. 'Mum's going to walk in and do a massive belch in the first five minutes, isn't she?'

'Probably.' Zoe caught the eye of the lady behind the reception desk, pleased to see the warm smile on her face.

'Hello. Are you Zoe? And Lily? I'm Nancy, the manager here.' The woman tucked a strand of grey hair behind her ear and held out her hand. She had bright brown eyes and an air of infinite calm. A good start.

'Yes.' Zoe nodded and shook her hand. Nancy's fingers were cool and steady.

'It's lovely to meet you both. Welcome to Woodleigh Place.'

'Thank you.' Zoe couldn't stop her eyes darting around. She was looking for flaws. She almost wanted to find fault with the place. To prove that it didn't live up to the impressive picture painted in the brochure Lily had given her last week. That way she could end this. Keep Mum at home. Carry on.

But deep down she knew she couldn't help her mum any more. Last night Zoe had found her running round the kitchen, opening cupboards and staring at the contents as if they were unfamiliar runes on a cave wall. It had taken hours to calm her down. She kept saying she had something to do, but she couldn't remember what it was. Zoe had cuddled her and been pushed away. She had reasoned with her and got nowhere. Even David Attenborough hadn't worked. In the end, Mum had fallen asleep at the kitchen table, her cheek pressed against the wood, hands balled on her lap as if in prayer.

As she had gently tucked a cushion beneath her head, Zoe had known she couldn't kid herself any more. This wasn't a life. And maybe Woodleigh Place could give her mum back something of what she had lost. A sense of a life lived.

Yet still the guilt made it difficult to look herself in the eye. However hard she searched for a right answer, she knew it would never be there.

Nancy walked round to the front of the desk. 'Now, as you might know from our website, every aspect of the home has been designed to improve the lives of the people who live here.' She clasped her hands together. 'We understand that families are placing a lot of trust in us when they leave their loved ones in our care, and we make every effort to reward that faith.'

She indicated the map on the wall beside them. 'This is a floor plan of the space we have. As you can see, the communal areas – the bistro, the dining room, the activity room and the lounge – are arranged in a figure-of-eight formation to reduce the feeling of being enclosed and to create a feeling of free flow for our residents.' She indicated the oval skylight above their heads. 'We have also maximised the light in every room, and we have plants and trees throughout to enable residents to feel connected to the natural world around them.'

She gestured that they should walk through the open door to their left, and Zoe saw that they were now in a big sitting room with huge windows opening out on to the garden. In one corner a group of men and women were doing the world's slowest session of aerobics, led by a teacher in an eye-watering pair of green and pink stripy leggings. Limbs waved and heads bobbed up and down as they moved, some smiling and some sporting clenched jaws more normally associated with aiming a gun on a shooting range.

An upright piano was set against the far wall with sheet music scattered on top, and throughout the room flowers and pot plants sat on top of tables and bookshelves, as if this was a country house just waiting for new guests.

New guests like her mum.

Nancy was watching her, amused. 'I promise you we keep things very clean.' Zoe jumped, embarrassed to find she had been running a fingertip along the top of a coffee table.

'Oh no. I'm so sorry.'

Nancy smiled. 'Don't worry. I know you want the best for your mum.' She sat down in a grey armchair by the window.

Zoe felt flustered. Caught out. 'Can she bring her own furniture?'

'Yes. Of course.' Nancy nodded. 'Residents make their own choices here. They can keep pets too, if they want.'

'Murgatroyd – that's my mum's cat – would love it here.'

More people to be stroked by. More titbits on offer. She wondered how enormous he would become.

'There are other benefits, too.' Nancy kept talking into the silence. She must have to do that a lot. Zoe thought of all the husbands and wives and children facing the stark choice between keeping a loved one close and keeping them safe. Forced to send them away to live surrounded by strangers with only one thing in common – the disease gradually cutting them off from everyone around them.

'And of course you can visit any time,' Nancy carried on. 'There are no set visiting hours here and the bistro is open to the public, so you can come and eat with her if you want to. I can take you there later if you like.'

'Thank you.'

Zoe attempted to smile but found she couldn't. The thought of their mum being in here was too much. Their mum, Snap demon, champion herb grower and mender of Wendy houses. Their mum, who should be beaming her way through her fifties, surrounded by friends and family and her beloved flowers and plants.

Zoe weaved her fingers in and out of the strap of her bag. The injustice never stopped stinging. The future had been stolen. Now Mum would be just another person in a place like this. Another person who couldn't remember what was real and what was not. Ever since that nightmare summer, Zoe had run flat out into the future, arms outstretched. Now she only wanted to look back.

She squeezed Lily's hand and the two of them sat down next to each other on a big purple sofa opposite Nancy. It was so soft that Zoe suspected she might never get out of it alive. She tried to sit up straight. The sofa had other ideas.

'Would you like any tea or coffee?' Nancy looked at them enquiringly.

'No thanks.' Zoe shook her head.

'So. Any questions?' Nancy smiled at them expectantly.

Zoe's mind was still stuck on regret. She fumbled in her bag and tried to find her list of questions. As her fingers closed around the piece of paper, she heard Lily start to speak.

'Can you tell us how residents' time is structured here?'

'Of course.' Nancy smiled. 'We wake residents at seven with a cup of tea or coffee, and then help them to dress and get ready for their day.'

Zoe nudged Lily, and they both grinned as they thought of their mum's legendary inability to be coherent before 11 a.m.

Nancy nodded. 'Most families worry about their relatives' capacity to adjust, but the fact is that they all do in the end.'

Zoe looked away. She didn't want their mum to have to conform. She wanted her to be able to be herself in whatever way she could. Just because her memory was fading didn't mean she was a different person. Her emotions were still there. Still real.

Nancy smoothed her navy skirt over her knees. 'After breakfast, there are various activities open to residents. We promote mental stimulation wherever possible, with a Sudoku group, a crossword group, music and movement – as you can see . . .' She gestured behind her. 'Then there's a drama group, cookery, gardening . . .' She came to a halt. 'You name it, we've got it.'

'Great.' As Zoe looked around, her eyes had come to rest on the CCTV cameras in the corner and behind the reception desk. The locks on the windows.

Lily was fiddling with the sleeve of her jumper, just as she had when she was a little girl entering the school playground. 'And do you ever see any improvement? When residents take part in these activities? Do they ever get better?'

Nancy's smile was kind. 'It depends on the individual, but the activities are certainly stimulating and enjoyable. Obviously all our residents are at different stages, and have varying symptoms, but it is possible to see improvements once they've settled in.' She steepled her fingers together and recrossed her legs. 'They have good food, lots to do, friends to spend time with but their own space too . . .' She gestured around the room. 'And of course we encourage relatives to take residents out and about in the local countryside. Walks. Museums. Whatever appeals to them most.'

'You've taken my chair.' A piercing voice cut through their conversation, and Zoe turned to see a tiny old lady in wire glasses and a pleated skirt holding on to the back of a floral armchair in the corner.

'It's mine.' A man in checked trousers and a green cardigan pulled a cushion on to his lap as if to wall himself in.

'No.' The first speaker grabbed it again. 'We agreed. Yesterday. When you ate my dinner.'

'I did no such thing. I've been here longer than you and . . .'

'Excuse me.' Nancy stood up. 'I won't be a minute.' She strode towards the pair, who both went up a key as she approached.

'Not quite as peaceful as she'd have us believe, then.' Zoe put her head on Lily's shoulder. 'What do you think of it, Lil?'

Lily's eyes glistened with uncried tears. 'I think it's the best place we've seen so far, but . . .'

'But what?'

'I just can't stand the thought of leaving her here.'

Zoe reached inside herself to see if she could come up with a more positive spin. No. Nothing.

Lily's forehead creased with worry. 'I mean, what are we going to say to her?'

'I have no idea.'

Lily flicked through the brochure that Nancy had placed beside her on the table. 'And have you seen these prices?'

Zoe looked at the little piece of paper in the loveliest possible font that contained the dreaded information on what a place here would cost per week.

'Bloody hell!' She dropped the page as if it were red hot. 'No wonder they don't send this information out before people come and visit. They'd have no clients left!'

Lily sighed. 'Know any millionaires?'

Zoe checked the page again. Just in case.

'I'm beginning to wish I'd asked for coffee now. And biscuits.'

The figures were hurting her eyeballs. She sighed. 'Well, if both of us were to give up eating and live in cardboard boxes, we might be able to cover a month or two.'

Lily's lower lip trembled. 'If only she owned her flat.'

'Yeah. Well. I'm not sure that was ever an option.'

'No.' Lily was chewing on a fingernail. 'Well, she'd hate it here anyway. So there's no point thinking about it, is there?'

Zoe put an arm round her. 'Lil, she hates being at mine now too. She doesn't feel safe.' She rubbed her eyes. 'I've tried everything I can, but the fact is, she's getting more unhappy every day.'

'But we don't have enough money for this, and she's

too young for the council accommodation. So what are we meant to do?'

Zoe didn't have any answers. Silence grew between them as she struggled to think of something.

'Dr Jones said she needs full-time carers if she stays at mine.' She felt a familiar surge of frustration. 'I could try the agencies again. Get a rota going?'

'No.' Lily shook her head.

'It wouldn't be so bad.'

'No.' Lily sat up straight. 'It's just as expensive, and besides - you've done enough.'

Zoe knew she could never do enough. Not to make up for all those years of shutting her mum out.

Lily ran a hand through her hair as the argument over the chair raged behind them.

'Mum would cause chaos in here.'

'I know. She'd be in that flowery chair in seconds and it would take a crane to get her out.' She peered over her shoulder at the two residents, still locked in heated combat. 'There might be bloodshed.'

Nancy came back, having instructed one of the staff to solve the chair war.

'Would you like to see one of the personal suites?'

'Yes please.' They might as well now they were here.

They followed Nancy as she led them to a sunny walkway that ran from the lounge round the rest of the building. There were pine handrails along the sides, and the whole length of it was warm and light. Outside, the garden was waking up after the winter – crocuses and snowdrops ran down to the green lawns, and Zoe could see a gardener mowing the grass on a small red tractor, his broad grin showing that he had definitely found his calling in life.

Mum would love this garden.

She tried to quell the thought, but it kept coming back.

Mum, who loved pruning and bonfires and pulling potatoes out of the ground and serving them half an hour later with parsley from the garden and a knob of butter. Mum, who loved planting and watering and the wet weight of earth between her fingers. Here, in this garden, she would thrive.

She might even be happy for a moment or two.

Tears glazed her eyes.

Lily stopped and whispered in her ear. 'Are you thinking what I'm thinking?'

Zoe gulped. 'That we're going to have to kidnap a royal?'

Lily grinned. 'Exactly.'

'And we're going to have to talk to Mum?'

'Yes.' Lily nodded. 'We are.'

They carried on until they came to a cream door with a glass box attached to the wall just outside it.

Lily pointed towards it. 'What's that?'

Nancy smiled. 'That's a memory box.'

'A what?'

'It's to help residents find their rooms. Sometimes it becomes more and more difficult for them to read their own names.' She bent down and picked up a feather from the floor as Zoe remembered her mum's pen poised over the cheque. Her eyes searching for answers. The way she'd put the pen down and walked away when none came.

Nancy straightened up again. 'So we have these boxes – cabinets, really – and residents can put whatever they want inside. The lady who used to have this suite had a feather boa in hers. From when she lived in Paris in the fifties.'

'I see.' A box for a life. It wasn't enough.

'I wonder what Mum would choose.' Lily's voice was a whisper.

Zoe wiped a tear away. 'Gardening gloves, probably. And Monkey.' She bit back a sob.

Lily's voice wobbled. 'And that God-awful photo of us on the beach when we were little.'

It was a relief to laugh. 'The one where I decided to hit you with the spade just as Dad took the picture?'

'And I started bleeding?' Lily grinned. 'Yep. That one. She loved it. Always pride of place on the mantelpiece, no matter where we tried to hide it.'

Nancy opened the door. 'This is one of our garden suites. There's a living room, a bedroom and a bathroom, with alarms and panic buttons in every room.'

They walked in, breathing in the quiet. It was beautiful. The living room had a shining wooden coffee table and cream walls. Double doors opened out on to the most glorious flower bed Zoe had ever seen. Whites and blues and yellows were everywhere as the world came to life again after the winter.

'We have light sensors to track movement, and residents are monitored centrally by our team. They can be here in seconds if needed, yet our residents still feel that they have their independence.' Nancy walked to the windows and sat in a chair while they looked around.

Zoe went into the bedroom, feeling the peace entering her bones. The orthopaedic hospital bed had a duvet and pillows piled up at its foot. Light flooded over the thick carpet. The bedside table. The cupboards for Mum's things. And there was a chair by the window. She could imagine Mum curled up in it, staring at the changing seasons.

It was a place where she might – just might – find peace.

Zoe looked at Lily, who returned her silent nod.

She turned to Nancy. 'Do you have any vacancies?'

'Not at the moment.' Nancy smiled. 'But would you like me to put your mum on the waiting list?'

Zoe and Lily looked at each other. 'Yes. Yes please.'

'Then let's go to the office and we can get the paperwork started.'

As they followed Nancy down the sunlit walkway towards the office, Zoe wondered what their mum would say. How they could afford it.

But she thought of the anguish on Mum's face last night, and she knew that they had to try.

Cosy flat

15th June, 2009

Dear Zoe,

Happy twenty-fifth, golden girl. At your age, I was
about to become a knackered mum, getting through
the days supported by cheese and pickle sandwiches
and a hell of a lot of Nescafé. But you? I'm guessing
you're a bit more organised. Rumour has it you have
an ISA (Lily told me that). That's grown up. Right there.

I saw Alistair and his wife Wendy at Hugo and
Andrea's wedding today. Sod's law dictated that I was
newly single, of course, so there I was all on my
lonesome when they appeared in the doorway to the
marquee. Bloody hell. They were bathed in sunlight
while I was trying to remove a canapé stain (damn you,
sun-dried tomato) from my very white River Island
jacket. I have a feeling she was probably in Dior or
some other designer I can't pronounce, let alone
afford.

She is pretty, isn't she? Wendy. That lovely shiny hair,
those big eyes, and so petite and demure and calm.
Honestly, I could actively feel myself sweating as they
came over. I quickly finished my champagne for a bit
of Dutch courage. Alistair was looking pained – no
surprise there – but she had a lovely smile on her face
and was doing a very good impression of someone
who was genuinely pleased to see me. Strange.

Mags had said they might be there but I don't think I

really took it on board. I looked around for her but she was off on the dance floor with Dominic. So I took a deep breath and waited for my ex-husband and Wendy, who used to model tights for Pretty Polly. Looking at the way she glided along in her heels, I have to say I could see why.

When they got to me, Wendy made small talk about the bride's dress (big) and the cake (big) – are you spotting a trend?! – while Alistair stood there doing an excellent impression of a hat stand. He has aged, hasn't he? The lines are cut deep around his eyes and I'm pretty sure his ears weren't that hairy last time I saw him. On the rare occasions his eyes met mine, I saw him wondering what he had ever seen in me. But *I* remember. The way his eyes followed me round that night. His hand on my arm and the passion in his eyes as he kissed me and asked me for my number.

Anyway, he started talking about you, about how much you're enjoying doing web development for some agency or other – I always forget details nowadays – and how you're so eloquent and competent, and all at once, as I stood there with the smell of marquee and wedding roses all around me, I found that I was crying. Bloody hell, how embarrassing. Alistair panicked and practically smothered me with his hand-kerchief before finding the nearest glass of wine, so poor Wendy had to take the lead. She took me to the loos and mopped me up. And as she chatted away, I wondered how he had done it. How he had convinced this kind-hearted woman to fall for him.

I was mortified, of course. I sat there sipping my water and hiccuping until the sobs had calmed down. I smiled at her and somehow I knew that she understood how much I'd lost. Then we went back to the party, and as Alistair put his arm round her shoulders and started to lead her away, I heard him say, 'She's been on the booze again. Sorry, darling.'

It hurt – of course it did – but I didn't say anything. No point. I have lost a daughter. And nothing hurts more than that. So I just sat there at my table. Alone. Thinking of you. Wishing I knew how to step out from behind the anger and the hurt and get through to you.

Next year, maybe.

All my love,
Mum x

Nineteen

'Yeah, but I could get a loan against the business.'
'Would that bring in enough, though?' She crept
back down the hall and put a blanket over her sleeping
mum, tucking it tight around her body.

'Well, we're doing a lot better now, but . . . no, probably
not.' Zoe felt an increasing sense of hopelessness. 'I don't
suppose you've got any spare cash lying around, have
you?'

Lily sighed. 'I work in a nursery now. The most I've got
lying around is a loaf of economy bread.' Zoe heard the
hiss of a can opening. Diet Coke. Lily's favourite. 'Fuck
it. I'm doing the lottery.'

'Me too.' Zoe put her keys down and peered at the
carrier bag that was waiting for her on the kitchen table.

She had spent so much time trying to make the numbers
add up. Playing with figures that weren't on her side. She
had put absolutely all of her savings into her company.
And the salary she paid herself would only keep Mum at
Woodleigh for about a week and a half.

'Oh well.' She shrugged off her jacket. 'There aren't any
spaces yet anyway, so even if we were billionaires we
wouldn't be able to get her in there.'

'True.' There was a brief pause. 'When are we going to
talk to her?'

'I don't know.' Zoe had tried to start so many times,

but her mum's distress levels were currently set to 'epic' and she didn't want to cause any more problems.

'I want to be there.'

'Of course, Lil. How about next Saturday?'

'Sure. And neither of us can cop out of it. OK?'

'OK.' Zoe grabbed a glass and filled it from the tap. She heard a door closing at Lily's end. Her sister shouted a hello and then came back on. 'Gary's home. Can I call you later?'

'Sure.' Zoe put her phone down and saw that a Post-it was stuck to the outside of the bag.

She knew that handwriting.

Jamie.

She dashed around the flat, allowing herself to pretend for a second that he might still be there – that he had somehow squeezed himself into a kitchen cupboard or into her wardrobe when in all reality he had probably dropped the bag and run away as fast as he could.

She had been so busy recently, she had barely had time to breathe, but her brain had still found far too many opportunities to revisit the painful memory of seeing Jamie and that girl. It was particularly fond of replaying it in slow motion at around 2 a.m. Zoe lay there, trapped, reliving her plummeting panic as they had pulled apart. The embarrassment on Jamie's face. The pain of knowing that he had moved on.

She walked slowly back into the kitchen and sank into a chair to read the message.

Hi, Zoe. Your mum called me to help her with the shower (she'd forgotten how to switch it off). Found these and thought you might like to read them? J.

She reached out and touched the plastic. Part of her hoped it was a gift. Part of her dreaded that it would just be a pair of tights he had found tangled up with his T-shirts or something. A hairbrush or a lipstick or one of the crime novels she loved and he resolutely refused to read.

Come on, Zo. She took a deep breath and looked inside the bag. It contained the purple box she had put all her treasures in when she was little. It had *Zoe* written on it in childish letters, and was decorated with silver leaves, intertwining in spirals across the lid. In one corner she had clearly decided to colour them in, and had unfortunately chosen orange. She smiled to herself, remembering how she had loved choosing a colour from a fresh pack of felt tips and gleefully finding a fresh piece of paper or cardboard to decorate.

Her heart quickened as she pulled the box out of the bag and set it on the table. She wondered about pouring a glass of wine. She wondered about tea. And then she realised she couldn't wait. Not even for the minute it would take her to get the glass out and open the bottle. No. She had to open this now.

She carefully took off the lid and put it to one side.

Inside she saw letters. Lots of letters. Scrawling, looping handwriting covering sheet upon sheet of plain A4. One had a red wine stain in the top corner. Another looked like it might have a dash of cigarette ash over the date. But that didn't matter. They were all in her mum's writing. And they were all for her.

She read the first paragraph of the letter on the very top of the pile. *So. You made it to one. Thank God for that. There were times when I wondered if you would.* She sat up straighter and kept reading as her mum told her about the past before Zoe's memories began. She read about nearly being born in the office, about her dad's joy on seeing her for the first time, about the way she slept in his arms and how her mum loved watching her when she slept. She sat at the table and didn't move an inch, lost in the love bound into every word, racing through line after line after line. until she reached the concluding paragraphs. *You blink at me with those wonderful catlike eyes, and you smile, and I can see that your heart is full of me. I can't wait for the day when you will say 'Mum'. When you will say 'I love you'.*

God knows, I love you too.

Zoe sat back and traced the writing with her fingers. Her eyes were heavy with tears. She dashed them away and picked up another. Then another. She read the story of a woman whose life hadn't been everything she had expected or hoped for, but who fought for the people she loved. Pride shone out of every page. She read about breaking aeroplanes and overwatering plants and then onwards through her childhood. Digging holes to Australia. Planting cress in yoghurt pots. Protecting Lily in the playground. Phrases leapt out that brought a sob to her throat. *I don't care about anything but the cord that ties us together. One to another. Mother to daughter.* And another. *My talented, big-hearted daughter.*

She read about her dad leaving the army, cinema trips, and then that awful night with Charlie. Her mouth was dry. She knew where this was heading. And she dreaded to see what her mum would say next.

And then she got there. Her sixteenth birthday. Her mum and dad's bed. Oh God. She could still feel the flush of shame. *But then I looked at you. So scared. All grown up and so damn angry with me, and yet still my little girl.* Zoe's throat tightened as she read on into that terrible night. *I hit him. Straight across the face.*

Go, Mum.

And here in her mum's words and sentences, she read

about how much she had been loved and about how much she was still loved. How her mum had been there at her graduation. How she had hoped to be forgiven, year on lonely year, settled in the same town where Zoe was living her life, doing her best to forget that the woman who had given birth to her even existed.

Her mum had never left her. Had never walked away.

No. Zoe had done that for the two of them. And now she was about to do something even worse.

She laid her head down on top of the letters, gathering them to her as if trying to breathe in the heart of her mum and take strength from it.

'Hello, Zo-bear.'

Zoe looked up, so lost in the past that for a moment she wondered where she was.

'Mum.' And before she could think or say anything else, she stood up and hugged her. The kind of hug that she would remember for the rest of her life. The smell of Imperial Leather. The softness of her mum's hair on her cheek. One moment. Here. In the kitchen, with the smell of curry wafting in from next door and her mum's memories scattered across the kitchen table. 'I'm so sorry.'

'What for?'

'Everything.'

'Have you eaten all the meringues again?' Her mum pulled away and frowned at her.

'No.' Even on this they couldn't connect. Zoe exhaled in frustration.

Then she got a surprise. 'I'm sorry too.' Her mum pulled her close again. 'For the terrible things I said. I was just trying to help.'

'I know, Mum.' Zoe squeezed her tight. It was such a relief to understand. 'Thank you.'

'Now.' Gina's knee clicked as she sat down in a chair. 'Tea, please. And one of those round things with the chocolate on.'

Zoe opened the biscuit tin and put it on the table.

Her mum took two and chewed happily.

'Do you like these?' She pointed at the letters.

'I love them.' It didn't matter how Jamie had found them. It just mattered that she would always have them now. Her mum's side of the story. 'I can't believe you wrote to me every single year.'

'Lily, too. I think I wrote to her too.' Gina pulled the biscuit tin towards her again and chose a chocolate digestive. McVitie's profits must have quadrupled since she had moved in.

Zoe put the mugs down on the table.

'Do you think we can just sit and talk for a bit? About when I was little?'

Her mum didn't need another invitation. She sat back in her chair, chewing thoughtfully on her biscuit.

'Do you remember when we taught Lily to walk?'

'No.'

'You must do.' Her mum was alight with the past. 'She was wearing those bumblebee trousers she loved. And you were there with a plastic beaker with Bagpuss on it.'

Zoe smiled. She remembered that beaker.

Her mum chuckled. 'I was at the other end of the room with Lily in the middle of us. And she loved us both so much that she couldn't decide which way to go. In the end she staggered towards you. She chose you.' She gave a contented sigh. 'You two.'

She looked around. 'Is Lily here?'

'No.'

'Oh.' Her mum sipped her tea and smiled contentedly. Obviously Zoe had finally learnt how to add enough sugar.

'She's with Gary tonight.'

'That's good.' She could see that her mum had drifted away.

Zoe looked at the letters and smiled.

Her mum leant towards her, eyes suddenly clear.

'Thank you, Zo-bear.'

'What?'

'Thank you for looking after me.'

Zoe thought of Woodleigh Place and felt a stab of shame. 'I . . .'

'You're being so wonderful.'

Oh God. Zoe had to tell her. Explain that she didn't know how to make her happy any more. What to do for the best. Now. Right now. She swallowed her tea and got ready. 'Mum . . .'

But her mum had already started talking again. Zoe listened as she described saluting tanks on the base and trips to the sandpit and Lego tunnels. She wanted to grab all the stories that still lived in her mum's head. To put up walls and doors and nail them in, until she had stopped the constant dribble of times and faces and places into the void.

Her mum took another biscuit and Murgatroyd jumped on to her lap. 'Everything changes, doesn't it? Look at you. Such a big girl now. So grown up.'

'Yes.' Zoe thought about the girl described in the letters and wondered how to get that happiness back. She had grown up on the pages in front of her on the table. From 'Twinkle Twinkle' to Oasis. From Monkey to a fake fur coat. From joy to fear.

She felt an ache of loss so intense she wanted to cry.

'Don't be sad.' Her mum shook her head. 'We'll go to the park tomorrow and it'll all be OK again.'

'Yes.' Zoe swallowed her tears as the doorbell rang. 'I'll just answer that.'

She got up. It had better not be that guy trying to hawk double glazing again. This time she really would slam the door in his face.

She opened the door.

And there he was.

'Dad?'

'Zoe.' He blocked the evening sunlight in his grey suit and purple tie. He was holding his briefcase and looking unusually ill at ease.

'Mum's here.' Zoe folded her arms. 'Do you still want to come in?'

'Yes.' He hovered on the doorstep. 'Please. If that's all right?'

'I suppose so.' She frowned, remembering his behaviour on their last two meetings. 'But you'd better not have a go at her this time.'

'I won't. I promise.' He stepped inside and put his briefcase down. 'I actually came to apologise.'

Zoe had to check she had heard him right. 'Apologise?'

'Yes.'

'As in saying sorry?'

'Yes.' He glared at her. 'You're not going to make it easy, then?'

Zoe shook her head. 'No, Dad, I'm not.'

'I see.' He took his jacket off and hung it on a peg. 'I suppose that's fair enough. You're still angry. About Sally.'

'Nope.' Zoe shook her head again. 'Not about her. God knows, none of us behaved very well back then, did we?'

'I want to explain, Zoe. About her.'

'It's OK, really . . .'

'We worked together. And things with Gina were difficult.'

'Dad . . .'

'You're right.' He held up his hands. 'There's no excuse. Gina was devastated and I always hated myself because of it, but I never really knew how to tell her that.' He blinked at her and she saw the tiredness beneath his tan. She had missed him. The solid comfort of him.

But she wasn't quite ready to tell him that yet.

'Seeing her again. Knowing that she still remembered such a bad thing about me. I felt terrible.'

'It's OK, Dad. We don't need to talk about it. I don't really want to know.'

'OK.' He peered into the living room. 'Is she in there?'

'No. She's in the kitchen, spending some quality time with the biscuit tin.'

'Right.' He coughed. 'Then can I just have a quick word in here?'

Zoe led him into the living room and stood with her arms folded. He sat down in one of her chairs and she remembered other happier times they had shared. Coming back from their Sunday runs and talking business over smoothies and porridge. Dinners. Films.

They hadn't done any of that since the non-wedding.

She sat down next to him.

'Dad, what really upsets me is that you shouldn't have been so harsh. At the lunch. Mum's ill. Don't you get that?'

He hung his head and didn't answer.

All action and no words. Her mum had summed it up well in her letters.

'Why did you come here, Dad?'

He straightened his watch. 'To try to explain to you, though I can see I haven't done a very good job. And to tell you I went to see Simon.'

Zoe blinked. 'What?'

He still wouldn't look her in the eye. He stared at the thick cream rug on the floor, jangling the change in his pocket. 'There were things I had to say.'

'Oh my God, you didn't punch him or anything, did you?'

He flicked his eyes towards her. 'No, Zoe. I'm in my fifties now. My Rocky days are well and truly behind me.'

Zoe pictured that blond hair. That caramel skin. She felt absolutely nothing now when she thought of him.

She looked at her dad and felt a rush of affection. She could imagine him now. Face serious. Eyes glinting as he looked at Simon. 'What did you say to him?'

No answer. She could see a muscle flickering in his cheek. 'Dad? How did you even find him?'

'I still have my contacts.'

'Really?'

He gave a dry laugh. 'No. Not really. He runs a company now. In Jersey. I just looked it up on LinkedIn.'

'And?'

'And if he hadn't had a cast on his leg, I think he would have run away.'

Zoe giggled, and Dad's eyes darted towards hers. 'I laid into him. For taking advantage of you. For lying. For not being the man I thought he was.'

'Wow.' Zoe smiled. 'He must have got the shock of his life.'

'Yes. I think he did.' Her dad's face softened for a second, before settling back into sadness. He took her hand. 'God, I'm so sorry, Zoe. For not seeing it. For not protecting you. For blaming your mum for so much when all the time it was my fault too.'

She saw the pain on his face and squeezed his hand. 'It's over now.'

'But I needed to say it.'

'I know.' She reached across and hugged him. 'I know.'

She breathed him in, feeling some of the tension of the last few months fall away.

'Now, Zoe.'

'Yes?'

'Can we stop talking about feelings now?'

She pulled away and saw the grin on his face.

'Only if you want to come through and see Mum.'

'Yes.' He nodded. 'I'd like that.'

'Good.' Zoe stood up.

'Oh, and one more thing.' Her dad reached out a hand to stop her.

'What is it?'

His eyes held hers. 'Lily talked to Wendy. Wendy talked to me. She's had an idea. About Gina.'

'What idea?'

'That we should pay for whatever care she needs.'

'What?'

'For your mum. For whatever she needs.'

'No. She wouldn't want you to.'

'I know.' His voice was clear and firm. 'But I don't care. It's the least she deserves after everything she's been through. You know, she was right when we were having tea. I didn't know how to let her in. I just blamed her instead. I'd never seen it from her side before.'

As Zoe opened her mouth to reply, she heard a word she hadn't often heard from him. 'Please?'

She thought for a second, weighing it up in her mind. Then she nodded. 'But only if I contribute too. Thank you.'

He didn't need to say anything in return.

She tugged him towards the door. 'Now can we stop

all this emotional stuff and go and play Pop Up Pirate with Mum?'

'Yes.' He nodded vigorously. 'God, yes. Is she still a demon at it?'

'Yep. Nothing changes.'

'Everything changes.' Her dad started to walk down the corridor. 'But Gina and Pop Up Pirate will live on for ever.'

'True.' Zoe started to follow him, then stopped to tap out a message on her phone.

Thanks for the letters.

She pressed send and waited for a reply.

Nothing.

Then a bleep, just as she reached the kitchen. **Thought you'd like to hear your mum's side of the story. She showed me the box and I just passed it on. Hope it helped. J.**

Kind. Friendly. Nothing more.

Zoe put her phone down and went into the kitchen.

Cosy flat

15th June, 2011

Dear Zoe,

I stood outside your work last night. Not in a stalker
way – I just wanted to say happy birthday. This year was
going to be the year I finally spoke to you again. I'd
bought you a bracelet. Two strands intertwined in
delicate silver. I'd thought it might be you and Lily, but
instead I see now it might be you and him. You and the
man I saw.

You were standing there in a green raincoat, hair
swept up from your neck in a ponytail. You were bent
over your phone and I could see the concentration on
your face. I was across the street, about to say to hell
with it and come over. Just as I started walking,
someone called your name and you turned and your
face just lit up. It stopped me in my tracks.

There was a man heading over to you. He had
blond hair, a canvas satchel over one shoulder, and he
walked as if he might be able to hold his own on a
dance floor. I saw him resting a hand on your arm for
a second as you talked. Then you shrugged and
laughed and let him persuade you to go to the pub.

I wonder who he is. I wonder whether he's good
enough for you.

He'd bloody better be.

As you set off, he put his arm around you and
kissed your hair. You turned to him, face glowing, and

my heart just sang. I've always hoped you'd meet someone. Someone who could finally put Simon behind you and make you want to live.

I put the bracelet back in my bag and headed home, warm in the knowledge that you were happy. Maybe I'll meet him one day. I don't know.

I hope so.

Happy twenty-seventh birthday.

All my love,

Mum x

Twenty

'Oh my God, is this you?' Mandy held up a picture from yet another one of the old photo albums they had found in Gina's living room. Zoe brushed the dust off her face with the back of her hand and went over to have a look.

'Yes.' She looked at the smiling girl dressed up in a purple curtain and gold sandals, a plastic tiara askew in her very red hair. She was thrusting her tummy forward and beaming at the camera in a way that showed she had lost all of her front teeth. 'That's me.'

'Wow.' Mandy looked at the faded snapshot in absolute wonder. 'I can't believe you always refuse to wear fancy dress now. You're a natural.'

Mags came by, a brown box in her arms. 'That's nothing.' She grinned. 'You should have seen her when she was Chewbacca.'

Mandy's eyes were wide.

Zoe shook her head. 'No, Mags. Not that picture. Anything but that. Please?'

Mags put the box down and knelt on the floor, her navy T-shirt riding up over her skinny jeans. 'I think it's in this red one.' She gave Zoe a glance of pure mischief. 'You should have let me have the last slice of cake earlier. Revenge is sweet, Zoe Whittaker.'

'You can have my last Rolo.' Zoe attempted to look

enticing as she held it out. She had to brush off a large piece of fluff. 'Mmm. Sweet chocolatey goodness.'

'Don't want it.' Mags stuck her tongue out. 'Besides, it's one of Gina's favourite pictures.' She turned back to Mandy. 'She must take it with her.'

As she turned the pages, the sheets of plastic protecting the photos crackled between her fingers. Zoe debated inventing an urgent call. A need for more milk. Anything to get out of here.

'Here it is!'

She put her head in her hands. 'Oh God.'

Mandy squealed. 'Is that eyeliner all over your nose? And your eyes?'

Zoe mustered what dignity she could and turned back to dusting the bookshelves. 'Yes.'

Mags snorted. 'She used up the whole bloody tube. Gina was livid.'

Mandy grinned. 'And is that a sheepskin rug you're wearing?'

'Yes.' Zoe sprayed some more Mr Sheen. 'I think it was pretty creative of me, actually.'

Mandy peered closer. 'If you say so. You didn't actually glue that wool to your face, did you?'

Zoe dusted harder. 'No. I used Sellotape.'

'She planned ahead even then.' Mags looked at her teasingly. 'It still hurt, though, didn't it? I can remember you screaming as Gina pulled it off.'

Zoe sighed. 'OK, OK, enough trips down memory lane, thanks. I'm starting to forget why we asked you lot to come round and help in the first place.'

Mags was still gazing at the picture. 'She had a rash for a week afterwards.' She grinned. 'God, we had some fun, didn't we?'

'Yes.' They held each other's gaze for a second, before Mags closed the album with a snap and turned away. All day it had been like this. Laughter to tears. Joy to grief.

The more they sorted and tidied, the more Zoe remembered the good times. The hugs. The adventures. And all the while, time ticked relentlessly onwards and Lily's car waited outside, ready to drive Mum to her new home.

'You OK, babe?' Mandy squeezed her shoulder.

Zoe turned to her and grimaced. 'It's been a long weekend.'

'Nearly there now.' Mandy folded her into a hug as Zoe thought of how this place had looked when they had arrived yesterday morning. The smell of dusty air. The stuff piled in every corner and on every surface.

They had barely stopped. Opening drawers to discover old school exercise books full of wobbly handwriting telling stories of 'What I did in my summer holidays' or 'Why I love my daddy'. Finding boxes full of babygros and soft pink blankets that made Zoe's heart ache with longing.

There had been so much more. A picture of Mum and Dad tucking into a cheese fondu, heads thrown back in uproarious laughter. And then a sunny snap of the four of them squeezed on to the bench outside their house at the base in Germany. All in flares and stripy tops, with Mum, Zoe and Lily sharing the same misguided pudding-bowl haircut. Zoe could still remember Mum placing the brown bowl on her head and literally cutting round it until it was done.

She carried on with her cleaning until she realised the shelf couldn't be any more spotless, then started on the one below. There were stains on the pine left by teacups or plates that her mum had clearly forgotten about, as they were practically welded on when they had arrived here. All the china was now piled up in the sink, ready for a final wash. Her mum's clothes were divided into piles – charity shop, recycling, and a much smaller one for Woodleigh Place. Gardening clothes. Tracksuits. The jeans and T-shirts Gina had loved all her life.

Zoe thought back to the conversation she and Lily had eventually managed to have with their mum a month before. They had cooked spaghetti bolognese with lots of Worcester sauce, just the way Mum liked it. They had bought the shop-grated Cheddar she loved. And then, in an increasingly rare moment of coherence, she had looked at them. No fog. No confusion. Just a mother asking her daughters for the truth.

'What is it, girls? Why are you looking at me like that?'

They had stared at her in the evening light.

'Come on.' She put her chin on her hand, and waited, at once so familiar and yet so unknown. 'It can't be as bad as the time you broke my bike.'

'It wasn't our fault!' Zoe looked at Lily for confirmation. 'The brakes were dodgy.'

Her mum raised her eyes skywards. 'Yes. You kept saying that. But they weren't.'

'No. But—'

Zoe felt Lily's hand on her arm and realised she was getting off topic.

'Sorry.' She hung her head.

Lily went first. 'Mum, we're worried about you.'

Their mum picked up the last shred of spaghetti from her plate.

'I don't know why.'

Lily continued. 'Last week. When you left the front door open. Anyone could have come in.'

Gina smiled indulgently. 'But they didn't.'

'Yes, but—'

'It's nice to be friendly.' She nodded as if that solved the problem.

It was Zoe's turn. 'And you get so scared, Mum.'

'No I don't.'

Zoe thought back to that morning at 4 a.m. The veins standing out on her mum's neck as she strained to see out into the night. The clutch of her fingers on Zoe's arm.

Of course her mum didn't remember. That was Zoe's burden.

'We just want you to be safe, Mum.'

'I am safe.' Gina spied another strand of spaghetti on Lily's plate and popped it into her mouth, chewing and swallowing with evident enjoyment. 'You're looking after me, Zo-bear.'

The trust on her face killed Zoe's appetite off for good.

'But I'm worried, Mum. I don't know how to help you.'

'You're always worried.'

'No. This is different.' Zoe tried to connect. 'I'm worried I can't look after you. I don't know how to make you happy.'

'I don't need you to look after me. And I am happy.'

Zoe stared pleadingly at Lily. She couldn't speak the truth. She couldn't say '*Mum, you're getting worse and we can't stop it and it's breaking my heart.*' Guilt made her brain sluggish. She wished there was a map for Alzheimer's. A compass to navigate by. She wanted to know that if she did X and Y it would equal Z. Instead there was just guesswork and relentless anxiety and a constant sense that she wasn't doing enough to save the person who was disappearing right in front of her eyes.

Lily tried a different tack. 'Mum, will you come out with us tomorrow? There's a place we'd like you to see.'

Their mum's eyes glinted. 'Of course. But only if we

have lunch.' She realised the pan was still on the hob and stood up to see if there was any more spaghetti in there. 'I do need my food.'

'We can see that.' Lily laughed.

'Where are we going?' Gina spooned more spaghetti into her mouth.

'It's a house. In Surrey.'

'A house?'

Zoe nibbled her lip. 'Yes. It's got beautiful gardens.'

'Are there daffodils?'

'Yes, Mum.' Lily was gripping her glass so tightly, her knuckles were tinged with white.

'Good.' Their mum smacked her lips as she ate the final piece of spaghetti.

'And there are some rooms we'd like you to see too.'

'Why?'

Zoe finally managed to speak. 'We just want to see if you like it there. That's all.'

She hoped this wasn't a lie. They were just following Dr Jones's instructions. Don't say too much. Take things one step at a time. Bite-size chunks. She hoped this wouldn't haunt her at 5.30 a.m. as she lay in her flat, breathing in the silence left by her mum's absence.

The next day, they had taken her to Woodleigh. And the week after that. There had been tears. And protests. But the garden had always won in the end.

Zoe came back to the present to find she was polishing the shelf to within an inch of its life.

Lily appeared in the doorway. 'You do know the flat's going to be professionally cleaned, don't you? You can probably stop now.'

'All right, all right.' Zoe picked up the Mr Sheen and her duster and put them into the cleaning bucket.

Bruno popped his head in from the hallway. 'You should see her at work. She even cleans the coasters with that stuff.'

Zoe hit him with the duster. 'Shut up! You're just as bad. That bloody coffee machine is so shiny I frequently use it to put my make-up on.'

'What a pair. The hours must just fly by.' Lily put her hands on her hips and smiled. 'OK. Washing-up's done. Are we nearly finished?'

'Yes.' Mandy got to her feet. 'This is the final box for the charity shop.'

Silence fell as they all realised this was it. The end. All that living and only one carload to show for it. Two suitcases, a rucksack, a pair of wellies and three cardboard boxes of photos and mementoes, topped with the jade necklace Alistair had given Gina when they had first met all those years ago, when shoulder pads were de rigueur and Viennetta was considered a sophisticated dessert.

Zoe and Lily looked at each other.

'So . . .' Lily drew Zoe into a hug.

The others tactfully melted away, leaving the two sisters together.

Zoe spoke into Lily's hair. 'I'm not sure I can do this, Lil.'

'Me neither.' Zoe could feel her sister's tears wetting her neck.

They clung together for a minute. Two. Then Lily pulled away and blew her nose.

'Come on, sis. Time to go.'

Zoe wiped her eyes. 'We can move her. If she hates it. Right?'

'Yes.' Lily nodded. 'Of course. But remember. She loves the lunches.'

Zoe tried to smile. 'True. She'll be the chef's best friend by tonight.' She knew she wouldn't sleep a wink thinking of her mum waking in unfamiliar surroundings, without anyone she knew to help. She had already emailed several pages of instructions to Woodleigh Place, and she knew she would be sending more.

None of it helped her to feel better. None of it could lessen the overwhelming feeling that she had let Mum down.

Bruno came in and put his arms round her. 'You'll visit her soon, won't you?'

'Definitely.'

He gave her a squeeze. 'Quite right too. She is your mum, after all. She's had a lot to put up with. Payback time.'

'Oi!' She thumped him on the arm, unable to tell him how grateful she was that he was here.

'Abuse.' He rubbed through his shirtsleeve. 'Did you see that, Lily? Abuse!'

'Oh be quiet.' Zoe tutted. 'You're so am-dram sometimes.'

Lily took her arm. 'Shall we go and see how she is?'

'OK.' Zoe led the way to the bedroom. The bed had been stripped, but Mum had taken a pillow from the pile by the door and was lying flat on her back, staring at the ceiling with her hands folded across her stomach. Her legs were crossed at the ankles and her red plaid shirt was unbuttoned at the neck.

'Are you OK, Mum?'

Her smile was calm and dreamy. 'Yes.' She leant up on one elbow. 'Are we going somewhere?'

'We are.' Zoe sat on one side of her, Lily on the other. 'We're going to get in the car and go for a drive.'

Bite-size chunks.

337

Zoe felt so dishonest.

She looked around at the faded walls, where the outlines of the pictures Mum had put up were still clearly visible. Their school photo had been by the door. Zoe going to university had been by the bedside lamp. And Lily giggling in the paddling pool had hung just to the left of the wardrobe. They were all packed. All ready to go.

The flat was just walls and carpets now. Just a building waiting patiently for a new person to come and give it life.

'Can we play my music in the car?'

'Of course.'

'Good.' Mum pressed her lips together, clearly satisfied. 'And you're both coming, aren't you? I don't want to go without you.'

The love on her face took Zoe's breath away.

'Yes, Mum. We're both coming.' She nodded.

She heard a loud sniff from Lily. 'There's no getting rid of us.'

'That's nice.' Mum pushed herself up to sitting. 'I like it when we go out together.'

Lily pulled out her car keys. 'Shall we go, then?'

As Zoe helped her mum to stand, Gina's forehead creased in that furrow she had seen so often over the last few weeks.

'Where are we going? Are we going to the beach?'

Zoe shook her head. 'No, Mum.'

'Oh.' She dropped her head and pouted like a toddler being forced to share her favourite toy.

'But we will go there. Soon.' Zoe looked over her mum's head to Lily. They needed to move quickly. To get this over with. This pain was too much. They had to get in the car and go – they could do their crying later.

But when they walked out into the corridor, they found they had a farewell committee waiting. Zoe had to bite deep into her lip to stop her tears. Because there they all were: Bruno, Mags, Mandy – all waiting to say a goodbye that felt like it would be for ever, even though Woodleigh Place was only thirty minutes away.

Her mum took them all in, and concern bit deep into her face. Her hands started worrying at her top. She knew this was a big moment. She knew something significant was on its way.

So naturally she did what she had always done. She dug in. Before Zoe could stop her, she grabbed hold of the door handle and fell to her knees.

'I'm not going.'

Shit. Zoe put a hand on her shoulder. 'Come on, Mum.'

Her anxiety spiralled so quickly now. 'I'm not leaving. You can't make me.'

Zoe took a deep breath. 'Mum? We need to get in the car now.'

'NO.'

Zoe looked at Lily and the two of them tried again.

'We've got honey sandwiches.'

'And crisps.'

'And Wagon Wheels.'

Zoe felt sick with guilt as she gently pulled her mum's hand, trying to coax her to move.

Her mum was swearing now, her face crinkling as she resisted. 'Don't. Want. To.'

This was getting them nowhere.

And then the music started from the car down below. Keyboard. Plucked strings. That rough-edged voice singing, '*It was a theme she had/On a scheme he had . . .*'

'China in Your Hand'.

Instantly her mum brightened. 'Oh. I love this song.' She let go of the doorknob. 'Where are we going again?'

Zoe saw Mandy coming back in and mouthed a heart-felt thank-you.

She led her mum to the front door and turned.

'Bruno? Will you drop the keys to the landlord?'

'Yes, boss!' He saluted.

'And Mandy, can you take the final boxes back for us?'

'Of course.' She nodded. 'Now bugger off and stop worrying.' She pulled Zoe close. 'And we'll all be in the pub later, OK?'

Zoe let herself rest for a second on her friend's shoulder. The last few days had been so miserable. Packing. Arranging. Terminating bills and contracts so that her mum would start her new life clean. Fresh. Ready.

She didn't want to think what she would have to be ready for.

'Thanks, Mandy. Make sure they have gin. Lots of gin.'

'Of course.' A final squeeze. 'I'll get a bottle. And . . .'

'Yes?'

Mandy couldn't quite meet her eyes. 'Do you want me to invite Jamie? Tonight?'

'Why would you do that?'

'I just wondered.'

'No.' Zoe felt a wave of panic. Not him and his new girlfriend. Not after all this. 'Definitely not.'

'OK.' Mandy held up her hands. 'Message received and understood.'

Gina was outside now, waving merrily at Mr Ames, who was standing on his tiny balcony enjoying the afternoon sun on his face.

Mandy watched her. 'She's quite a lady, your mum, isn't she?'

Zoe smiled. 'Yes. Yes, she is.'

She turned and followed her mum and Lily down to the grey car waiting on the street below. Murgatroyd was already inside, asleep inside his carrier. Lily helped their mum to climb in and fasten her seat belt, and Zoe waved up at her friends as she slid into the back. She wondered what they would all look like in thirty years' time. Who would be married. Who would be divorced. Whether she and Lily would be following in their mum's footsteps and receding into their own misty worlds, locked away from those who loved them for ever. God, she hoped not.

Lily started the engine and beeped the horn. The group on the balcony waved down in reply. Zoe saw Mags putting a hand to her eyes, and Bruno and Mandy laced their arms around her, keeping her warm. Giving her comfort.

'Karma Chameleon' boomed through the speakers.

'I love this one!' Their mum started swaying from side to side.

And so they left. Driving slowly down the side road that was the beginning of her mum's journey to her new home. To a place with sunlight and a garden and kind faces and capable hands.

Zoe stared out of the window as the houses and play-grounds started to speed by. She thought about her mum dangling keys to so many homes, always talking about the good things that were going to happen in whatever place they had landed in this time. Unpacking the kettle. Starting again.

This time she had Lily and Zoe to help her. They would always make her feel loved, even as the fog descended and her world was reduced to the sun on her face and the roses growing outside her window.

For once, Zoe was certain. She knew what she had to do.

She leant forward and squeezed Mum's shoulder.

Then she started to sing along.

Cosy flat

15th June, 2012

Dear Zoe,
~~I'm worried about Lily.~~
~~So, I hear you're really happy now.~~
~~I've had enough of this.~~
I miss you. I've run out of words to say how much.

Love,
Mum x

Twenty-One

'Hello, Zoe.'

Zoe looked up from her screen, squinting against the sun that was beaming in through the window.

'Dad. Nice to see you.' She stood up and hugged him. 'I'm afraid I don't have Pop Up Pirate here.' She remembered how ecstatic he had been a few weeks ago when he had finally managed to win a game. Her mum's glee as she had thrashed them both time after time.

Mum. The flat seemed so quiet without her.

She sighed. 'Why are you here?'

'I've come to take you out for the day.'

'What?' She looked at him suspiciously. He was dressed in full office regalia. Dark navy suit. Polished brogues. And she knew without looking that his socks would be grey and wrinkle-free. 'Where to? The Stock Exchange?'

'No.' He coughed. 'It's a surprise.'

'Sorry, Dad.' She didn't have time. 'I'm working.'

She sensed Bruno's ears flapping as he sat on the sofa clicking through some graphics from a meeting the previous day.

'I know. But this is something special.'

'You're carrying a briefcase, Dad. It's not screaming adventure to me. And I do have a lot to do, so . . .'

In actual fact, she was struggling to concentrate. Ever since they had dropped Mum off the week before, she had been watching her phone like a hawk, waiting for Nancy to tell her that Gina had run away or was refusing to eat. But Nancy hadn't been in touch at all. And when Zoe called her mum every night after dinner, she was full of talk about the garden. The flowers. The trees. And the food. She was very happy about the food.

Sometimes, at the end of a call, she would ask when Zoe was going to pick her up. And Zoe would walk into the empty spare room and sit on the cold bed and say she would visit at the weekend and that they would have a day out soon. And she would keep saying it, hating herself more with every second, until her mum moved on to something else. She wondered if she would ever stop feeling like she had betrayed her.

Her dad shuffled from foot to foot. 'I'm afraid I have to insist.'

She shook her head. 'Dad, we've just landed a new client and we're working to a very limited time frame, so—'

'Zoe.'

She stopped. 'Yes?'

'You're not going to want to miss this.'

'Well, I don't have a choice. I can't come.' Zoe looked back at her screen. More emails were pouring in. She would be eighty-five before she managed to get through them all.

She felt a tap on her shoulder and turned to see Bruno hovering at her side. He spoke in the kind of stage whisper that was perfectly audible to her dad and probably to the people in the next office too.

'You should go with him, Zoe.'

'Bruno. That's really kind of you, but I need to stay here.'

'No.' He picked up her bag and held it out to her. 'You should go.'

345

'Why?' She was talking in the ridiculous whisper too now. 'We have so much work to do. I can't take any more time off.'

'I'll cover it.' He grinned. 'Besides, you know I like sitting in your chair. It's way more swivelly than mine.'

She couldn't help smiling. 'Just as well you don't say things like that in pitches.'

He drew himself up to his full height. 'Well I am very professional.' He winked. 'You'd better watch out. I'll be ousting you in a boardroom coup before too long.'

She laughed. 'Bruno, we *are* the boardroom. And there'll be no coups here, thank you very much.'

'Boring.' He pointed towards the door. 'Now run along and play.'

Zoe turned back to her dad. It didn't look like play was on the menu. A funeral, possibly. Not fun. God forbid.

'No.' She started to sit down, only to see that Bruno had whipped her chair away.

'Bruno!'

She could see a smile playing on his lips.

He arched an eyebrow. 'See you tomorrow.'

'But . . .'

'BYE.'

She sighed and picked up her bag. 'OK.' She turned towards the door, feeling a mixture of curiosity and irritation. 'Let's go.'

'Good.' Her dad turned and held the door open for her. 'I've got coffees in the car.'

'The car?'

'Yes.' He nodded. 'Thought it would be quicker than the train.' He led her to his grey Audi and the two of them got inside and set off.

*

Two hours later, they were stuck in a traffic jam just outside West Wittering.

'Well, this is a lovely day out.' Zoe drummed her fingers on the passenger door. 'We must do this more often.'

Her dad was doing his best to appear patient, but Zoe knew better. She could see the tension in his jaw. She noticed the tap of his fingers on the wheel as the exhaust fumes built around them.

Conversation on the journey had been stilted. Traffic had never brought out the best in her dad. She had made several attempts to establish where on earth they were going, only for him to refuse to tell her and start berating the English motorway system. They had sallied into Wendy's latest book group antics – some Dutch thriller that nobody had managed to finish – and finally segued into politics, which had made Zoe sorely tempted to open the car door and get out, even though they had just breached the road-works barrier and hit the heady heights of 50 mph.

Now Zoe was staring at the back of a particularly battered red lorry and wondering why on earth she had agreed to get into the car in the first place. She didn't need a day in a traffic jam. She needed to be at work.

They moved forward a foot. They would be very lucky to get anywhere by dawn.

'Dad.' Zoe decided it was time to try again.

'Yes?'

She wondered if she was brave enough to ask.

Sod it. He couldn't exactly go anywhere.

'Tell me about when you met Mum.'

Silence.

Well that went well. She folded her arms and leant back against the seat, vowing never to ask him anything ever again.

'OK.' His voice was husky. Hesitant. 'She was absolutely beautiful.'

'Really?' She swivelled and looked at him.

He nodded. 'I couldn't take my eyes off her when we met, I really couldn't. She had those big eyes and that amazing hair, and she was just the happiest and funniest girl in the room.' His blue eyes softened and his lips curved into a smile.

'I asked her to dance.' The car inched forward again. 'And she said yes and I felt like the luckiest man alive.' He shrugged. 'I hated dancing, but that night it was all I wanted to do.'

He was glowing. Sitting in a traffic jam recalling a night that had taken place well over thirty years ago.

'So it wasn't always so bad? You two. You were happy?'

'Yes.' He glanced at her and then back at the road. 'It was wonderful.'

Zoe felt a clutch in her chest as she realised that she used to light up like that when she talked about Jamie. She would get used to this hurt. She would. However long it took.

At least she had stopped counting the days since they had split up. That had to be progress.

She wanted her dad to keep talking. To help her to block Jamie out. 'So what happened? Why do you think it all went wrong?'

'Oh, I don't know.' Her dad broke off a piece of chocolate from the Dairy Milk on the dashboard between them. 'The army happened. Richard died. And Sally. . .' He coughed. 'We fought all the time after that. And I think it was hard for Gina. Being an army wife. Toeing the line.' He reached down and adjusted the heating. 'It wasn't her natural style. She always liked to speak her mind. And I was away so much that I couldn't help her as much as I might have.' He sighed. 'And when I came back, I was never the easiest. It's hard to adjust to being home. Not just for me – for her, too.'

'I see.' Zoe could remember it now. Her mum's nervous face as they waited for Dad to arrive. The way she tidied for a week beforehand, trying to make everything perfect for him. The joy in her eyes as she ran over and threw herself at him. And then her dad, face shadowed as he tried to forget whatever it was he had seen. Mags bent over the kitchen table after Richard died, crying all the tears her dad could never set free.

'I was always so happy to see you all.' Her dad touched her hand. Just once. Lightly. Lovingly. 'I loved seeing you and what you were getting up to. Building your forts or playing with your pretend sword or commanding your troops of soft toys into action.' He grinned. 'It made me so proud and so hopeful for what you might do with your lives one day.'

'Did you hope I'd join the army?'

'I did, yes.' He nodded. 'But then I left and I realised that I wanted you whole and real and here. Not out there in the Gulf or in some Afghan desert with sand in your eyes and no idea at all who the enemy was.' He got the car into second gear. 'I may have a funny way of showing it, but I just want you to be happy. Both of you.'

In the car next to them, a chocolate Labrador stuck its head out of the window, tongue lolling from its mouth. A motorbike whizzed past through the traffic, a girl with long brown hair riding pillion, a purple helmet on her head.

'Nearly there.' Her dad spun the wheel and they turned on to a smaller road, which snaked along the beachfront.

'Nearly where?' She cupped her chin in her hand and

stared out at the water. The blue sky arced above them. The sand was golden. She felt that old childish excitement at the prospect of the taste of salt on her lips. The whip of the wind on her face. Names written in the sand. Cartwheels. Hide-and-seek amongst the dunes.

'Here.' Her dad turned into the car park.

She stared at him. 'What?'

He smiled. 'You'll see.'

'You do know it's March, don't you? And it's about five degrees out there.'

'I am aware of that, yes.'

'So what on earth are we doing here?'

'Look over there.'

'Where?'

'To where they all are.' Her dad put one hand either side of her head and gently turned it to the right. 'There, Zoe.'

She strained her eyes, peering towards the sea. She saw a lone man being taken for a walk by his bounding bundle of a dog. She saw an elderly couple holding hands, bracing themselves against the wind. She saw a kite surfer whirling around on the water near the cliffs.

She pressed her face against the window. Beach huts. A red flag flaring in the wind. Seagulls crying overhead.

It was beautiful.

And then she saw them, and the beauty only increased.

Because there on the sand, setting up the ancient red windbreak she remembered so well, was her mum. Lily. Gary.

And him. Blond hair. Back bent as he planted his spade in the sand. Mouth open as he turned round to talk to Gary. Feet planted wide. That huge navy coat she'd bought him for Christmas two years ago.

Jamie. Jamie was here.

She put her hand on the door handle and fumbled to open it. She got nowhere. Swore. Tried again. In the end her dad leant across and she scrambled out. She had no clear thoughts in her head. No words on her lips. No hesitation whatsoever in her heart.

She ran down the pathway to the beach, not caring about the wind cutting through her coat. Not caring about the drizzle that was just starting to fall or her bag sliding off her shoulder until its contents spilled on to the sand.

No. For once, the way forward was crystal clear.

The way forward was him.

Cosy flat

15th June, 2013

Dear Zoe,

So, you've started your own company.

Sometimes I get out the red exercise book with 'Zoe Whittaker, aged 7, Sycamore Class' in your handwriting on the front and I flick through the pages till I get to the page where you say that when you're older you want to be like your mummy. I'm so glad you're not.

Happy birthday, Director Zoe.

Mum x

Twenty-Two

'**B** agsie the strawberry one!'

It was amazing how quickly being on a freezing beach in March had transformed them straight back into their childhood selves.

'I want it.' Zoe reached out her hand. 'You know I don't like vanilla.'

'No, me!' Lily made a grab for the cone. 'It's mine.'

'Girls, girls.' Their mum shook her head and her hair flew around her face in the blistering wind. 'WAIT.'

Jamie leant across to Gary, speaking in a stage whisper. 'Aren't you feeling so proud of your girlfriend right now?'

Gary blew warm air on to his reddening fingers. 'That's one word for it.'

'Cheeky git.' Lily butted him with her head and he picked her up and held her upside down before whirling her back on to her feet. Zoe saw the affection on her sister's face as they kissed. She looked away, so happy for Lily, yet wondering what lay ahead for her.

She tucked her hands into her pockets. The drizzle was turning to rain and she hadn't been able to feel her feet for the past hour. Her face felt like it was being razored and the windbreak was no better at keeping the chill out than it had been twenty years ago. The same old holes were gaping open. And Jamie's great idea of using his scarf to block up the biggest one hadn't helped the situation in the slightest.

Gina looked at Zoe and Lily and grinned impishly. She was her younger self again. Adventurous. Free. 'I'll have it. Problem solved.'

'NO.' They both looked at each other and made a dive for the cone.

'Too late!' Gina licked the soft ice cream just as they both landed against her, and soon the three of them were a twisting, giggling flurry as they rolled around fighting for the cone. Eventually they came to a breathy halt and lay there panting, faces slathered in dripping white ice cream.

Zoe leant up on one elbow. 'You know, that was mine really.'

Lily punched her on the arm. 'No. Mine.'

Gina rolled her eyes and settled on her back, staring up at the sky. 'You two.'

'What?' Zoe lay back down again, head comfortable against the golden sand. She wriggled towards her mum until she was nestling at her side. 'What do you mean, "you two"?'

Gina folded her hands on her tummy. She laughed a low, contented laugh. 'Always wanting the same thing.' She sighed. 'Doing the same things too. When Zoe fell into the swimming pool and hit her head, you did the same a week later, Lily.'

'Did I?' Lily narrowed her eyes. 'I don't remember that.'

'I do.' Alistair loomed over them, a tiny orange spade in his hand. 'You had matching bandages.' He shook his head. 'Now can you move? You're getting in the way of my moat.'

'Oh bloody hell. Not the moat.' Zoe rolled her eyes.

'Stop him now, someone, or we'll all be digging solidly for the next twenty-four hours.'

Lily reached out to take Zoe's hand. 'This is good, isn't it?'

'Definitely.' Zoe nodded. Here she could forget the future. Apart from the fact that she was gradually turning to ice, she couldn't remember feeling this relaxed in a very long time. She loved being here with these people, all the anger and resentment gusted away by the wind and the sand and the sea. The spirit of her mum's letters filled her heart and made her see how tightly knit they would always be. No matter what.

'I'm going to have one of those cold white things.'

Her mum still had vanilla on her cheek. Nobody told her. Nobody pointed out that she had only just finished her first one.

Zoe looked at her – at the warm glow of excitement on her face. She could relive the joys in life over and over again. It was their job to make sure they gave her every opportunity they could.

Not only bad things repeated themselves.

She swallowed and felt tears start to form. She looked towards her dad, Gary and Jamie, who were locked in intense discussion about the sandcastle at their feet. Gary had dared to query whether it was the correct distance from the sea, and was rapidly learning the error of his ways.

She turned back to her mum and Lily. 'So tell me, you two. Whose idea was it to come here?'

Silence fell. A seagull shrieked above them and a wave crashed towards the shore. The sky felt infinite. The world was theirs.

'Hello? Earth calling?' Zoe prodded them both. 'Whose idea was this?'

'It was Jamie's, of course.' Lily shook her head. 'Doesn't take a genius to work that out. You must have been wondering why on earth he's here too.'

'Yes.' Zoe shifted. The fact was, she had run up to him earlier and then had no idea what to say. She was too unsure of herself. Too much hung on his reply.

'Such a lovely boy.'

'Yes.' Zoe nodded. 'He is.'

Her mum was staring at the men. 'They're building . . .' She stopped. Tried again. 'Building sand things.' She tutted. 'Alistair always made them too complicated.'

Zoe propped herself up on her elbow again and looked across. The men were utterly absorbed. Now her dad and Gary were constructing a moat from the sea to the sand-castle, while Jamie seemed to be doing his best to ensure that the sandy turrets were fit for royalty. He had even fashioned a flag out of seaweed and planted it on top of the highest tower. His pink *Frozen* bucket didn't seem to be cramping his style at all, and he was wandering around scouring the beach for tiny shells, which he was collecting in what must have been very cold hands indeed.

Zoe's heart swelled.

'How did he know this was what we needed?'

'Me.' Gina settled back down on the sand. 'Maybe.'

Zoe looked at her. 'Did you talk to him about our trips?'

'Probably.' Her mum flicked a chunk of hair out of her eyes. She needed a cut, but that didn't seem important any more. 'Yes.' She nodded. 'I did.'

Zoe smiled. 'Thank you, Mum.'

Lily grinned. 'Why do you think he did it, Zoe?'

'Don't know.'

Lily reached over and slapped her on the forehead.

'Oh my God, sis, you can't seriously be saying that, can you?'

'Yes, I can.' Zoe knew that she could never explain her doubts. She knew they would make no sense when laid out to her family on this cold beach, with fresh air in their lungs and ice cream on their lips. This was a place for acting on instinct. For following your heart.

Gina levered herself up to sitting, staring happily at the waves. 'I like it here.'

'Good.'

'I like it in my garden, too.'

Zoe and Lily looked at each other.

'Which garden, Mum?'

'The one with the flower beds by my window.'

Zoe reached out and held her sister's hand.

Gina grinned. 'Anyone for a paddle?'

Lily reached down and started to take her boots off. 'I'll race you, Mum!'

'You're on!' Gina whooped into a gust of wind. She flung off her trainers and ran towards the sea. As the two figures receded in a cloud of sand, Zoe looked at the sandcastle. At the man with the bucket who had done his best to set her world to rights. She walked towards him.

'Have you seen any white shells anywhere?' Jamie's face was furrowed in concentration. 'I need more white.'

'No.' She had to do this. She had to be brave.

She dared to reach out and touch him. Freezing fingers around freezing fingers. Between them, a tiny spark of warmth. He looked at her, and she saw something in his eyes that hadn't been there during their last meeting. An openness. A way in.

She just had to find the courage to take it.

She fell into step beside him, hands swinging, palms pressed together. 'Do you think we could leave the shells for now?' She stared at the patterns on the sand. Curving arcs left by the morning's waves. Sticks marooned by the tide. Doggy footprints. Seaweed curving into pebbles and shells.

And above it all the biggest expanse of sky she had ever seen.

Jamie sighed. 'I don't know.' She felt herself sagging, but then heard him laugh. 'I'm not sure your dad will ever forgive me if I don't finish the decorations properly.' He put his mouth close to her ear. 'He seems to take sand-castles very seriously.'

'Yeah.' She nodded. 'When we were little, he used to enter us in those sand sculpting competitions. He made us build Darth Vader once.'

Jamie blinked. 'Wow. No wonder he's not that impressed by my efforts so far.' He smiled, and she felt a wave of relief so intense that she wanted to sing. She had missed him so much. The curve of his lips. The mischief in his eyes. The certainty of holding his hand.

'Jamie?' Sand had blown across his cheek, and without thinking she reached out and brushed it away.

He looked at her. 'What?'

'Thank you.' She smiled. The world was suddenly a simple place. The sky. The sea. The two of them. Mum and Lily jumping in the waves.

'For what?'

'For knowing that we needed this.' She felt her heartbeat pounding as she tried to get the words right. To get this moment right. To make him see.

'Jamie . . .'

'Come over here.' He kept hold of her hand as he walked over to a deserted hut on the far edge of the beach. 'You're frozen.'

'I'm OK.'

He looked at her and laughed. 'You always say that. Even that time when I was driving you to hospital with severe gastroenteritis. You had your head stuck out of the window like a carsick bloodhound, but you still kept telling me I should head off on the night out I'd planned with my mates.'

She hung her head. 'I would have been OK.'

'I know, but wasn't it more fun with me around? Well, as much fun as constant vomiting in an A&E waiting room can be.'

'True.'

They reached the beach hut. He tried the door. Inevitably it didn't open.

'Let's just hunker down outside, OK? I'm not sure I'm manly enough to kick this open.'

'Yeah, you are. You're just too polite.' She was starting to shiver but didn't want this moment to end. Being cold was nothing compared to a life without him.

They lowered themselves to the concrete. The low wall around the hut provided some sort of barrier from the wind, and she could feel a modicum of feeling returning to her nose.

'Look, Zo, I'm sorry.'

'*You're* sorry?'

'Yes.'

'No.' She huddled closer to him as a seagull wheeled on the breeze above them. 'No. I'm the one who's sorry. For walking out on the wedding. For not telling you about what happened when I was sixteen.'

359

She searched his face for anger. There was none.

'I should have trusted you, Jamie.'

He stared at the horizon. 'Wait, Zo.' A dog went running across the sand below them, woofing in circles as it chased its own tail. 'Please? Let me talk.'

'OK.' She could feel sand in her shoes. Sand in her shirt. Probably sand in several other places she'd rather not think about.

'First of all – that girl you saw me with.'

'Yes?' She was barely breathing.

'She was someone from work. From the last contract I did.'

'OK.' She folded her arms tightly across her chest.

'I went out with her a couple of times.' He shifted uncomfortably on the cold concrete. 'It never went anywhere and I knew it was all wrong, especially when we bumped into you that day. All the time I knew I was kidding myself and that the only person I really wanted was you.'

'Are you sure?' She didn't dare to believe him. 'In spite of everything I did?'

'Yes.' He rubbed his hands together and Zoe could see the white tinge on his knuckles. 'I ended it that night, pretty much. But then I knew you'd seen us and I didn't know what to do next. How to talk to you.'

'That makes two of us.'

'And I wasn't ready, I suppose.' He turned, and his eyes searched her face. 'That's why I'm sorry – I knew you must be going through such shit with your mum. And I wanted to help and I couldn't see how. Until that afternoon when I helped her with the shower and she told me about the beach and the letters and I knew that at last I could do something. Try to make a new memory that was a happy one.'

Zoe looked at her mum, who now seemed to be splashing Lily with freezing-cold water. Lily was shrieking and laughing and now Gary was walking across to join them.

It was an idyllic scene. A mum and daughter cackling in the waves. Zoe wondered how many times she had looked at a family having a picnic or sitting in a car and assumed a perfection that simply wasn't there. How many times she had taken things at face value when there were always secrets lying beneath.

'I didn't know how to get back to you, Zo.' He was staring at her. So close. So warm. 'You seemed so sad when I last saw you. I wanted to make you smile. To make you all smile. Even Mr Psycho King of the Sandcastle Major Alistair over there.'

Zoe grinned. She looked again at her mum, her hair flying free as she jumped into the waves. 'It's been so hard, Jamie. Ever since I first saw Mum again. I knew we were losing her.'

His voice was steady. Calm. Just the way she remembered it.

'Well she's still here, as far as I can see.'

'I know.' She bit her lip. 'But I'm so ashamed of myself. Ignoring her for all those years.'

He took her hand. 'You've done so much for her, Zo. You've looked after her. You've been the daughter she needed. You should be proud of that.'

She shook her head. 'Right now I'm not proud of anything.'

He squeezed her hand. 'So what's new?'

He moved closer to her and she dared to allow herself to hope. 'You know, Zo. If you ever want her to move back, just tell me. We'll work something out. OK?'

'OK.' She drank in his face. His eager, tanned wonder of a face. A face to wake up to. A face to live for.

Her voice was so low it nearly got lost in the wind.

'I've missed you.'

He smiled. 'I've missed you too.' He ran a freezing finger down her cheek. 'Let's not waste any more time, OK?'

There was more she needed to say. 'But what about kids?' She felt the old anxiety rise. 'It might happen again, Jamie.'

He pulled her close and she breathed him in. So strong. So precious.

'Yes. It might. Or it might not. We might get our baby, Zo. Our second chance baby.'

'I know.' She clung to him. 'But I'm scared that if we didn't it would break us.'

'It won't.' She loved his confidence. 'And if – and it's a big if – if it happened again, we'd do other things. Wonderful things.' He raised his eyebrows. 'And we'd have more money too, and that's never a bad thing, is it?'

She tried to smile.

'We'll be OK.' He stroked her hair. 'I promise.'

Something in her believed him.

He pulled away, pressing her fingers in his.

'Do you know what your mum told me that day?'

'I dread to think.'

'She told me that you were her golden girl. That I would be lucky to have you.'

Zoe shook her head again. 'Well, her mind *is* wandering . . .'

'No.' He was serious again. 'She wanted to say it now, you see. Before . . .' He drew her closer and she snuggled into his warmth.

'Before it's too late.' She felt a tremor pulse through her.

'Exactly.' He nodded.

'Why? Why did she want to tell you that?'

He raised his eyes and looked her full in the face. He was so close, she could feel his breath on her cheek.

'So I'd do this.' And he bent his head and kissed her.

The day swelled and her heart filled and the waves came and went on the shore. Her dad carried on building a moat with his smart City trousers rolled up and his shoes and socks arranged neatly beside him. Gary stood dabbling his toes in the waves. And the sun shone and the windbreak rattled and in the ice-cold sea beyond, two women splashed each other in the waves.

This was what mattered. Her family. The here. The now.

No matter what came next. Kids. No kids. A mother fading into the past. Zoe couldn't change any of that. She couldn't get it right or wrong.

She could only try.

She pulled Jamie closer.

Now was what mattered.

Right now.

A man and a woman kissing on a beach with their family around them.

Life.

Home, 2014

Darling Zo-bear,

I'm scared. At work I forgot my password and left a whole load of meetings out of the team calendar. I know everyone forgets passwords. I know I shouldn't worry. But I can't help it. Sometimes I search for words or names and they're just not there – all I get is blanks and gaps and a vague sense that my brain isn't on my side any more. And here I am at home alone and I don't have anyone else to tell but you.

Some days I'm fine. I bustle into the office and there's nobody more efficient and organised than me. I might make the odd mistake but I finish all my work and help other people if I can. But more and more I'm in the middle of something and suddenly I have no idea – not even a clue – what I'm trying to do. And in those moments the clouds surround me and I can feel people looking at me and sometimes I can't even remember their names.

I want to call you and ask you to help but sometimes I can't work out how to switch on the thing I call with. I know you would be there for me if I asked. You always were when you were little. I'd say 'Come and help me wash up' and there you'd be happily sloshing water into the bowl. I'd say 'Come and help me put the washing away' and up you'd pop, throwing clothes into enthusiastic piles. 'Help me make the beds,' and you'd appear, merrily flinging sheets around and putting your head in a pillowcase and pretending you were a ghost.

Why aren't you here?

Sometimes I dream. We're on the beach. You, me and Lil. The air is crisp. We have pies and those crunchy things and flasks of tea. You're wearing your green cords and that pink frilly jumper you loved so much when you were small. Lily is in polka dots. And you're looking at me as if I hold the key to all the questions life could ever ask. We're in freeze-frame, of course. You can't see the big slobbering dog about to steal our sandwiches. You can't see the wave about to knock our sandcastle over. It is one moment. And it's perfect.

Sometimes I wake up and I think we're going on that trip. You, me and Lily. Invincible.

Then I remember. I remember that we're not a trio any more. I remember the years of silence. I remember that Alistair and I aren't married now. It all comes back. Slowly. Painfully.

Sometimes forgetting makes things better.

I love you. I wonder if you and your boyfriend will ever get married. I can't wait to come and see you, my golden girl. My wonderful daughter. My Zoe.

Mum x

Twenty-Three

Lily sipped her tea. 'I think you've probably texted him enough now.'

'No.' Zoe pressed send. 'I can never text him enough. Not considering what I did last time.'

Jamie's reply came straight back. *In bar contemplating fleeing the country before you get here. Tit for tat. You know?*

She looked up, smiling. 'He's making jokes. Operation Make it Down the Aisle is right on track.'

'Glad to hear it.' Lily headed for the bathroom.

Their mum wandered back in, clutching yet another piece of toast.

'Do I look OK, Zo-bear?'

'You look great.'

Zoe eyed her in the mirror as she put her mascara on. Pink dress. Hair that had recently had contact with a hairbrush. A cream hat that wouldn't look out of place in *Gone with the Wind*.

Gina sat on the edge of the sofa and took a bite of toast. 'It feels funny wearing this.'

'I know.' Zoe twisted the top back on to the tube and started on her lip gloss. 'But your jeans will still be there tonight. Waiting for you.'

'I suppose so.' Her mum took a happy bite of toast. 'God, this stuff is good. What is it again?'

'Er . . . toast.'

'I know that.' She frowned. 'I mean the brown stuff on top.'

'Nutella.' Zoe grinned to herself. Her mum had asked the same thing twenty minutes ago. She finished her lips and turned round. 'How do I look?'

Her mum stopped chewing.

'Mum?'

Silence.

Zoe put her hand up to her hair. 'Is there something wrong?'

'You look absolutely beautiful, golden girl.'

'Really?' Zoe smoothed her dress with her fingers. Simple. Cream. The same dress she had been wearing the day Jamie walked into her office for the very first time. Her hair was down. Daffodils and primroses made up her bouquet. Everything felt calm. Simple. True.

She reached out and hugged her mum. She was so happy that she was here. She couldn't imagine getting married without her.

Her mum went back to the important business of eating her toast. 'Where are we going again?'

Zoe began to explain. Then she saw the smile.

'Mum!' She huffed. 'Honestly. You're not meant to wind me up today. Bloody hell.'

'She's going to get all Bridezilla now.' Lily appeared, earrings in hand. 'I've done this before, remember? I know what she's like.'

'I'm not a Bridezilla!' Zoe pouted. Then she caught sight of herself in the mirror. Hands on hips. Flushed face.

'Oh. Maybe I am.' She smiled sheepishly. 'But at least there aren't a hundred and fifty people waiting this time. Forty is much more like it.'

'Thank God.' Lily settled into Zoe's sofa. 'Fewer people to laugh at me when I inevitably fall flat on my face.'

'Don't be an idiot, Lil.' Zoe reached down and squeezed her sister's hand. 'You don't trip up in normal life, do you?'

'No.' Lily examined her fingernails. 'But in normal life I don't wear heels.' She made them sound like some form of torture device. She waved her feet in the air. 'I'm going to need crutches just to get me into the cab.'

Zoe grinned. 'Oh, just wear your beloved flip-flops if you want to.'

'Do you mean that?' Lily sat up and stared at her. 'Are you serious?'

'Yep.' Zoe nodded. 'If it makes you happy, wear those hideous old things. I don't mind.'

'Oh my GOD.' Lily started capering around triumphantly. 'This is amazing. This is SO much better than last time.'

'Isn't it?'

Zoe stared out of her living room window. The sun was shining. She looked up at the sky and she felt – deep down in her bones and her heart – that the world was kind. A feeling from long ago. Before Simon. Before the arguments and the loss and the loneliness.

She knew that today, nothing would go wrong. That this time it would happen. That this was their turn. Their moment.

Her mum might not remember it tomorrow. She might not remember the hat on her head, or the music, or the speech that Jamie would make about the girl she had once dandled on her knee. But Zoe hoped – with all her heart – that she would remember the feeling. The pride. The joy.

And sometime in the future, her mum would see a new picture on her wall. A photo of a girl with red hair and a cream dress, embracing a man in a purple waistcoat. She would look at it and she might not know the names of the bride and the groom, but maybe that wouldn't matter. She would see the love. She would see the trust.

And she would know that these two people were made for each other.

Then she would move on and gaze at other pictures. Her and Mags rocking their babies in a sunny garden. Her and Alistair brandishing a new set of keys as they moved into their latest home. Lily and Zoe sporting matching pigtails and sticking their tongues out at the camera on the first day of the school holidays.

Her eyes would wander back to the man and the woman. To another snapshot of a life full of love.

And she would smile. And life would carry on. Moment by moment. Towards whatever the future held.

Acknowledgements

This book has been a very personal and challenging story to write, so thanks must go first to my husband Max for being my counsellor, my supporter and my personal chef when deadlines are looming and I am in danger of only eating food out of cans. All my hugs and love also go to Evie – my own personal Tigger. Long may our storytelling continue. I am constantly indebted to my wonderful parents and to my outrageously inspiring brother Richard, who consistently sets me such a fine example of what it means to be a writer.

I am very grateful to my editor, Emily Kitchin, for her energising and insightful help from first draft to final full stop. Thank you to Emma Knight, Naomi Berwin, Anna Alexander and everyone at Hodder for working with such passion and commitment to bring this book out into the big wide world. I am also endlessly thankful to my brilliant agent Hannah Ferguson for working so hard to make my dreams come true.

Thank you to the wonderful friends who have supported me along the way: Alice Jarvis, Jo Rose, Nijma Khan, Helen Winterton, Diana de Grunwald, Myoung Rhee, Maria Nicholson, Tanya de Grunwald, Kate Holder and the incomparable Rhian Fox. I couldn't have done it without you all.

I am enormously grateful to the book bloggers who

have given me such heartfelt support over the past year – you are a wonderfully warm community and have made a world of difference. Particular thanks go to Anne Cater, John Fish, Victoria Goldman, Sophie Hedley, Linda Hill, Agi Klar, Laura Lovelock, Nina Pottell, Sandra Robinson, Michelle Ryles, Kelly Spillane and Sharon Wilden. I would like to send enthusiastic hugs and promises of wine to my cheerleading wonder writers: Isabelle Broom, Cesca Major, Lisa Dickenson, Cressida McLaughlin, Miranda Dickinson, Amanda Jennings and Kim Curran. You are the best support I could ever hope to have.

Finally, heartfelt thanks to the many people who helped me to research this novel: Mary-Anne Driscoll, Claire Pollard, Louise Forbes, Andrea Marlow, Georgia Best, Tamara Bathgate, Rachel Kingston, Deborah Wolverson, Tom Davie, James Thomas, Rebecca Jarvis, Dr Hugo De Waal, Andrew Goodson, Hannah Mitchell and Dr Sophie Edwards. Thank you all for your honesty and for your time. You have helped to bring this story alive.

Reading Group Questions

- Zoe leaves her wedding in the first chapter. Given the circumstances, can you empathise with her decision?

- The novel is split into two sections: the present, and the past as narrated through Gina's letters. What is the effect of this stylistic device? Does it make you feel closer to either Gina or Zoe?

- Gina is diagnosed with early-onset Alzheimer's Disease aged only 56. How do you feel society reacts to people dealing with mental health issues?

- Both Gina and Zoe make mistakes. Who do you think is more to blame for the breakdown in their relationship?

- Each member of the Whittaker family struggles to come to terms with Gina's diagnosis. Do you feel that they have made progress by the end of the novel?

- Discuss the theme of bravery in the novel. Where is bravery most needed? Who displays the most bravery?

- 'At its heart, this is a novel about mothers and daughters.' Would you agree with this statement?

- What do you think the future holds for Zoe and Jamie?

- Do you feel that Zoe and Lily make the right decision in moving Gina into a home? Can there ever be a 'right' decision in these circumstances?

Katie Marsh

MY EVERYTHING

'Devastatingly good – wonderfully warm, heartbreakingly real and completely uplifting' Miranda Dickinson

On the day Hannah is finally going to tell her husband she's leaving him, he has a stroke . . . and life changes in an instant.

Tom's only 32. Now he can't walk or cut up his own food, let alone use his phone or take her in his arms. And Hannah's trapped. She knows she has to care for her husband, the very same man she was ready to walk away from.

But with the time and fresh perspective he's been given, Tom re-evaluates his life, and becomes determined to save his marriage. Can he once again become the man his wife fell in love with, or has he left it too late?

My Everything is an unputdownable debut novel. It will make you cry, laugh, and stop to think about what's really important in life.

Out now

HODDER